Darker Than Love

He touched his fingertips to her cheek, turning her gently to meet his gaze. She looked at him steadily. His lips were set in an arrogant half-sneer, and his black, inky eyes glittered with callous joy. She saw in that expression how sure he was of his hold over her, of his ability to master her, body and soul. His confidence was unshakeable. It incensed her, it crushed her, and it thrilled her.

'You see, in your innocence you think love the greater force,' he said softly. 'And, true enough, it binds many couples. Although there are plenty who do not even have that. But as man and wife, Clarissa, you and I will be bound by something so much darker than love, so much stronger.'

Darker Than Love

KRISTINA LLOYD

[For SD]

Black Lace novels are sexual fantasies.
In real life, make sure you practise safe sex.

First published in 1998 by
Black Lace
Thames Wharf Studios,
Rainville Road, London W6 9HA

Reprinted 2001

Typeset by SetSystems Ltd, Saffron Walden, Essex
Printed and bound by Mackays of Chatham PLC

ISBN 0 352 33279 4

Chapter One

Clarissa Longleigh stood by the window, her nervous fingers toying with the crimson drapes. The dipping sun had at last touched the tallest mast at Chelsea Wharf, and to the east Battersea Bridge was busy with a flow of hansom cabs and carriages. The afternoon was almost over.

A paddle steamer gliding downriver sent clouds of drifting smoke into the azure sky. Silvery water cascaded from its churning wheel, and fishing boats, dwarfed by the ship's great bulk, bobbed gently in its rippling wake. How slow it was, thought Clarissa. As slow as time spent waiting. If the weeks leading up to her marriage were as long as the hours had been today, then summer would be interminable.

She sighed restlessly, her thoughts surging ahead. Would Lord Alexander Marldon be everything she wanted him to be? 'Sophisticated and handsome,' her father had said. 'Dark,' Alicia had said, and that pleased Clarissa greatly. A fair man was not to her taste.

She prayed she would meet with his approval. The prospect of returning to the Sussex countryside at the close of the season filled her with the dread of boredom. Clarissa had no desire to spend her nineteenth year stitching dull little samplers, marking time while her father sought another worthy suitor. She wanted to be wed in the autumn, as proposed. She wanted to be the wife of the sixth Earl of Marldon and live at Lockstone Hall on his grand Wiltshire estate.

Tonight at supper, under the disapproving gaze of her father, she would dazzle Lord Alec. She would wear the daring blue silks which her new stepmother, Alicia, had insisted upon. Her ebony hair would be curled and piled high, and she would be elegant, witty and charming. How could the earl be anything other than impressed? Perhaps, in a summer of dancing, he would feel compelled to lure her into things more intimate than polite conversation. Away from suspicious eyes, he would embrace her passionately and press lingering kisses to her lips.

Clarissa frowned, and flicked at a golden tassel hanging from the curtain-tie. It was unlikely to be quite so easy. Her father and stepmother were soon to embark on their honeymoon tour and, in their stead, Hester Carr was to act as guardian and chaperone. A maiden aunt, seldom without her good Bible, was not rich with promise.

A clatter at the door broke into her reverie. Kitty Preedy, struggling with a tall, copper pitcher of steaming water, shuffled into the bedroom. Her elfin face was flushed with exertion.

'Lord ha' mercy,' she muttered. 'I'm not cut out for this.'

Clarissa smiled, her rich-blue eyes softly sympathetic. The Longleighs' town house had been closed since the death of Clarissa's mother, some fifteen years ago. While it was pleasantly situated and of a good size, the facilities were somewhat lacking, and the family were having to wash in primitive hip baths.

Kitty placed the jug by the half-filled wooden tub and swept a thin forearm across her damp brow.

'Lordy, I hope you won't be after smelling sweet every

2

day, miss,' she gasped, kneeling on the fireside rug and readjusting her mob cap. Several limp strands of corn-coloured hair fell free and she tucked them behind her ears. With a grunt, she poured water into the bath, muttering oaths as a cloud of steam enveloped her.

Kitty – Pretty Kitty, they called her – was one of the few servants from Sebdon Hall who had accompanied the family to London. Back home she was a mere scullery maid but here, at Alicia's insistence, she'd been promoted to housemaid. It was rather odd to see her in a neat black frock and crisp white pinafore instead of shabby hand-me-downs. She looked almost presentable.

'So how does London suit you, Kitty?' enquired Clarissa.

'I don't know much about London, miss,' the maid sighed, sitting back on her heels. 'I haven't seen anything but muck and dust for days. Haven't even had a chance to find myself a fancy man yet.'

'If I know you, Kitty,' replied Clarissa, 'I dare say that will happen within a short enough while.'

'Not at this rate, it won't,' she countered. 'I'm fair run off my feet, I am. If the master doesn't get some more help in sharpish, I'm going to be as badly off as you. Who'd have thought it, eh? Me and you, both twiddling our buttons until harvest time.'

'Kitty!' reprimanded Clarissa, putting on a frown. 'If you continue to speak in such a manner I shall be obliged to take that soap and water to your mouth.'

Kitty grinned. 'Does all this London air come with graces in it, then?' she teased. 'I ought to go and take a few breaths for it's fairly turned your head, miss.'

'Someone might hear, that's all,' cautioned Clarissa in a low voice.

She was glad to have Kitty in town. In recent months they'd struck up an odd sort of friendship. It was thanks to the young maid that Clarissa, one shy September morning, had learnt all about the mysteries of love. She now knew exactly what to expect on her wedding night.

To her shame the prospect, though somewhat daunting, filled her with a hungry ache.

Whenever she dwelt on it, as she often did, the place between her thighs grew heated and damp. But it hadn't taken Kitty to tell her that, even without a man, there were ways to calm those feelings. She knew that it was sinful – shamefully, wickedly sinful. A lady of breeding, her governess often said, is fortunate in that she does not suffer from nor submit to the demands of vulgar, bodily appetites, as men and animals do.

But Clarissa suffered. And the cravings of her body were such that, in moments of privacy, she was prepared to forfeit her status as a lady of breeding. She was becoming quite an expert at pleasuring herself.

'I don't think you need worry overmuch about your chores,' she said, guiding the conversation back to safer ground. 'More staff are to arrive later in the week so your burden should be eased.'

'It isn't my burden that wants easing, miss,' replied Kitty, getting to her feet and shaking out her skirts. 'It's this darn ache in my cunny.'

Clarissa shot her a disapproving glance but it was a weak effort and Kitty paid her no heed.

'Anyway,' she continued, crossing to join Clarissa by the window. 'If these new folk are anything like your French miss, I don't much fancy my chances. Looks like she's got a broom handle up her fundament, that one.'

Clarissa gave a tiny gleeful laugh. Alicia had taken it upon herself to appoint Clarissa, now she was of age, a lady's maid. Pascale Rieux had arrived only yesterday and Kitty was quite right: the young woman certainly didn't have the friendliest of airs.

'Well I never,' breathed Kitty, pressing her nose to the glass. 'Your old man's turning into a dandy little lapdog.'

Clarissa followed the housemaid's gaze to the wide pavement of Cheyne Walk below. Fine silks and linens strolled in the shadow of elm trees and there, standing beside a dray horse and cart, was the stout figure of her father, his brow creased in dismay.

'If that's what love does to you,' murmured Kitty, 'I don't think I'll be wanting much.'

Eager to take a closer look, Clarissa jerked up the sash. Kitty wrinkled her nose in distaste.

'That river's in need of a few rose petals,' she complained, backing away. 'Think I'd rather be fetching up more hot water.'

Clarissa knelt to lean over the sill. Her father, a powerful shipping magnate, was generally regarded as a strong-willed, authoritative man, with a touch of the tyrant about him. But, since Alicia had entered his life, he'd changed almost beyond recognition.

Alicia sparkled. She was a flame of red hair and a swish of beautiful gowns. It was she who had persuaded Charles to reopen his town house, saying Clarissa really ought to be introduced to London society. On their arrival she'd declared, 'The only way to improve this place is by burning half the contents.' 'Absolutely not,' Charles had replied. 'A preposterous notion.' And yet here he was, gazing on mutely as men in shirtsleeves removed the offending pieces of furniture. It was a delight to behold.

'*Qu'est-ce que vous faites?*' came a demanding voice. '*C'est une odeur infernale. Tish! Fermez la fenêtre, mademoiselle. Immédiatement!*'

Clarissa bridled. Pascale Rieux had yet to learn her station.

'You close it,' she replied, maintaining a dignified calm and rising to her feet. 'And I'll thank you to remember you are in England, Pascale. We speak English here.'

Pascale, without replying, busied herself at the washstand. When Kitty staggered in with another pitcher of water she turned on the housemaid with flashing dark eyes.

'*Et toi,*' she snapped, clapping her hands to chivvy the puzzled girl along. '*Vite! Vite! Et fermez la fenêtre!*'

Kitty pouted. 'What's she saying, miss?'

'She is saying,' sighed Pascale, 'to please hurry up and to please close the window.'

'But without the "please",' added Clarissa tartly, sliding the window shut with a vigorous heave.

Kitty set down the jug and, making a face at Pascale's back, left the room with the merest of curtseys. The French maid planted herself on the plush-seated chair by the dressing table. For a few moments she closed her eyes and drew long, deep breaths.

Clarissa gazed at her, intrigued by the faint quivering of the young woman's nostrils. What a curious creature she was, she thought, and how strangely beautiful. Her face was delicately boned, yet she had a strong Roman nose with the slightest sideways bend to it. On anyone else, that nose would have been monstrous, yet on Pascale it was perfect.

'Mademoiselle, forgive me,' she said at length, looking at Clarissa with an unwavering gaze. 'I do not wish to be rude. It is simply that I want you to be very beautiful for tonight. And this house, it is ... it is *chaotique*. It makes me too furious. Forgive me.'

'Please,' corrected Clarissa sternly. 'Forgive me, *please*.'

Astonishment flickered on Pascale's face. Then she smiled faintly. 'Ah yes,' she said. 'Please.'

Kitty huffed in frustration and crept away from the bedroom door. So much for the good telling-off she'd been hoping to hear.

She stomped down the stairs, her jaw clenched, her brows drawn in a sharp frown. Oh, if she were high-bred, she'd give the French bit a damn good hiding. That would sort her out. Kitty grinned, an even better idea occurring to her. What Pascale needed was a good firm prick inside her. That would turn up the corners on that tight little mouth of hers.

Then again, if there were any lusty young men going spare, Kitty was going to be first in the queue. Fingers

6

were nice enough and they did the trick, but there was nothing like a proper thrusting to get a girl all hot and dizzy.

As she stepped on to the tiled floor of the hall, there was a loud rapping at the front door. She ignored it. That wasn't her job. Then a holler from below stairs told her it was. She swore volubly. Housemaid, parlourmaid, cook's skivvy and, now, the cursed butler. She should have stayed at home. Slopping out suds was a lark compared to this.

She opened the heavy oak door to find a top-hatted cabman standing before her. Kitty smiled coquettishly and looked at him from beneath lowered eyelashes. Well, he was under thirty years, she thought. But the man, unmoved, merely handed her an envelope, stating it was for Charles Longleigh, Esquire. Then he bid her a curt good day and made his way down the steps.

Kitty sighed and closed the door. These Londoners weren't up to bantering the way country folk were. She stared at the envelope, not quite knowing what to do with it. Then she remembered: letters went on the hall table.

She turned smartly, smug to think how quickly she was learning. But it had gone. The table had gone. Kitty scowled at the empty space. The new missis must have had it carted off, along with everything else she didn't much care for. What a waste of good polishing.

There was a shout from the basement stairs. Cook, her fat cheeks bulging, emerged from the doorway at the far end of the corridor.

'Kitty Preedy,' she yelled, wagging her finger. 'If I find you shirking once more, I'll have your guts for garters. Get down here. There's work to be done.'

Kitty groaned and pushed the letter into the deep pockets of her skirt. When she had a spare moment she'd breathe. Then she'd give the master his letter.

* * *

Dusk had yet to fall but in Clarissa's bedroom the long, crimson curtains were already drawn. The waning sunlight filtered through them as a soft red hue. It turned the oak dado into mahogany and the gilt picture frames into rose-gold.

In the grate a small fire burnt. It had been lit not for heat, but for the curling irons. Clarissa sat before it in the hip bath, feeling deliciously languid. Her long legs, crooked over the front of the tub, gleamed like amber in the flickering light. Her head lolled against the sloping back. Her eyes were closed.

Pascale had a magical touch. She didn't just cleanse. She massaged and soothed, her touch both firm and gentle. While she worked, she murmured soft compliments and hummed lazy melodies. Any friction between them had now melted away. They shared a calming lassitude, undercut with the tension of anticipation.

Pascale, kneeling by the tub, dipped the sponge into the soapy, attar-scented water. With a slow, sensuous movement she swept it up, through the valley of Clarissa's breasts and briefly over the full, high mounds. She rubbed it across her shoulders and the flat of her chest, squeezing lightly.

Rainbow-glinting foam slithered down Clarissa's body, back into the water which frothed about her waist. Pascale lifted a wet arm and ran the sponge along it, twisting and turning so as not to miss an inch. Then the sponge slid over to Clarissa's breasts and lingered, just a little longer than it had done before.

'Such a beautiful bosom,' said Pascale in a husky whisper. 'So firm and young.'

Clarissa felt a slight awkwardness tighten her body. But Pascale had now moved her attention to one of Clarissa's hands. She was sponging between her fingers, admiring the pearly sheen of her almond-shaped nails. Clarissa relaxed again, chastising herself for being so bashful. When the sponge returned to her breasts and circled over the yielding white globes, she ignored the niggling self-consciousness. She would have to grow accustomed to this style of bathing, and Pascale was merely being thorough.

'Your betrothed is a handsome man, no?' asked Pascale quietly. 'And young also?'

'I'm told he is very handsome,' murmured Clarissa. 'Though I believe some years older than myself.'

'Ah, an older man is good,' replied Pascale. 'A virgin bride does not want a virgin groom. No. She wants a man with experience. Your husband will give you much pleasure, I think.'

As she spoke, her thumb grazed lightly over one nipple, then the other. The sensitive crests tingled and puckered. Clarissa felt a flutter of nervous excitement at both the reminder of her wedding night and Pascale's illicit touch. For a brief moment she considered expressing her disapproval. But the touch had been too fleeting and the sensation too pleasant for it to matter.

Pascale, gently holding an ankle, raised Clarissa's right leg. She sponged back and forth, soaping the slender length of her calf and thigh. Clarissa wondered how it would feel to have a man's caress. When her husband made love to her, would his hands glide along her flesh like this? Would he be slow and attentive or would he just take her quickly, the way Kitty said so many men did?

Pascale slid the sponge down Clarissa's leg, beneath the water, and pressed it between her thighs. Clarissa shifted in discomfort but the maid pressed more firmly and began rubbing at her intimate parts.

'I'll do that, thank you, Pascale,' she said thickly, trying to ignore the heat swelling in her groin.

Pascale made no move to obey. She tightened her grip on Clarissa's ankle and kneaded the sponge against her soft folds.

'Do not be shy, mademoiselle,' she purred. 'I can show you many things. From me you can learn something of what your husband will do. It is not good for a bride to be too *naïf*. The husband, he will grow bored.'

The sponge bobbed to the foamy surface. Pascale's diving fingers sought out Clarissa's sex, swiftly parting her lips. Clarissa yelped and wriggled, sending water sloshing over the edge of the tub.

'No,' she urged breathlessly. 'Stop it at once.'

With a power that belied her petite frame, Pascale held on to Clarissa's writhing ankle. With a calm smile she turned aside, blinking rapidly, as the water splashed her face and clothes. Her persistent fingers glided along Clarissa's slippery cleft.

'The lady should learn,' she said, above Clarissa's protests, 'that a husband does not always hear the word "no". This is a good lesson, mademoiselle. Very good.' Her questing fingers probed at the narrow entrance of Clarissa's vagina.

Clarissa squealed and, with a violent jerk, wrenched her leg free. Pascale recoiled, a hand cupped to her cheek where she'd received a glancing blow.

'Tish, mademoiselle,' she said, without a trace of anger. 'Such a fuss.'

'Pass me that towel at once,' ordered Clarissa. 'And in future keep your hands to yourself.'

Pascale shrugged. 'I meant no harm, mademoiselle. I thought my touch was giving you much pleasure. Forgive me. Please.'

Ignoring her, Clarissa took a jug of clear water and stood to rinse the soap from her body. Her sex pulsed with light sensation and she could not deny that a part of her had wanted to surrender to Pascale's invasive caress.

'I'll dry myself,' she snapped, stepping out of the tub and wresting the towel from the maid's extended arms.

Pascale raised her brows in an ironic arch. 'And will mademoiselle also dress herself and arrange her own hair?' she enquired pleasantly.

Clarissa, cursing under her breath, briskly rubbed

herself dry. She could hardly do without Pascale's help, especially tonight. But the girl wasn't getting away with such insubordination. Perhaps Alicia should deal with it later. She was the one who had appointed the bossy little wretch.

Dropping the towel to the floor, Clarissa snatched up her chemise from the bed. It was a delicate garment, of white China silk threaded with pale-blue ribbons. She jerked it over her head and punched at the armholes.

'Please, mademoiselle,' whined Pascale. 'You will tear your beautiful new clothes. And do not frown so. You will make an ugly line there. Think only that I made a silly mistake. In France, a maid helps her lady with many things. Perhaps here it is different. Come, say it is forgotten and let me lace you.'

Clarissa, somewhat reluctantly, acquiesced. She feared Pascale's touch and the tiny spark of need it had aroused. But the maid, insisting on doing everything, set about her task without a hint of suggestion in voice, eyes or hands. With a firm action, she unrolled silken stockings along Clarissa's outstretched legs then secured silver-grey garters at her thighs. She was reassuringly strong in lacing up the stays, and nimble-fingered in pinning the heavy petticoats so they trailed just so. Perhaps, conceded Clarissa, Alicia had been right to appoint the Frenchwoman.

Almost two hours later, Clarissa, dressed in her finest and groomed to perfection, was quite certain her step-mother had been right. Her gleaming black hair was pinned into a high chignon and woven through with ribbons of ice blue. Wispy tendrils curled about her face. Her indigo gown, fashionably smooth in front, sheathed the dips and curves of her body. At the back, a mass of elaborate draperies fell to the ground in a train of lace-edged flounces. The neckline, low and square, hinted at the merest shadow of her cleavage.

'*Magnifique*,' trilled Pascale, her face glowing with

11

satisfaction. 'Your betrothed will demand an earlier wedding when he sees you tonight.'

'Thank you, Pascale. That will be all,' said Clarissa coolly. 'I shall ring if I need you.'

Clarissa crossed to the window and opened a chink in the curtains. She would not descend until Lord Alexander arrived. Then she would sweep into the room and he would rise to greet her, a smile of admiration and desire lighting up his handsome face.

She watched the carriages rumbling along the cobbled road of the Embankment below. Each one sent her hopes soaring and plunging. He was late, perhaps only ten minutes, but nevertheless he was late. While society might consider that fashionable, Clarissa couldn't help thinking it was just a little rude.

She brushed her cheek against the velvet curtains, imagining the touch was that of Lord Alexander, a gentle caress. Her lips skimmed the soft fabric in a breath-light kiss.

'Please, my love,' she whispered, 'don't be too fashionable.'

In the flock-papered drawing room the gaslights purred gently in their sconces. Alicia Longleigh, in silks of caramel and gold, sat in a deep-buttoned armchair. Her head was bowed over an open book and her smile was serene. Standing before the marble chimney piece was Charles Longleigh, thickset and bewhiskered, his thumbs stuck in his waistcoat pockets. Occasionally he rocked forward on to the balls of his feet, pulled out his watch, or cleared his throat.

On the mantelshelf, the ormolu clock ticked with loud impatience.

The kitchen window was open wide. The heat from the range and smells of roasted meats drifted upwards into the yellowing gas-lit street. Kitty and cook sat at the enormous pine table, each cradling a glass of sherry.

Scullery maids weren't allowed sherry but Kitty wasn't a scullery maid any more. She was a housemaid and she was the best housemaid that ever there was. All day she'd been rushing round, fetching this, cleaning that, polishing the other, and not once had she complained. She'd helped lay out all the crystal, the hams and the jellies. And she'd done marvels in fancying up the dining table with flowers and candelabras. It looked a treat upstairs and, like cook said, they'd earned themselves a drink.

The sherry, rich and syrupy, warmed her insides like nothing else. The first glass had slipped down so quickly she'd had to ask for a second. Cook had looked a little doubtful, then she'd said, 'Ah, bugger it,' and poured some more. Kitty was beginning to feel all soft and giddy.

Cook wasn't in much of a mood for talking though. Her face was one big scowl, but Kitty didn't mind. She was happy enough just sitting there, dreaming about her farmhand, Tom. He had a lovely prick and a good hard thrust in his body. And he was a dab-hand at finding sneaky places to do a bit of sweethearting. Kitty's thoughts drifted until suddenly she cocked her head to one side and frowned at the tureen.

'Why hasn't that soup gone up yet?' she asked. 'Aren't they hungry upstairs?'

'It ain't gone up yet,' said cook, straightening her back defiantly, 'because his lordship ain't bloomin' well arrived. Hasn't even sent word on to say as he'll be late. No manners ain't rich folk. No bloomin' manners.'

'Oh,' said Kitty, draining the last of her sherry. It was to be hoped the meat didn't get all dried up. Then her blood turned to ice and a great mallet thumped in her guts.

'Oh, lord,' she breathed, fumbling in her pocket. She rose unsteadily to her feet and pulled out the crumpled letter. 'Oh, lord ha' mercy.'

* * *

13

There was an almighty shout. Clarissa's stomach lurched. She hurried to the bedroom door and, picking up her skirts, hastened down the stairs. It was almost an hour past the time appointed by Lord Marldon and her father hadn't made such a noise in months. Something had gone dreadfully wrong.

At the drawing-room door she caught a warning glance from Alicia and came to an abrupt halt. Her father, oblivious to her presence, was towering over Kitty, his face red with fury.

'You great scatterbrained loon,' he raged, waving a piece of paper inches from the young girl's face. 'You jumped-up little scarecrow. I knew you'd never make a housemaid. I bloody knew it.'

Kitty, her eyes cast to the ground, sniffed convulsively.

'Your brains are in your drawers,' continued Charles. 'Didn't anyone ever tell you about letters? They're meant to be read. You put them on the hall table, where I can see them. Do you understand? Do you? On the hall table.'

Kitty wiped her forearm across her nose and looked up at him, her lower lip trembling.

'But, sir,' she wailed, 'we haven't got one any more.' Her voice trailed off into great heaving sobs.

'She's quite right, Charles,' said Alicia placidly, stroking damp strands of hair from Kitty's tear-streaked face.

Charles glowered at his wife. 'And whose fault is that?' he bellowed.

Alicia sighed and placed a consoling arm around Kitty's shoulders. 'What's done is done,' she said. 'Now go and clean yourself up, Kitty, then tell cook we shall have dinner presently. And chew some fresh mint while you're at it.'

Kitty bobbed a quick curtsey and scuttled away, avoiding Clarissa's eyes as she passed her in the doorway.

'Clarissa dear,' said Alicia. 'I'm afraid Lord Marldon

has been delayed. He won't be coming down until the end of the month.'

Clarissa stood motionless, a wave of desolation sweeping over her. The end of the month? But that was weeks away. Oh, the wait would be intolerable. She dug her fingernails into the palms of her clenched hands, determined not to cry. 'Oh?' she said softly, the word catching in her throat.

Her father jerked his head round and opened his mouth to speak. But the words were unforthcoming and he simply stared at her, his eyes wide with astonishment. 'What the . . .?' he began.

'Charles,' said Alicia in a cautionary tone. 'Keep calm. She's a woman now. Remember?'

'A woman?' he spluttered. 'God damn it, I can see that. The barefaced monkey's got her wares out in a fine old display. A woman? I do not want my daughter to be a woman. I want her to be, for God's sake, a lady. Do you hear?'

Alicia laid a gentle hand on his arm and he shook it off with a snort of disgust. 'This isn't the Haymarket, my girl,' he bellowed at Clarissa. 'This is your father's house. Get upstairs. Get something decent on. I'll not dine with a harlot.'

Clarissa flew, unshed tears blurring her vision. Her father railed after her. She was a strumpet and a fool. Those clothes were for men with no imaginations, didn't she know that? And Marldon, damn him, he had imagination enough for a score of men.

Reaching the calm of her bedroom, Clarissa slammed the door shut and leant against it, breathing rapidly. Oh, her father's insults were cruel and ill-timed. How could he have said such dreadful things when already she felt perfectly terrible? The end of the month? It was only the first week of June. She kicked her heel against the wood.

She hoped Lord Alec, whenever he chose to arrive, would be more appreciative of fashion. She'd spent hours being primped and preened and it was all for nothing. She couldn't even wear the gown for supper.

Clarissa turned the key in the lock, dashed away a tear and took several deep, steady breaths. If she could not dress as she pleased, then she would not go down for supper at all. It was a beautiful gown. Both Alicia and Pascale had said so. And it was her colour because her eyes, Alicia said, were all cornflowers and violets at midnight, and the blue silk enhanced their depths. It wasn't tawdry in the least, and only the most puritanical mind would deem it indecent. Besides, modish women wore things far more revealing. In Regent Street, they paraded in dresses so snug there barely seemed space for underclothes.

She crossed to the cheval mirror. She would be as daring, once her father had gone. She would wear the dress again, and she would order dozens more in the same cut.

Passing her hands lightly over her body, Clarissa considered her figure in the glass. According to Alicia, she had a shape well suited to the new style of gown. Her shoulders were wide and her curves graceful, rather than generous. 'Statuesque,' the dressmaker had said.

Her chin tipped up stubbornly. What did her father know? She unlooped several tiny buttons of the bodice, baring the lace trim of her stays. Then she pushed the shoulders of her chemise and gown against her arms and carefully adjusted her breasts. When a hint of rosy nipple was peeping above the lace and her pale flesh was spilling over her corset, she was satisfied.

There, that was more befitting to the insults her father had hurled at her. A little paint and she could turn professional. She would sneak out of the house when the moon was up and join the molls in the glittering heart of London. Turning, she slid her gaze sideways and offered her reflection a coy smile. 'One gold sovereign, sir,' she breathed. 'And you can do with me what you will.'

A wanton thrill shivered through her and she scooped her breasts free from their final restraints. Unbidden, the memory of Pascale's trespassing fingers flashed in her mind. The insolent maid had sparked a tingling in her loins with her sly and forceful touches. A moment's irritation tweaked at her before she pushed the thought away.

Closing her eyes, she stretched back her head and smoothed a hand from her slender neck down to her jutting breasts. She palmed the taut, high orbs. The caress was Lord Alec's. He was kissing her, whispering that she was beautiful, so ready for loving. Fingers teased her nipples, rousing them to hard, prickling peaks. Her sex glowed exquisitely, answering the sensations with a gentle throb. He would surely die of wanting her, he was saying, and, oh, their wedding night was an eternity away. 'Then take me now, my lord,' she murmured. 'No one need ever know.'

Clarissa slipped off her drawers. She moved the mirror, tilting it to reflect the chintz-hung bed, and lay down. The soft mattress dipped beneath her weight, and she dropped one foot to the floor. Raising her other knee she drew back her skirts, surrounding her open thighs in a foaming nest of white guipure lace and indigo ruffles.

The image of her secret place was enchanting. Against her evening finery, it was all the more naked. Fringed with black curls, it was a dusky flower, pouting brazenly and gleaming at its crimson heart. She traced her hand down her bended leg, gliding from silken stocking to silken skin. It could be, she thought, that her husband could not control his passions. He had thrown her on to the bed, too impatient to allow her the time to disrobe.

She twined her fingers in the crisp dark hair of her mons and sighed heavily. Oh, why hadn't he come tonight? She should be chatting amiably to him now and he should be smiling at her with his deep-brown eyes.

His eyes would be brown, she decided. And so would his hair.

Her head dropped back on to the pillows and she trailed her fingertips over the contours of her breasts. Her other hand dipped to the swollen petals of her lips and eased them apart. She stroked along the hot, satiny crevice then pressed at the scrap of tender flesh above. A gentle moan escaped her lips as sensation, rich and fierce, flared in her groin. Beneath her rolling fingertip the hard little bead swelled to erection and pulsed insistently.

Downstairs the dinner gong clanged dully. Clarissa tensed. Would someone come for her when she didn't appear? She listened for the sound of footsteps, her finger gently rocking. But no, there was nothing.

Lifting her hips, she drew moisture from her split dewy crease and swirled it over the inflamed knot of her clitoris. With a quick, light friction, her fingers rubbed. Her breathing shortened to tiny gasps and the air sweetened, heavy with the scent of her need. A quivering anticipation coiled within her.

Arching her back, she drove a finger into her tight heated passage. In just a few months it would be a man she felt there, strong and hungry. She thrust urgently back and forth, her thumb nudging at her pleasure bud. He would slide wet kisses over her eager, naked body. He would take her to heights such as this.

Clarissa stifled a cry as the delicious tension surged and unleashed itself. Her body jerked, the ripples of her crisis spilling through her. Then, all too quickly, they ebbed away. She slumped against the bed, her breasts rising and falling with her shallow breath. An enfeebling glow soothed her body and her mouth curved in a warm, gentle smile.

For some time she lay in abandoned repose, until a soft tap at the door roused her. Alicia called her name. Clarissa straightened her clothes and repositioned the mirror.

'I must have fallen asleep,' she mumbled, turning the key. Her stepmother swept in, trailing wafts of lavender perfume.

'I thought you might be hungry,' she declared, setting down a salver on the bedside table. 'Take no notice of your father, my dear. He's a fool sometimes. As is Lord Marldon for not showing. But take heart. You can have just as much fun – heavens, probably more – without him. Cousin Lucy is quite looking forward to seeing you. She said she'd be delighted to introduce you to London.'

'But Cousin Lucy's a scandal,' exclaimed Clarissa. 'Father would never agree to it.'

Alicia tapped the side of her nose. 'Your father need never know,' she said. 'We'll be gone soon enough and then you can do as you wish.'

Clarissa gazed at her stepmother in awe. How was it that she could never allow a problem, no matter how big or small, to exist for more than a moment? Then she frowned.

'You've forgotten something,' she said wearily. 'Aunt Hester. She's hardly Lucy's greatest admirer.'

Alicia smiled mysteriously. 'Leave it to me. You may find there's more to Aunt Hester than meets the eye.'

Chapter Two

*B*eneath the flaring gas jets of the Haymarket, theatre-goers spilt onto the pavement. Top hats and jewelled chignons bobbed above sombre suits and shimmering gowns. Arm in arm, elegant couples made their way between the columns of the portico to step into awaiting carriages. Others strolled away in a sea of frothing silks, up to Piccadilly or down to Pall Mall.

Lucy Singleton, recognising a handsome face, smiled with downcast eyes then quickly resumed the conversation with her tawny-haired companion.

'And what is more,' she breezed, 'I hear she is to attend Octavia's ball.'

Sir Julian Ackroyd glanced back at the crowd. 'Who is?' he asked vaguely.

'Why, Miss Eulalie Crane, the American heiress!' Lucy tapped his chest with her closed fan. 'I see your attention is wandering, Julian. Can your Parisian whores truly be so memorable?'

'Not at all,' he replied equably. 'I was simply wondering who the young swell was. The one who deserved such an alluring smile.'

'Ah, him!' Lucy adjusted her boa and pulled her black velvet mantle over her arm. For a brief moment she thought he might be jealous but then she remembered this was Sir Julian. He was never anything other than mildly curious.

'Nothing of present interest,' she said. 'I'm afraid he's now wed. Like you, dear Julian. But, unlike you, he's a tiresomely faithful husband.'

'I see. Then that explains the frosty glare you received from his lady friend.'

'Did I? Oh, how I should like to reassure her. "He is truly devoted to you, Mrs Wife," I would say. "Why, the last time he bed me was on the eve of your nuptials. After that, nothing!"'

'What?' exclaimed Julian in mock horror. 'Not even a stolen kiss? I can barely believe it.'

'Well, maybe just a small farewell between the ceremony and the honeymoon. It was of no consequence.'

'Then I'm sure she'd be much assured. A husband able to resist the charm of Mrs Singleton shows true fidelity indeed.'

'Precisely! And is not Mrs Singleton quite irresistible tonight?' Lucy knew she was. With a cluster of blonde ringlets hanging from her flower-entwined topknot, and dressed in her new gown of lilac taffeta, she had caught many an admiring eye. And her daringly low décolletage had not gone unnoticed by Julian.

In the privacy of their box, he'd spent a great deal of Act Three printing kisses on her bare shoulders and neck. In Act Four his hands had strayed beneath her skirts as far as her thighs, and by Act Five his fingers had played deliciously within the crotch of her silk drawers. She hoped no opera glasses had been trained on her face at the time.

'Quite irresistible,' agreed Sir Julian, drawing to a halt and turning to face her. Beneath the lurid glare of a street lantern he looked down at her, his china-blue eyes narrow with desire, and pressed her hand to his lips.

'Then am I to have my *cadeau* from your bawdy jaunt?'

asked Lucy. 'I fear the suspense will kill me before long. Won't you give me just a tiny clue?'

'Very well. I have it about my person.'

'Goodness! Do you wish me to search you?' she gasped, trailing her hand down the front of his cape. 'Here in the street? That would be most indecent of me.' A passing drunk jostled her and she seized the opportunity to press herself to Julian's strong, broad body. She clung to him, gazing up with sparkling green eyes.

'Decency has never been a strong point of yours,' he said, offering her his arm.

'I'll have another clue, if you please.'

They strolled further along the Haymarket. Beyond the windows of the gin palaces, coffee rooms and oyster shops, chandeliers sparkled in enormous rococo mirrors. Revellers from the smoke-filled establishments stumbled out on to the street and, above their din, flower-sellers and sundry hawkers touted their wares. Sir Julian and Lucy, moving closer together, threaded their way through the bustling crowd.

'It is long and sturdy,' he said after a moment's thought.

'Pah!' she scoffed. 'I've had that before.'

'It has the potential for affording you exquisite delights.'

'So, you have brought me nothing but your cock? Daubed in all the flavours of France, I shouldn't wonder.'

'*Au contraire, ma chérie.*' He leant close to whisper in her ear. 'My cock has a taste for only the finest English honey-pot.'

'Why, you lie so beautifully.' She smiled. 'Then what do you have for me?'

'What I have, my darling, is something so delightful that you shall have to wait for it.'

Lucy mused on the various options. In the past, Sir Julian had presented her with deliciously lewd books, French chocolates and liqueurs, underclothes from the finest Parisian fashion houses and, best of all, a magnificent kid-leather dildo. 'That,' he'd said, 'is for the times when I cannot be there to satisfy you.'

She had laughed at those words. Many times she'd made it clear to him that, when he could not be there, she had no shortage of lovers to pleasure her. While Lucy was not averse to lying, her claim was now sadly less accurate than it had been some months ago. At present she had only one other beau, Gabriel Ardenzi, and he'd been somewhat inattentive of late. She would have to find another handsome man, or continue with her teasing half-truths, if she were to keep Sir Julian on his toes. After all, if he could not devote himself to her, then she was certainly not prepared to devote herself to him.

'Oh, I have news of great import,' she cried excitedly, suddenly recalling the help Alicia had asked of her. 'Remember me talking of Clarissa?'

'Your prim little cousin,' replied Julian, encouraging her with a raised eyebrow.

'Well, she's in London and she's to be wed. And you'll never believe who to.' Lucy paused, eager to create dramatic effect. 'To Lord Marldon. Isn't it perfectly dreadful?'

Sir Julian whistled between his teeth. 'Well, well. I never thought I'd hear those words. Marldon getting wed, eh? Still, I'd heard his coffers were rather low. I assume the dowry is quite substantial.'

'Oh, but of course,' said Lucy gravely. 'And, in return, Clarissa becomes a countess. Apparently her father is as proud as punch.'

'An excellent match, as they say,' said Julian. 'And dear papa? Is he also delighted at the prospect of gaining a son-in-law whose tastes are . . . how shall I phrase it, a little rare?'

'Pah!' said Lucy in a sharp, cross breath. 'I doubt he's given much thought to that. Why, the lovelorn fool merely wants Clarissa off his hands, and quickly.

Wouldn't you with a wife like Alicia, eager to mete out punishment at your slightest wrongdoing? A woman always ready to –'

'Not my taste, I'm afraid,' interrupted Sir Julian, squeezing her hand and smiling suggestively. 'You of all people should know that.'

Lucy, for once unable to summon up a breezy, flirtatious quip, sighed despondently. For a moment she fell silent, her thoughts turning bitterly to her own ill-treatment at the hands of Charles Longleigh. He was a selfish browbeater and, worse still, he was a hypocrite. Here was a man who, having once denounced *her* for all manner of indecencies, was about to marry off his own daughter to the most notorious debauchee in London. Was he completely shameless? Devoid of the merest scrap of conscience?

Why, a woman of the loosest morals would be hard-pressed to keep pace with Lord Marldon, and poor Clarissa was but a sweet young virgin. And, according to Alicia, she was utterly blind to her father's scheming ways. She had not the faintest notion of what lay ahead of her.

As they turned into Piccadilly Lucy's spirits rose. 'But all is not lost,' she exclaimed, taking a couple of sideways skips. 'Alicia has hit upon a most wonderful plan. She thinks it prudent to try and make Clarissa somewhat more amenable to Marldon's demands. And guess who's been charged with the task of, shall we say, introducing her to a little of what's to come?'

Julian laughed and shook his head. 'You haven't, have you? What on earth for? Marldon's hardly going to reject the girl, is he? He needs the money. I would have thought he'd take her if she were riddled with the pox and as coarse as a sailor's drab.'

'Well unfortunately she isn't,' replied Lucy, hooking her arm over Julian's. 'So she won't have the luxury of being cast aside or locked in a broom cupboard. No, apparently – and more's the pity – the poor girl's grown

24

into quite a beauty. Alicia, dear Alicia, simply hopes to ease Clarissa's suffering, reduce the trauma of the conjugal bed.'

'How very benevolent,' said Julian, smiling. 'So, my little Jezebel, what is the plan?'

'Ah,' said Lucy enigmatically. 'First you must show me my gift. Perhaps then I may consider telling you.'

'I shall hail a cab at once,' he replied, fingers clicking in the air.

At Chester Square the hansom drew to a halt. To Lucy's relief, the stucco terraces looked sleepy and the streets were quiet. Nevertheless, she kept her head bowed as Sir Julian reached up to hand the cabman his fare.

Belgravia could be such a gossipy neighbourhood and her reputation was in no need of scandalised embellishments. She'd enlivened quite enough afternoon teas when she'd failed to complete her year of mourning. But Lucy knew that dear old Robert, God rest his soul, would not have wanted it any other way. Black, quite frankly, didn't suit her, at least not head-to-toe black. Far better, she thought, to pursue all the rich pleasures to which Robert had introduced her. It was a much more sincere and personal tribute to his memory.

Lucy unlocked the door and was satisfied to find the house in hushed semi-darkness. Her servants had long since learnt when to be discreet and when to tend to her. There was no one standing by to take their cloaks and nothing but an oil lamp awaiting her return. Lucy clasped its heavy gilt base and crept up two flights of stairs, forging a path through the gloom with the lamp's bleary incandescence.

In the bedroom, shadows leapt and Julian's stretched silhouette momentarily reared up to the high coved ceiling. Either side of the fireplace mirror, gaslights burnt within frosted half-cups, suffusing the room with a honeyed glow and gilding the brass bedstead. Lucy stood the oil lamp on a pier table and turned its wick low.

Oh, how inviting that bed looks, she thought. But she knew she would have to wait. If Julian had a gift, then she was in no position to make demands.

'And so?' she said, draping her mantle across the ottoman. 'Am I to receive my present now?'

Julian, setting down his beaver hat, ignored her. The silence lengthened as, without hurry, he removed his gloves, his bow tie, and finally the high, starched collar of his shirt.

'Indulge my prurience,' he said, seating himself in a velvet-cut armchair. Slowly he folded one leg over the other and laid his walking cane across his lap. 'Tell me, in lurid detail, how you intend to educate this country cousin of yours.' He smoothed a finger over his pencil-fine moustache, calmly awaiting her reply.

Lucy stood by the dressing table, her mouth curving in a challenging smile. She recognised Julian's disdainful manner as the prelude to a game in which she could do no right. He would conjure up whatever misdemeanours he could and then, oh how deliciously, she would be punished for them. Her stomach fluttered with apprehension and her groin thrilled with lust.

'I shall reveal nothing until I receive my present,' she said, deliberately antagonistic.

'Do you think you deserve it?' asked Julian, his stern blue eyes raking her body. 'I wonder, how did you conduct yourself during my absence?'

Lucy opened her mouth to speak but Julian stopped her with a raised hand.

'No. Let me guess. Impeccably?' he asked in a voice heavy with sarcasm. 'Or perhaps imperfectly? But no. Only a generous soul could say such a thing. Come here.'

He indicated with a tap of his ebony cane where she should stand. Wordlessly, Lucy complied.

'Or . . .' Julian pointed the jewelled tip of his walking

stick at the tiers of lace hanging below Lucy's ruched overskirt. 'Immorally?' He lifted her petticoats. Her shoes were lilac satin, a matching rosette adorning each square toe. Her openwork stockings were of the palest blue.

'Such dainty feet,' he mused. 'I should dearly like to know how many times they've been up in the air of late.' He touched the cane to an ankle then trailed the slender staff along the inside of her calf, lifting the weight of the fabrics.

Lucy shuddered as, with agonising slowness, he reached the frilled knee of her drawers.

'For I am quite sure,' he continued, raising her layers higher and higher, 'this is not the only stick you have felt in recent days.'

The cane slid over her silk-clad legs then lightly nudged at the juncture of her thighs. Arousal, warm and dewy, moistened her sex, and her labia twitched with gathering hunger.

'How many cocks have you had in here?' he asked, pressing the ebony shaft into the split of her drawers. He slotted its cold, hard length into the damp cleft of her pouting vulva and moved it back and forth.

Lucy, murmuring pleasure, widened her stance.

'Ah, but still hungry I see. How many?' Julian tapped the cane against her. 'How many?' he repeated fiercely.

'Why, you do me an injustice,' replied Lucy, adopting the air of one offended. 'Or do you pay me a compliment? You've been away only nine days.'

'Tell me about Clarissa.'

Lucy shrugged. 'I haven't seen her for some three years, though I'm told she's a beauty. A beauty, of course, whose naivety is unlikely to appeal to Marldon.'

'And?' urged Julian. 'Your role in solving this slight problem is . . .?'

'Is divulged when I receive my *cadeau*?' she said imperiously.

Julian teased her pulsing sex with a soft, skimming

caress of the cane. 'Has Gabriel had you during my absence?' he enquired, his face devoid of all expression.

'But of course,' said Lucy airily, wondering if perhaps this time she might provoke him to jealousy.

'Then your *cadeau*, my sweet, is between your legs.'

Lucy could not understand him. Did he mean to chastise her with a common walking cane? Surely not. He knew her passions were roused by only the finest implements. Then maybe he was jealous – actually jealous! And he was to torment her by offering a mere stick with which to satisfy her needs.

'Are . . . are you to deny me?' she asked.

'What do you feel here?' He pushed the tip into the vent of silk and rubbed it over her tender flesh. 'Concentrate. What do you feel?'

Lucy felt the smooth glassy end rubbing against her folds and nudging at her engorged clitoris. She felt her plump lips separating, and then the object gliding along her slick, wet crease. She felt it hard and round, poised at the aching mouth of her openness. It felt as if it would slide into her far too easily and she said as much.

'Like this?' he suggested. Swiftly, he drove the cane into her moist depths.

Lucy gasped. Though the shaft was slim the head pushing before it was large and bulbous. Julian moved the rod in small rotations, stirring it against the walls of her vagina, teasing her with its strange, shifting pressures. Glorious tremors rushed within her and her desire liquefied with heavy slowness.

'Does it feel like a cock?' asked Julian.

'A little,' she replied hoarsely.

'A little cock you mean? Perhaps like Gabriel's?'

Lucy smiled inwardly. 'Not at all,' she breathed. 'Gabriel has a most handsome cock.' He *was* jealous, she thought exultantly. Measurements had never concerned him before.

'Of course,' he said smoothly. 'How foolish of me to

think you would accept anything less. Then does it feel like a cane, an ordinary cane?'

'I've never –'

'Close your eyes,' he clipped. He withdrew the ebony rod and Lucy's skirts rustled to the ground. 'Kneel before me.'

Lucy, her eyes shut, her sex burning, allowed herself to be manoeuvred into place. She felt his open thighs snug against her arms and heard him fumbling with the buttons of his fly. Then his hand cupped her head, bringing her mouth down to touch something rounded and smooth.

It was the cane, salt-sweet and hot from her own body. At Julian's command she sucked her wetness from the hard knob and explored its contours with her tongue.

'And now this,' he said, clutching a handful of her curls. He guided her into a new position.

This time the touch was familiar: it was the satin-smooth head of Julian's stiffened prick. With an eager mouth, Lucy sheathed his warm length, closing her lips firmly about the thick root. His coarse hair brushed against her nose as she nuzzled deeply, breathing in his musky closeness. Heeding Julian's words, she sucked back and forth, then played her fluttering tongue over the lines and folds of his swollen glans. Ah, now she understood.

Julian tugged at her hair, forcing her to pull back. Before her eyes was his tumescent flesh, potent and glistening. Next to him was the cane, its purple glass tip moulded and scored to represent the unfurled head of a phallus.

'Why, it's stupendous,' breathed Lucy. 'What a delicious idea.'

'And even better,' said Julian, unscrewing the tip, 'is this.' From a hollowed-out shaft slid a short ebony handle followed by six thin leather thongs. 'An exquisite little martinet,' he said, curling his fingers to the sculpted haft. 'As yet, unused.'

Lucy cooed in delight. She watched him draw the strands lovingly across his palm, her skin tingling with anticipation. Oh yes, this was a fine instrument indeed. Sir Julian had chosen well.

She reached out to touch the whip but was sharply rebuked. This might be a gift for her, said Julian, but he was the one bestowing it. He draped the thongs over one of her shoulders then trailed them behind her neck. Lucy shivered. The leather swept lightly across her skin, its soft caress a mockery of the pain it could inflict. Ah, she would have no hesitation in baring her flesh to its stinging kisses.

'Take off your frippery,' ordered Julian.

Lucy obeyed. Layers of silk and taffeta pooled to the ground. She unclasped her stays, cast them aside, then slipped off her beribboned chemise. Standing in her drawers, stockings and shoes, she paused and fixed Julian with a lascivious smile. She cupped her hands to her breasts and kneaded the heavy, orbed flesh. She scuffed her thumbs over her nipples, bringing the coral tips to tight points of pleasure. Her body thrilled to her indulgent touches and she murmured with unabashed arousal.

Julian, the trace of a sneer on his lips, drew the thongs of the martinet through his loosely curled fist. When the ends disappeared beneath his fingers, he opened his palm, lashed the air softly, and once more trailed the leather through his large hand.

With teasing slowness, Lucy untied the string of her drawers then let the silk slide down her legs. She ran her hands over the lush contours of her body, lingering at the point where her neat waist flared out to the swell of her hips. Then, turning to offer Julian a view of her plump rear, she stroked the peach-smooth cheeks of her buttocks.

She was about to remove her garters when Julian

demanded that she stop. He didn't want her naked; he wanted her as she was but with her stays against her skin. Lucy smiled obligingly and picked up the garment, panelled in peacock-blue and emerald satin. Sucking in her breath she managed, after some fumbling, to refasten its hourglass boning around her own softer curves.

As she paraded and twirled she stole glances at her reflection in the pier glass. In the half-light the curls of her pubis had the lustre of spun gold, and her ample buttocks jutted below her corset like two pearly moons. She looked well, and she knew that beneath Sir Julian's cool exterior there was a man churning with lust.

'How obedient you are,' he said, rising from his chair and striding towards her. 'I can see you are eager for your *cadeau.*' He pushed a foot between her ankles, nudging her legs apart. 'Do you wish to know the reason why I am to punish you so severely?'

'Yes,' she said boldly, excitement clutching at her heart.

Julian pressed a firm hand to her hot, pounding sex.

'There are three reasons,' he said with dispassionate calm. 'One, because you refuse to share your bawdy plans concerning some dear virgin cousin.' As he spoke he slipped his index finger into her humid passage. 'Two,' he continued, pushing in a second broad finger, 'because you're screwing an artist whose prick, so you tell me, is most handsome.'

The mention of Gabriel, again with that possible note of envy, caused Lucy to smile with secret delight. Was he actually growing fond of her? Enough to be covetous of her body?

'And three?' she breathed.

Julian merely smirked. Slowly, he drove his fingers into her, again and again. The pad of his thumb rocked her clitoris, intensifying its rich, aching pulse. There was no sound, save for Lucy's light gasps and the soft clack, clack of her molten sex.

'And three . . .' he said at length.

He removed his fingers and played them teasingly across her distended outer lips. He stroked her with a maddeningly light touch, as if he were handling gossamer. It was unbearable. When he pressed his fingers into the wet seam of her folds, Lucy whimpered with gratitude. Pleasure coursed through her entire body before sinking to engulf her fiery loins. It throbbed there, a percussive heavy beat. She waited, her heart drumming wildly, for the announcement of her third unforgivable sin.

'Because you conduct yourself like a whore,' said Julian at last. He pushed once, hard. His three compacted fingers slammed into her.

Lucy groaned, her sex stretched around the awkward girth of his penetration. He shoved again, his knuckles banging into her soft, hungry flesh. When he next spoke he punctuated his words with a thrusting hand.

'And I want you – over the table – your cunny wide for me. And I'm going to whip you – twice for every sin.'

In one swift movement, Julian caught hold of Lucy's wrists and, twisting her sharply, clasped them behind her back. He pushed her towards the writing desk, mocking her when she stumbled, and leant her body across the green leather surface. The busk of her corset dug viciously into her belly, and she shifted herself in search of greater comfort.

'Don't dare to move,' he said severely, sliding open a desk drawer – a drawer he knew contained no writing equipment. He withdrew several lengths of silken cord and murmured, 'Perfect.'

Sir Julian stretched Lucy's arms either side of the table and secured each wrist to a finely carved leg. She lay there, moaning faintly, as he repeated the bondage on her wide-spread ankles. The indignity and vulnerability of such a position thrilled her. She felt deliciously open, brazenly wet, and completely at the mercy of Sir Julian.

She listened to the sound of him moving about the room, undressing without haste. When he returned to stand behind her she instinctively clenched her buttocks. But he did not touch her. He laughed.

'Hasn't your Italian artist taught you the first rule?' he scorned. 'One must prepare a canvas before painting it.'

He spanned his fingers to her legs and edged slowly upwards, his thumbs trailing over her damp inner thighs. He massaged whorls over her skin, nudging inwards but never quite touching her seething sex. Then, moving to the swell of her rump, he caressed and pummelled the pliable twin globes.

'So pale and succulent,' he murmured. 'So ripe.'

He nipped her twice and Lucy jerked with the sharp pain. Then his touch grew gentle, lulling her into relaxation. He blew cool air over her skin and gently parted her rounded cheeks. He breathed soft lines along her open crevice, lingering over her tightly pinched hole. Following the lines of his breath, his tongue trailed moistly along her deep furrow. His moustache rasped lightly, and he lapped at her wrinkled centre.

Lucy tensed, wondering if he would invade her most secret orifice. The thought inflamed her and, squirming against her restraints, she pushed herself towards him.

Abruptly Julian pulled away. 'You expect to *take* your pleasures?' he scoffed. 'As and when you wish? Remember, Lucy, I am the one who gives. You are the one who receives.'

He fell into silence. The room grew heavy with tension. Lucy could not feel him, see him nor hear him. She stiffened, knowing the sweet onslaught was imminent.

'Two for every sin,' he said sternly. 'On each side of your luscious arse.'

Lucy turned her head, pressing her cheek to the table. From the corner of her eye she saw him raise his arm. The leather strands flicked back. She braced herself. With a soft swish the whip arced down and cracked loudly across one plump buttock. Lucy yelped, stripes of pain searing into her flesh.

Julian waited, allowing the smarting impact to subside. Then again he whirled the martinet back and the second lash fell, as cruel and swift as the first. The fanned-out thongs moulded to her curves and the sting, hot and sharp, rushed back to the surface.

Lucy whimpered as the pain transformed itself into smouldering pleasure. Then a third and a fourth lash. The scorching impact bit into the glow suffusing one half of her bottom. Two more deft strokes and a deeper radiance uncoiled to meld with the intensity burning in her sex.

Julian paused. 'Oh, what a fine artist I am,' he said. 'One virgin canvas, the other streaked with blushes.'

He moved away from the periphery of her vision, his hand rubbing the cool area of her other cheek. Then another six lashes rained down on that untouched side. Each one rekindled the sting of the previous stripe, building up a savage heat until her two mounds were a symmetry of crimson fire. Then he stopped.

Lucy lay still, listening to Julian's ragged breath. When she felt his hands again, they were no longer those of a chastiser but those of a tender lover soothing her raw, prickling flesh. Her blazing skin, alive with sensitivity, took his caresses deeper. Flames of desire licked around her womb and her juices ran freely. She shifted her hips, striving to press her simmering clitoris to a surface. But her tethered ankles would not allow for it.

'Please,' she begged, raising her pelvis high. 'Take me.'

Julian grunted a short, scornful laugh and laid the length of his prick, heavy and insistent, against the split of her arse.

'For one who prides herself so on shocking her noble peers,' he teased, beginning to slide back and forth, 'your language is remarkably coy. Will you say what you mean, Mrs Singleton?'

'Fuck me,' she said, through clenched teeth. 'Please, oh, Ju – oh fuck me.'

The thick head of his phallus dropped and hovered momentarily at her wetly gaping entrance. 'Such a pretty request,' he breathed huskily. Then, with a vigorous lunge, he buried himself to the hilt. She cried out, the force of him shunting her forward. At once he pulled her to him and held her steady.

Lucy clenched her muscles to his swollen prick, and he drove into her, his thrusts long and hard. His flat belly pounded against her sore buttocks, and his hand reached around, seeking her clitoris. With a quick, fretting finger, he chased the urgency beating in the tight little bud. On the edge of extremity, Lucy uttered a staccato of shrill, breathy bleats. The hot spasms gripped and she wailed as their fierce, trembling energy consumed her. A growl echoed in the wake of her cry and Julian's orgasm pumped into the final throes of her own.

Her tormented body sagged with blissful relief. Julian held his position, caressing her inside with a soft rhythm while gently stroking her tender rump. All his movements were perfectly in tune with the warm tranquillity bathing her senses.

'Julian,' she murmured when her breathing had steadied. 'I adore your *cadeaux*.'

'And I adore handing them to you, my sweet.' He began unlacing her stays, adding to her sense of lazy release. 'Though, if you recall, generosity alone was not my motive. You are now obliged to divulge your plans for cousin Clarissa?' He withdrew from her and set about untying the cords at her ankles.

Lucy murmured a languorous half-groan. She'd forgotten their earlier bargain, and in truth she didn't really have much of a plan. Alicia had merely expressed a hope that Clarissa, given the right encouragement, would yield to a little pre-marital dalliance.

After running various names through her mind, Lucy had concluded that Gabriel Ardenzi was probably the best option. If Clarissa didn't mind a man who wore his hair too long and who had a tendency, to say the least, to be capricious, then maybe she would succumb to his seductions. Persuading Gabriel to agree to it, however, would not be an easy task. A country virgin was hardly his usual choice of lover.

'Pray tell,' encouraged Julian, helping her to her feet.

Lucy unclasped her loosened corset, stepped out of her shoes, and rubbed at her reddened wrists. 'Is there no end to your lecherous curiosity?' she asked, standing on tiptoe to press a kiss to his lips.

'You should know better than to ask,' he said, smiling fondly and tangling his fingers in her dishevelled curls.

Lucy sighed and padded across the room to sit on the edge of the bed. 'The strength of it is this,' she said, rolling down her stockings. 'I'm to find her a beau, and quickly, before Marldon arrives. I thought perhaps Gabriel would be suitable.' She looked at Julian provocatively and said deliberately, 'After all, there are few women able to resist his dark good-looks. And he *is* a most skilful lover.'

Julian raised his eyebrows, affecting surprise. 'I didn't realise that you were willing to share your bedfellows. I'd be more than happy to assist.'

'*You* are a married man,' said Lucy, with only half-feigned severity. 'I already share you.'

'Such a pity,' he teased, joining her and playfully biting her neck.

'And besides,' continued Lucy, 'I've been prevailed upon to take merely the edge off her innocence, not corrupt her completely. That prerogative belongs strictly to Lord Marldon.'

Chapter Three

Clarissa, steeling herself for disappointment, pushed tentatively at the door of the breakfast room. Please, Aunt Hester, she willed, don't be sitting there.

Since Charles and Alicia's departure, Aunt Hester, with her pinched, sour face, had presided over the household with a fearsome impassivity. She'd insisted on taking Clarissa to some dull afternoon teas and some even duller soirées, and summer had seemed to hold all the promise of a wet Wednesday. But yesterday Aunt Hester had taken to her bed, complaining of a dreadful fatigue. This morning she'd failed to appear for breakfast and Clarissa's hopes were rising.

In the breakfast room, Kitty was leaning across the table, sweeping a cloth over its oak surface.

'What on earth are you wearing?' exclaimed Clarissa, catching a flash of red beneath Kitty's crisp black uniform.

The housemaid grinned and hitched up her skirts, proudly displaying a pair of scarlet stockings.

'Dandy, aren't they?' She beamed. 'Real silk. Missis gave them me afore she went away. To say sorry for the saucing I got. Didn't you get anything?'

'I got Aunt Hester,' replied Clarissa grimly. Then she hissed, 'Has she been seen yet?'

'Lor, has she!' cried Kitty. 'Came down to breakfast in her nightgown and wrapper, she did. And she was all of a moony flutter. I've never seen the like.'

Kitty pulled up a chair and sat before the table, her chin resting on steepled fingertips. Cocking her head to one side, she batted her eyelashes at Clarissa and smiled.

'Could I harf another hegg, please, Hellis,' she mimicked. Then she shrieked with glee and slammed her hands on the polished surface.

Clarissa laughed, protesting it was untrue.

'On my mother's grave,' insisted Kitty, crossing herself. 'And you have to say he's a bit of a looker, isn't he? Bit oily for my tastes, mind, but all the same he's a looker.'

Sebastian Ellis was their new footman, another of Alicia's appointments. Undoubtedly he was handsome, as a footman ought to be, but the idea of Aunt Hester falling for his charms was absurd. Still, if he kept her occupied then Clarissa wasn't going to complain.

'So where is she now?' she enquired.

Kitty, her lips pursed, shook her head in sardonic pity. 'Dreadful fatigued, miss,' she replied. 'Dreadful fatigued.'

Clarissa's thoughts raced. There were new gowns to collect from the dressmakers, gowns that Aunt Hester would be sure to frown upon. Then perhaps later she could pay a call on cousin Lucy. Without Lord Marldon there was no one to introduce her to London society. And Alicia had said Lucy knew everyone there was to know and went to all the very best parties.

'If she gets out of bed,' continued Kitty, noting Clarissa's expression, 'then I'll give her a mighty kick on the ankles.'

'Thank you, Kitty,' she said. 'That would be much appreciated.'

Gabriel Ardenzi could never decide if taking a house in the suburbs of Chelsea had been a superb idea or a terrible one. Away from the city smog, the air was good and clear. But on days like today the sunlight glancing off that damned river was infuriatingly harsh. He'd spent far too long this morning fiddling with oiled paper, stretching it across the windows in a bid to diffuse the glare.

He should have chosen the north-facing room instead. But no, he reminded himself, it was too small for a studio; it would have felt like a prison cell. At least here he could rack his unfinished canvasses against the walls and remind himself of things he'd rather be painting.

He stepped back from his easel and looked dully at the incomplete portrait. A society miss gazed back at him with bland eyes and a vapid smile. A good enough likeness, he thought bitterly. He tossed his brush on to a table cluttered with mixing bowls, phials and bundles of charcoal, and, yawning widely, wiped his hands on a rag. Christ, he'd been at work less than two hours and already he was bored. Commissioned portraits were the bane of his life and summer invariably brought a glut of them.

He wandered about the room in a desultory fashion before throwing himself full-length on to a damask chaise longue. He raised his unseeing eyes to the ceiling and sighed heavily. What he needed was a wealthy patron, some old duke with money to burn and an interest in decent art. And that, he decided, was as likely as England's dear Queen casting off her widow's weeds and dancing down the Mall.

Hell, he would have to start working harder. He'd already lost two lucrative commissions this summer. Some accused him of idleness, but it wasn't that. Or if it was, he mused, it was brought about by his talent and imagination, two things utterly wasted on the commercial market. He tugged at the string which kept his chestnut locks from falling about his shoulders and shook free the loose curls.

Pushing himself up from the chaise, he crossed to

where the oiled paper closed him off from the outside world. Impatiently he tore down several sheets, squinting as brilliant sunlight flooded the room behind him.

He opened the tall casement window and stepped out on to the wrought-iron balcony. For a moment the blare of a ship's horn cut through the clangs and shouts from the wharf. Gabriel leant his bare forearms on the warm metal railings and noticed, with a nagging sense of guilt, his exposed skin. He was bronzed, a sure sign he was spending too few hours at his easel and too many here, gazing idly at the bustle of the Embankment.

No, he decided, it wasn't a patron he needed, but someone truly inspirational to paint, someone like the new girl on Cheyne Walk. Yes, that would bring the passion back to his art. If ever there was an Attic beauty, then it was her. She was fit to adorn a Grecian coin. Oh, how his fancy would roam with a woman such as her sitting for him. All the other stuff, the oils and watercolours that kept the roof over his head, would be a breeze. Fuelled by the love of just one painting, he could be ruthlessly industrious with the others. He would rise early, work until twilight rendered it impossible, and –

There she was again, hair black and glossy as a pool of Indian ink. Damn it, who was she? Turn this way, willed Gabriel. Look at me. But she didn't. She glided down the steps to an awaiting brougham, its door held open by a footman in silver-blue livery. Then, with the merest lift of her skirts and a dip of her head, she stepped into the carriage and out of view.

Gabriel sighed. He ought to make some discreet enquiries and find out who she was. Perhaps she could be persuaded to sit for him. He would paint her as – what? Helen of Troy? Or Cleopatra – on a barge like a burnished throne, surrounded by purples and gold. No, he would paint her as herself. But it wouldn't be a stiff smiling portrait for the drawing room. It would be a work utterly free of society's trappings.

There would be no pins in her hair or her gown. Her

dark locks would tumble freely about her shoulders and she would be simply attired, in a length of gossamer-fine chiffon. He envisaged the wispy fabric draped about her reclining body, offering filmy glimpses of her nudity beneath. He would use pastels to capture the subtle nuances of shade, to hint at a shell-pink nipple and at the darkness cloaking her sex.

A surge of arousal clutched at his loins and in his mind he stripped his model of her chiffon folds. He imagined running his hands over her smooth creamy flesh and kissing her full, rose lips. His cock lifted with a rushing pulse of blood and thickened to hardness. What colour were her eyes? he wondered. How would she look when ecstasy seized her?

For several minutes he stood there, the sun warming his skin, lulling him into fantasies both lustful and romantic. Then a smart rap at the studio door broke violently into his thoughts.

'Hell's teeth,' he spat, stalking angrily into the room. Hadn't he told his staff often enough never, ever to interrupt him in such a manner? Not when he was working. Christ, that could have been a streak of cobalt across some peach-toned cheek.

The door swung open and Lucy, smiling widely, breezed into the studio, pompadour heels clacking on the oakwood floor.

'Good morning,' she said buoyantly. 'I trust I find you well. Delightful weather, is it not?'

Gabriel's exasperated valet appeared in the doorway, spilling profuse apologies and flashing angry looks at Lucy. Dismissing his servant with a flick of the hand, Gabriel rounded on her.

'What the devil do you think you're playing at?' he exclaimed. 'No one, but *no one*, interrupts me when I'm working.'

'Oh, such charming hospitality,' she rebuked gaily, peering into the chimney-piece mirror. 'Such impeccable manners.' She brushed an invisible speck from the tip of her nose and adjusted her frivolous little hat. 'Anyway, you weren't working. You rarely are, Gabriel. And don't even attempt to deny it. I saw you from the street. Besides, the reason for my visit is a matter of some urgency.'

Gabriel exhaled sharply, his anger waning to mere irritation. For Lucy the slightest thing became a matter of some urgency if it so happened to be uppermost in her mind. She was either acting upon a whim, he thought, or she was scheming. The suspicion formed in his mind that it was more likely to be the latter.

'I'm inviting you to dinner,' she continued, turning to him brightly. 'Along with the de Laceys, James Cargill, his two ravishing sisters, Captain Dennett and perhaps –'

'Why, Lucy?' he asked coolly. 'You've never invited me to dine before. Would I be correct in assuming you intend me to neighbour someone at the table? Surely not yourself? No, a ridiculous notion. Perhaps then some whey-faced miss, new in town and in need of a guiding hand.'

The flicker of annoyance on Lucy's face suggested he was quite close to the mark. 'How quick you are,' she said, a note of petulance in her voice. 'It's actually a dear cousin of mine. She's uncommonly handsome. Why, everyone says so, and very respectable too. It would make quite a change for you, Gabriel.'

Gabriel laughed derisively. 'Respectable? I take that to mean a simpering little virgin. Out of the question, I'm afraid. I work hard enough for my pleasures as it is.' He gestured contemptuously towards his easel. 'Do you really think I could be bothered to do the same in my leisure hours?'

Lucy sidled over to him and ran the flat of a hand down his loose cambric shirt. She gazed beseechingly into his brown eyes as her fingers trailed further down his body.

'Come to dinner,' she implored, cupping his groin and rubbing gently. 'Please.'

Gabriel's phallus, only recently stirred by his thoughts of the raven-haired girl, responded quickly to her touch. His shaft twitched and swelled and he pressed himself against Lucy's palm. She murmured her approval of his burgeoning erection and Gabriel, noting the gleeful spark in her eyes, smiled to himself. No doubt she was working on her principle that a man's mind is ruled by his prick. Well, if she wanted to play that game, he was happy to oblige. The pleasures Lucy afforded him were often welcome.

'I would need an awful lot of persuasion,' he said in a low, suggestive tone.

'Would you indeed,' she purred, raising her mouth to his.

Their tongues entwined and she pressed her yielding bosom to his lean, muscular chest. Rubbing herself against him, she planted a series of flirtatious kisses on his neck.

'Do you have an engagement Tuesday next?' she enquired. 'If not, then I could arrange dinner.' She moulded the broadcloth of his trousers to the hard, straining ridge and stroked along its length.

'Try a little harder, Lucy,' he mocked. 'It's going to take a deal more than your fingers playing about my crotch to persuade me.'

'Oh, but I intend more,' murmured Lucy. She dropped to her knees and nuzzled against his imprisoned cock. 'Much more.' Her delicate fingers worked on his fly then pushed beyond to unbutton his drawers. 'Let me pleasure you, Gabriel. In return, I ask no favours, only a promise from you to dine at my house. Soon.'

Gabriel was silent, relishing the coolness of the hand which slipped into the vent of his garments. Lucy released him, her small fingers curling around the veined column of his prick. The smooth, silky skin moved beneath her caress and her breath wafted, soft

43

and warm, over the rosy head. A droplet of clear liquid seeped from the tiny eye and hung there, glistening.

His stiffened penis jerked eagerly, seeking out the promise offered by Lucy's parted lips. Gently, she licked away the shimmering bead of his desire. She teased the glossy acorn tip, skimming its wrinkled collar and fretting the fine membrane beneath. Then the warm, moist cavern of her mouth enveloped him.

Gabriel moaned faintly. His glans nudged deep as, with steady luxury, her lips moved wetly along his engorged staff. Her tongue lashed and an exploring hand reached into his loosened clothes. She hammocked the tight, wrinkled purse of his balls and stroked the pad of flesh behind with teasing fingers.

A rush of sensation filled Gabriel's cock and he closed his eyes. Unbidden, an image came into his mind of the Embankment girl kneeling before him. For a brief moment the fluttering lips, sucking him closer to his peak, were hers. Tension quivered in his thighs and a guttural rasp sounded in his throat.

At once, Lucy withdrew. She made a tourniquet with her fingers and thumb, and squeezed back his climax.

'Damn it,' cursed Gabriel through gritted teeth. His thoughts had wandered, allowing him to forget the truth of his situation. He wasn't being pleasured at all; he was being bargained with.

'Well?' asked Lucy sweetly. 'Do I hear you accepting the invitation?'

Gabriel gave no answer. His cock throbbed with insistent pressure and he craved fulfilment, but he was loath to yield so easily. If Lucy was so desirous of his company, then she would have to work a little harder to secure it.

'It's only dinner,' she chided, looking up at him with big, pleading eyes. 'And perhaps a touch of light flirtation. Nothing you're unaccustomed to.'

'I'm unaccustomed to virgins,' he retorted, but his voice lacked the determined note of earlier.

'So,' began Lucy, her tongue flicking over the flushed head of his penis, 'you are to refuse my kind offer?' She circled her fingers about his thick root. 'Such a pity,' she murmured. 'Such a beautiful young woman, with so much to learn.'

Then, once again, the liquid heat of her mouth engulfed him. With a practised caress, she sucked him quickly back to the border of his crisis. Gabriel felt his semen rising, clamouring to be unleashed. Then he felt the shock of cool, empty air on his straining length.

'Curse you,' he hissed, clutching at Lucy's thick golden curls. His penis, painfully hard with thwarted desire, butted at the closure of her lips. He would have his satisfaction. 'Dinner would be delightful,' he snapped, then he was driving urgently into her pliant, open mouth. He crushed her head into his loins, his hips pumping furiously.

He gasped as the liquor of his release coursed along his shaft and, with a triumphant snarl, he spent his pleasure. His seed jetted over Lucy's searching tongue and she drank deeply.

Gabriel sighed in a long breath and placed his massaging hands on her shoulders. 'If you could teach your cousin such tricks,' he said, 'then perhaps this business would hold a little more appeal.'

Lucy drew back and smiled. 'Oh, I'm sure you'll be a much better tutor,' she replied.

'Dinner,' he said firmly. 'That was my promise. Nothing more.'

Lucy shrugged and rose to her feet. 'There really isn't much more,' she said, brushing at her skirt. 'But, once you meet her, I'm quite certain you'll want more. A lot more.'

Gabriel grunted his doubtfulness and buttoned up his flies.

'There is one small thing though,' continued Lucy, her voice hesitant and unsure. 'If you should take it upon yourself to try and woo her, please tread carefully. It's really her mind – rather than her legs – I want you to open. Well, not quite, but –' She paused and looked at him, guilty and awkward.

With a measured gaze, Gabriel watched her toying with her wedding ring. 'I'm intrigued,' he said flatly. 'You, a woman quite adept at lies and deception, are plainly hiding something. What is it?'

Lucy inhaled deeply. 'Well,' she began, clasping her hands before her, 'my cousin is shortly to be married and –'

'And she must go virgin to the altar?' he interrupted. 'I see no problem there, particularly since I've agreed only to dinner. Who's the lucky groom? Anyone we know?'

Lucy cleared her throat and smiled weakly. 'Lord Marldon,' she said.

Incredulous, Gabriel stared at her. But, before he could utter a sound, Lucy silenced him with an outpouring of desperate persuasion. 'But it need not be a problem. Marldon has yet to arrive. Why, he won't visit London for several weeks. No one will know of it, I give you my word. You could –'

'You expect me,' said Gabriel crisply, 'to attend your dinner? With a view to romancing Marldon's bride-to-be? You must take me for a fool, Lucy.' He walked away and tugged on the bell-rope. 'Would you care for some tea? It might help restore your sanity.'

'Please listen, Gabriel,' she protested.

'Absolutely not,' he said curtly. 'Not dinner, not dominoes. Not anything.'

'But you made a promise,' she whined, plaintively wringing her hands.

'And I've just broken it,' he replied. 'Rather that than my neck.'

Lucy's drawing room was furnished with an abundance of little tables, tasselled footstools and trailing ferns. Nearly every surface was draped in sumptuous, glowing fabrics, and the walls, papered in delicate florals, were covered with paintings and photographs. There were far too many to count. Clarissa knew; she'd tried.

She sat on the plumply stuffed chesterfield, her hands folded demurely in her lap. Mrs Singleton wouldn't be long, the maid had said. And she'd expressly asked that, if a Miss Longleigh were ever to call, refreshments should be served until her return. Unless of course, Miss Longleigh had a pressing engagement.

Clarissa had no such thing. Oh, Lady So-and-So was holding an at-home, and Mrs Barchester was receiving guests between the hours of two and four, but neither prospect appealed. Clarissa would far rather sit alone, waiting for Lucy.

She was a little perturbed about meeting her cousin. It had been some three years since they'd last met, and that was at Mr Singleton's funeral. Since then Lucy was rumoured to have been out with several different men, yet had married none of them. Her husband had left her well provided for and she'd once said, according to Aunt Gwendoline, that she had no need of a man except in her bedroom. That had been the final straw for Charles Longleigh and he'd declared that, under no circumstances, was Clarissa to associate with such a low-tongued light-skirt.

But Clarissa couldn't help but think what a delight it would be to talk to someone closer to her own age. She wondered if cousin Lucy was acquainted with Lord Alec. She knew but little of the man chosen for her. She'd been patient, expecting their meeting to be imminent. But now it wasn't and her curiosity was piqued. She couldn't bear the thought of spending the next few weeks knowing only that the Earl of Marldon was dark, handsome and somewhat sophisticated.

There was a chattering commotion in the hall. Clarissa's stomach flared and danced with nervous expectancy. Would her cousin have changed much? she wondered. Would she really be pleased to find her sitting on the sofa?

The door flung open and Lucy, a froth of tulle and lace perched atop her corkscrew curls, bustled into the room. Exclaiming her delight, she wove a hasty path through the furniture, pursued by the soft whisperings of her magenta gown. Clarissa rose to greet her.

'Gracious heavens,' sparkled Lucy, clasping both Clarissa's hands. 'Alicia said you'd grown into quite a beauty but she neglected to say how beautiful.' She stepped back to run admiring eyes from Clarissa's dark tresses to the flounced hem of her muslin day-gown. 'Ha, dearest cousin, such looks will get you into trouble some day, of that I'm sure. How are you finding London? And dear Aunt Hester? Why, I hear Marldon's been somewhat tardy in presenting himself. Men! Do sit down, Clarry. Tell me everything. I'll ring for some tea. No, no. Some Madeira, don't you think? This calls for a little celebration.'

Clarissa nodded mute compliance, unnoticed by her cousin, who was already making her way to the door. Ignoring the bell-ropes, Lucy called out for wine and cakes. She hastened back into the room, unpinning her hat and chattering gaily about all the places Clarissa ought to go, the people she ought to meet. Really, London was the most marvellous place to be in summer. And, if Lord Marldon couldn't be in town, then Clarissa ought to jolly well have some fun until he deigned to grace her with his presence. There was absolutely no point in moping around, waiting for his lordship, was there?

Clarissa was grateful when the wine arrived and cousin Lucy paused for breath. It gave her the chance to respond to the stream of questions, and the two of them giggled over Hester's dreadful fatigue and the changes Alicia was wreaking on Mr Longleigh. Then Clarissa, nervously fingering the stem of her diamond-glinting goblet, asked, 'Have you ever met the Earl of Marldon?'

'Mmm,' mumbled Lucy, licking cake crumbs from her fingers. 'But it was some time ago, and I confess to having paid him scant attention. He's very handsome, of course. But, cousin, allow me to offer my advice. Do not think on him overmuch. Why, if you do, you'll be quite frantic with impatience before the month is out. Find something to distract you, perhaps a young beau to while away the time. After all –'

'Lucy!' reproached Clarissa, making no attempt to conceal her disapproval. 'How could you say such a thing?'

'Oh, what's the harm in a few secret kisses?' she said, shrugging. She poured out more of the rich, golden wine, despite Clarissa's insistence that one glass was perfectly adequate.

'London's quite different to the country, you know,' she continued blithely. 'Why, it's only the nobodies, poor fools, who are faithful here. Discretion is the only virtue. Ha, and some don't even bother with that. Anyway, how will you know if you truly desire Marldon when there's been no one else to compare him to? Why, sweet innocence, I'll bet you've never even kissed a man, have you?'

Clarissa shook her head, desperately wishing she had. She suddenly felt herself to be the dullest, most prudish person that ever drew breath. Lucy Singleton knew all about life and men, whereas she knew nothing. No doubt her cousin regarded her as scarce more than a child.

'But I – I do know . . .' faltered Clarissa. She was eager to befriend Lucy and desperate to prove she wasn't a mere innocent, a poor foolish nobody. With a surge of determined courage she spoke, her words tumbling over each other in her haste to finish. 'I know about it. I mean, about men and women. I know – in bed. I know about that.' She felt two hot patches colouring her cheeks but was gratified by Lucy's smile of approval.

'Well, you do surprise me, Clarry,' she replied. 'And

do these things you know of appeal to you? Are you eager to experience them?'

The heat still burnt in Clarissa's face but she was resolute. 'Yes,' she said, her eyes fixed on Lucy's, a smile of daring playing about her lips. 'I am.'

Lucy clapped her hands together in delight. 'Ha!' she shrieked. 'How perfectly wonderful. Cousin, I think perhaps you're ready to meet some friends of mine. Are you engaged the evening after next?'

Clarissa was not.

'Then we shall go to a ball,' announced Lucy. 'Octavia Hamilton's ball. It's to be a very fine affair, I promise you.'

'And who,' enquired Clarissa, 'is Octavia Hamilton?'

'She's an actress,' replied Lucy with a wicked grin.

Clarissa felt herself warming to Lucy's irreverence and disregard for decency. To say someone in society was an actress was as good as saying she was a harlot.

'An actress!' she cried with exaggerated shock. 'Goodness, my father would be horrified.'

Emerald shards twinkled in Lucy's eyes. 'And your father,' she said, 'is by now probably in Biarritz. Besides, Octavia is a very good friend of Alicia's. Why, didn't you know? The two of them used to tread the boards together.'

Octavia Hamilton lived in Berkeley Square, in a house of some consequence. The ballroom was a wedding cake of lofty pillars and gilded stucco swirls, with garlands of flowers draping the walls. From a low stage fringed with palms, musicians in hussar costume played gallops, waltzes and polkas. On the dance floor, twirling jewels and gold-studded shirt-fronts glittered in the blaze of chandeliers.

Gabriel, languidly self-assured in white tie and tails, leant against a towering Doric column. Society events usually bored him and invitations he received were, more often that not, answered with his regrets. He would far rather spend an evening at Solferino's or the Six Bells. At least you got decent conversation there. But an invitation from Octavia, profligate and scandalously wealthy, had proved more tempting than most.

As he'd hoped, the action was lively and there was drink aplenty. Footmen in powdered wigs, their calves bulging through white stockings, circulated with skilfully balanced trays of refreshments. Gabriel beckoned one over and took a flute of champagne from his salver.

'Who's that?' hissed Lord Farringdon, reaching for a glass.

Gabriel followed his nod to beyond the dance floor. 'Well, well,' he said, recognising the mass of blonde ringlets. 'If it isn't Mistress Singleton. How surprising to see her amongst such dissolute –'

'No, you fool,' interrupted Farringdon. 'The one with her.'

'One of her beaus, I shouldn't doubt,' said Gabriel, looking incuriously beyond the whirling crowds.

Impatiently, Lord Farringdon took his elbow, jogging his champagne a little, and nudged a path through the chattering clusters of people. 'Feast your eyes on that,' he urged.

Gabriel saw her. It was the girl from the Embankment, in diamonds and mulberry satins, and, oh, she was exquisite. Her gown was cut low, its sleeves scarce more than rosebuds and ribbons. Above the lace edge, her creamy white bosom crested in a gentle curve. Her hair, piled in a heap of tumbling coils, gleamed like jet. And her face was sheer perfection.

He had to capture her. 'Hold this, Algie,' he said, thrusting his drink into Farringdon's hand. He patted his coat and rummaged through a couple of pockets before drawing out a pencil and a slip of card, bordered with gold. His invitation – that would suffice. Gabriel turned it to the blank side and laid it against his companion's back.

'Keep still,' he hissed. 'Lean forward.'

Lord Farringdon grudgingly obliged, allowing Gabriel to sketch soft, fluid lines on to the card. From time to time he glanced up at his unsuspecting model and glowered when anyone threatened to step too close. Moments later, the drawing was complete, or as complete as his patience would allow.

Clarissa was embarrassed. Lucy's London was dazzling and fast, a far cry from Aunt Hester's. She'd fended off countless admiring comments, both murmured and bold, and had refused far more dances than she'd accepted. Yet still her feet, in new brocade slippers, ached. Her mind was spinning with names and faces, none of which seemed to match up, but she was quite sure she hadn't been introduced to this man.

She would have remembered someone who looked so outré and wore such a splendid gardenia in his buttonhole. So why, then, was he demanding a waltz? It flew in the face of all protocol.

'Manners, Gabriel,' reproached Lucy, coming to her rescue. 'Allow me to introduce you: Gabriel – Clarissa. Now go and dance.'

Clarissa, hesitantly placing her fingertips on Gabriel's outstretched arm, allowed herself to be escorted on to the dance floor. The paucity of their introduction alarmed her a little. At a glance you could see this man wasn't ordinary. He was clean-shaven with dark, wavy hair caught in a ponytail. Unruly strands hung about his cheekbones and there was an angelic clarity in his finely boned face. She found his rakish air oddly arresting, thrilling even; and beyond that, something deeper tugged at her, stirring her heart to excitement and making her glow warmly within.

The violins played Strauss, and Gabriel led the steps with strong, easy grace. His hand, pressing against the small of Clarissa's back, was firm, on the threshold of drawing her body close to his. Although he chatted lightly, when he looked at her, his brandy-rich eyes lingered with mesmeric intensity.

'You have a rare beauty,' he said quietly, guiding her into a spin. Clarissa had heard such things before, but nonetheless she missed the beat of the music and her footsteps faltered slightly. Gabriel stumbled with her and laughed. 'You ought to learn to dance,' he teased. 'Then you would be truly perfect.'

His attentions left Clarissa tongue-tied, and the depth of his gaze kindled a flame of longing, confused and illicit, within her. She found herself guiltily wishing her husband would be a man such as this. He was witty and charming, and she fancied his eyes concealed a restless, hungry passion. She thought perhaps it would be wise to reveal that her hand was promised to an earl. But something stopped her. She didn't want to risk losing him so soon to another dancing partner.

And besides, she reassured herself, his words were mere flattery, harmless society banter. How foolish to appear to be taking them seriously.

She wondered if she was being disloyal to Lord Marldon by thinking of this man in such a way. She convinced herself it could not be so, particularly since Lord Marldon was as yet unknown to her. And thoughts alone could not be an act of betrayal.

The music reached its crescendo and Gabriel whisked her into a final, breathtaking spin. As Clarissa sank into a curtsey, he bowed low over her head and whispered, 'Would you care to stroll in the garden? I think fireworks are about to commence.'

For a moment Clarissa thought he'd read her desire. But his meaning was literal, safe. By the French windows a chattering crowd was gathering and spilling out on to the patio. Clarissa was relieved to join them.

After the heat of the ballroom, the evening air cooled her burning cheeks. The leafy garden, decorated with statues and urns, was strung with Chinese lanterns. Their coloured lights swayed in the breeze and glittered like gems in the fountain's shimmering jets. A sudden whoosh heralded the first firework. The onlookers squealed then cooed as starbursts of red, green and silver shattered the night sky.

'Come,' said Gabriel, his gloved fingertips pulling gently on her own. 'There are things far more brilliant away from here.'

Clarissa, driven by a reckless hunger, followed as he squeezed a path through the enraptured crowd and skirted along the shadows. She knew it was wrong. Aunt Hester would be mortified; her father quite unforgiving. But then, wouldn't cousin Lucy be perfectly delighted? A forbidden dalliance, she'd said, was quite accepted in society. Indeed a woman with but one man would be deemed quite undesirable by the fashionable set.

A belt of trees stretched along one part of the garden, and there Gabriel slipped between two slender trunks, encouraging her to follow. After a moment's doubt, she did so. A leafy colonnade stretched ahead, its darkness coloured by the pastel hue of lanterns. Statues, eerie and stern, frozen in their near nudity, loomed from the foliage.

'A little further,' he urged.

The distant strains of the orchestra drifted on the night air and fireworks popped gently overhead. The noise of the people grew low and muffled. Clarissa's blood pounded with fear and excitement. She wanted him, had expected him, to kiss her at once, and yet he seemed intent on taking her deeper into the garden. Perhaps, she thought, he believed her to be one of those disreputable ladies who, in the seclusion of a few trees, would offer up her body. Panic speared her.

'Mr Ardenzi,' she began. 'I have to . . . I'm not what –'

'Hush,' he said. 'I know.'

He drew her aside into a pergola thickly entwined with greenery and honeysuckle. The delicate blossoms filled the air with their rich spicy fragrance, and the entrance, lit by a single lantern, glowed with a ruddy mist. Gabriel stripped off his gloves, let them fall, then lifted Clarissa's chin with one slim finger.

'I want to paint you,' he whispered. 'Will you promise to sit for me soon?'

Relief and disappointment thudded in Clarissa's stomach. How handsome he was, she thought, with his dark hair haloed by a ruby haze and his skin bathed in warmth. But was that all he wanted? For her to be his model?

'I don't always ask for consent,' he said when he received no reply.

Clarissa squinted at the gold-edged card he offered and, with a start of recognition, saw herself sketched in pencil. Heavens, how composed and dignified she looked. She felt sure, at that moment, her face was far from such.

'And the same goes for kisses,' he said, embracing her swiftly. 'Though I see consent in your eyes.'

His mouth bore down on hers and a rush of pleasure weakened Clarissa's every limb. She clung to him, responding hungrily to the questing of his velvet tongue. His hands moved on her back, smoothing over the silk of her gown and up to the naked skin. Her flesh thrilled to the light touch of his fingertips. Then, gently, he cupped her buttocks, drawing her hips towards him. She felt a little fearful but she did not resist.

Through the layers of her petticoats she could feel the hardness of his arousal. It pressed insistently, just above the swell of her pubis. A dart of pleasure pierced her and an aching sweetness pulsed low in her body. Tremulous moans echoed in her throat and then, to her shame, she realised she was rocking her pelvis, grinding herself against his swollen lust.

Struggling to quell her passions, she pulled away from him, breathless and wanting. Her deep-blue eyes, full of needy frustration, looked into his.

'No more,' she pleaded in a whisper that shook, 'I beg of you.'

Gabriel stroked her face, his expression one of bemused confusion. 'A few moments ago,' he said, smiling faintly, 'I was with a woman I assumed to be an innocent. Such a kiss tells me otherwise.'

The night was warm but Clarissa's skin prickled as if it were winter. 'No,' she protested. 'Your assumption was quite true. Please, ask no more of me.'

Gabriel's playfully arched brows suggested he'd heard such coquettish games before. 'Then why, innocent, do your lips speak so fiercely of lust and hunger?' He lowered his head and pressed tender kisses to her neck. 'And, even more difficult to explain,' he continued, his tone mischievously challenging, 'why do you associate with one such as Lucy Singleton? She's hardly famed for the respecta –'

He halted, took a step back, and stared at Clarissa. The amusement drained from his eyes and his jaw sagged with the shock of realisation.

'Christ, no,' he breathed, drawing out the words. 'You're not . . . You're Lucy's cousin, aren't you?'

Clarissa nodded, confused and fearful.

Gabriel, his fists clenched, his eyes closed, raised his head skyward.

'Dear God,' he murmured. 'Dear God, why?'

In the ballroom, Lucy stood with a small, chattering group.

'And do you know,' gushed Lady Neville, fanning herself rapidly, 'the wretched woman was actually received at court?'

'And she was carrying Bertie's child?' exclaimed Augusta Pritchard, jubilant with horror. 'Oh, the temerity of it.'

'Quite shameful,' added Lucy, feigning interest.

She was vexed that Julian had not shown a spark of jealousy when Gabriel, handsome and brusque, had appeared. But then, she reasoned, he'd little cause to. It was perfectly apparent that Gabriel's interest was in her cousin alone. While that was all perfectly delightful, and Lucy had hoped for nothing less, it left her with but one lover, one married lover. Another beau was needed, someone whose attentions would make Julian more appreciative of her desirability.

She scanned the milling crowds, half-heartedly searching for someone suitable, and caught sight of Octavia Hamilton, tall and auburn-haired, gliding towards her. Her brows were knit in a worried frown.

'Lucy darling,' she boomed, snapping on a smile as she edged her way into the group. 'Do let me introduce you to Lady Tranter.' Taking hold of Lucy's elbow, she steered her away from the gossip, the smile dropping from her face. She glanced over her shoulder. 'I think your charming cousin may have a slight problem,' she said in a low voice.

'Whatever is the matter?' demanded Lucy, a little irritably. She could only think that Clarissa had done something foolish. Perhaps she'd swooned over Gabriel's intensity, or cried out for help when his hands had grown too hungry.

'Quite unexpected, I assure you,' said Octavia, pressing her splayed fingers above the swell of her bosom. 'But it's Lord Marldon. I'm afraid he's just arrived.'

Chapter Four

*L*ord Alexander Marldon was known more by his reputation than his face. Yet people, some cross, some curious, still edged aside as the tall figure forged a path through the crowds.

Lucy, although she hadn't seen him for some years, recognised the earl at once. His hair, swept back from his strong angular features, was as thick as ever and, save for a few greying streaks about the temple, just as black. His dark, half-lidded eyes held the same cruel glint, and the arrogant sneer had not faded from his lips. Along the right side of his face ran a thin scar, a silver line following his jaw and dipping an inch or so into his neck. Any other man would have worn a beard. But Marldon didn't; he had only neatly clipped sideburns. He knew the power of that mark.

Octavia crackled open her fan and slipped away with a murmured excuse. Marldon moved towards Lucy, his stride confident, his gaze purposeful.

'Mrs Singleton,' he said in a voice that was menacingly soft. He took her gloved hand in his and touched a kiss to her fingertips, his eyes never once straying from hers. 'I believe we are soon to be related. Your cousin, isn't it?'

Lucy flashed him a smile, the brilliance of which belied her disquiet. 'It appears so,' she replied calmly. 'And I'm told she expects you at the end of the month. Your presence, my lord, is untimely.'

Lucy struggled to keep her attention fixed on Marldon. She was desperate to survey the room in search of Clarissa, and her thoughts raced to find a way of keeping the two apart.

'Business brings me here, Mrs Singleton,' said Marldon. 'Nothing more. I'm not one for the niceties of courtship, as you may imagine. I have no intention of presenting myself quite yet.' His eyes flicked briefly over the mass of heads, then returned to Lucy. He regarded her with a steady challenge. 'Although, if Miss Longleigh *were* here tonight, perhaps a glimpse would whet my appetite. Is she present?'

'Of course not,' blurted Lucy, immediately regretting the zeal of her reply. 'The company she keeps is far more respectable.'

'Oh?' said Marldon, arching his brows. It was only one word but it was imbued with mocking disbelief.

Panic fluttered in Lucy's stomach. Did he know that Clarissa was a guest? And, if he did, was he here for that reason? She trusted him not one iota. It was only a little after midnight, but it was imperative that her cousin return home. She could not bear to think that the two of them might meet, not when Clarissa seemed to have embarked upon an intrigue with Gabriel. It would ruin Alicia's plan of lulling her gently into an acceptance of the earl's depravity.

Relief flooded over her as Julian approached and clapped Marldon on the shoulder. The two men exchanged greetings and shook hands warmly.

'And how is your dear lady wife?' asked Lord Marldon. 'Locked up somewhere in Oxfordshire for the season?'

'Her health troubles her,' answered Sir Julian, giving a smile which did not reach his eyes.

'Still?' said Marldon. 'How unfortunate. I've yet to meet anyone who's seen Lady Ackroyd fit and well. In fact, I've yet to meet anyone who's *seen* Lady Ackroyd. A curious state of affairs, don't you agree?'

'My wife doesn't much care for London,' replied Julian tetchily. Then he brightened a little and added, 'Baccarat, my lord? There's a promising game about to begin upstairs. Perhaps your luck will be better this time round.'

Marldon gave a scornful laugh. 'The devil take you, Ackroyd. Yes, revenge would be very sweet.' Then he turned to Lucy. 'Do you gamble, Mrs Singleton? Ladies tend not to but – well, I don't suppose your presence would raise many eyebrows.'

Lucy bristled at the veiled insult then caught a sly, urging nod from Julian. For a moment she was confused, then comprehension dawned. Ha, what a sweetheart he was. Julian's invitation to cards was a diversion, an attempt to lure Marldon away from the ballroom. Her heart lifted.

She took a deep breath and smiled. 'Yes, my lord. I most certainly do gamble.'

The balloon-shaped lamps in the games room were shrouded in a fog of blue smoke. The place was a babel of noise. Amidst rumbling chatter, shouts and laughter, balls rattled on roulette wheels and bagatelle boards clattered incessantly. Men, some in shirtsleeves and waistcoats, were hunched over tables, intent on poker, baccarat or piquet.

It was unusual to find a place so shamelessly boorish in a house with such pretensions to grandeur. But, thought Alec, it was perfectly apposite to Octavia Hamilton. She knew how to keep men happy – it was her trade – and that skill had taken her from gutter to glitter. Remarkably the woman hadn't lost a shred of vulgarity on her way up. Quite a feat.

He rocked his chair back and yawned. His contemptuous eyes surveyed the unruly stacks of coins either side of the long table. The stakes were tediously low and the men, excepting Julian Ackroyd, lacklustre players. He stretched to take a decanter of whisky from the chiffonier, poured himself a measure, then drank it at a draught.

Lucy, sitting opposite, glanced anxiously from him to Julian. He smiled inwardly, gratified to have unnerved her. Loyalty was not a concept he set much store by and it was amusing to see her so protective of a cousin. He wondered, with idle curiosity, how far she would go in her bid to keep him entertained. The woman was renowned for her free and easy ways. It would be interesting to see if she could take her pleasures without that spirited air which dogged her social persona. More interesting, at least, than playing baccarat with buffoons.

With a smirk, Sir Julian scooped up his winnings and flicked the used cards into the wastebasket.

'I find the banker's lucky streak somewhat dull,' said Lord Marldon, addressing Julian at the head of the table. 'Perhaps you'd be prepared to change your coinage. Mrs Singleton would prove a more enticing wager than a handful of sovereigns, don't you think?' As he spoke he surreptitiously levelled his cane beneath the table and touched its jewelled head to Lucy's belly.

Lucy inhaled sharply and silence fell upon the table. Lord Trimmingham screwed a monocle to his eye and the assembled company turned their gazes to her. She stared at Marldon in astonishment, her mouth agape, her bare shoulders lifting with her quick angry breaths. Marldon's lips twisted in a half-smile and he lowered the cane a few inches until it nudged into the juncture of her thighs.

Animosity flickered in Lucy's sharp, green eyes before, with hasty determination, she softened her expression. She smiled evenly and gave a defiant toss of her curls.

61

'Very well,' she said, nodding at Julian's winnings. 'I do not see a man about to lose.'

Clarissa stood on the patio listening to a heavily powdered woman prattle about the latest beauty to find herself in the Prince of Wales' bed.

Gossip and flirtation, it seemed, were fashionable society's two modes of communication. At that moment, Clarissa didn't much care for either.

Foolishly, she'd fancied that Gabriel was different. But, shortly after the kiss they'd shared, a kiss which even now lingered on her lips and glowed in her sex, he had made his excuses and left. He would, he'd said, leave his card 'sometime' and perhaps, if she were willing to sit for him, they could agree upon her fee – 'sometime'.

Clarissa struggled for an explanation. He had appeared so genuine, interested in her, and as desiring as she had been. Did being Lucy's cousin mean she was to be shunned by certain people? No one else seemed to mind overmuch, so why should he? Perhaps she could not kiss properly. But no, her body and the way he'd responded said otherwise. She could only conclude that he was the same as all the other men, all those who'd pressed her to sit on the stairs awhile, come look at the stars, dance one more time. He was a cad, a rakehell, seeking quick pleasures and nothing more.

Clarissa wanted to go home, but finding Lucy had proved impossible.

She asked the powdered woman to please excuse her – though she need not have bothered – and drifted away from the gaiety in search of quieter, darker parts. She would be alone. She would bide her time until their carriage returned; and she would not think on Gabriel. She wandered over to the far side of the house, each calm curtained window taking her further from the party. There were a few stragglers on the lawns, couples tempted by the privacy night afforded.

Two or three steps around the corner of the house was an arched wrought-iron gate and, beyond it, the gloom of an alleyway. Clarissa clanged the latch. Nobody stirred. Lifting her trailing skirts, she moved cautiously, edging past a hand-cart and a pyramid of barrels, glancing at black windows. The music and noise of the party was faint, blissfully faint.

She wondered what Gabriel was doing. Was he over there, swirling about the glittering dance floor? Or had he lured someone else, a woman more prepared to give, into the seclusion of the pergola? Perhaps, she reflected, it was well that he bid her goodnight when he did. Nothing could ever come of it, and in future she would be more guarded in her imaginings.

Ahead, yellow light from the house cut a wedge through the darkness. She would rest there, enjoy the stillness, before returning to seek out Lucy. No one would bother her, and she would pretend she'd had a wonderful time.

At the tall window, Clarissa cast an idle glance through the slightly parted drapes. She froze. The gap in the curtains showed a slice of a book-lined library and there, seated in a stiff-backed chair, was Lucy, her naked breasts exhibited above her emerald gown. Her hands were clasped behind her head, exaggerating the thrust of her bosom, and her face was clouded with anger. But her eyes were uncertain, fearful. She spoke words that, through the glass, were silent to Clarissa.

A man stepped into view and Clarissa bit her lip. It was not Julian. He was taller; his hair was black. With a slow, stealthy gait, he moved to stand behind Lucy, his mouth set in a thin, bitter smile. His face was powerful, square-jawed, but the skin sagged ever so slightly. Ten years ago he would have been handsome and ten years from now his features would doubtless be slack with dissipation. Looking down, he addressed Lucy's head, again in words Clarissa could not hear. Lucy dropped her arms to her side.

Clarissa glanced guiltily over her shoulder before returning her gaze to the dumbshow. They would not see her standing there. To them, from their lighted room, she would be as the night.

The man reached over Lucy's shoulders and laid the length of his thumbs above each plump breast. A diamond glinted on his left hand. His mouth murmured silently as his thumbs slid down the twin, pale slopes to the lift of her beaded nipples. There, he flicked away from the tight crests before repeating the action – a lingering glide, a flick, another glide, flick.

Clarissa stood there mesmerised, of no place, of no time. The lack of sound glazed the scene with unreality. The two people were phantasms, moving in a hushed aqueous world. Floating from far away, came the merry jangle of a polka. It clashed discordantly with the unfolding tableau, enhancing its strangeness.

She watched avidly as the man cupped Lucy's milk-white bosom and squeezed the flesh into a deep cleavage. He kneaded, massaged, and teased rotations over her erect peaks. There was scorn in his expression and a cold indifference to his caress. But, despite that, Lucy responded. Her eyes dropped shut, her shoulders sagged and she mouthed a gasp. The sight tugged at Clarissa's loins.

She saw cousin Lucy cry out as her raspberry-pert nipples were crushed between thumb and forefinger. The man twisted and tugged with efficient brutality, ignoring Lucy's obvious pain. His cruelty shocked Clarissa, but more shocking still was the rush of tingling heat which invaded her sex.

She wondered how it would feel to be touched and treated so harshly. Her pulse quickened. Clarissa knew she ought to look away, but she could not. Something held her there, something more than fascination. It unfurled from deep within her, a sombre desire, winding eerie tendrils about her body.

The man stepped back from Lucy and regarded her

reddened nipples with mild satisfaction. He stalked circles about her, his mouth moving occasionally. There was tension in his legs and buttocks, a suggestion of hard muscularity beneath his black evening trousers. His shirt was collarless, its sleeves rolled back, and under white cotton the broad power of his shoulders and the strong jut of blades were clear.

Clarissa blanched when he leant to touch Lucy's knees. She saw, for the first time, the violence of a slash mark scarring his face. A shiver crawled across her skin and set the downy hairs at the nape of her neck prickling.

He eased Lucy's knees apart and his hands slid quickly along her thighs, bunching up her green and white silks. He smiled, spoke, then reached one arm into the midst of frothing lace. Lucy's back arched and her mouth gaped desire. The man, his face close to Lucy's, his lips speaking nothing, caressed her. His elbow moved in lazy nudges.

Clarissa swallowed hard, trying to ignore the fluttering in her sex. Lucy was shaking her head, whether in protest or refusal Clarissa did not know. But, whatever her meaning, it was belied by her writhing body and the passion contorting her face. Then Lucy was suddenly nodding her head and her lips shaped 'Yes, yes'. The man, his arm still softly jogging back and forth, laughed at her. His white teeth flashed; his shoulders shook and the bump in his throat quivered and bobbed.

There was a metallic clank at the gate. Clarissa started. Her head jerked to the dark end of the passageway then back to the scene within. In the library, a flash of military scarlet moved across her view. Her blood surged. How many people were in the room? She turned again. At the far end of the alleyway were shadows and muted giggles. She looked back at the window. The man in uniform was standing astride Lucy's lap, his fingers fumbling over his swollen crotch. The dark, scarred man was behind her, pushing her head down.

Clarissa gasped, her heart thudding. The shadows and giggles were approaching. She stole a last glance. The man's hips were pumping and his stiff, fiery penis was thrusting into Lucy's mouth.

She stepped away from the window and coughed. There was a squeal and a hushing. With her head lowered, her face burning, Clarissa scuttled past a pair of patent-leather lace-ups and a frilled, dragging hemline, then out through the gate.

Oh, cousin Lucy was a disgrace. How could she allow the man to do such things to her when there were eyes watching? It was humiliating, degrading. Clarissa leant against the wall of the house, gulping the night air. A pulse, surly and insistent, beat in her loins, and the image of the man laughing at Lucy was branded in her mind.

Something, something she had a strange budding sense of, had held Lucy there, imprisoned by that man's contempt. What it was exactly, Clarissa did not know. But she knew she feared it.

'Miss Longleigh,' came a deep female voice. 'What on earth are you doing here in the dark? Your companions have been hunting high and low for you.'

Octavia moved towards her, slow and Junoesque. Clarissa greeted her with a feeble smile. 'I needed air,' she said quietly.

The woman looked at her for a silent moment, her face full of sympathy. 'Your cousin had to leave some time ago,' she said. 'Dreadful bloody headache, I'm afraid. Poor thing. Too much champagne.' She brushed a long dark curl away from Clarissa's shoulder. 'Perhaps you should do the same. You don't look at all well. I could arrange a carriage.'

Clarissa nodded meekly. 'Yes,' she whispered. 'I think that would be wise.'

Kitty dawdled into Clarissa's bedroom. With a sigh she set down her bucket and, hands on hips, flexed her spine. At least she wouldn't have to do Hester's room today, not with the old maid still abed. And long may she stay there, she thought, ambling over to the cheval glass.

Kitty hitched up her skirts and shuffled half-circles before the mirror. Yes, the scarlet stockings from Mrs Longleigh were well worth getting into trouble for. She really ought to save them for Sundays but they were so difficult to resist. She wished it could be Sunday for ever, except without church.

Better still, she'd be rich. She'd have petticoats of lace, a gown of poppy-red silk and a matching ostrich feather in her hair. And the men who chased her wouldn't be lowly farmhands; they'd be proper gentlemen who'd buy her diamonds and furs.

Her eyes scoured the room, searching for inspiration to perfect her vision of grandeur. Draped over a chair back was a gown of slate-grey silk. Kitty couldn't help but take a closer look. She fingered it lightly, delighting in the smooth fragility of the material. That hem needed laundering though, she thought, an impish grin playing on her lips.

The silk crackled as gingerly she lifted up the dress and held it against her body. The yoke was richly braided and ribbons streamed from the skirt. It was better than anything she possessed. Kitty swayed gently. Then, with a twirl and a swish, she was sweeping across the room, gliding in the arms of an imaginary suitor at the finest imaginary ball. There was a blur of dark grey as she whisked past the mirror and Kitty felt a pang of regret that it wasn't poppy red. She wondered if the young miss had any colours more to her taste.

At the bedroom door, Kitty paused and listened. Silence. No one would know if she took a peek at Clarissa's gowns. Throwing the grey silks on to the bed, she crept to the sturdy oak wardrobe. The hinges squeaked slightly. A rainbow of lustrous fabrics opened up. Amidst all the colours there were soft reds, deep reds, corals and crimsons, but nothing quite so bright as poppy red. Nonetheless, those reds weren't grey.

Hurriedly, Kitty slipped out of her uniform. Well, she reckoned, there was no point in just wondering. With Clarissa in town, Aunt Hester fatigued, and the servants all busy below stairs, she may as well find out. Standing in her flannel petticoat and shift, she mulled over the problem of whether to try on the rust with black buttons or the dark pink with an enormous bow on its skirt.

A noise from beyond the bedroom door wiped the dilemma clean from her mind. Her stomach lurched; her heart thundered. There were quick, light footsteps on the stairs, growing louder, nearer. Oh, if someone caught her she'd be well and truly done for.

In two swift steps she snatched up her bucket, her discarded clothes, and bundled them into the wardrobe. Then she stepped in herself, crushing the hanging gowns into a space, and crouched low. Her fingers curled around the door in a bid to pull it shut, but a stubborn strip of light remained.

She heard a muted giggle and cursed silently when she saw Pascale, dark eyes flicking shiftily, slink into the room. What was she up to, the haughty little piece? The Frenchwoman smiled furtively and whispered at the door. Then the new footman sidled in, shrugging off his blue and silver frock coat as he did so.

Pascale closed the door softly and leant against it, her head back, her bosom thrust provocatively forth. At once Ellis embraced her. They scattered feverish kisses over necks and faces, murmuring of love and lust. Their hands, urgent and searching, roved over each other's contours, tugging frantically at clothes.

From the semi-darkness, Kitty peered through the gap, transfixed by disbelief. So Pascale wasn't such a starchy piece after all. And, lordy, she was a quick worker, getting her claws into the poor fellow like that. He hadn't been here a week. Hardly daring to breathe, Kitty watched with bewildered attention.

Ellis massaged and squeezed his lover's breasts while Pascale, gasping and groaning, fumbled with the buttons on his breeches. Her head lolled from side to side then gently she moved him away. The footman's cock, erect and uncapped, sprang from his flies.

Kitty moistened her lips, feeling a stab of hot need. That was a strong, randy stalk, she thought bitterly. Given the chance, she wouldn't say no. With slow stealth, she moved the heel of her hand to her groin, and pressed at the rumpled fabric. Her face screwed into a resentful pout when Pascale, with a flurry of white lace, hitched up her skirts. Her stockings, like her high-heeled boots, were black, gloriously, wickedly black. Scarlet, decided Kitty, was not the best colour.

Pascale clasped the footman about the neck and, with a nimble leap, circled her legs about his hips. He pinned her to the door, his knees bent, and fumbled beneath her petticoats. Then with a jerk of his pelvis, he thrust upwards.

The woman grunted as Ellis began pounding vigorously, his plush-clad buttocks tensing and flexing. She scrabbled with the buttons of her dress and lifted free her nipple-hard breasts. Muttering in French, she caressed herself with wide-spread fingers and pummelling hands.

Kitty chewed her lower lip. Her sex was swollen and wet, throbbingly hot. Inching back her petticoat, she opened the split crotch of her drawers and eased two fingers into her juicy warm orifice. Slowly at first, then with an urgency to match Ellis's, she pistoned back and forth, fighting desperately against the impulse to gasp.

The sight of the impatient, grinding lovers urged on her lust. She fretted the nub of her clitoris and deftly brought herself to a small but satisfactory climax. As she peaked, she allowed herself a soft whimper, safe in the knowledge that the rising clamour of Pascale's passion would drown it.

Oh, how she envied that woman. Ellis, with his

slicked-back hair and fancy clothes, wasn't exactly her cup of tea. But he'd got a fine thrust on him and a lovely looking prick, and those things mattered. It wasn't fair. For Kitty, the Longleigh town house was as good as a nunnery.

She scowled as Pascale, with a thin reedy whine, spent her pleasure. Ellis thundered on then, moments later, snatched himself away. His creamy seed spurted to the ground in diminishing arcs. He smiled and with a buckled shoe rubbed the viscid white puddle into the carpet.

Kitty clenched her fists. How dare he, the grease-haired dandy? Didn't he realise that some poor skivvy had to take care of this place? She'd make damn sure she took some hot suds to that patch later on. He wasn't going to leave his mark like that, not in Miss Clarissa's bedroom.

Pascale slid down the door and sat, her legs wide, her knees bent. 'Ah, Sebastian, it is so good you are here at last,' she breathed. 'For those many days when you did not come, I missed you terribly. It was an agony to me.'

Kitty strained to listen. So these two had known each other before they arrived. Well, they'd certainly kept that one quiet, the sly old devils.

'God, I hated it too,' returned Ellis. 'But, as I said, blame his lordship. He was the one who detained me.'

'Hmmm,' said Pascale. 'Then your agony, ah, it was nothing compared with mine.'

'Console yourself,' replied Ellis, buttoning his breeches and smoothing back his dark oiled hair. 'My agony's about to get much worse in this place.'

'Ah, *oui, mon pauvre petit*. This Hester is no beauty,' said Pascale, pushing her breasts back into her corset. 'Do you think it will be possible? Because, if you cannot keep her diverted, my task will be so very difficult. I cannot do it if she is watching all the time.'

'I'll make it possible, my love,' he said, grinning. 'Anyway, I suspect that, deep down, the old spinster has the makings of a whore. Once I've fucked away the cobwebs there'll be no stopping her, more's the pity. Tell me about yours. Will she make a suitable wife?'

'Pough,' scoffed Pascale. 'Clarissa has much distance to travel. She is too stubborn, too – too independent. She will need to be broken first. But . . . ' Her mouth turned down and she shrugged heavily. 'It can be done. I think the girl, she is like this Hester. She has the makings of a whore.'

Ellis grinned and reached out his hand. 'Then perhaps Alicia's money will be the easiest we've ever earned.'

Pascale clasped his hand and allowed herself to be pulled to her feet. 'I doubt that,' she said, buttoning her gown to the neck. 'Very much, I doubt that.'

Kitty remained in the wardrobe long after they'd gone. She wanted to follow them to see what they did next but she didn't quite have the pluck. It didn't make sense at all. The new footman was after bedding Aunt Hester? What to goodness for? And the French bit talking about Miss Clarissa in that way. They were trouble those two, that was for sure.

Kitty was going to keep a sharp eye on them. And, right now, she was going to give the carpet a darn good soaping.

Another ball, and another evening of wasted emotion. But at least the host had the decency to keep the bedrooms unlocked. Misspent lust was a welcome addition to the grim pleasures Gabriel sought.

He slammed into the woman beneath him, driving with a passion that was not for her. Pulsing wet flesh massaged his cock, and the legs hooked to his back were tight and strong. Constance Yates, groaning and squealing, bucked eagerly to meet his thrusts. Gabriel kept his eyes resolutely shut. Whenever he opened them he saw a face frantic with excitement, and eyes that were light brown. He wanted other eyes, eyes that were soulful, eyes that were bluer and more precious than lapis lazuli. But Clarissa could not be his.

Constance reached her orgasm with a long screech. Her vagina contracted hungrily but it was not enough to milk the pleasure from him. Gabriel powered into her rich slippery depths, ramming himself high. Angry resentment fuelled his search for release, spurring him on to rough urgency. The woman whimpered. Whether it was in pleasure or protest, Gabriel did not know. Nor did he care. The woman had come to him full of greedy lust and he was determined to claim satisfaction, just as she had claimed hers.

'Grip me harder,' he hissed, and Constance clamped her sex muscles to him. The tightness drew him closer to his peak. He thrust with bitter determination, his arse lunging furiously, until his hot seed raced along his shaft. He cursed hoarsely, taking relief rather than pleasure from the moment.

Within seconds, he pulled out of her and flung himself on to his back. He was grateful that Constance never bothered with sweet talk or made any attempt to pet. She was, at least, honest in her desires. She wanted Gabriel for his prick, nothing more, and that was fine by him.

'You exhaust me,' she said. 'I'm thirsty. I need a drink.'

'Then go and get one,' muttered Gabriel.

'You go for me,' she wheedled. 'It'll take me an eternity to get dressed. Go on, Gabriel. Be a treasure. Pop down for a glass of champagne.'

Gabriel grunted dismissively. Clarissa was somewhere downstairs, and tonight he didn't know if he could trust himself. His plan to make her hate him was proving difficult to follow. The logic of it worked against itself. Whenever he knew Clarissa would be attending a function, Gabriel made sure he was also there, just so he could spurn her. But the more he saw her, the more he wanted her, and the harder it was to be cold. Yet he had to do it, for both their sakes.

Gabriel had no desire to make an enemy of Lord Marldon, but it was not fear which kept him from Clarissa. He suspected he could love her, and her him. The pain of parting, weeks or maybe months from now, would be unbearable. It was easier to stop things before they started. And, with Clarissa's feelings uppermost in his mind, Gabriel thought the kindest way to do that was not with open explanations but with cruelty.

'Champagne,' he repeated, jerking on his shirt. 'I shall return with two glasses. But only if you promise me a dance later.'

Constance gave a short bray of laughter. 'A dance?' she exclaimed, affectedly fluffing at her ash-blonde curls. 'Gracious me, I didn't realise you cared.'

'Oh, I do,' said Gabriel, thinking of Clarissa. 'I do.'

Clarissa thought she had hardened her heart to Gabriel. Every time she'd seen him flaunting his latest conquest, every time he'd cut her dead with his eyes, her protective shell had grown stronger. She dwelt on his rejection of her and did not avert her eyes when he paraded and flirted with the other woman. It was a painful process, like cauterising a wound. Better that, she thought, than have a weeping sore.

But now she craved for a word, a look, a touch. Earlier, she'd caught him observing her and his eyes had held such tender yearning that she could no longer believe he didn't care. In that brief moment all her defences had crumbled.

She hovered by the doorway of the music salon, within view of the broad staircase. Men, elegant and gloved, milled about, sipping wine and chatting. But none of them was Gabriel. He had disappeared up the stairs some time since, the blonde on his arm – a blonde, thought Clarissa, which had not been achieved without a frisette or two and a good deal of gold powder.

It had hurt her deeply to see them ascend, laughing and touching just a little too much. No doubt they were seeking out one of the many bedrooms rumoured to be on offer. Clarissa wished she could be as brazen and daring. Perhaps then Gabriel would look upon her more favourably. Or, better still, she would not ache so profoundly for him. She would be a woman who pursued pleasures with casual lightness and did not suffer from the heart's demands.

She spotted him and her stomach leapt excitedly. He was at the head of the crowded stairs, tall and slender, hair curling at his shoulders – so different from all the others.

Clarissa stepped back and, screened by people, she watched him make his way down, relieved to see he was now alone. His eyes swooped over faces, acknowledging some with a nod and a tight-lipped smile. As he neared the bottom, Clarissa nudged a path towards him. She was calm and bold, knowing only that she had to speak with him. Gabriel's roaming eyes met with hers, and immediately he looked away.

Clarissa surged forward, ignoring the muttered complaints, and grabbed at his wrist.

'Why do you treat me so?' she pleaded in a hushed voice.

Gabriel swung round, vexation twisting his face. He stared at her with haughty disapproval before tugging away his arm and moving on. Clarissa followed him along the corridor and, when the crowds began to thin out, she clutched his wrist again.

'Why?' she asked. 'Just tell me why.'

Gabriel shook off her hand. There was a dishevelled air about him, more so than usual. His clothes were not as crisp as they had been earlier, and his chestnut curls were a little tangled. Clarissa felt a hot stab of jealousy, and hoped she might delay his return to the blonde.

'I find it better not to court women when they're about to be wed,' he replied stiffly. 'The intrigue invariably proves quite tiresome. With you, it would be more tiresome than most.'

'Please, Gabriel,' she began, unsure of what to say. Surely she did not deserve such opprobrium for withholding the fact of her marriage. Yet, what could she ask of him? He was perfectly correct. Within three months she would be wed.

'Can't we at least be civil?' she asked weakly.

'Civil?' he scoffed. 'You want civility? Oh, charming little party, isn't it, Miss Longleigh? Are you enjoying your London debut? I do hope so. When are the banns being read? I would dearly like to attend. Have you found yourself a gallant for the evening? You'll want to keep up with the kissing practice if you're to satisfy your –'

'Stop it! Stop it!' she shouted, emotion stinging her eyes.

'And perhaps there's more you should practise,' he continued over her protests, his tone increasingly caustic. 'Have you found anyone willing to probe beneath your petticoats, Miss Longleigh? You ought to loosen up before you tie the knot. You hardly seem a ready piece to be sharing a bed with that . . . that heartless old roué.'

'No,' she whispered, shaking her head. 'No. Lord Marldon is a worthy man. My father has chosen him.' A tear rolled down her cheek and she gulped a stifled sob.

The angry lines disappeared from Gabriel's brow and the scornful twist to his mouth vanished. He looked at her softly and she thought she discerned a glint of moisture in his caramel eyes.

'You're too trusting, little one,' he said in a low, sympathetic voice. 'Far too trusting.' He stroked away her tear with a gentle caress, watching her with compassion and desire. His gaze flickered longingly over her face and he bent towards her, his lips parted in readiness for a kiss.

Clarissa's mouth lifted; her heart drummed wildly. This was what she wanted. She didn't care who saw.

But Gabriel drew back. He smiled, a nasty narrow smile. His eyes burned.

'Grow up, Clarissa,' he spat, with a lashing venom. 'You'll need to.'

Chapter Five

*I*t was Hyde Park, an hour or so after noon. The season was well under way, the weather was glorious, and it appeared all of London was out to see and be seen.

On the far banks of the Serpentine, the Bayswater crowds lazed under trees or took skiffs out on to the weedy waters. London's fashionable, however, stayed clear of that area. Their gleaming horses and lacquered carriages jangled around the gravel drives. On lawns and walkways, ladies in pastel silks strolled, twirling their parasols and smiling serenely as flurries of top hats greeted them.

Clarissa, in a black habit cut like a glove, cantered along the dusty tanbark of Rotten Row. Her face was flushed and radiant, but her heart was lead.

Lucy had counselled her to ignore Gabriel's taunts. Lord Marldon was not the man he'd said, of course he wasn't. Pah, Gabriel was a twenty-six-year-old bachelor and probably jealous. And he was an artist, a typical artist – fickle, moody, selfish and impossibly passionate. In short, he was perfectly hopeless. She must forget him and find herself another beau.

But Clarissa could not forget him and she did not want another beau. At the very least, she wanted an explanation. At the most, she wanted – what? Would half a summer of secret meetings and stolen caresses be enough? She doubted it, but it was the best she might hope for.

As she rode along the burnt-orange strip, the young swells lounging elegantly over the railings followed her with approving eyes. Clarissa did not care for them; she hated their attentions.

'Whoa there, Brandy,' she said, reining in her hack as she approached Hyde Park Corner. There faultlessly tailored horsewomen gathered. They chatted in little groups or wheeled around their horses for another turn.

She stroked the chestnut mare's sleek neck and spotted Lucy, her golden ringlets spilling out beneath the veil of her dainty tricorn. Trotting over, Clarissa smiled politely at the faces that had become familiar in recent weeks.

'There's a gentleman in a red carriage,' she said, drawing up her horse near to Lucy's. 'At the far end. His footman has requested that we speak with him. Please come. He mentioned your name.'

'Did you notice the crest?' asked Lucy suspiciously.

'I'm afraid not. I wasn't close enough.'

Lucy touched her crop to the gelding's flank and Clarissa followed suit. Hooves softly thudding, they cantered a mile or so until they reached a part of the row where the bordering trees thinned out. In the shade of an oak stood a pair of dappled greys harnessed to a deep-claret barouche. Its small hood, unusually drawn for such fine weather, cast darkness over the occupant. On the box a coachman in a gold-banded top hat, his whip angled high, stared blankly at their approach.

Lucy reined in alongside the carriage. From the gloom of the seat, a man leant forward and propped an arm on the carriage door. A diamond flashed on his hand. It was Lucy's secret lover, the man in the library.

Clarissa's head span with guilty recollection and her pulse surged to a rapid beat. The man surveyed Lucy with a cool interest and smiled knowingly. Remembered arousal coursed through Clarissa's body – arousal which, though it warmed her loins, chilled her blood and froze her heart.

Lucy lowered an extended hand. 'Lord Marldon,' she said in a hostile voice.

Clarissa felt the colour drain from her face, leaving her cheeks cold and ashen. Her stomach clenched on itself and swirled with a heavy sickness. Her senses reeled. This could not be her husband. It was impossible.

'Won't you introduce us?' said the man, disdainfully pointing his chin towards Clarissa. 'She has the makings of an excellent horsewoman. Sits too low though.'

His eyes were beads of jet, watching her from hooded lids. His gaze was coolly assessing, predatory. Clarissa felt that stare as fingers of ether, slithering between her silks and her skin. Though her mind urged her to look away, she could not.

Lucy pulled her horse back a couple of steps, obliging Clarissa to move closer. She recalled now Alicia's single word: dark. And yes, in appearance he was. But the darkness went beyond that. It was in his eyes as a malevolent glint and on his lips as a cold, cruel smile. And it was doubtless the architect of the drawn cynicism which etched his face.

Gabriel had spoken the truth.

She held out her hand, hoping her black kid gloves would conceal the tremors within.

'Alexander van Ghent, the Earl of Marldon,' said Lucy stiffly. 'Allow me to present Miss Annabel Stanton.'

Clarissa felt faint with relief. For the moment she was safe, her identity unknown. She was not the woman he would take as his bride. Sooner or later he would discover who she was. But for now that did not matter.

Lord Marldon smiled thinly and took her tentatively proffered hand. He looked up at her while his lips lingered on her fingertips. Clarissa cast her eyes to the ground and heard her own soft voice saying, 'Delighted to make your acquaintance, my lord.'

Then suddenly, somehow, the buttons on the underside of her glove were undone. A sharp breath caught in her throat and she felt the cool lightness of his touch. The shock of the intrusion paralysed her, and her hand would not move from his. It stayed there, allowing him to stroke ticklish rotations on the thin, veined skin of her wrist.

She swallowed hard. As he rubbed gently, a growing sense of doom crept upon her, a stealthy realisation that this man would be, not her husband, but her master and tormentor. While the thought filled her with dread, an unfathomable desire, deep and fierce, twisted like a knife within her.

She moved to snatch away her hand but the earl was quick. His grip tightened, his mouth slid down, and his teeth closed around the very tip of her gloved middle finger. He nipped once then released her.

Clarissa clutched her hand protectively to her body, gazing at him in stunned disbelief.

Lord Marldon leant back and laughed.

'Delighted to meet you, Miss . . .?' Beneath his raised, questioning brows, his dark eyes mocked her.

'Stanton,' interjected Lucy. 'Miss Annabel Stanton. Now, if you'll excuse us, my lord, we have a pressing engagement.' She touched her whip to her horse and wheeled it away from the carriage.

'Such a pity,' said Marldon, with the merest lift of his hat. 'I do hope we meet again, Miss . . . Stanton.' He tapped his cane on the carriage floor. The coachman cracked his reins and the barouche rolled away, its red wheels sending up tiny clouds of dust.

Clarissa was motionless. She saw her future closing in like a box. She felt dreadfully afraid, and amidst that fear was a deep seam of hurt. She had been betrayed – by her father, by Lucy, by all those who had withheld their knowledge of Lord Marldon.

Lucy trotted over to her. 'Sorry,' she said with a light apologetic shrug. 'Nobody thought it fair to warn you.'

Clarissa looked away, her eyes brimming with tears. Nobody, she thought bitterly, except Gabriel.

Clarissa rapped the brass knocker with furious impatience. She'd left her horse in the mews and, without bothering to change, had hurried directly to Gabriel's address. Everything was clear to her now. At least she hoped it was; otherwise she was about to make a terrible fool of herself.

The door opened and the valet informed her that Mr Ardenzi was, alas, not at home to visitors. Clarissa had no inclination to bargain with him, nor to leave her card. She edged briskly past and, from the hall, shouted out Gabriel's name. The valet swore under his breath and closed the door.

Gabriel, looking bewildered and annoyed, appeared at the top of the stairs. His loose white shirt was collarless, open at the neck, and his glossy brown hair fell in ragged curls about his shoulders. A tide of desire swelled within Clarissa and her heart spurred her on. She flew to him.

'I know,' she gasped, throwing her arms about him. 'I understand.' She shook Gabriel's stiff, unyielding body. 'It's not that I'm to marry. It's that I'm to marry him, isn't it? Isn't it?'

In a rambling explanation, she told him everything, from other people's reticence to the scenes she'd witnessed at the ball. As she spoke, Gabriel's strong arms encircled her. He held her tightly, nuzzling into her neck, murmuring solace, regrets and passions in her ear.

Clarissa's mouth, half-speaking, half-kissing, fluttered over his chest and throat. She tasted the saltiness of his warm, silken skin and smelt the closeness of his masculinity. When she fell silent her body was trembling.

'I've never known a woman so honest,' said Gabriel softly. He pressed his lips to her brow. 'You've broken all the rules, Clarissa. Don't you know you're supposed to lure me into your arms by smiling coyly and seeming unobtainable?'

'We have not time for that,' she breathed, her lips lifting in search of a kiss.

His mouth descended on hers and their tongues snaked together in questing hunger. Clarissa's hands roved over his back, her fingers thrilling to the heat of him beneath fine cotton. She felt the tension in his strong, lithe body and quivers of sharp, sweet lust tumbled through her. She wanted him. She didn't care about the future.

'Gabriel,' she said shyly. 'Will you ... will you teach me things?'

There was a flicker of consternation in his amber-brown eyes. 'No,' he said firmly. 'I will not teach you things. I want to be your lover, Clarissa, not your mentor. But I will show you things. That is if you wish me to.'

Clarissa looked at him hesitantly. She did not know how strong was the promise that tied her to Lord Marldon. Once, she would not have believed her hand could be offered to a man such as he. But now she saw things differently. Her father had acted with blatant disregard for her feelings. Could he have made a commitment from which she could not escape?

'Your maidenhead will be safe,' said Gabriel, noting her reluctance. 'God forbid that you should ever marry Marldon, but we would do well to tread cautiously until the matter is resolved.' He held out his hand to her. 'Come. Once I told you not to be so trusting. Now I urge you to trust.'

Nervous, excited, her fingers hooked in his, Clarissa followed Gabriel up to the second floor. She was not sure if she could trust him to keep her honour; she knew she could not trust herself. But she would take the risk.

Gabriel showed her into a room of bottle-green walls, its oak floor covered with a square of Turkish carpet.

The brass bed seemed to dominate the space, not because it was big or unusual, but because it was a bed. Clarissa's heart would not calm.

He stood before her, clasping both her hands. He gazed down with a hungry intensity. 'So many times I've dreamt of you,' he whispered. 'I've dreamt of your flesh against mine, of my lips on your skin. I've dreamt of your face, trying to picture how you would look when I make you come. But I never imagined it like this. I never once dreamt that you would offer yourself so, that you would ask me to give you pleasure.'

'Nor I,' murmured Clarissa. 'It was ... It is bold of me. Though I fear my courage fails me now.'

Gabriel took her in a soothing embrace and kissed her for a long, tender time. Then he passed his fingertips over her face. 'Don't let modesty be a barrier between us,' he said. 'I will not do anything you do not wish me to. You have my word on that.' He toyed with the white ruffles at her neck.

'But I scarce know what I want,' she replied in a timorous voice. 'All I know is ... is I want you.'

Gabriel unpinned her hat and set it down. 'That could be difficult when you are dressed for riding,' he smiled, brushing back errant strands of hair.

Then his slim, elegant fingers began working down the buttons of her pelisse.

He lingered over undressing her. With every discarded layer, he rained soft kisses over the newly bared skin and murmured his delight. He drew swirls over her arms, tickling the smooth white underside with the lightest of touches. His tongue lapped at the hollow of her throat and licked along the lines of her collarbone. Cloths of black and white whispered to the ground.

Clarissa stood trembling. His slow movements were reassuring, exciting. His gentleness sensitised her flesh and her nerves leapt beneath each trailing caress, each moist imprint of his lips.

Gabriel knelt before her, murmuring promises and

words of desire. He stroked her silk-stockinged legs, moving cleanly upwards from her finely boned ankles to the slender line of her calves. The deep-frilled hem of her chemise lifted and he reached beneath to untie her ribboned garters. His fingers strayed to the naked flesh above and he drifted languid circles there, teasing with an encroaching proximity.

She shivered to feel him so close. Moisture warmed the cleft of her sex, filling her out, making her lips pout needfully. But he did not touch; nor did he look. Instead he wrinkled down her stockings, divesting her of everything save for her flimsy, laced shift. Then he guided her to the bed and bid her wait for him. She was grateful. She did not want to be fully disrobed before he was.

Eager, yet a little afraid, she knelt there while he stripped off his clothes. Every revelation of his body intensified her longing. As he moved, his muscles rippled beneath honey-dark skin. A streak of sparse, deep-brown hair ran from his navel to merge with the cluster of thick curls at his groin. His cock jutted forth, sturdy and vital.

A dart of lust pierced her. Abandoning modesty, she gazed at the column of flesh. The skin was tightened to a porcelain sheen and beneath was a tracery of blue veins, some thin and delicate, some strong and pulsing. The orbed crown glistened with the purple-red rawness of a peeled plum, and the whole thing was so unashamedly male – arrogant almost in its bold, upright thrust. She found the sight fiercely exquisite.

The bed creaked as Gabriel moved to kneel opposite her. Coaxing her to raise her arms, he lifted her chemise over her head. He drew a sharp breath. His eyes, drowsy with lust, wandered over her pale, graceful contours and rested on the damask-rose tips of her bosom.

'God, but you're heavenly,' he said, his voice catching huskily. Then his hands followed the tracks of his gaze. He swept meandering, easy movements over her body, tracing the dip of her waist and the swell of her hips. He palmed her high, satin-skinned breasts and skimmed her nipples. They sprang to erection, tingling.

Clarissa moaned lightly. Her stiffened peaks were cones of sensation, spilling shards of pleasure into her glowing sex. A heavy, sweet yearning coiled inside her and somewhere, buried within the growing wetness of her folds, a pulse beat hungrily.

With a timid gesture she reached out to him. His body was firm and his skin was waxy-smooth, so smooth that Clarissa's touch could not rest on it. Growing in confidence, she mirrored Gabriel's sinuous explorations. She snaked her hands over the slab of his chest down to his flat, ridged abdomen. She stroked the angularity of his lean hips and the tautness of his flanks and buttocks. Then a spark of daring impelled her to touch his engorged penis. She rubbed lightly and it bobbed in searching little jerks.

Gabriel pushed his pelvis towards her. 'Hold me,' he breathed.

Clarissa curled her fingers around the warm shaft and nudged her fist up and down. The feel of marble-hardness under skin, velvet skin which moved when she did, delighted her. She glided along his stiffness, relishing the straining potency. Then she brought her other hand to cup the plushy weight of his balls. They tightened and drew up hungrily. Gabriel hissed and pulled back.

'When I refused to be your tutor,' he said, 'I failed to realise you had no need of one. Let me take you to ecstasy, Clarissa. But please, just for now, do not touch me so.'

His head dipped to her taut, full breasts and his hand eased into the humid juncture of her thighs. Simultaneously, his lips closed about one nipple and a finger pressed into the deepest crease of her vulva. Clarissa gasped at the sudden ferocity of the double pleasures. On her rigid pink crests, his tongue lashed and his teeth grazed lightly; between her legs, the length of his finger moved along her slippery crevice.

Clarissa was an hourglass of desire. She whimpered faintly, barely able to hold herself upright. He circled at the opening to her vagina, stirring just within its fleshy red throat, then drew back to tease the fierce little knot of her clitoris. Her arousal flared to greater heights, making her weak with hot, rushing pleasure.

'Lie back,' he whispered, leaning his free hand to her shoulder.

Clarissa sank supine on to the bed, her knees raised and parted for him. Gabriel lowered himself over her, his mouth moving and sucking on her neck, nibbling at her earlobe. She pressed tremulously upwards, and the touch of their bodies, warm and damp in the afternoon heat, suffused her with longing. Their limbs entwined before Gabriel drew back. Poised above her, he moved down her flesh in kisses.

He laid his hands to her thighs, spreading her still wider, and gazed upon the crinkled petals of her sex. Clarissa felt herself opening to him, like a rosebud in sunshine. Her back arched and she lifted her loins, hungry for more tangible attentions. Gabriel shifted and dropped within the space of her legs.

His breath was warm there, then his tongue, hot and wet, swept up the valley of her labia to press on her clitoris. She uttered gentle moans of bliss as he rocked licking rotations about the tiny throbbing bump. His mouth opened over the length of her split lips and pulsed rich suckling kisses. His saliva mingled with her seeping juices. It streamed through her tender grooves, bathing her folds in sliding heat until she lost all sense of her body there. She felt only a union that was friction-less, almost fleshless. And she felt too the feverish rise of her impending orgasm.

Her hands clutched at the counterpane and her head rolled from side to side. Gabriel brought a finger to his liquid caress and slowly slipped it into her snug, succulent passage. He thrust gently back and forth, stroking her inner walls, and she writhed against him. It seemed like for ever that he kept her there, hovering on the shivering brink of ecstasy. The prolonged intensity was almost more than she could endure. Then his mouth closed over her clitoris, and with a quick eager tongue he pushed her beyond the edge.

Clarissa tangled her fingers in his hair, crying out as she came. Tremors soared and clutched, before crashing into a flood of delirious pleasure. She clasped his head to her loins, her body racked by convulsions. When the shuddering violence melted to a gentler throb, she released her hold on him and fell limply into the softness of the bed.

She lay there languishing in a dazed afterglow, her shallow breath gradually calming. Gabriel crawled up the bed and leant over her. His chin and parted lips were glazed with her secretions and his face had paled. His eyes spoke of lust, but more than that, of pain. He trailed a soothing hand over her creamy-white breasts and shook his head.

'Dear God,' he breathed, gazing at her. 'You've surpassed my every dream, Clarissa. And now I fear you'll leave me with nightmares. How will I ever keep my promise?'

Clarissa reached out to slide lazy hands over his shoulders. 'Then maybe you shouldn't,' she ventured.

'No,' he said quietly. 'A woman of your standing needs her honour intact. Whether you marry Marldon or some other, the loss of your virginity would ruin you.'

Despondency darkened her mood. She wished her father would hurry back from the Continent. She could tell him she disapproved of his choice, that she cared for another. Her face brightened with hope. 'But, maybe we could –'

Gabriel silenced her with a kiss. She tasted herself on his lips – musky and salty with a hint of sweetness.

'Don't even think it,' he said. 'I'm a humble painter and you're an heiress.' He lay beside her, his head propped on one elbow, and smiled playfully. 'Your fortune would be most welcome to me, of course. But, alas, there are others with more to offer for it than I.'

Clarissa sighed heavily. She tried to convince herself that her father would understand, but in her heart of hearts she knew he would not.

'Then what do we have?' she asked.

'We have this,' he murmured, drifting a finger down her belly. 'We have the moment. And we shall have more moments, because that's all life is. Moment after moment. But we shall seize them, Clarissa, use each one as if it were our last. We shall make them into every-thing.' He smiled roguishly. 'And we also have an erection, my angel, desperate for your touch.' He guided her hand to his groin. '*Quid pro quo*?'

Clarissa took his phallus in a gentle clasp. '*Quid pro quo*,' she agreed softly.

Madame Jane's did not open until eight o'clock. It was late afternoon and a group of whores were putting their final touches to some new performance.

They were in one of the salons, deep within the bowels of the building. The room had few windows and those that existed were screened with heavy green drapes, ruched and tasselled with gold. Lavish gilding and scrollwork was in abundance. It edged panels on the cream walls, swirled thickly around long mirrors, and twisted the lines of every chair and couch. Louis Quinze: vulgar but very popular.

A gallery lined with private booths ran along two sides of the room. Lord Marldon, in his office at one of the furthermost corners, stood at the small window, looking down on the rehearsal. The show was called, apparently, *A Tale of Love in which Venus rises from the Sea and meets the Nymphs*.

'Venus', swathed in flimsy lengths of blue and green,

stood within the curve of a papier-mâché shell, affecting a pose. One hip was thrust out, one hand was laid to her breast, and her languishing gaze was set low. Her wheat-coloured hair streamed down her back to her waist. Fluttering about her were the 'nymphs'; chiffon of brown and yellow hues wafted as they moved. A man in a frock coat sat watching sternly, his arm resting on a table. Another was seated before the pianoforte, his back to the tableau vivant, playing a lugubrious air by Liszt.

Slender fingers reached out to Venus and the fabric began falling away, a wisp of sapphire, a wisp of jade. The woman was majestic, motionless, as the veils slipped from her. Her nudity emerged gradually, strong sensuous curves and flawlessly pale skin. When she was naked, she stepped out of the cloths frothing at her feet and moved forward. Venus had risen and she was shaved.

Her pubis was a bare swell divided by a carmine split, and the nipples of her full, handsome breasts were wantonly rouged. The nymphs, half-crouched, slid a multitude of hands up and down her gleaming white thighs. Venus threw back her head and began gently rotating her hips. She swept a caress up over the small pout of her belly then circled fingers around the globes of her bosom. She fondled the dark crimson tips, teasing them to puckered crests.

Below, a hand edged up towards the pendulous lips of her vulva. Venus widened her stance, allowing fingers to move within the plump flesh. She shivered and ground her loins with rising urgency. Her mouth parted and her face slackened with arousal that was clearly not assumed. The pleasuring nymph crammed her fingers into the cavern of the woman's vagina. With a jerking arm she thrust upwards, again and again. The pianist crashed dramatic low notes and Venus writhed, her breasts lifting with deep, heaving sighs.

'What price are we selling Moselle?' asked Marldon without turning.

'Twelve shillings a bottle,' came Madame Jane's quick reply.

Beneath, Venus was running delicately about the room, stretched like a cross with a nymph supporting each arm. They moved with light-footed grace, whisking the naked woman before an imaginary audience. Ripples of diaphanous chiffon trailed after them, and the music fluttered, shrill and fast.

'And champagne?' he enquired.

'The same, my lord.'

Venus was brought to a halt before the chair occupied by the watching man. She swayed provocatively before him and planted one foot on to the table. Her sex was open to the man's gaze. She fondled her breasts in a licentious display before her hand drifted down to her parted thighs. She slithered two fingers along the glistening scarlet furrow then dipped them into her gaping passage. She drove into herself, her speed increasing. Her pumping fingers shimmered with her secretions and she panted wildly.

'Put it up to fifteen,' said Marldon, striding over to his desk. 'Profits are down.'

Madame Jane huffed and her plump cheeks flushed with indignation.

'They'll never buy it,' she protested. 'It's expensive enough as it stands.'

Marldon threw her a sharp glance and at once she acquiesced. He drew his leather armchair up to the table and ran a meditative eye over the open ledger. He flicked back the lid of a silver box and took out a slim cigar, clipped it and set it to his lips.

'Well?' said Jane with undisguised testiness. 'What do you think of our new show?'

Marldon lit a match to his cigar. The tip glowed red as he inhaled. 'Medici will be turning in his grave,' he said, releasing a cloud of smoke.

'Bah,' she snapped. 'One day they will perform something and you will declare it superb.'

He turned a page of the ledger. 'That I very much doubt,' he said, idly scanning the figures. 'Leave us now, Jane. And close the curtains.'

'*Non*,' said Pascale, stepping from the gloom. 'My lord, I cannot stay long. It is impossible. I am on an errand to buy ribbons. I will be missed.'

Marldon looked at her contemptuously. 'With the curtains open,' he began, 'I can see the chandelier stem. It is annoying me. Do not flatter yourself, Miss Rieux. I tired of your charms long since. You grunt too much.'

Pascale scowled at him as Jane set a taper to the gas brackets, drew the curtains and left.

'Well?' said Marldon, resting his cigar in an onyx ashtray and leaning back in his chair. 'I'm waiting.' A thin plume of smoke wreathed upwards into the dimness.

Pascale moved to stand before the desk, her hands clasped at her waist.

'Miss Longleigh is in love, my lord,' she declared. 'I heard her say it to the maid. And it is as I suspected – with the artist.' She looked at him, smirking with pride.

Lord Marldon leant forward and steepled two fingers below his chin. A sweep of hair fell across his brow. In the haze of smoky gaslight it hung there, a raven's wing, shimmering blue-black. His dark eyes narrowed with malicious intent and a calculating smile played on his lips.

'So the girl's in love, is she?' he said. 'How quaint.'

He fell into a contemplative silence. His head nodded gently and his fingers rubbed over the strong bump of his throat. Pascale, save for a slight wringing of her hands, stood perfectly still.

'And tonight?' he asked, reaching for his cigar. 'Where does she go?'

'Tonight, my lord, she will go dancing at Cremorne.'

'Delightful,' said Marldon. 'I think I shall take my bride early.'

* * *

It was a velvet-black night but Cremorne Pleasure Gardens were ablaze with light.

It was as if the stars had tumbled from the heavens to nestle in the scattered trees. The open-air dance floor, encircled with ornate ironwork arches, was as elegant as a birdcage. And those who danced there, thought Gabriel, were exotic birds. Trapped.

He muttered something to his companions about trying his luck in the shooting galleries and sloped away. They'd detained him too long and Clarissa would be growing impatient. Discretion was not easy but it was vital. Society gossip spread like wildfire, and when Lord Marldon was your adversary it was folly to take too many risks. But, away from the crowds, under the canopy of darkness, they could be alone together.

Gabriel wound his way past candlelit supper booths, marquees, marionette theatres and freak shows. Above the noise of orchestras, of soft applause, of the music of a hurdy-gurdy, and laughter, voices called out: 'Step this way! Step this way!' 'Sherry Cobblers at sixpence!' 'Buy my sweet cherries!'

Further beyond, away from the hubbub, were the more sedate areas of ferneries and groves. The arbours and leafy avenues would be in deep shadow and there they could embrace in the thick protection of the trees and the night. Gabriel quickened his step.

It was costing him all his willpower to keep Clarissa's honour. Her beauty, and the passion with which she took her pleasures, aroused him beyond belief. They'd shared only a few intimate moments, but the last time he'd allowed his prick to hover, nudging, at the entrance to her sweet, hot vagina. She'd pleaded with him to take her. And, so easily, he could have done. It would have been a split second's thought, just one deep thrust. But, somehow, he'd restrained himself.

Clarissa could relieve him in other ways. Sometimes she used pleasuring hands; at other times her wet, mobile mouth. Her tongue would flutter delicately about his shaft and her firm sucking lips would drive him to blissful heights. It was not the ultimate fulfilment they both craved, but for now it had to suffice. They must wait until her father returned and then, perhaps, maybe, there was the remotest of possibilities that their union would be sanctified.

Gabriel was far less hopeful than Clarissa but he would not give her up. If necessary they could flee the country together and live in poverty.

Quick breaths and light footsteps hurried towards him. An urgent hand grabbed his wrist and he swung around.

'What have you done to Clarissa?' demanded Lucy.

Gabriel shook himself free and stared at her in confused aggravation. 'I've done nothing to Clarissa. What on earth do you mean? Has something happened? Christ, is she hurt?'

Lucy glared at him. 'No, you fool. But I have suspicions which make me uncomfortable. I've seen the way you two look at each other. I asked you to seduce her a little, prepare her for Marldon, and I fear you have taken things further. I sincerely hope the pair of you are not falling in love. Things could get awfully complicated. And I, for one, would not wish to endure the wrath of Lord Marldon.'

'In love?' scoffed Gabriel. 'Don't be ridiculous, Lucy. Since when have I been a man to fall in love?'

'You do it all the time, Gabriel,' she said waspishly. 'You fall in love with a melody, a flower, with . . . with raindrops in a spider's web. And then you fall out of love. Where is she? Do you have a tryst in the avenues?'

'She's gone home,' he said, thinking quickly. 'She was tired.' Lucy was the last person in the world he wanted to discover the truth. She didn't exactly gossip: she simply shared secrets. As did many other people. And he did not relish the idea of his secret being shared with the Earl of Marldon.

Lucy eyed him distrustfully. 'Then where are you

going? Why, it looked to me as if you were making for the trees.'

'And yourself?' he teased. 'Out here all alone, Lucy? There must surely be someone awaiting you. Why else would you leave the delights of the dance floor?'

Lucy smiled brightly and her chin tilted in defiant pride. 'Lieutenant Gresham,' she said. 'He's quite a gentleman, actually.'

'You have the principles of Messalina,' Gabriel replied with disapproval only half-feigned. 'Still trying to make Sir Julian jealous?'

Lucy pouted. 'Well? Where are you going if it's not to meet Clarissa?'

'Mrs Singleton,' he said. 'Excuse my indelicacy, but I'm merely going to take a piss.'

Lucy flounced away. As if taking Clarissa under her wing wasn't already enough trouble! She had devoted herself to ensuring the girl was kept apart from Marldon. And now it looked as if she might have to do the same where Gabriel was concerned.

She drifted across the lawns towards the crowds and found a group of friends to chatter with a while. Lieutenant Gresham would have to wait; she was in no mood for him now. Gabriel and Clarissa were in love, she was sure of it, and the whole thing was becoming too much of a responsibility.

She had utterly debased herself at Octavia's ball, just to prevent Clarissa from meeting the earl. Marldon had humiliated and shamed her. He had forced her into innumerable acts with the watching men, so obscene that even Julian had looked disgusted at some points. And this was the thanks she got. If she did not care so much for her cousin and Alicia she would wipe them clean from her mind and leave Clarissa an innocent at the mercy of a monster.

'Ah, here comes Sir Julian now,' piped up Miss Thorpe. 'Didn't I say he was looking for you?'

Lucy excused herself and went to meet him, wanting his company more than anyone else's. The two of them strolled among the flowerbeds: tranquil parterres and crunching pathways lit softly by gas lanterns. Julian listened patiently to her grievances. When she had finished she felt a great deal better.

'Forget about them,' said Sir Julian. 'I can see only one good thing to have come of this affair so far, and that is that it's made you cross. And, when you're cross, your breasts heave and quiver so deliciously.'

Lucy paused by a cascade of rocks and ferns, and turned to him with a seductive smile. 'Why, I don't think you've heard a word of what I've been saying,' she chided.

'Oh, but I have,' he replied. His eyes, made deep blue by the shadows, twinkled mischievously. He dropped his gaze and stared deliberately at the bulging shelf of her bosom. 'I have a remarkable ability to concentrate on two things at once, Mrs Singleton. However, it was not listening to your complaints which has made my cock so hard.'

Excitement arrowed to Lucy's groin. She loved it when she aroused him with the slightest thing.

'Then perhaps a stroll in the avenues would ease the swelling,' she ventured.

'Of that I'm sure,' said Julian. 'But I would far rather have you sprawled naked before me, groaning with abandon. I fear a few dark bushes would not grant me such a privilege.'

'Then I shall take you home,' she cooed. She felt a pang of regret that she was wasting an opportunity to pique him with tales of the lieutenant. But, she decided, she could always invent something if she felt so inclined. Her lust was for Julian now, and Julian alone. And, besides, she ought to make the most of him while he was in London. His ailing wife could summon him at any moment.

'And Clarissa?' asked Sir Julian, wearily dutiful.

'Oh, she's already left,' said Lucy. 'There's no need to wait.'

'Delightful,' he replied, raising his forearm. 'Then home it is.'

'On one condition,' breathed Lucy, wrapping her arm around his and sidling close. 'Which is that on the way there, in the back of the hansom, you will allow me to suck your prick.'

'I shall ask the cabman to drive very slowly,' replied Sir Julian.

Clarissa was lost. 'The sixth avenue,' Gabriel had said. But it depended on where you started counting and what you defined as an avenue. She'd ventured part way down a rough track and a broad walkway, but to no avail. And she had seen no sign of him either. 'Five minutes,' he'd said. But much more time than that had elapsed.

She looked towards the distant panorama of lights and scanned the shadowy figures wandering about the trimmed lawns. There was nobody familiar moving in this direction. She would wait a while longer, then she would go in search of him. But she would wait further down one of the avenues. Loitering on the edge of the trees was doing little for her dignity.

To the right a gloomy pathway, flanked with bushes and overhung with leafy branches, faded to a menacing blackness. Berating herself for being nervous, she took a few stealthy steps into the darkness. Underfoot was well-trodden grass with patches of hardened earth. She moved cautiously, reluctant to alert any hiding lovers to her presence. At the third tree she paused. She would count to sixty then tiptoe back to see if Gabriel were approaching.

As she reached twenty-nine a rustle in the foliage startled her. She held her breath, listening. But there was nothing. It was a bird, or perhaps a courting couple. Thirty, thirty-one . . .

'Clarissa!' came an urgent voice.

Her heart lifted. He was here. Gabriel was here. 'Where are you?' she hissed, looking about her and advancing towards the sound.

'This way,' he whispered from bushes deeper along the track.

Clarissa giggled and moved swiftly. So he'd found a place that was truly secluded. She halted where she thought the source of his voice was.

'Gabriel?' she said in a soft, eager tone.

There was a loud crackling and quick springing footsteps behind her. Before she could turn, his hand closed over her eyes. Her pulse jumped.

'Stop it,' she laughed. 'Stop playing games.'

But the hand pressed more firmly, drawing her back. Then something thumped across her belly. Clarissa doubled over, winded, her breath gone. Panic seized her; her mind raged. The ground spun and she saw two pairs of feet, a flash of Oxford brogues, a flash of sturdy boots. This was not Gabriel. She was going to die.

She wheezed, struggling for air. A hand clamped the lower part of her face then something was forced between her teeth. It was fabric, thick and dry, filling her mouth and stretching her lips into a rictus of muffled protest. She caught a glimpse of a grizzled beard before a blindfold plunged her into a black void. It was too tight. Hazy purple spots dilated in the darkness. She jerked and writhed as an iron grip hooked back her elbows, pinning them inflexibly.

'Keep still, bitch,' someone growled in her ear.

The man smelt of horses and tobacco, and his stale, sour breath was hot on her face. His coarse whiskers scoured her cheek and she squirmed to be free of him, squealing dully into her gag, hardly able to breathe. A punishing hand caught her wrist; her arm twisted and searing agony tore through one shoulder. It was useless, useless. Her body heaved with muted dry sobs. She was too young. She did not deserve it. She prayed only that her end would be painless.

'You're going on a little trip, Miss Longleigh,' sneered a second voice. 'Your presence has been requested. And, if you want my advice, don't bother struggling. You'll need your energy to do that later.'

Chapter Six

Clarissa's heels clattered across a hard floor – tiled, she thought: it had that clean sound, that slippery feel. Behind her a door creaked and closed with the dull thump of heavy wood. She heard the grating rasp of bolts being drawn and the stuttering clicks of keys in locks. Feminine footsteps clipped away. Every noise rose high and came back to her as a harsh echo.

She knew she was still in London, although she did not know which part. The carriage she'd been bundled into had driven along the King's Road – it was the only route out of Cremorne – and her sense of direction told her she was now somewhere north of that. But where exactly – and more to the point, why? – she did not know.

'Welcome to Asham House,' said the voice to her right.

Clarissa's heart lurched. Asham House, Asham House. The name danced and swirled in her brain, repeating itself senselessly in the turmoil of her panic. It was Lord Marldon's town residence. He knew who she was. He had sent for her. She was in Piccadilly, in his mansion.

It was confirmation of what she feared the most. A rush of terror made her writhe violently against her

99

captors. She made urgent noises of protest but the gag kept the sound trapped within her mouth.

Hollow, condescending laughter greeted her futile struggles.

'Hold still, bitch,' came the other gravelly voice. Then a cold, metallic edge rested against her neck. 'Or I'll slice you from ear to ear.'

It was a knife; she had a knife at her throat. An overwhelming urge to swallow tormented her. The more she thought about it, the more her cheeks seemed to fill with saliva. Desperately she fought against the impulse, fearing even to breathe lest the movement should cause the blade to pierce her skin.

'This will be your home for some time,' continued the clearer voice. 'Although I doubt you'll be allowed to treat it as such.'

No, Clarissa told herself. He could not keep her here against her will. She would be missed. She had not kept her assignation with Gabriel and, even now, he would be combing the Pleasure Gardens in search of her.

The knife moved away from her throat and she swallowed; there was no moisture. Viciously strong fingers forced her arms behind her back. Others looped twine about her wrists and tugged a series of knots, each pull of the rope making the rough bondage cut deeper into her flesh. Her body wriggled: a gesture of resistance. She knew it was hopeless.

Then someone fumbled with the blindfold and whipped it from her eyes.

'If you behave, my lady, we might do the same to your mouth.'

Clarissa blinked rapidly. She was in a lofty white entrance hall and, although the lights in the girandoles burnt low, the room came as a glare after her enforced darkness. Enormous, heavily framed paintings adorned the walls, and a grandfather clock said it was a quarter past midnight. Before her a broad marble staircase with a gilt and glass balustrade swept up to a columned gallery. Above was a second gallery and higher still was a domed ceiling patterned with golden-edged honeycombs.

Clarissa craned her neck, expecting to see Marldon sneering down from one of the balconies. But he was not there.

'Brinley Jefferson,' said the man to her right. 'Lord Alec Marldon's loyal valet. I expect we'll be seeing quite a lot of each other. Forgive me if I don't kiss your hand.'

Clarissa whirled her head around to the man. He was a willowy creature with a crop of short dark curls, and strange green-grey eyes. She glared at him, her heated look conveying the anger her bound mouth could not. He merely smiled, his lips thin and sensual, and nodded towards her other abductor.

'Jake Grimshaw, stablemaster,' said Brinley. 'I hope he hasn't been too rough with you.'

Jake Grimshaw leered at her. A brown-toothed smile gaped within his mass of grizzled whiskers and a lecherous snigger gurgled deep in his throat. He stretched his callused hand to Clarissa's face. She shrank back on the instant.

'Easy, Jake,' warned the valet, stopping the other man's hand with his own. 'When we remove this gag, Miss Longleigh, if you so much as squeak it goes back on. And I won't be quite so gallant in controlling Jake's eagerness. He likes a pretty girl, don't you, Jake?'

The burly stablemaster grunted agreement and the valet untied the knot at the nape of her neck. Clarissa drew deep, free breaths and ran her tongue around the inside of her dry mouth. She did not cry out, nor did she rail against those who had brought her there. She merely whispered, when she could, a hoarse 'thank you'.

But it was not the men's threats which made her compliant, for their danger, although it was real, was also crude. It was her dread of Lord Marldon which stilled her. She felt the subtlety of his menace as an aura within the house, oppressive and all-pervading.

Her heart thundering, she allowed herself to be escorted up the shallow slabs of the staircase. She feared Marldon might be covertly watching her, trying to gauge her reaction, and her face was as stone. The men led her from the gallery landing down a long red corridor lined with portraits and Chinese urns, then into an anteroom hung with striped yellow silks. Before double doors of oak and studded leather, they stopped.

'You ought to look your best for Lord Alec, don't you think?' said Brinley with a sneer.

In one swift movement, he grasped the low neckline of her gown and jerked the purple silks from her shoulders. The fabric tore a little and he jammed the lacy froth around her arms, trapping them at her sides. She gave a shocked gasp and the valet, laughing quietly, shoved a hand into her underclothes. His cold thin fingers spanned the swell of her right breast, then he heaved out the pale globe.

A burning anger pounded through her veins. Breathless with outrage, she backed away, stumbling against the great bulk of the stablemaster. His brawny forearms circled her waist, squashing the air from her. She shouted and kicked but her struggles had no impact. With the same cruel enjoyment, Brinley dug his fingers beneath her chemise and scooped free the fullness of her other breast.

She could scarce believe what was happening.

Jake released her and Brinley stepped back. His covetous gaze hovered on her soft white orbs, swooping over their curves, darting from nipple to nipple.

'How dare you?' fumed Clarissa, petulantly stamping her foot.

The valet grinned, his eyes flicking from her juddering bosom to her face.

'Orders are orders,' he said with an ironic lift of his brows. 'You wouldn't want us to defy his lordship, would you now?'

Clarissa tried to stem the tide of her fury. He had

ordered this, actually ordered his servants to expose her. Well, if he was determined to humiliate her, then she could be equally determined not to respond. She assumed an air of glassy composure, and looked steadily at the valet. Lord Marldon would not get the better of her. She would meet him defiantly, not cowering in shame and terror.

'Lovely,' growled Jake. His clawed heavy hand reached for her bared mounds, and Brinley at once slapped it away.

'She's not yours to touch,' he admonished.

'Just a lil' squeeze,' argued the man gruffly, batting away Brinley's arm. 'They're so darn lovely.'

With a lunge, his coarse stubby fingers fastened on to one breast. He pummelled vigorously, chuckling mildly, clutching and tugging as if he were trying to wrest the flesh from her.

Clarissa screamed, her cool veneer forgotten.

Brinley barged into the stablemaster's hulking frame and the brute lurched back, his arm flopping to his side.

'Damnation,' hissed the valet. 'I've seen dogs with more finesse. Now look what you've done, you cursed oaf.'

'Bitch made me,' mumbled Jake, looking contritely at the ground.

Clarissa's white flesh was streaked with red. Sapphire chips blazed in her eyes and her face was dark with rage.

'You'll answer for this, Grimshaw,' said Brinley, turning the gilded ring of the door handle. 'I'm taking none of the blame.'

He ushered Clarissa forward. Her boiling blood simmered down, swamped by fear as she stepped into an immense salon, softly lit and stretching either side of the entrance. Three vast chandeliers swept a line down the room, cascading crystal, dripping beads of ice blue. Clarissa scanned sharply from left to right, hunting for Lord Marldon. She could see no one, yet she felt the presence of many.

The salon was irregular, full of places to hide. There were no walls as such, but rows of archways, divided by gilded pilasters, and decorated in rich mosaics of turquoise and gold. Above a frieze inscribed with Arabic lettering, the ceiling too was set with tiny tiles, forming geometric patterns which glinted in the light. Tall, fringed palms stood here and there, and divans and ottomans, upholstered in figured crimson silk, were scattered about the room alongside fragile lacquered tables. Everything was exotic and palatial, and the furniture seemed almost to languish.

Brinley guided her deeper into the salon. The thick red and gold carpet, as soft as a bed of moss, soaked up the sound of their footsteps. Candles flickered in ornate sconces, each one a mirror of her own fluttering pulse.

Then, slowly, figures stepped into view. They emerged from the arches' shadows or rose from couches which had until now concealed them. There were women, clearly naked beneath gauzy wrappers and peignoirs, and men in livery, lounge suits and high-buttoned frock coats. They drifted silently towards her, snaking among the furniture and smiling lasciviously.

Clarissa could not quell her embarrassment. She coloured hotly, the flush creeping up from her bared breasts to stain her face. Frightened, she edged backward and felt the valet rest a gentle, stilling hand against her back. His touch was not coercive; it was merely a reminder that she was utterly powerless, and it worked on her all the more forcefully for that. She gave a little whimper of defeat, and was rendered motionless, mesmerised, petrified.

The valet dropped away, leaving her in isolation as the people – perhaps twenty or so – formed a wide, uneven circle about her. They ogled her with unabashed lechery. She caught the eye of a swarthy fellow with a great drooping moustache. He smiled and licked his lips, his tongue slow and salacious. A brunette in transparent green rolled her hips suggestively.

Their hungry stares burned into Clarissa's naked bosom, infecting her with a flare of sensuality. The response of her body appalled her. It was sordid, wicked, beyond comprehension. Dropping her eyelids, she stared at a fleur-de-lys on the carpet, willing the moment to pass. There was a stirring within the group. For as long as she could, Clarissa ignored it. But the compulsion to look was overwhelming.

Lord Marldon strode forward. His face was stern, devoid of the sneer she remembered him having, and beneath his shock of sable hair his ebony eyes were fierce. Candle flames from above cast shadows on his harsh, cynical features, and his scar, after the rectangle of one sideburn, was silvery white. It lay across his strong, solid jaw, gleaming like a tiny sliver of moonlight.

He moved towards her with intimidating indolence. His arms, corded with muscle, were bared to the elbow and his shirt gaped to reveal a triangle of his hard chest.

An image of Lucy, sitting in the library, meekly accepting the invasions of his fingers, jumped into her mind. Desire crawled over her skin, leaving goose bumps in its wake. Her heart hammering against her ribs, she glared at the earl's approach. Ready insults swam to the fore of her mind but, as he drew near, his sloe-black eyes rendered her mute with fear and awe. She bowed her head, her lashes sweeping down.

Marldon stood before her, held light fingertips beneath her chin and lifted it. He stepped back and surveyed her, his face impassive, his gaze roaming at leisure, taking in every inch of her. He stared at her exhibited breasts. A frown of disapproval creased between his dark brows. Clarissa was stock-still, her chin just as he had positioned it, fixed in a brave thrust.

He reached out to touch the underswell of one taut, high globe. Her skin tingled beneath his cool fingers and a frisson of arousal coursed through her body. It was the breast the stablemaster had sullied, and its striations, though fading, were still visible. Marldon lifted its weight. Gently, he bounced the fullness of her mound in a cupped hand, regarding it with a contemplative expression. A gasp caught in Clarissa's throat. Then, tenderly, he set the flesh back.

He looked beyond her shoulder. 'Grimshaw,' he said blandly. 'Come here.'

A murmuring ripple spread through the onlookers and Jake, his head hung low, shuffled into the centre of the circle.

Lord Alec curved his hand to Clarissa's flushed breast and addressed the stablemaster with dead eyes. Before the hushed crowd, he kneaded her soft orb with a gentle caress. He teased her roseate nipple and it crinkled to a throbbing point of pleasure.

Clarissa could not stifle a light moan. She drew soft, shaky breaths, for a moment losing sense of her audience. Marldon smiled faintly. Silently, bitterly, she cursed him.

'I doubt the lady appreciated you mauling her,' he said to Grimshaw, his thumb scuffing over her hardened nipple. 'Yet note how her flesh rises to a more practised touch. Did the sight prove just too tempting, Jake? Does it tempt you still?'

Jake's anxious eyes darted from his master's face to Clarissa's jutting bosom, and his spittle-flecked lips sagged with appetite.

Marldon fixed him with a cold expression and spread his hand over Clarissa's other breast. With undulating squeezes, he slowly rotated the yielding globe. Her nipple tensed beneath his massaging palm. Then his stroking fingers played over the stiffening crest, enticing it to full erection.

A violent need inflamed Clarissa's body, a need that was somehow fiercer for the watching eyes and Marldon's arrogant dispassion. Her cheeks glowed with shame and rage, but she did not move; she did not speak. He would only crush an outburst with mockery.

'You must learn, Jake,' he began serenely, 'that Clarissa is mine, and mine alone. Permission must be granted before other hands can touch. And I did not grant you such permission, did I?'

Before Clarissa could protest, Marldon startled her with a swift movement.

He stepped away and, with a swoop of his arm, swiped the back of his hand across the stablemaster's face. It might have been just the blow of a master chastising his servant. But it was not, for Marldon wore a diamond ring on his middle finger.

The crowd chorused a hiss of indrawn breath as Grimshaw recoiled with a guttural cry. Recovering his balance, the man gingerly patted his cheekbone then stared in dismay at the viscid red mess coating his fingers. An inch or so below his eye a raw gash pouted with swelling blood. Clarissa winced.

'Get out of here,' said Marldon levelly, examining his left hand and rubbing at the gemstone.

The wounded man lumbered away. Lord Marldon turned to Clarissa.

'I cannot abide insubordination,' he said. 'Allow me to apologise for his trespass.'

'I am not your chattel,' she returned sharply, her revulsion spurring her to boldness.

'No?' replied Alec with quizzically arched brows. 'Forgive me, but I believed we were to be married soon. I planned on a honeymoon in Venice before we take up residence in Wiltshire. What do you think, Clarissa? Personally, I'm rather fond of Venice and I thought it might suit your romantic sensibilities. I toyed with the idea of Paris but, really, the city isn't what it used to be.'

'My father will never permit a marriage when he hears of this,' she said, her voice low and angry.

Lord Marldon gave a short, hoarse laugh.

'Oh, how spirited women rouse me,' he said, trailing a finger over her breasts.

He drew her close in a tight embrace, bearing down on her mouth. He forced a sultry, probing kiss into her mouth. Clarissa tensed her muscles in rigid defence but every thrust and lash of his tongue conspired against her. She felt the insistent power of his body, so hard against hers, and a devastating lust melted her. She smelt his masculinity, sharp and tangy beneath warm, woody cologne, and she inhaled deeply, a voluptuous throb surging through her veins. When he broke away, she was as limp as new death in his arms.

'Do you need to sit?' he enquired briskly.

Clarissa shook her head, staggering a little as he released her.

'Good,' he replied. 'Then meet some of my household: the upper servants.' With a matador's flourish, Marldon gestured part way round the ring of spectators. 'Think of them as friends, Clarissa. I would introduce them personally, but I'm afraid Jake has set my patience at rather a low ebb. Excuse my discourtesy, please. But, in the days to come, we shall have plenty of time for the humdrum of formalities.'

Clarissa's eyes swooped over the greedy faces in cursory acknowledgement.

'You cannot keep me here,' she said quietly, still enfeebled by the kiss. 'What is it you want? Is it money? Do you intend holding me to ransom?'

Marldon laughed. 'I confess, money has its attractions, Clarissa. In fact that was the first, most tempting thing about you. Would you believe my funds are so low I was actually considering selling this place? That is, until your father came along with his very generous offer. What was it now? Twelve thousand a year until his death? Yes, I think so. And then, after that, let me see, his estate in Sussex, his properties, his holdings in Pacific Steam, his fortune, and ... something else ... Oh, yes, how forgetful of me: his daughter. She would be thrown into the bargain too.'

Clarissa jerked her wrists against the ropes in a storm of fury. 'Then you have lost it all with this,' she replied through clenched teeth.

Marldon stroked over her brow and down one scarlet-hued cheek. 'Oh, I think not,' he said. 'You see, the second most tempting thing was you, Clarissa. I received quite an enchanting photograph. You were wearing pearls. Do you recall it?'

'Then may it satisfy you as a keepsake,' she snapped, turning sharply from his touch. 'As a reminder of the woman who refused to be your bride.'

'You will capitulate,' he stated confidently. He held her chin, compelling her to look into his narrowed, black eyes, and leant close. 'I see desires in your body, so deep that you do not even dream of them. I will open up those delights to you, Clarissa. I will explore every shadowy recess of your appetite. I will awaken lusts so base that you would rather die than share them with another.'

'No,' she said faintly.

'And awakened lusts,' he continued, 'no matter how shameful, can sleep only in nightmares – secret nightmares which will haunt you, plague you and corrode the very depths of your soul. You will find the prospect of a life without me intolerable. I predict a willing bride.'

Clarissa shivered. 'No. It is not so. It will not be so.' Her words fell away into a whisper.

Marldon slid an arm beneath her bound wrists and pulled her to him. She bent backward in a show of rejection and he seized the opportunity, bending to cover a rigid nipple with his warm, hungering mouth. His teeth pressed and scraped on the roughened cone, and his hellish tongue lapped and teased. He moved slowly from breast to breast, lavishing kisses over the soft, satin curves, and all the while a thumb rubbed steadily in the small of Clarissa's back.

A murmuring groan escaped her lips, needful and despairing. She felt hot sensation tumble through her, and the creases of her sex filled with wanton appetite. Her moisture gathered inexorably, a swelling silkiness bathing her vulva in rich fluidity, easing her folds to openness. Her body had betrayed her.

She closed her eyes, blotting out the audience, blotting out him. She tried to think of dull things, of whist parties and Sundays, but her mind could not hold them. So she concentrated on Marldon, listing every reason she had for despising him. But reason deserted her, vanquished by lust. The only thing she knew was the fierce, demanding ache which engulfed her. Gasps echoed in her throat and her breath grew ragged. A flicker stirred between her thighs, growing to a pulse, then stronger still to a frantic throb.

Lord Marldon moulded a grasping hand to the curve of her buttocks. He caressed her through layers of silk, drawing her loins closer to his. Clarissa felt his desire, a stern hard rod, digging into her belly. She imagined that imprisoned shaft of flesh violating her maidenhead and a bittersweet intensity tugged deep within her. Gabriel had valued her honour but Marldon would place no store by it. In the haze of her arousal, Clarissa was thankful for her bondage. If he should attempt to ravish her, she would be unable to fend him off.

'Hardly a good start,' murmured Lord Marldon, smudging kisses over her neck, 'considering you're supposed to be resisting me.'

Clarissa moaned weakly. His hand roved over her breasts. His lips brushed against her ear.

'Are you wet?' he asked softly. The closeness of his mouth blurred his voice to a low intimate tone, thick with warped sensuality and so darkly threatening. The sound speared Clarissa's groin with a shameless clutch of longing. 'Are you?' he repeated. 'Shall we find out, Clarissa?'

Marldon stepped away from her and clicked his fingers. 'Marcus, James, get rid of her drawers.'

Clarissa shrieked as a couple of strong, slender youths stepped forward, flexing their fingers and smiling eagerly.

'No,' she begged, her eyes wildly beseeching. 'Not here. I entreat you. Let us be alone, my lord. Then you can have me, I swear. But, please, not here.'

Lord Marldon could not contain a faint gleeful smile. 'You must accustom yourself to it,' he said. 'I'm afraid the prospect of coupling beneath the bedclothes fails to excite me.'

Clarissa writhed, continuing to plead, as the two men hooked their arms in hers. She hated Marldon with a savage, burning passion. He could not do this to her, not before so many eyes; he could not.

The men, battling against her protests, dragged her to an ottoman and forced her to lie back on the padded red silk, an expanse almost as wide as a bed. Hands clamped her kicking feet to the ground while others rummaged beneath her petticoats, fumbling with the waist-cord of her drawers. Her tied hands pressed a lump into her back, and she twisted and flapped like a dying fish. More than anything she wanted to conceal her seeping moisture. Marldon would doubtless torment her with it, brandish it like a trophy.

One of the youths dragged down her drawers and, with the noise of shredding silk, ripped them from her legs. Then there were hands on her ankles and shoulders, pinning her jerking body.

Lord Alec toed the heap of white fabric contemptuously.

'While I'm not averse to taking my pleasure from a woman who kicks and screams,' he said, 'I'd rather you stop this charade of reluctance. Or I'll be obliged to spread your ankles and bind them. A moment's work, granted, but all the same rather tiresome, don't you think? And so degrading when one has an audience.'

Clarissa held her muscles tight, pushing against the restraining hands, until the sense of his words filtered into her mind. If she resisted him with force, no matter how hopeless, it would be met with force. Her body sagged in defeat and the two men released her at Marldon's bidding. Then she would resist him with passivity.

Lord Marldon flung up her skirts, baring her ivory-pale thighs and the stark black curls of her mons. She could not help but clamp her legs together. She lay there, staring up at the ceiling's blue and gold tiles, striving to find a steadiness of breath. The eyes on her vulnerable half-nudity seemed to increase with every beat of her frightened heart.

The earl moved around her, a panther waiting to pounce. He stood by her feet, put his hands to her knees and stretched her wide. She felt his rapacious gaze feasting on her vulva, split, glistening and ripe with desire. He slid up her tensed thighs and brushed lightly over the tremulous pouch of her labia, tickling the fronds of hair. Then, with his fingertips, he opened her plump rosy lips. He held them apart like a shining red butterfly, assessing the view. The heel of each hand rested in the hollows of her splayed inner thighs.

Clarissa was rigidly immobile.

Marldon's finger slicked through her ready fissure and teased at the entrance to her warm opening.

'Delicious,' he breathed.

She made a noise of anguished pleasure, feeling the tension thaw. Her thighs lolled open. Her hips strained to rise but she would not let them. She smothered every groan as his subtle, tricksy fingers explored her tender flesh. He nudged her pouting clitoris and, with insidious slowness, began revolving the pad of his thumb over the tiny bead, tempting her to succumb, to relinquish control.

Clarissa whimpered and her hot, pulsing loins lifted, pursuing his clever ministrations. Marldon laughed quietly and dipped a pale, lean finger into her narrow opening, finding her succulence, her eagerness.

'I see the artist has left me your virginity,' he said with calm detachment. 'How generous. Remind me to thank him sometime.'

He began to drive in and out, taking strokes that were long and indulgent. He stirred and tickled deeply, then trailed back, finding the sensitive pad of her inner wall.

He lingered there, rubbing and teasing. Clarissa cried out, her sex pounding, her head tossing wildly on the silk. Marldon's thrusts grew faster and faster. She was lost, abandoned to pleasure.

'Good,' drawled Marldon, watching her keenly. 'Good, Clarissa. Give in to it.'

The ropes about her wrists chafed as she drove herself into his hand, her feeble curses lost in her urgent gasps. She craved wider, deeper penetration. She wanted him, yearned for him with an all-consuming hunger.

His finger plunged on with infernal sweetness while his thumb pressed and rolled her clitoris. Her groin tightened in a soaring flurry of bliss, and she wailed, her body hurtling towards its peak.

He slid out of her vagina and ploughed upwards, through her aching wet seam to the simmering knot of her pleasure bud. He smeared her creamy juices there and stimulated the engorged tissue, fretting it with quick shifting pressures. Clarissa felt her crisis rush, and immediately his caress slowed. He held her there, tarrying on the threshold, tormenting her with nudges that were never enough, never enough to send her spiralling into ecstasy.

Then he pulled away.

Clarissa gave a howl of disappointment. 'No,' she cried. 'No.' She wriggled frantically, struggling to right herself in senseless pursuit of him. 'You cannot deny me so. Please, my lord, I'll do anything.'

Her tethered hands unbalanced her and she tumbled from the ottoman, falling to her knees as if in supplication.

'Anything?' he enquired derisively. 'Do you mean to say I have the future Countess of Marldon at my feet?'

Clarissa stayed as she was, hunched forward, shoulders heaving. Her dark hair hung in a tangled curtain of curls and pins, shielding her face.

'No,' she managed to sob. 'You do not.'

Then she tossed her head back and looked up at

Marldon, breathless and wild, her face glowing with passion.

'Perfect,' he said. 'That's exactly how I want you.'

With a start of recognition Clarissa recalled her surroundings.

The circle of spectators had broken up. They were strewn about the salon, draped on couches or sprawled across divans. Some watched her avidly, while others partook of their own lewd pleasures. Some did both. A woman with clothing crumpled high toyed with the wet pink folds between her spread legs. She grinned obscenely at Clarissa. Another lay bent over a huge malachite table, her body jolting with the lunges of the rangy creature behind her. Subdued gasps whispered on the air.

Clarissa averted her gaze. 'Take me away from here,' she pleaded softly, hoping her voice would not carry to any ears but his.

'Away?' he scoffed. 'But, Clarissa, I fear you are not quite ready for me.'

Clarissa whimpered. She could not fight both herself and him. 'My lord, I am,' she said humbly.

The earl gave a wry smile. He pulled an object from his pocket, a handle of tortoiseshell, and flicked it open. It was a shaving blade. He turned it ponderously, finding angles where its sharp steel edge caught glancing stars of candlelight.

'You misunderstand me,' he said, moving to stand behind her.

Dryness choked Clarissa's throat and she swallowed hard, her heart drumming furiously. Was her surrender insufficient? Did he intend forcing her into wickedness and depravity? Relief sank into her when she realised he was merely cutting the ropes from her. He had seen the truth of her desire; he knew she would not retaliate. Perhaps now he would take her elsewhere.

'Truly, I do not doubt your willingness to offer me your body,' he said smoothly. 'I expected nothing less.

114

But it does not follow, Clarissa, that you are now ready. You must understand, I require more than a mere orifice for my pleasure.'

He signalled across the room. The valet sauntered over, a leering curl on his thin lips, and stood before Clarissa. His crotch, level with her face, bulged against pearl-grey trousers. Clarissa turned away, rubbing at her sore, reddened wrists.

'No, no,' said Marldon, lowering himself to one knee. He squeezed a hand to Clarissa's jaw and twisted her head, forcing her to confront the valet's swollen groin.

'At your service, my lord,' said Brinley, opening the buttons of his fly.

Clarissa squealed in horror and Marldon's grip tightened. The valet reached into the vent of fabric and withdrew his penis. Stiff and unfurled, it jerked from his clasp and its thick purplish head brushed over Clarissa's lips. She pulled back, pressing her lips together and murmuring fervent protests in her throat.

'I cannot abide an untutored mouth on my cock,' said Marldon. 'Yet this is a skill you must acquire for me. Shall we see how quickly you learn, Clarissa? There are, let's see, thirteen men in this room – excluding myself, of course. Do you think that will be sufficient practice? Or will I be rousing the grooms and bootboys at dawn?'

His merciless fingers dug into her face, but Clarissa fought the pain and kept her mouth resolutely shut.

'Stubborn, eh?' he said. 'There are two ways to do this.' He sank his teeth into her neck, a long, hard bite, until she yelped in pain.

'Force,' he declared, 'is one. And that was but a kiss when compared to other methods I could use. Persuasion is the second.'

His hand fluffed her skirts wide and stole beneath them to find her moist, pulsing flesh. Her need for him flared. She moaned repeatedly while his slender fingers worked, teasing out the urgency he had not satisfied.

'Which one do you prefer?' he whispered gently, his caress slipping down to massage a thigh.

Clarissa did not reply.

Marldon's teeth grazed over the stinging skin on her neck, then pinched hard and strong. He churned a finger within the humid well of her vagina.

'Which one?' he repeated, scuffing her clitoris before removing both the pleasure and the pain.

Clarissa closed her eyes. 'The latter,' she said in a tired, beaten voice.

'I thought as much,' he said crisply. 'Now take him.'

She parted her lips a fraction and the valet's cock at once pushed beyond them. His stout, quivering stem filled her mouth and began slowly to drive back and forth. Lord Marldon's fingers slithered along the furrow of Clarissa's aching sex. He murmured instructions in her ear: flutter your tongue about his shaft, Clarissa, lash at the tip, breathe now, yes, and suck, make your lips firm, clasp him, good, now sheathe him, take him deep, Clarissa, relax.

His finger rimmed the entrance to her molten tunnel then he penetrated her, thrusting into her slippery hunger.

'Keep time,' he said, and he plunged upward with a quickening rhythm.

Clarissa took the valet's prick deep and fast, willing Lord Alec to match her tempo. Brinley grunted like a beast, ramming vigorously. His cock's head banged ceaselessly against her throat, and she struggled for ease of breath. But she was so near to her peak, so frantically near, that she could not draw back from him. Marldon's finger, driving relentlessly, urged her ever closer. Then with a long rumbling groan the valet climaxed. His loins tensed and shuddered and the bitter liquid jetted over Clarissa's tongue.

Marldon shoved his finger. 'Swallow,' he snapped, and she did.

He stopped his stimulation of her and the valet snatched his phallus from her mouth.

Clarissa coughed and dashed her hand across her lips.

'Well?' enquired Lord Marldon, wiping his hand on Clarissa's skirt. 'How was she?'

Clarissa trembled with ill-disguised rage, hot tears welling in her eyes.

'Hmm,' said Brinley with a sneer in his voice. 'Satisfactory, my lord.'

'Then send Rupert over,' replied Lord Marldon. 'Satisfactory isn't quite to my taste.'

It was too much. Clarissa turned on him with a cry of anguish, battering her fists furiously against his solid chest. She hated him, she hated him from the depths of her being. He was a wretch, a despicable, heartless fiend. May Satan take him and may he burn in hell.

Marldon laughed wildly, deflecting her flailing blows. Then he caught her wrists in a harsh grip and, with a twist, pinned her to the ground. Her skirts frothed about her knees. He lay over her, supporting himself on arms which held hers down. His thick black hair hung about his face as he gazed at her, breathing quickly, his jet eyes flashing with pleasure.

'Hell could be closer than you think, Clarissa,' he taunted. 'But, when the flames lick, I won't be alone.'

She cursed him virulently, writhing and bucking in a bid to unbalance him.

'Good,' he said. He lowered his tumescent groin to press between her thighs and rubbed himself hard against her thrashing body. 'It seems you're a natural. Go on, thrust up to me again. What? Tiring so soon?'

Clarissa fell slack beneath him, sobbing in frustration.

'What is it that offends you so?' he enquired. 'Are you particular about the cocks you taste? Do you prefer those attached to gypsy artists? Perhaps you do. Because something tells me this mouth isn't as chaste as I'd

117

imagined.' He lunged to press a forceful kiss to her lips. 'You took to Brinley like an old whore. What would your lover say to that?'

Clarissa's mind reeled to imagine Gabriel seeing her like this.

'Why do you torture me in this manner?' she cried, choking back her tears.

Lord Marldon affected surprise. 'Because I enjoy it,' he said. 'Hadn't you realised?' His hips dropped and once more he ground the powerful ridge of his trapped cock into her parted thighs. 'What would soothe you? Is it me? Do you want me inside you?'

'No,' lied Clarissa.

'Are you sure?' he teased, still sliding his erection into her bunched silks.

Clarissa felt her petticoat, sodden with arousal, clinging to her pounding sex. She wanted him and she loathed him. But with so many people about – watching now, delighted by the fuss – she could admit to only one emotion. She turned her head aside and clamped her teeth on to the flesh of his forearm, a bite so long and vicious that her jaw trembled.

With a hiss, Marldon wrenched his arm away. Crimson beads of blood oozed through the punctured skin, and she tasted its copperiness in her mouth.

'Termagant,' he snarled, rising swiftly to his feet.

He tugged roughly at Clarissa's arm and she scrambled to stand up, her heart thudding in terror.

'You set my temper on edge, Miss Longleigh,' he breathed, his eyes flinty, his lips tight. 'May I recommend that you tread more cautiously in future.'

He stalked away from her. 'Get rid of her, Brinley,' he said, flicking his hand towards the door. 'I'm not in much of a mood for rape.'

Alec watched as the squirming girl was escorted out.

She was proving harder to break than he'd anticipated. Most women would have crumbled and begged

118

for mercy by now. Oh, she'd been close, very close. Yet, in the end, she'd still managed to hold out. It could only be a good sign.

He rubbed at his throbbing forearm, idly smearing the warm blood over his pale skin. Yes, there was no pleasure in dominating women who yielded too quickly. While eagerness and surrender had their place, it was not at the beginning. Marldon liked to see eyes full of rancour, not assent. Clarissa's determination was perfect.

He caught the gaze of one of the housemaids observing him with sly expectancy.

'What the hell are you looking at?' he growled. 'If you've nothing better to do, then get out of here.'

The woman shrugged indifferently and wandered away. Doubtless she thought he'd have use of her now Clarissa had gone. Another time he might have done. But why bother with sluts when there was a supremely beautiful and deliciously stubborn virgin on offer?

What a joy it had been to see Clarissa's elegance fracturing. Her frenzied attack, her dishevelled hair and unfettered emotion – oh, the girl had no idea how that roused him. There was nothing more exquisite than abasing someone of refinement, someone who valued their dignity. They had so much further to fall.

It had taken him a great deal of self-control to dismiss her like that. Her sex was weeping for him and his cock was ferociously hard.

But it would be far better when they were alone. Spectators worked well enough to humiliate her, but she seemed almost to be growing used to them. And she was too bold.

A little intimacy was required to bring the fear back into her eyes.

Absently, Lord Marldon snuffed a candle flame between thumb and forefinger. He'd given the maid ten minutes to disrobe her. He glanced at the clock and smiled. She would be almost ready.

Chapter Seven

*T*he room selected for Clarissa was on the second floor, with windows that did not open and a door with bolts on its corridor-side.

Old Spanish leather lined the walls, and the furnishings were of oak and ebony. The heavily carved tester bed, curtained in fiery-red damask, was softly lit by the feeble white glow of an oil lamp. On the embroidered coverlet lay Clarissa, naked, half in shadow. Her loose hair fanned midnight-black waves on the lace pillow. Her hand moved between her spread thighs, driving into that sweet little slit. Near-ecstasy racked her face.

Opposite her was a tiny hole bored into the wall, a mere speck in the worn leather hangings.

Alec stood in the long passageway, a hand holding back a heavy tapestry, an eye pressed to the aperture. The girl's rounded breasts were tipped with hard beads of lust. He smiled to see her massaging them with an urgently roving caress. She was greedy for fulfilment, beyond the subtleties of a light, teasing touch.

Her mouth fell open and she raised her hips, unwittingly offering more of herself to his stolen observations. Her splayed vulva gleamed like the pulp of a split juicy fig, and a slender finger slipped rapidly into the tight, scarlet hole of her vagina.

Lord Marldon moistened his lips. True virgins, women who were untouched and reluctant, held no appeal. But a virgin roused to heights of grasping appetite was a rare and splendid treat. Her untried sex, once he'd torn its resistance, would be deliciously snug around his prick, sheathing him with wet, clinging heat. And she'd respond to him with the zeal of a debauchee.

But he would allow her to climax first. His desire was already too strong, and he did not want the girl's orgasm to push him to quick release. He wanted to prolong the pleasure he would take inside her, savour every moment. And she would still be eager. A single masturbatory peak was hardly going to slake her thirst for him. He had roused her to a passion which required far more than that.

Clarissa's body lifted and she leant her head back on the pillow, stretching the pale slender line of her neck. Her fingers worked furiously until she cried out, her hips pumping, her thighs trembling. Then she slumped into the bed, breathing fast, her lush peony lips parted in blissful ease.

Marldon watched, grinning with satisfaction. He could not have hoped for a better bride. Not only was she beautiful, particularly when aroused, but she had a deep seam of wantonness that was begging to be tapped. While a frigid widow who left him alone might have been easier, this was going to be much more fun.

Clarissa sat up sharply, her lips curving in a smile of sly resolve. Her eyes flashed about the room, then she sprang to her feet and began tugging open drawers, overturning the silks within, pulling them out in rippling streams. She seemed not to notice or care that the contents were her own.

Alec frowned in confusion. What the hell was she up to?

She snatched up a silver-backed hairbrush from the

dressing table and circled her fingers around the slim handle. She eyed it thoughtfully, before tossing it on to a heap of petticoats. She grabbed a hand mirror and repeated the process before standing still, hands on hips, gazing about the room. Then her mouth twisted with devious pleasure. She rushed to the fireplace, stepped over the brass fender and clasped one of the mantelshelf candelabras. From its centre she pulled a stout, unlit candle.

Her fist gripped its thick length and her shoulders dropped with a huff of relief. She widened her stance and cupped her other hand between her legs.

Damn it! The artful minx was about to deprive him. She was going to take her own virginity.

Clarissa screamed as the door banged open. Lord Marldon was on her like a cat, wrenching the stick of wax from her hand and bearing her back on to the bed.

'My compliments on the delightful show,' he snarled. 'However, I'm afraid at this point I must intervene.'

Clarissa thrashed beneath him, horrified to think that he had somehow watched her. 'I will not give you my maidenhead,' she cried breathlessly.

'Who said anything about giving?' replied Marldon with a scornful laugh. He pinned her down and pressed a fierce kiss to her unresponsive lips. 'Come now, Clarissa,' he said. 'Enough of the prim-little-miss act. It fails to convince and it's beginning to grate.'

He edged up her body and knelt heavily on her spread arms, rendering her defenceless. She squealed in pain, the weight of him crushing into her delicate tendons. In one swift movement, Alec pulled his shirt over his head and let it fall. His chest was pale and taut, polished ivory tapering from wide shoulders to a trim waist. His hips were narrow, and beneath his black broadcloth trousers his groin bulged demandingly.

Leaning back, Lord Marldon sought out Clarissa's sex.

He watched her, scrutinising, while his skilful fingers probed, teasing folds that were soaked with desire.

His unremitting tyranny thrilled her, and the receding throbs of her climax blazed to his touch. Her hot flesh drew his caress deeper and the last vestige of defiance ebbed from Clarissa's body. Her eyelids dropped. She moaned gently. Her loins rose in small, questing nudges.

Marldon smiled and shifted his knees from her arms, straddling her breasts.

'Undo my trousers, Clarissa,' he said in a gentle command. 'Release me. Explore the tool which will deflower you.'

Clarissa's compliant fingers drifted nervously over his crotch. His prodigious length lay angled across his belly, a hard unyielding line. She craved to see him, to handle him, and yet she feared him greatly. Marldon urged her on with an impatient jerk of his hips. She fumbled with the buttons. His erection sprang free of his garments, proud, virile and dauntingly large. The flaring glans shone like a huge amethyst, and the veins entwined about his shaft looked ready to burst. Hot excitement shivered through Clarissa and she reached out to clasp him.

'I trust you find it preferable to a candle,' he said.

Clarissa nodded dumbly. His warm, stiff potency pulsed fiercely within her fist. She moved firmly along the sturdy length, wanting to please Lord Marldon; then he would please her.

'Your changed attitude is most encouraging,' he said, his hand still playing between her parted legs. 'I may propose marriage before the night is out.'

'Then I will refuse,' she whispered.

A clear bead of fluid trembled at the slitted end of his phallus. She ached for the first taste of him and, with brazen hunger, she stretched to lick the droplet away. Her tongue tingled with his saltiness and she lingered there, lapping at the contours of his stout, glistening tip.

'Control yourself,' he hissed sharply.

He stood, crossed to the door and locked it.

'Privacy seems to appeal,' he said, pocketing the key. 'So, for the moment, I shall guarantee it.'

He stripped off his remaining clothes and moved towards the bed. A ladder of muscle ran from his chest to his stomach, his thighs flexed with strength, and his cock reared massively from a nest of rich, black curls. He leant over her, light slithering from his broad shoulders, and his hot mouth suckled on her breasts. Her nipples ached with shame and need.

Clarissa pressed upward in an arc of giving, her body crescent-like.

Marldon threw back his head and gave a long laugh of conquest.

But it didn't matter; she didn't care because he was scooping her to him and, with disarming speed, he had flipped her on to her front. Clarissa, crouched on all fours, scrunched the coverlet in her fist, tensely awaiting the rip of his penetration.

He held her buttocks apart and slicked moisture from the valley within her labia up to the puckered indent of her anus. She whimpered plaintively. This was not what she wanted; she did not want delay. His finger nuzzled at the crinkled rose, and pressed damply against it. Clarissa flinched at the intimacy, her breath heavy and desiring.

'That virginity will be the next to go,' he said huskily.

Then, to her relief, she felt the orbed head of his cock nuzzle within her pounding sex-lips. She moaned impatiently, so eager and open for him, so wet. Taking a vigorous lunge, Marldon pushed into her. His stern iron prick breached the closure of her flesh and Clarissa cried out, a note of pain lost in a wail of pleasure as he plundered her tight, eager tunnel. His rigidity crammed into her, filling her utterly, stretching her wide.

He moved in deep half-thrusts, nudging repeatedly at the neck of her womb. Keeping the whole of his cock inside her, he ground his loins, circling his thick shaft against her slipperiness. Clarissa sobbed, snatching gasps of ecstasy.

'Ah, you like that, don't you?' he breathed. 'Tell me, Clarissa. Tell me you like it.'

His pelvis continued to roll and she wailed without restraint. Marldon drew slowly back and gave one hard slam. His phallus butted deep, and the power of it spread through her like the quivers of a gong.

'Tell me,' he urged. 'Tell me you like it.'

Lodged high, he gave little shoves, prodding at the core of her.

'Yes,' cried Clarissa. 'Yes, I like it. Yes.'

She felt his withdrawal and instinctively she gripped him, moulding her muscled passage to the density of his prick.

Marldon forced a gasp into a quick laugh.

'Good,' he said throatily. 'Hold me tight, Clarissa. Don't let me go.' As he spoke he drew further back.

Clarissa squeezed him hard, relishing the suck of resistance. The bulb of his glans lingered within the entrance of her vagina. She was pliant and awash with juices, receptive to his next leisurely glide. Then she was clenching him feverishly, her sex clamped around his retreating staff. She moaned with new delights and pushed back, meeting the next hungry surge of his cock.

Marldon grasped her hips, moving her to his rhythm, driving into her depths with steady luxury. Her glossy wet walls tensed and slackened, a fluttering intuitive caress. She shoved against him, banging her buttocks into his flat firm belly, urging him to a quickness, as quick as the pulse which hammered in her blood.

She heard him trap a groan in his throat. He dug his fingers into her haunches and his stroke shortened; his tempo rose. The weight of his balls swung into her vulva, sending shudders to her clitoris. Her pleasure mounted; her crisis swelled.

Marldon slowed. He tunnelled a finger down the deep cleft of her buttocks and began stirring pressure over the ring of her anus. Clarissa moaned with black excitement, feeling the tight portal relax beneath the insistence of his massage.

'No,' she whispered lamely. 'No.'

'You've abused the word far too much,' said Alec. 'It no longer has any meaning, Clarissa.'

His questing digit invaded, sliding to the knuckle, boring deeply into her dark secret passage. She cried out helplessly as he drove it back and forth, slowly at first then with increasing speed until his finger matched, thrust for thrust, the rhythm of his hard, pounding cock.

Clarissa heaved and squirmed, gasping in mortified enjoyment. Hot intensity flooded her loins and belly, and Marldon's flesh, plunging remorselessly into both openings, blurred all boundaries of sensation. She could scarce distinguish one hole from the other. Her body seemed to be melting into a tumult of sweet, burning confusion.

She drew frantic breaths. Her gathering rapture shortened, converging on a deep, whirling centre. Then the tension lashed its release. She wailed, soaring on a heady plateau, before the moment shattered and precious, tumbling waves devoured her.

Marldon gave her no quarter. He drew his finger from her anus and reached around to claw at her breasts. He pressed and squeezed their hanging softness, his cock powering into her with brutal ferocity. His body slapped harshly against her fleshy cheeks. His hands clutched in an animalistic frenzy. Then he uttered a roar of gratification, held a long jerking thrust inside her, and released the scorched seed of his pleasure.

'Christ,' he said, slipping out of her. 'I'm glad your father does not know you intimately. If he did, he would not have offered such a generous dowry.'

The cold, crude remark stung like a whip. Clarissa snatched a pillow to her nudity and twisted around to face him, her eyes narrowed with contempt.

'You foul man,' she blazed. 'You foul, repugnant man.'

Marldon's brows flicked in a quick arch, and he feigned mild surprise.

'You didn't seem to mind too much,' he jibed.

Clarissa's shameful conscience overwhelmed her. How could she have surrendered to him? No, it was worse than surrender. She had responded to him with greedy, unconcealed lust; she had delighted in his every action. She hated him bitterly for making her succumb to his base, heartless appetite.

'This means nothing,' she said vehemently. 'You forced me to it. And even if you do it again and again I will never, ever be your wife. You could put a pistol to my head and still I would say no. The moment I contact my father, he will withdraw his promise.'

'I think it might be a little late for that,' said Alec. He moved away from the bed and rummaged in the heap of his discarded clothes. 'I have the dowry contract here if you'd care to see it,' he said, producing a sheet of folded paper. 'Look at these signatures. They are far more valuable, albeit less charming, than your angry words.'

Clarissa looked at the swirl of her father's name and the scratch of Lord Marldon's. 'My father cannot, would not have done this,' she gasped. 'There is no reason to it.'

'You think too highly of him, Clarissa,' he replied dispassionately. 'He's really no different from all the other parvenus in society: desperate to introduce a little nobility into the family, to add a touch of refinement to his vulgar wealth. Businessman first; father second.'

Clarissa shook her head. She knew it made sense and yet she could not comprehend it. She had not thought her father a man to pursue those ends so ruthlessly. The truth hurt more than anything: he had signed her away.

'I shall refuse to go along with it,' she said defiantly.

'Then he'll disinherit you.'

Clarissa turned her head aside. 'I don't care,' she said sulkily.

'I'm afraid I can't quite see you as a seamstress,' he mocked. 'Nor a governess. Of course, you could try whoring. But even your appetite wouldn't be enough to keep you in the pretty frocks you're accustomed to.'

'Then why am I here?' she asked, still without looking at him. 'If it's all so cut and dried, why not just meet me at the altar?'

'I thought I'd try my hand at the preliminaries of courtship,' he said. 'An old-fashioned notion, I know. But I thought it only polite.'

Kitty could swear something strange was going on. She hadn't seen hide nor hair of Clarissa since she'd gone off to the Pleasure Gardens the evening before. And that Frenchwoman was definitely up to something.

Pascale had declared that mademoiselle was too tired for breakfast that morning. That didn't concern Kitty overmuch and, when she'd crept up the stairs to tap gently on the bedroom door, it was only because she'd hoped to find Clarissa there, drowsing in a happy haze. Kitty was always eager to hear her stories of dancing and romancing. But no one had answered and Kitty, a little concerned, had peeked into the room. Clarissa's bed had not been slept in.

She'd said nothing, though she'd thought it mighty funny. But funnier still was that when she'd returned to clean the room – later than usual because 'mademoiselle' kept on sleeping – the bedsheets were all rumpled and the pillows all bashed at. Had Clarissa done that? Or Pascale?

And then, according to Pascale, Miss Clarissa had gone off to spend a few days with her cousin who was unwell. Well, Kitty hadn't heard her leave.

After some thought, she could only conclude that the young miss had cooked up a plan to spend secret time with her new lover. Perhaps that was what Alicia paid Ellis and the Frenchwoman for. *He* kept Aunt Hester diverted while *she* covered for whatever Clarissa was

128

doing. But it didn't seem right, and the whole thing nagged at Kitty. She couldn't put it from her mind and she'd been skulking about all morning, trying to catch the footman and Pascale off guard.

She stood now on the landing, hidden from view, listening intently to the conversation at the front door. It was Mr Gabriel Ardenzi, Clarissa's sweetheart, and Ellis was giving him some cock-and-bull story about Clarissa being poorly. Kitty had done well to be vigilant.

'As I say, sir,' said the footman stiffly, 'such things are not at my discretion. And I assure you the matter is not serious. Miss Longleigh merely needs to rest awhile. If you wish to leave a message it will be conveyed to her.'

'Half a crown, then,' came the other voice.

Kitty was eager to steal a glance. She peered cautiously over the balcony and looked at the dark slender figure leaning against the door jamb. Lord, he was lovely.

'Sir,' said Ellis. 'It embarrasses me to have to make my meaning clearer: I am above bribery.'

'Five shillings,' persisted Mr Ardenzi, jangling the money in his cupped palm.

'The honour of those I serve means more to me than a pocketful of coins,' replied Ellis pompously.

And there goes another lie, thought Kitty. What the devil was going on here?

Gabriel thanked the footman and, promising to return on the morrow, bid him a sharp 'good day'. As Ellis closed the door, Kitty made her presence known.

'I thought she was staying with Mrs Singleton,' she said, making her way down the stairs.

Ellis turned quickly, unable to conceal a spark of annoyance in his eyes.

'She is,' he retorted. 'But, if I told him that, he'd never be away from the place. Miss Longleigh's reputation could be ruined by the attentions of such a raffish character.'

'He looked all right to me,' said Kitty defensively.

Ellis smiled and moved to block her way. 'So the Latin type appeals to you, does it? Tell me, what else do you like in a man, pretty Kitty?'

'I like good manners,' she snapped, trying to edge past him.

'Hush, hush,' he said softly, mirroring her sideways shuffles. 'I only want to talk to you. We hardly know each other, do we?' He rested his hands on her shoulders. 'That doesn't seem right to me, not when we're in the same house and there's so little work for us to do –'

'Speak for yourself,' she replied, vigorously shrugging off his hands.

'Oh, Kitty. Wouldn't you like to spend some time with me?' he cooed, stroking a finger down her cheek. 'I find you a remarkably attractive woman. Ever since –'

'Get out of my way,' she said. She heaved a shoulder against his chest and pushed past him.

Ellis stood back and sighed longingly. 'You're too cruel, dear Kitty. Too cruel.'

She walked briskly along the hallway, feeling his foxy eyes on her back. The smarmy popinjay was trying to win her over, do an Aunt Hester on her so she wouldn't be any trouble. Well, he had another think coming if he thought she'd fall for that one.

Down in the kitchen, cook was sweating and swearing over the range, and Pascale was bustling around, complaining that someone had stolen her tea allowance. The under-footman, buffing up the silver and crystal, was quietly glowering at her. No one liked Pascale. She was a nasty piece of work; thought she was too good for everyone else. Serve her right if her tea had been filched.

'Is Miss Carr having lunch in bed or at the table like normal folk?' enquired Kitty.

'At the table,' growled cook. 'So hop to it.'

Kitty busied herself in the laundry room, finding cloths and napkins. Aunt Hester was getting stranger by the day. Everyone knew the footman was popping in and out of her bed, and the old maid seemed determined to spend as much time there as possible. Whenever she emerged – to eat or to take a glass of port with the housekeeper – her eyes were glazed with bliss. Kitty was convinced she'd taken to laudanum. Ellis couldn't be that good.

A clatter of the door knocker sounded through the house. Kitty grabbed a half-filled laundry basket and, mumbling that she'd forgotten some sheets, darted up the stairs. It was Mr Ardenzi again. Kitty sauntered down the passage, singing a music-hall tune. Ellis flicked his head around and glanced at her, his face full of nerves. Kitty grinned.

Gabriel handed an envelope to the footman. 'For Miss Longleigh,' he said crisply.

'Thank you, sir,' replied Ellis, putting his fist to a little cough. 'I'm sure it will be much appreciated.'

Kitty approached them. 'I'm going up there now, Mr Ellis,' she said, smiling brightly. 'I'll give it her if you like. She could do with a little something to cheer her up, poor mite. Nothing but a nasty wheeze for company. If you ask me, it's this London air. Gets right inside –'

'Thank you, Kitty,' snapped Ellis. 'But there really is no need.' He put the letter in his top pocket. 'I'll make sure Miss Longleigh receives it.'

'Suit yourself,' she said. 'Just trying to save your legs.'

My dearest Clarissa,

It pains me deeply to hear you are unwell, almost as much as it pains me to be apart from you. Yet it consoles me too, for when you did not come to me at Cremorne I had only demons in my mind to answer my question, 'Why?' The blackest and the loudest demon of all said you no longer loved me. My sweet flower, my precious jewel, I could bear anything but that. Please, I implore you, send word to say –

Clarissa's vision blurred. A tear, then another, splashed on to the paper, spreading words into fragile inky spiders. She turned away and fixed her gaze on one of the rows of calf-bound books, trying to focus. The guilt and shame she'd felt on waking yesterday were nothing compared to this.

'Would you like me to read it to you?' asked Lord Marldon, reaching across the vast library table to take the letter.

'No,' she whispered. She'd betrayed Gabriel; she'd defiled their love with her squalid carnality.

'Are you sure?' he asked. 'It's really quite a touching piece.'

'No,' she repeated in a voice just as soft and small.

For a day and a night she had not seen Lord Marldon. He had left her alone, with nothing but bitter thoughts and regrets for company. In those bleak, lonely hours she had berated herself for yielding to her desires. But now, more desperately than ever, she berated herself for having them. She found Lord Alec dangerously compelling. She could not help wanting him; she could not stop anticipating the cruelties he might impose on her. And, even with Gabriel's words of love spinning in her mind, she knew she would yield again.

Marldon placed an inkstand by her hand and laid a sheet of paper before her. He pushed her loose, wavy hair over one shoulder and curled a hand to the back of her neck, massaging gently.

'The pen, Clarissa,' he said.

She shivered at his touch and dipped the nib into the inkwell. It was another surrender to him, but surrender was not the worst of it. She might, somehow, be able to resist his lewd demands, but what good would it do? The desire would still exist; a dark part of her being that separated her from Gabriel, not physically but emotionally. Finding the self-control to fight both herself and Marldon could never be enough.

'My dear Gabriel,' Alec began, dictating slowly.

'Thank you so much for troubling to write. I'm afraid I am rather weak at present and I fear visitors would only tire me.'

Clarissa saw the words forming on the page, flowing meaninglessly from the nib. The doctor has advised complete bedrest ... you must refrain from calling ... time to reflect ... a little overhasty ...

'In declaring my devotion to you,' continued Marldon. 'It was a moment's infatuation, a foolish caprice which must be for –'

'No,' said Clarissa. 'I cannot say that. I will not. And, besides, he will not believe it.'

Lord Marldon leant over her. The stripe of a neatly clipped sideburn grated on her cheek. She smelt his closeness, masculinity blended with woody cologne, and it roused her. She held her breath as slowly he slid a hand beneath her silks and spread his fingers around a naked breast. He palmed the soft flesh.

'But, Clarissa,' he whispered with sardonic tenderness, 'it's the truest part of the letter.'

His touch set smouldering a need, a need shadowed with black remembrance of her first night at Asham. She shuddered imperceptibly. It was Gabriel she loved. It was he who had captured her heart. Yet Lord Marldon had captured something else and, with him standing so close, caressing her that way, it seemed a stronger thing.

'And don't you think,' he continued, nuzzling into her neck, 'it would be unkind to offer him false hope? You must realise you have no future with him. Your father, for one thing, would never permit marriage. But that is not reason enough. No, no. The reason, Clarissa, is that you have extraordinary desires. Most men would not understand them, let alone be capable of satisfying them. I can do both.' His voice was gentle, comforting. He held out his hand. 'Come, let me show you. You can write to the gypsy later.'

Clarissa did not reply but she placed her hand in his. Her shameful heart quickened.

Lord Marldon led her along a wide corridor, its walls hung with great Gobelin tapestries and ancestral portraits. He stopped occasionally to point out the significance of various people. This was the first viscount, and that was Lady Buckley who sired eleven children. Ah, here was one. She became Duchess of Westminster at the age of fifteen.

His words, thought Clarissa, were not intended to provoke awe. They were merely another part of her education, a display of his conviction that she would soon be his wife. She must learn about the family she was marrying into, just as she must learn how to enjoy his depravities. Well, he was wrong. She would never consent to be his bride, no matter what settlement her father had arranged. It was about the only thing she was certain of.

Before a vast oil painting of a young man with a flamboyant ruffle at his throat, Marldon paused.

'And this is the fourth earl,' he said. 'If it weren't for him, Asham House would not be as you see it today. He's responsible for much of the decoration, his tribute to a whore from Cadiz. A magnanimous gesture, don't you think?'

'He's your grandfather,' stated Clarissa flatly, not wanting to appear impressed.

'That's debatable,' Alec replied, guiding her away. 'But she was quite certainly my grandmother.'

Clarissa looked at him, shocked by the admission of impurity in his family.

'What does it matter?' He shrugged, catching her expression. 'After all, it was bastardy which brought us to the peerage. I'd have the blood of Charles the Second in me if it had not continued.'

'So instead you have the blood of a bastard,' said Clarissa acidly. 'How fitting.'

Marldon laughed loudly. The sound soared in the great entrance hall and hovered on the air, enveloping the clack of their footsteps. Shafts of dusty sunlight slanted across the room on to the tiled floor. The immense double doors were bolted and padlocked.

'How well we're getting to know each other,' he said as they ascended the broad curving staircase. 'Perhaps one day I shall pay homage to you in the manner of my cuckolded forefather. If I still desire you in, say, four months, I might think about replacing the curtains in the drawing room.'

Clarissa did not rise to the insult in the way she might have done previously.

'And if you still desire me in five months?' she said with challenging aplomb.

'I won't,' he replied matter-of-factly. 'All women have their limits, even you. We'll go to your room, shall we? It's a little more conventional.'

The moment they were in Clarissa's bedroom, Lord Marldon began deftly unlooping the tiny buttons which ran down her back. He turned her this way and that, swiftly removing layers and talking of Disraeli and some bill the House had overturned. She did not understand him. He showed no desire; he did not tease.

'Get on the bed,' he said when she was naked.

Clarissa sat on the edge, nervously watching as he stripped off his clothes. His brusque efficiency confused and alarmed her. He fell on her, pushing her back and spreading her legs wide. His erection butted at her vulva.

'Please, I'm not ready,' she implored.

Lord Marldon spat on his hand and rubbed it briskly against her sex.

'Better?' he snarled.

His stiffened penis found her entrance and he shoved hard, to the hilt. Clarissa moaned in protest as he began thrusting rapidly, his head raised, his eyes fixed grimly on the head of the bed. His manner, so disinterested and remote, made her feel worthless and small. He took her as if it were a chore. Why didn't he indulge her with his cruel seductions? Why didn't he show how she excited him?

She begged him to desist, yet even as she did so she felt her body thrill to the heavy plunges of his great, swollen cock. Its thick solidity, driving urgently into her depths, stimulated her within. She clutched her sex on his pounding shaft, gasping with rising pleasure. The pit of her belly pulsed and throbbed, and she tilted her hips, hungry to take his thrusts.

'Be still,' he snapped. Then a moment later he withdrew, leaving Clarissa breathless and wanting. He had not climaxed.

'Are you satisfied?' he asked, sitting back against the mass of pillows. 'No? Nor I, but a lesser man might have been.'

Clarissa pressed a hand to his pale, muscular chest, and stroked quickly downward, imploring him to continue. He spurned her, flinging away her touch, and she shrank away in bewilderment and fear.

'And that is what you would get from the marriage bed,' he went on, a note of irritation in his voice. 'Though in such a situation you'd be wise not to respond quite so ardently. A husband will take a mistress if he wants those sorts of antics. He expects his wife to show, at worst, modesty; at best, revulsion. Do you think you're suited to the role, Clarissa?' He turned to her with a mocking smile.

She shook her head. She knew Gabriel was not such a man. But at that moment her thoughts were more concerned with Lord Alec. She ached for him; she wanted him to give her delight as he had done before. Yet she dared not admit to it. He would only use it to prove how right he was.

'Then you're fortunate in that you will have me as a husband,' he said. 'I can show you pleasures far superior.'

'You mean perversions,' said Clarissa sullenly, casting her eyes down. 'They're hardly a basis for marriage.'

'Ah, but that is where you are wrong,' he replied.

He touched his fingertips to her cheek, turning her gently to meet his gaze. She looked at him steadily. His lips were set in an arrogant half-sneer, and his black, inky eyes glittered with callous joy. She saw in that expression how sure he was of his hold over her, of his ability to master her, body and soul. His confidence was unshakeable. It incensed her; it crushed her; and it thrilled her.

'You see, in your innocence you think love the greater force,' he said softly. 'And, true enough, it binds many couples. Although there are plenty who do not even have that. But as man and wife, Clarissa, you and I will be bound by something so much darker than love, so much stronger.'

He moved her hand to his groin and held it against the warm sac of his balls. She massaged the pouch, delighting in the tight weight rolling within the shifting skin. Her fingers explored, stroking lightly and running along the bridge to his anus.

'Suck me, Clarissa,' he rasped. 'Brinley was rather complimentary about your mouth. Show me what you can do.'

She flinched inwardly at the reminder and pitched him a hurt look. There was a moment's reluctance in her eyes, only a moment's, but it was enough. Marldon lunged forward and tangled a fist in her hair, tugging her towards him. She yelped, her body twisting, as she struggled on to all fours. He pulled her head between his bent, open legs and held it there, inches from his formidable, jutting member. Gnarled veins pulsed beneath the skin and she smelt his musky sexuality. The hungry power, so densely packed in his rigid organ, made her sex flush with longing.

'Come now,' he said with a touch of asperity. 'I'm not asking for much. I merely expect you to get rid of what you've roused. It threatens my plans for you.'

Clutching her dark tresses, he forced her down. She

137

parted her lips to take him, and his taut, hard cock surged fiercely into her mouth. He clasped her firmly and thrust his loins upward, pounding relentlessly as if he were coupling with her. Clarissa's throat contracted. Tears burnt her eyes. She clawed at his thighs, fearing he would choke her. Yet still, there was some part of her which relished his brutality.

Marldon stopped and raised her head. 'Don't try my patience again,' he said. 'I can usually control my lust, but seldom my temper. Now do to me as you wish. But make sure I come in your mouth.'

Clarissa licked teasingly along his shaft, from hair-collared base to smooth, swollen tip. She explored his glans, lashing around the circlet of retracted skin and probing the tiny opening. Her fingers stole in to caress his testicles, and she sank her mouth to the thick root of his phallus. She drew back slowly, indulging in the feel of him: the throbbing heat, the unyielding virility. She kept her lips tight to his girth, and her agile tongue moved ceaselessly.

Marldon glided into her caress with restrained lifts of his pelvis. 'A little faster,' he urged. 'Go with me.'

Clarissa complied. She took him in sweeping gulps, matching the gathering rhythm of his jerking hips. Her arousal soared in response to his urgency, and she felt her labia thicken with honeyed humidity.

'Yes,' he hissed. His cock plunged quicker and deeper. She kept pace, sucking and swallowing, firm and deep. She heard him groan, a husky sound of bliss, and it pierced her groin with stabbing fire. His balls tightened beneath her fingers and his prick throbbed to a sudden hard swell. He drove furiously and, with a grating shout, spent his release.

His cock twitched and pulsed, and his semen flooded over her tongue in hot, tearing spurts. Its pungency burnt in her throat. She drank deeply and Marldon gave a low sigh of contentment.

For a long time he did not move or speak, and neither

did she. She kept him in her mouth, lapping idly at his decreasing solidity.

'I expect you'll be wanting your pleasure now.' His words were cold and functional but his tone was gentle. He curled tendrils in her hair with lazy, distracted fingers. 'Come here,' he murmured.

His eyes smiled drowsily into hers and he played his hands lightly over her contours, skimming her nipples and hip bones. This was a new mood for Clarissa, one she liked. Her body tingled with eagerness and she was glad she had pleased him.

She widened her thighs and tilted her hips to him.

Lord Marldon huffed a quick laugh. 'Patience, patience, child,' he whispered. 'I want to take my time over you. We have an evening and a night ahead of us. I want to indulge your desires.'

Clarissa flexed her spine in anticipation of luxury. She reached out to him and slid her hand over his chest in slow, sinuous motions. His gaze roved over her pale curves.

'You're delectable,' he said quietly. 'Ah, what times we shall have together.'

He smoothed a finger over her lips and she sucked softly on it. Her hand travelled up to his face and stroked over his features. She traced the slope of his nose, over the slightly raised bridge, down its straightness. She swept along his cheekbones and drifted to the line of his scar, wondering, wondering. Her finger followed the silvery ridge almost parallel to his jaw, then dipped down to his neck.

'How did you get such a mark?' she enquired, her voice scarce more than a breath.

Marldon smiled. A sparkle of glee replaced the tenderness in his eyes.

'From a woman, would you believe?' he said. 'A lover. She slashed me while I was sleeping.'

Clarissa drew back her hand and looked at him aghast.

'She didn't try it again,' he added, rising from the bed. He picked up his shirt and began to dress.

'Where are you going?' pleaded Clarissa. He had promised her pleasure. He could not leave.

'I'm taking you somewhere special,' he said, stepping into his trousers.

Clarissa leant to gather her shift from the floor but Marldon lightly kicked it away.

'Don't bother,' he said. 'You'll only have to take it all off again.'

'I can't go anywhere like this,' she hissed, crossing her arms over her breasts.

'It's only the servants,' he scoffed. 'And they've already seen most of it.'

'No,' said Clarissa, pulling the coverlet to hide her body. 'Don't let them watch us. I don't like it.'

'You do,' he replied, shrugging on his waistcoat. 'But don't let that concern you. Tonight, Clarissa, they will not be watching.'

Chapter Eight

Clarissa hesitated in the doorway, fingers linked over her groin, and gazed upon the small room before her.

It was a windowless octagon, its ebony-panelled walls inlaid with tall plate mirrors. Sconces, carved into naked figures, held purple waxlights in outstretched arms, and a patchwork of dead animals, sleek and black, covered the floor. The only item of furniture was a low couch, its frame scrolled silver, its upholstery midnight satin.

Lord Marldon put a hand to the small of her back. A shiver started there and chilled through her body.

'Go on,' he said, easing her forward. 'There's much to admire.'

Her bare feet padded soundlessly across the silky carpeting. The room ran to infinity in the depths of the mirrors, and so did Clarissa. She saw her every movement, her nervously darting eyes, her fruitless attempts to turn from her reflection. Somewhere in the distance she was a tiny thing, a fluttering insect trapped in a confusion of candle flames.

Marldon closed the door. In the glass Clarissa saw the ebony panel beside it. She whirled to look, hoping it was an illusion, a trick of the light. It was not.

Hanging from the wall at six points were sturdy leather plaits attached to broad leather cuffs. They dangled limply, the lower two trailing across the floor, patiently awaiting their next captive. Clarissa drew a sharp breath and cursed herself silently. She should have known better. When Marldon said he would indulge her desires, he meant the desires he read in her, not the desires she knew.

She turned to him, full of trepidation. 'What do you intend?' she whispered.

Alec began folding back his shirtsleeves and smiled. In the mirrors, a hundred cruel faces gave a hundred cold smiles.

'You have too much control,' he replied evenly. 'No, let me correct that. Too much self-control. At times it deserts you, but that is nothing special. It happens to us all. Ecstasy and desire are great equalisers. Everyone is overwhelmed; everyone is debased to mere carnality.'

He paced the room, hands clasped behind his back, addressing an imaginary audience. 'You see, I do not wish to have a woman who governs herself. When I see such a person, I want to strip her of that protective shield. I want to remove everything mankind has toiled to develop, the things we believe elevate us above the animals: dignity, self-possession, the revered intellect, the sacred soul. I want to reduce her, degrade her to nothing but flesh and appetite. Strange, isn't it, the way some things appeal?'

He turned to Clarissa. 'Sit there,' he said. He nodded to a mirror which ran from ceiling to floor.

Clarissa knelt before it, her guarded eyes following his reflection.

'On your arse, miss,' he ordered. 'And open your legs.'

Clarissa acquiesced. Her compliance dismayed her but rather this, she thought, than be shackled. Marldon crossed and knelt behind her. His hands moved around to cup and fondle her breasts.

142

'Look at yourself,' he urged.

Reluctantly, she did so. The subdued orangey light tinted her pale skin, and her crinkling nipples peeped through Alec's caressing fingers. Her sex, so flagrantly exposed, seemed to glare back at her, commanding attention. It nestled within her parted white thighs, a deep-pink lily fringed with fine black curls. It pouted lasciviously. It flaunted its wetness.

'Now touch yourself,' he whispered.

Clarissa shook her head. 'No, I cannot,' she breathed. 'Not when you are watching.'

'Yes, you can,' he said in a soft, cajoling tone. 'I've watched you before. Remember?'

'But then I did not know it,' replied Clarissa, bitterly resentful.

'Touch yourself,' he repeated. 'Keep your eyes where they are and spread your sex for me.' He rolled her nipples between thumb and forefinger, teasing her arousal, challenging her to disobey. 'Or I'll bring in one of the servants to do it,' he added.

Clarissa flashed an alarmed glance at his reflection but Alec did not see. His gaze was fixed on her secret place. She dared not refuse him, for without doubt he would summon a servant. Drawing a deep breath of courage, Clarissa touched timid fingers to her moist, tender flesh and splayed her labia for him. She saw flattened glossy lips, smooth and crimson, and the dark hungry shadow of her vagina. The lewdness of the image she offered dismayed and enthralled her.

'Push your fingers inside yourself,' he said. 'Touch your clitoris. Make yourself come.'

'I cannot,' she insisted. 'I won't be able to . . . to come.'

'Try,' he snapped, massaging her breasts with a sudden harshness.

Clarissa whimpered in objection then inserted a finger into her humid passage. Awkward and embarrassed, she began driving slowly. Marldon watched her avidly in the glass, a vague smile playing on his lips. With lazy enjoyment, his hands caressed her pale orbs, scuffing their rigid tips. Clarissa's lust swelled with heavy heat.

Tentatively she slid in a second finger and moved her thumb to her engorged and needful clitoris. It tingled lightly in response. She teased and fretted the sensitive tissue, but could not push her arousal any further. Desperate to fulfil Alec's vile command, she tried imagining herself elsewhere, alone. But it did not work. Her discomfiture held her pleasure in check.

Lord Marldon shook his head disparagingly and gave a reproachful tut. 'What's the problem, Clarissa?' he enquired. 'You were eager for satisfaction not long since. Is it because I'm watching, or because you are?'

She looked at him askance. 'I don't know,' she said ruefully. 'Both.'

'You must learn to let go,' he replied. 'Perhaps a third party will help you find a little distance from yourself.' He rose to his feet.

'No,' implored Clarissa, twisting round to him in a panic. 'Don't let anyone watch. It's hateful. I'll try harder, I promise.'

The earl turned a boss on one of the mirrored walls and it opened partially, revealing shadows of a closet. 'An inanimate third party,' he said, shutting the door.

He returned and knelt at her buttocks, an object in his hand. Reaching his arms around her, he weighed the thing in upturned palms. It was a column of stout, phallic ivory, sleekly carved with a rounded end. It gleamed in the half-light, obscene and threatening. Clarissa uttered a faint squeak of horror.

Lord Marldon gripped the tool at its root and stroked its smooth blunt crown across the upper curves of her bosom. 'You will use this,' he said, brushing a taut nipple with the cold ivory shaft. He swept it up to her throat then slowly trailed it down, nosing its tip through the valley of her breasts and over her belly.

Clarissa shivered as the phallus, stern and hard, lingered at the curls of her pubis. Her sex flushed with desire, and a thick, hungering beat blossomed there, urging her to take the foul object, to push it high into her aching depths. Marldon drew the dildo back up her body then clenched it upright in his fist.

'Go on,' he said. 'Use it.'

Spots of colour burnt in Clarissa's cheeks and she took the fake cock with a petulant snatch. Lord Marldon moved away. He sat beneath a mirror, watching, waiting, smiling.

Clarissa held her breath and nudged the hard domed head at the flagrantly wide portal of her sex. Her body yearned for the crude invasion and she could not suppress a gentle moan. Her lust guided her. Swiftly, she dropped back to lie on the floor, spreading her bent legs. The soft carpet caressed her skin, silk slipping on silk.

Her hips lifted and she eased the dildo into her hot, receptive well, taking the full measure of its strong, solid length. Its inflexible girth stretched her and she groaned wantonly, feeling her moisture slide over the cool, polished bar. She drew the tool back then pushed high, again and again, delighting in the thrust of unyielding rigidity.

'Yes,' hissed Marldon. 'Yes.'

She no longer cared that he watched. Her fast-rising arousal flamed and throbbed, taking precedence over modesty. She pounded on, driving herself to climax, cramming in the phallus with fast hard shoves. The curved tip bumped deep, exquisitely brutal. She clamped her muscles around the cock's rigidity. She arched her spine, her loins heaving as she pistoned shamelessly.

A long, keening sound broke from her lips. Her orgasm peaked, spilt over, and blissful tremors coursed through every part of her body. She was motionless for a while, gaining her breath, then she curled on her side and hid her face in her arms. The dildo slipped from her.

The room was silent. Clarissa's self-loathing grew ever

stronger as the stillness lengthened. Then Marldon began a slow handclap.

'Encore,' he said flatly. 'Encore.'

Clarissa drew herself into a tighter ball, embittered and ashamed. She should not allow him to push her to such extremes nor to treat her with such contempt. Yet Marldon's cold dominance made her powerless. It vanquished her because it thrilled her. She wished it were otherwise.

'I can still see you,' said Alec, nudging a cold shoe into her buttock.

She unfurled herself and sat in a huddle, glaring up at him with defiant eyes. 'I despise you,' she hissed.

'I expected nothing less,' he said, smiling. 'Now stand up.'

Clarissa rose. Her lower lip trembled but she fought back the tears. She would not give him an opportunity for further amusement. Marldon took both her hands gently, then with a sudden twist he was clutching her wrists and bearing her backward to the wall – to the wall affixed with straps and shackles. Her toes crushed under his quick footsteps and she yelped, hopping to avoid further pain. He slammed her against the ebony panel, and pressed his powerful body to hers. His clothes felt rough against her skin and his cock was a hard bulky mass, digging into her belly.

He lifted one of her arms and deftly wrapped a leather cuff round her wrist, pulling the buckles tight. With quick skill he pinned up her other arm and fastened the second thick strap, grinding his erection into her as he worked. Clarissa barely had space to struggle.

'There is no need for this,' she gasped, squirming uselessly against him.

'Oh, there is,' said Alec, dropping to his knees. He leant heavily against her right leg and secured a fetter about her ankle. Then he did the same to her left ankle and stepped back, breathless, to look at her in the opposite mirror.

146

The candles poured their light on to Clarissa's naked body, and she was a star of flesh. She could move her limbs, a few inches this way, a few inches that. But she could not make the body staring back at her any less exposed. A thick tress of her dark hair hung over one breast. Marldon, still watching in the glass, swept the loose curls behind her shoulder.

'That's better,' he murmured. 'Are you comfortable, Clarissa?'

'Oh, perfectly so,' she said dryly.

'Good,' he drawled. 'Because I have some business to attend to. You're going to be there a while.'

Clarissa cursed. The leather restraints creaked as she tugged. His devilry was impossible to match. Every time she predicted his next move, he outwitted her.

'You cannot go,' she cried. 'You cannot leave me like this.'

But her protests were heedless. Lord Marldon had gone.

Alec strode briskly down the corridor. His lust pounded fiercely in his trapped prick, demanding relief.

The girl roused him too much. Her beseeching, fearful eyes brought the blood pumping to his cock. And those tormented writhings as she'd thrust with the dildo had made him savagely hard. Everything about her delighted him: her splendid body, her fights to quell her passion, and the beauty of her when she succumbed. Ah, they were exquisite things. They were also novelties and within a short enough time they would fade. He would tire of her, as he tired of all women. But, for now, that disenchanted future seemed far away. His appetite for Clarissa was strong and sharp.

If it were not for his plans he would have taken her in the Octagon Room, but that would have spoilt things. She would have enjoyed it.

He ran his hand along the balustrade and turned to

descend the stairs. He caught sight of a dark-haired maid below.

'Charlotte!' he called out. 'Don't move.'

He jogged down to the first-floor gallery. The girl stood motionless near the head of the marble staircase, holding a tray of silver tea things, eyeing him warily. He approached rapidly and her worried gaze flicked to his swollen crotch. She backed away.

'Who's taking tea?' he demanded.

'Brinley, my lord,' replied Charlotte, still retreating along the gallery. 'In the blue drawing room.'

'Damned boy's getting ideas above his station,' said Alec, catching the young maid's arm.

She squealed. The tray crashed to the floor, shattering china and splashing pools of tea and cream. Lord Marldon pushed the girl back against a marble column, clutching a fistful of her thick, brunette curls.

'That will be docked from your wages,' he snapped.

He took a moment to savour the fear in Charlotte's face, then he twisted her around, forcing her upper body to lean over the balcony's glass rail. The spreading tea trickled past the gilded balusters, over the edge. It dripped on to the tiled floor of the hall beneath. Marldon flung up the maid's skirts and with a violent wrench tugged at her drawers and let them fall to her ankles. Her arse was taut and white, as deliciously skinny as a young boy's.

'No,' protested Charlotte. 'Not here.'

'It's what I pay you for, isn't it?' he snarled, quickly opening the buttons of his flies. 'Are you handing in your notice, girl?'

Marldon released his pulsing erection and widened the maid's legs with a swift kick of his foot.

'No, my lord,' she conceded in a breathy voice.

Her pink folds hung lasciviously below the split of her buttocks. Without delay, Marldon levelled his thick, angry glans at her yawning entrance and drove himself hard, penetrating her hot, fleshy depths. She was wet;

she wanted it. Or she'd just had it from Brinley. Lord Marldon thrust furiously, indifferent to her pleasure, hungry for his own. Her tightness clung to his surging cock and he plunged deep, his belly banging against her little quivering arse.

Charlotte's shrill cries, punctuated by Alec's husky grunts, soared to the domed ceiling. Their noises echoed back and an orgy of sounds filled the air. The maid grasped the rail with her small hands, her knuckles gleaming like the crystal. Her slender cheeks lifted and rocked with Marldon's merciless slamming. His strokes were heavy, increasingly fast. His fingers were fastened to her hips like claws. The pressure of his impending climax swelled in his phallus. He thundered on, chasing fulfilment.

The maid beat a hand against the banister, shaking her mane of glossy curls. Her cries shortened to frenzied gasps then she released a long, bitter wail. Her vagina spasmed wet ripples around his shaft, milking the hot lust from him. Lord Marldon thrust deep, growled, and came.

His shoulders heaved with his recovering breaths. He slipped out of the maid and tidied his prick away.

Charlotte was motionless, her buttocks still bared. Alec eyed the white flesh, reddened at the sides with the imprints of his fingers. The girl mewled pathetically. Marldon raised a hand and swung it down to crack across one cheek.

Charlotte yelped and cursed him openly.

'That's for spilling the tea,' he said in a dull tone. 'Get it cleared up at once.'

'For God's sake, Gabriel, will you please sit down?' snapped Lucy, clattering her teacup in its saucer. 'I can't think with you pacing about in that manner. It's driving me to distraction.'

Gabriel stalked over to an armchair, perched himself on the edge and glowered at her and Julian.

'I fail to see why we can't involve the police,' he said, slicing a hand through the air in exasperation. 'I don't give a damn if they raid his whorehouse and shut the place down. I don't give a damn if they lock him up and throw away the key. I don't – I just want Clarissa, safe and well. It's perfectly, perfectly simple.' He threw himself back into the armchair and exhaled impatiently.

Lucy twirled her wedding ring. A few weeks ago, she would have relished this friction between the two men. But now it was plain to see Gabriel no longer had eyes for her, and the situation was far graver.

'My dear fellow,' said Julian, calmly pouring tea. 'The closure of Madame Jane's would be another nail in London's coffin. There's hardly a place left which dares flout the licensing laws so unstintingly and with such panache.'

Lucy gave him a scathing look. 'Sir Julian is being either incredibly selfish or utterly facetious,' she said in a brittle tone. 'Or quite possibly both.'

'Quite possibly.' He smiled and took a genteel sip of tea. 'But at least we've moved on. Mr Ardenzi is, I assume, no longer contemplating murder.'

Gabriel fixed him with a black, angry stare.

'I think he might be,' mumbled Kitty.

Sir Julian laughed. 'Forgive me if I'm being infuriating. But surely you see the sense of my argument. Alec Marldon is a clever man. He has friends in high places and he has influence. How else could Madame Jane's have survived? Every brothel in Panton Street, barring his, has either closed or operates illegally. Heavens, we could send a cartload of constables to Asham House and he'd probably be on first-name terms with the lot of them. He'd offer them some bawdy delights, then they'd dance off into the night as merry as sandboys.'

Gabriel stood quickly. The little housemaid, sitting awkward and tense, followed his every movement with big anxious eyes. He combed his fingers through his hair and began striding between the two fireside armchairs.

Lucy fought the urge to upbraid him. 'I'm afraid Julian's correct,' she said sympathetically, hoping to defuse the tension. 'We have to catch Marldon unawares, play him at his own game. And, however we do that, I for one would dearly like to see him squirm and suffer.'

She had not forgiven Marldon for the night at Octavia's ball. She'd insisted to Julian that she'd done it solely to prevent Lord Alexander from meeting Clarissa, but the truth of it was otherwise. He had aroused her greatly. He had built her appetite to such a fever that she had readily demeaned herself to quench her lust. He was remarkably adept, and she detested him for it. She could only hope that cousin Clarissa had substantially more willpower than she herself did.

'Any bright ideas then?' asked Gabriel, thrusting his hands deep in his pockets.

Silence fell upon the room. A carriage rumbled by in the square below. The hall clock chimed half the hour.

Lucy stood up and turned to the Longleighs' housemaid. It was thanks to her that they'd learnt of Clarissa's whereabouts. She'd rushed to Gabriel's house within moments of overhearing the servants' gossip. The girl was obviously loyal to her mistress.

'Do you enjoy your work, Kitty?' enquired Lucy affably.

Gabriel groaned and sat heavily in the armchair, his head in his hands.

Kitty shrugged. 'It's all right, ma'am,' she said. 'I get Sunday afternoons off and once a month I have a Wednesday. Don't much care for Mondays though, as then it's laundry day.'

Lucy smiled. 'Would you like to spend long mornings in bed, wear elegant clothes and drink chilled champagne in the evenings?'

Julian rose to join Lucy and stroked a hand down her spine. He looked intently at the pretty, young maid, his smile broadening.

'Course I would,' replied Kitty, her lower lip pouting. 'Who wouldn't?'

Lucy swung around to Gabriel, her face bright with enthusiasm. She was about to speak when she stopped herself and looked at him thoughtfully.

'I have two plans,' she announced at length. 'Both of which Marldon will never guess at. Both of which involve Octavia Hamilton.'

Gabriel sank back into his seat and released a heavy sigh. 'Lucy,' he said wearily, 'you have my undivided attention.'

The Octagon Room was hot and airless. Clarissa's arms tingled with lack of blood, and a dull ache weighed on every part of her.

The image of her body, spread and helplessly bound, would not leave her mind. Even when she closed her eyes and blocked out the mirror opposite, she could see herself. And the creamy-white phallus lay on the black floor, grotesque, mocking.

Clarissa did not know how long she had been there. There was no natural light to judge the hours by, no clocks, no sounds of the house. One candle had died and now another was guttering. Its dancing flame flickered light and shadows over the pale curves of her flesh. The room seemed to shudder.

Clarissa's emotions had run from anger to frustration and now to listless despair. She was thirsty and tired. Whenever she thought of sitting down, a sob of wanting rose in her throat. If only she knew when Alec would return, then it might be more bearable. Would it be shortly, tomorrow, or a week from now? Perhaps he intended to starve her into submission. He would propose marriage when she was irrational, delirious with hunger. And, she thought sourly, he would do it on bended knee.

A long, heavy breath drifted from her dry lips. She tried to sink her body lower, allowing the cuffs to take her weight, but the strain on her arms was too much. She tried grasping the leather plaits which joined her to the wall and slumping down. A few seconds was all she could manage.

If she had the strength, she would hate Marldon. And she would hate that duplicitous French maid, Pascale. How well they had organised her disappearance, bothering even to send on some clothes before her arrival. And, back in Chelsea, a carefully woven tissue of lies veiled her absence.

She recalled Gabriel's letter and her heart lifted a touch. Marldon could not keep her bound for long: she had a reply to finish writing. He would surely not take the risk of arousing Gabriel's suspicions.

To her left, the door swung slowly open. Fresher, cooler air wafted into the room and the spluttering candle at last petered out. Clarissa turned, hope and fear mingling in her stomach. A woman entered, a woman she vaguely recognised, with a cascade of rich-brown curls. She wore a maid's plain blue linen, and in her hands she carried a glass pitcher, brimful of water. The amber half-light glowed in its transparency, and beads of dew misted the surface.

Clarissa moistened her lips.

The young woman looked at her with sullen indifference. 'Tired?' she asked. 'Thirsty? Hungry?'

Clarissa nodded. 'Could I please have a drink?' she said softly.

The maid smiled, her jade eyes sparkling. 'That makes my task easier,' she replied.

She lifted the jug to Clarissa's mouth, tipping it slightly. The liquid washed over Clarissa's parched throat and chilled an exquisite path to her stomach. It trickled from her lips as she drank, spilling sweet, icy droplets on to her breasts. She gulped her fill and murmured satisfaction, murmurs which grew more urgent when the pitcher was not withdrawn. She moved her head back and the glass rim followed, pressing to her lips. She locked her throat. Water streamed over her chin, coursed down her neck, and splashed on to her body.

The young woman pulled the vessel away and sighed.

'Enough,' gasped Clarissa through coughs and splutters. 'Thank you. Enough.'

The maid paused, watching her recover. When Clarissa's breath was steady she raised the jug once more.

'His lordship's request,' said the girl, regarding her with an unwavering gaze. 'You're to drink it all.'

Clarissa swallowed some of the liquid in shock then pursed her lips, resisting. She could not understand why Marldon would want such a thing.

'Damnation,' hissed the young woman, lowering the pitcher. 'I thought you were thirsty. Brinley!'

The door opened and Marldon's weaselly valet came into the room. His smoky-green eyes raked Clarissa's helpless, naked body.

'Being difficult is she, Charlotte?' he said gleefully, shrugging off his frock coat and dropping it to the ground. He tugged the tie from his neck and began hastily unfastening his shirt studs.

Panic swam in Clarissa's mind. He was going to threaten her. He was going to violate her if she disobeyed. Her shackled legs felt suddenly more open than ever. 'No,' she pleaded. 'Let me drink.'

Charlotte immediately tilted the jug to Clarissa's lips. She drank urgently, fighting the instinct to choke it from her mouth. The water was hard to swallow. It flowed ceaselessly into her, bloating her belly to leaden heaviness. When she'd drained the contents, the young maid stepped back and smiled contentedly.

'His lordship invariably gets his own way,' she said, setting down the empty jug.

'So I hear,' said Brinley, flashing the girl a knavish grin.

He was naked now, his lean buttocks reflecting endlessly in one of the mirrors. His prick, clasped in his fist,

154

was stiff and upright. Its gleaming purple tip swelled above his fingers, and he fixed Clarissa with bright, taunting eyes. Slowly, he moved his hand up and down the turgid stem.

Clarissa whined in soft complaint and turned away, remembering her first night when she'd sucked the valet's penis. The memory revolted her, and terror ran quick and cold in her veins. Had Alec ordered him to do worse things to her? Was he going to ravish her? She jerked on her manacles in panic and fury, and felt the volume of water sloshing inside her. She wished she could close her legs.

'Miss Longleigh,' said Brinley lightly, moving into the range of her vision. 'I see you've been enjoying yourself.'

He stooped to pick up the ivory phallus and held it to his nose, his nostrils flaring as he inhaled deeply. A hot flush swept from Clarissa's bosom to her face. She felt as if he and the whole world had witnessed her earlier disgrace. Oh, why had Marldon ordered this torment, for doubtless he had?

'Whatever he's told you to do,' she said angrily, 'will you do it quickly and leave me be.'

Brinley laughed and exchanged conspiratorial glances with Charlotte.

'Very well,' he said. His wide, thin-lipped mouth twisted in a satyric smile. 'To be honest, I'm more than ready.'

He crossed to the young maid and began unfastening the blue buttons of her dress. Clarissa released a soft breath, her dread and horror easing. Perhaps she was not to be subjected to the insolent fellow's phallus. She was alarmed to think her expectations were worse than Lord Alexander's plans.

Charlotte assisted the valet, eagerly casting off linens and silks. Her body was slender, her breasts small and pert with pinched cherry-red nipples. The couple embraced, sharing fervent kisses and dashing hands over each other's flesh.

Their passionate, carefree nudity heightened Clarissa's sense of shame and vulnerability. She felt so distanced from them, somehow more naked, sickeningly exposed. When the two broke apart and turned to her, those feelings rushed to an acute pitch of horror.

Brinley stood behind Charlotte, palming the scant globes of her breasts and gazing over her shoulder. They both looked so alike, slim-hipped and pale, with elegantly boned faces and dark-brown curls. But worse than that was the similarity of their expressions. Charlotte watched her just as Brinley did: sensual wet lips curving in an avaricious smirk, grey-green eyes leering, shining with appetite.

Clarissa's heart pounded. She made a gasp of fear and wriggled against her bondage. The movement was uncomfortable, reminding her of the liquid weighing in her belly.

'Told you she had good tits,' said Brinley, studying her.

He edged forward, his hands still on the maid's breasts, ushering her closer to Clarissa. When the girl was just inches away, the valet scooped her white half-globes high. Charlotte leant in a little, allowing Brinley to touch her rigid nipples to Clarissa's. Lightly, he brushed them back and forth.

A sob caught in Clarissa's throat. She twisted her head aside, avoiding the maid's lustful face, and blinked back the threat of tears. She could feel the heat of the girl's breath on her cheek and smell the cleanness of her hair. Occasionally their hips and bellies nudged together and Charlotte's pubic curls tickled her own.

Brinley continued moving his lover's breasts, scuffing their hard peaks across Clarissa's rose-pink flesh. The persistent strokes sensitised and teased, and she felt her nipples puckering to aroused points. It embarrassed and shamed her.

Charlotte murmured delight and slid her hands down Clarissa's contours, moving from the dip of her waist to the smoothness of hips and flanks. Stepping back, she bent to take a nipple in her warm, wet mouth. Her streaming brown tresses swept softly against Clarissa's skin, and her tongue lashed, her lips suckled. Clarissa moaned. Her body tingled in response, little tremors of pleasure radiating from her sweetly aching tips. Heat stirred in her sex, and her wide-spread legs began shaking gently. Her hips rocked of their own accord.

'Alec said she'd like it,' breathed Brinley. 'Come on, Lottie. Let me join you.'

'No,' whispered Clarissa, shutting her eyes and resting her head against the wood. It was a perfunctory protest, born out of feeble embarrassment, not rejection.

The valet's lips closed over her other nipple, bathing it in heat. A long groan rumbled faintly in Clarissa's throat. Hands snaked over her creamy, satin curves and she relaxed into the spreading bliss. Immediately, she tensed, aware of the fullness in her bladder. She hoped no one would lean against her belly.

But their caresses stayed gentle, luxurious, and arousal began to pulse at her groin. Charlotte licked a slow, wet path down her bloated stomach and drifted kisses over her hips, her thighs. She knelt on all fours and nuzzled her head between Clarissa's parted legs. Her mouth, damp and soft, pressed there. A flash of sensation speared Clarissa's loins and she gasped in shock and excitement. It was not right that another woman should touch her so, yet that very thought seemed to increase her excitement.

Charlotte's tongue slipped into her folds and squirmed along the sleek, hungry groove. With a moist, warm caress, she tantalised the engorged flesh, nibbling and sucking.

Clarissa writhed in torment. She chafed to give herself up entirely to the pleasure, yet she was not free to do so. The pressure of the water she'd consumed was too much; it forestalled her ease.

Brinley dropped away from her. Clarissa watched in the opposite mirror as he stooped over Charlotte, stroking along her back then kneading her slender rear.

'Oh, Lottie, Lottie,' he said in a voice full of longing. 'I need to fuck you. I really need to.'

The half-crouched maid edged her shins wider, opening herself, and the valet dropped to his knees behind her. His fingers toyed briefly between her thighs and she mumbled her pleasure into Clarissa's hot, slippery sex. Then he shuffled close, his prick poised at Charlotte's entrance and, with a jerk, slammed into her.

In the glass, Clarissa saw the reflection of his buttocks, tensing with each strong, eager lunge. The image of their coupling, raw and bestial, added a spark to her own pleasure. She turned her gaze away, fighting the nearness of her crisis. Her body pleaded for her to relinquish control, yet she dared not do so for fear her bladder would empty. No doubt her suffering was intended. Lord Marldon had commanded that she drink so much.

With greedy enthusiasm, the maid lapped at Clarissa's inflamed vulva. Brinley drove rapidly into her, grunting in time to his thrusts, his eyes set on Clarissa. He watched her keenly, judging her reactions, his face contorted with ecstasy and exertion.

'God,' he gasped. 'I'd like to have you on your knees. I'd like to be hammering into you, Miss Longleigh. I can't wait until Marldon tires of you. We'll have you then, no limits, and God, what a day it will be.'

Clarissa's curses were lost in the clamour of her agonising desire. Brinley laughed at her torment between hoarse, gulping breaths. His hips pumped hungrily and he scratched red weals along Charlotte's back, spitting obscenities.

In the mirror, his sinewy haunches flexed. His noises grew to a frenzy, and his urgency increased Clarissa's own. She felt herself on the verge of an orgasm she could not, dared not have.

There was a movement at her side. She turned to see Lord Marldon slip quietly into the room and close the door. He wore a long dressing robe of black silk and clearly there was little else beneath it. His long muscular legs flashed through the front split as he moved. He leant against the wall, his arms folded, and ran a connoisseur's gaze over the scene. His head nodded, approvingly, and he smiled at Clarissa.

A surge of self-consciousness dampened her need. For once, she appreciated his cold scrutiny: it made the task of curbing her lust easier.

Brinley glanced at his master. He screwed his eyes shut and pounded fiercely. Alec crossed the room and draped himself along the low couch. He rested his arm high on the silver frame and, with one foot on the satin, the other on the floor, affected a pose of languid nonchalance.

'Get on with it, man,' he said. 'Or finish her off in the kitchens.' His weary tone belied his obvious arousal. The silk over his crotch twitched and lifted with the swelling of his erection.

The valet gave an exultant shout and buried himself deep inside the young maid. She wailed into Clarissa's throbbing wet flesh before pulling away, breathless and shuddering.

'Now scram,' said Marldon evenly, as the two drew apart.

Charlotte looked up at him with a challenging smirk and crawled towards her heap of clothes. Lord Alec leapt up and grabbed at the crumpled garments. Flinging open the door, he hurled them outside.

'And do it quickly,' he snapped, kicking at strewn bits of fabric.

Charlotte protested and snatched up her remaining clothes while Brinley hurriedly collected his. From the corridor, the maid hurled angry abuse at him.

'And tell your sister to shut up this instant,' said Alec, slamming the door on the departing valet.

'Sister?' echoed Clarissa in shock. 'You mean –' She broke off abruptly, replaying the word in her head. It made sense; the two were so alike.

'Didn't you know?' asked Marldon, crossing to stand before her. 'I thought it was obvious. In fact, their incestuous love was the reason I took them on. No one else in the land would touch them. Personally, I find it quite endearing. And they are, of course, eternally indebted to me. A most useful thing in a servant. Did they treat you well, Clarissa?'

Marldon slipped a hand between her thighs, and dabbled his fingers in her seeping wetness. Clarissa writhed, squirming to fight her arousal and the urge to relax her bladder.

'Ah, I see they did,' he murmured.

He slicked along the glossy seam then probed into the eager cavern of her vagina.

'Please,' she entreated, 'unfasten me. Allow me my freedom.'

Marldon moved his hand up and pressed it to her liquid-swollen belly. 'Why?' he enquired with a knowing smile.

Clarissa gritted her teeth and squeezed her inner muscles tight. The near-bursting pain was excruciating. It made her eyes water, her stomach burn. Lord Marldon stepped back and untied the cord at his waist. The black silk slithered, like a cat in the night, from his hard alabaster body. His cock, enormously stiffened, surged from his dark bush of hair, its tip blood-violet.

'I'll release you in a while,' he said, running his hands over her flesh. 'Once I've taken my pleasure inside you.'

'No,' said Clarissa. 'Do not, my lord. I need . . . I have to –'

'To piss?' ventured Alec, arching his dark brows.

'Yes,' she snapped. Clarissa could not understand why he wished her to suffer in such a distasteful manner.

'How long do you think you can hold on for?' he said, pressing his body to hers.

He bent his knees, nudging the fleshy knob of his prick at her pouting sex. With slow control, he pushed his tumid phallus into her. The bulbous crown forged a steady path, widening her to take his stout, solid shaft, until he was sheathed to the hilt in her loins.

He grinned at her. 'How long?' he repeated, with a quick upward shove.

Clarissa groaned. His rock-hard stiffness filled her, accentuating the pressure and the need for relief. She contracted her sex muscles, gripping him in a bid to quell the demands of her full, aching bladder.

'Not long,' she said. 'Please don't do this. It hurts. I need to go.'

'Your modesty is most amusing,' he replied. 'Particularly considering that, but a few hours since, you were so shameless and wanton. Surely if you can masturbate before me, Clarissa, you can piss before me.'

He began to thrust, taking long measured strokes, his prick inflaming both her bladder and her lust. The glass across from them showed the power of his body. Muscles rippled across his shoulder blades, and his thighs tensed in firm curves. His working buttocks hollowed to shadows as his hips tilted up to her and his cock plunged high.

Clarissa's outspread limbs were white on black, a broken lily plastered on mud. She was helpless. She could not even push against him, so delicate was the tension which kept her from urinating. She cried out incoherently and Marldon drove on, hard and furious. His scattering hands brushed over her flesh. He crushed and twisted her nipples; he slipped his fingers between their joined bodies and frigged her clitoris. He bit into her shoulders and neck.

Every fibre of her being screamed for release. But she knew the zenith of her pleasure meant also the depths of shame. She felt she was on a tightrope: her dignity was her balancing pole and beneath was an abyss, so tempting and terrifying.

'Lose control,' urged Marldon. 'Give yourself to me, Clarissa. Surrender to your needs.'

Tears of rage spilled down her cheeks. Lord Marldon slammed into her. He grasped her buttocks with ruthless delight and pulled her soft mounds apart. Clarissa whimpered for mercy as he ran a finger between the wide gap of her cheeks and found the creased aperture of her anus. He pressed there, threatening to invade.

'Let your body be master,' he whispered.

For a moment, Clarissa clung on to the torturous brink of her climax. Then she gave a long, despairing wail. Her muscles could not hold. Her vagina loosened and she was slippery, easy about his powering phallus. Convulsions seized her body and relief gushed from her in a fast warm torrent. In the mirror she caught sight of her pale golden liquid. It wreathed down Marldon's jerking legs; it streamed and splashed from their union and pattered loudly on to the floor.

The humiliation of it hardly concerned her. The double release was bliss beyond compare. Marldon gasped harshly and plunged deep into her. He snarled, baring his teeth, snapping wildly at the air. Clarissa's belly deflated with slow-sinking ease and the clenching tremors of her sex continued, transporting her on a wave of dizzying euphoria. With a bestial roar, Marldon reached his peak. His buttocks shivered as his jets of need spurted inside her, hot and fierce.

Clarissa's crisis fell away around his, plunging her into the heaviness of fading delight. Her stomach glowed with dispelled pain and her water trickled thinly, dying away until it was nothing but drips. She rested her head against Alec's shoulder, gasping for breath, feeling his penis slackening within her.

For a long while, Marldon said nothing. In the silence, with their bodies still linked, Clarissa experienced a doomed sense of oneness with him. He had provoked her into abasing herself then had shared in it so utterly, without a trace of disgust or scorn, that she felt grateful to him, strangely beholden.

Lord Marldon withdrew from her. 'I can see my style of courtship enchants you,' he said, picking up his robe. 'Your cries of joy are wedding bells to my ears.'

Chapter Nine

*H*eavy curtains screened out the street lanterns and the candles were few. On the sideboard stood a range of bottles containing vile-coloured liquids, together with numerous clay bowls heaped with lurid powders.

A purple cloth covered the round table and opposite sat Dr Irfan Paya, hunched within his hooded robes. A long greying beard poked from his shadowy face, and from his neck, strung on a thick silver chain, dangled a long twisted piece of metal.

Octavia's palm was upturned in his slender bejewelled fingers.

'There have been many men in your life,' said the doctor after an interminable silence.

Octavia snorted. 'I don't need a soothsayer to tell me that,' she said, her bass voice resonant. 'It's common bloody knowledge.'

The doctor raised a hand for silence, and resumed his contemplation of her palm.

'Many have pleased you; many have charmed you.' The doctor inhaled deeply, his head raised, his eyes closed. His skin was like tanned leather, dark and lined, and his eyebrows were thick and grey.

'I see a man watching you,' he continued. 'And you are ... Diamonds ... Wearing nothing but diamonds. Laid across a long table. He is a royal man, not a king. He is waiting. One day he will be king.' The doctor dropped his head abruptly and drew a long, shuddering breath.

Octavia paled. She had told, at most, three people of that episode in her life. Or was it four? Gallantry with the Prince of Wales was not something one discussed. A courtesan who gained a reputation for gossiping would not be welcomed again in high circles.

'Only one man has truly satisfied you,' murmured the strange doctor. 'I see a scar on his face. He wanted you to submit to him.'

'And I did not,' said Octavia vehemently, snatching her hand away.

'No, no. You did not. You did not.'

Octavia was beginning to think this was not the enjoyment Lucy had promised. Memories, painful ones, were best left alone. They belonged to the past, not the present. And Octavia was a different person now from the eager chit Marldon had first taken in hand.

He had taught her a great deal, much of it unwittingly. Dominating others and turning them into snivelling, pleading wrecks was something she'd learnt purely by following his example. It had proved a lucrative skill, but less satisfying than learning how to conceal hatred. Smiling indifference was something Marldon could not endure. It left him with nothing to feed off and Octavia had, where he was concerned, become superbly, charmingly cool.

She was, after all, an actress.

Such a talent served her well in society: nobody knew the real Octavia; nobody knew about her innermost desire or how she took her pleasures, unless of course they were participating. She hoped the doctor couldn't read too deeply.

'Are those your medicines, Dr Paya?' she enquired

brusquely, nodding to the sideboard. 'A most interesting selection.'

'You do not need medicine,' he replied. 'Although there are some who would disagree. They see it as diseased, an unnatural act. Abhorrent.'

'No,' exclaimed Octavia, jumping to her feet. 'No more.' The chair thumped to the ground behind her. She spun on her heels and headed for the door. If this got out it could ruin her career.

'Octavia, stop,' came a soft, urgent voice.

She drew up short and turned slowly, disbelievingly, to the man. He pushed back his hood, unhooked the beard from his ears, and smiled apologetically.

'Mr Ardenzi,' she whispered. 'You ... you contemptible swine.'

'I know,' he replied. 'I'm sorry. Please, Tavi, let me explain.'

Octavia returned and picked up the chair, her shocked gaze never leaving his painted face.

'Who told you?' she breathed. She sat down as though she were old and fragile, and gently patted her bright auburn hair into place. 'How much do you want?'

Gabriel shook his head. 'Some of it was gossip, some of it was guesswork.'

'And my ... my unnatural acts?' she said, her fingers fluttering with the jewelled choker at her neck.

'A hunch.' He shrugged. 'Something about the way you looked at Lucy before. But, if you recall, I didn't really say anything, Octavia. My words could have meant any number of things to any number of people. Although your reaction did much to confirm my suspicions.'

Octavia sighed and looked into the gloom. She had a name to keep as a sophisticated, man-hungry harlot. At the age of forty-four, she could not command the fees she once did. If her burgeoning taste for women became known, it could consign her to the scrap heap.

'We need your help,' said Gabriel abruptly. 'We need

better make-up, theatrical stuff. And we need some dirt on Lord Marldon. Intimate things.'

She jerked her head to him, her eyes narrowed with mistrust and anger. 'Is this bribery?' she snapped.

'No,' he replied. 'I pledge you my word, I'll say nothing of what I know. I simply need to get into Asham House.'

'In heaven's name, what for?' asked Octavia.

Gabriel called Lucy in from the adjoining drawing room and together they explained.

'The grasping cur,' muttered Octavia when the two of them had finished. 'And your cousin, such a charming thing. I dread to think what he – Oh, so sorry, Gabriel. So sorry. Of course I'll help you, though I suggest the good doctor gain himself a reputation before attempting a visit to Asham. Marldon's curious about this sort of thing, but mainly because he likes to spot a charlatan. You'll have to be good, my boy, damn good.'

'It doesn't matter if he thinks Gabriel's a fraud,' said Lucy. 'As long as he doesn't think he's Gabriel. And there's a second part to our plan. That is, if you'll help us.' She crossed to the door. 'Miss Preedy. Do come in.'

Miss Preedy, her fair hair curled, pinned, and woven with tiny flowers, glided into the room. She wore a gown of brilliant red, and a sumptuously laced train dragged on the floor behind her. She held her head high and she smiled at the three of them.

Gabriel looked at her in astonishment and whistled. 'Hell's teeth, Kitty,' he said. 'And I thought my disguise was good.'

Kitty beamed a wider smile. 'Dandy, isn't it?'

Lucy coughed disapprovingly. 'Tavi,' she said. 'Do you think, with your contacts, you might manage to secure Kitty a position at Madame Jane's?'

Octavia's critical eyes wandered over the young girl, assessing her from head to toe. 'I can try,' she said, nodding thoughtfully. 'Yes, if it means Marldon getting his just desserts, I can try my bloody hardest.'

Clarissa stood at her bedroom window, gazing beyond Piccadilly to Green Park. Its calm, rolling expanse seemed a world apart from this one. It was close, but not close enough for her to attract anyone's attention; and in everything else it was far, far away.

The people who strolled there were everyday people, taking the air and going about their business. Their normality made Clarissa feel her imprisonment and the strangeness of her lusts all the more acutely. Those elegant swells knew nothing of her plight; they did not have desires as sick and hungry as hers. It was inconceivable.

She felt utterly, irrevocably changed. And she did not know if Marldon had created her corrupt appetites or merely discovered them. But she was quite sure they would be forever with her. Some day she would walk among those people below, but never again would she be of them. Inside she could count herself as nothing but a fairground freak.

She turned away from the view and sat on the bed, her knees bunched to her chest. The early-July sunshine cut two pale slants across the room, and a fat bluebottle buzzed intermittently against one of the windows. They don't open, you fool, she thought bitterly. But, if they did, would she shout for help? If she could leave, would she? Clarissa dared not think about it. She preferred not having the choice.

She flicked back the cover of a book beside her and shut it without a glance at the title. She was in no mood for reading. She was in no mood for anything.

Asham House was a place of extremes, and on days such as this it defeated her. For thirty-two and three-quarter hours, she had seen nothing of the earl. He had ordered her out of his bed, just as she was falling asleep in his arms. It was a cruelty she should have expected.

But after a night when he had taken her to peak upon peak, indulging her in pleasures that were pure and untainted, his command had been all the more callous. But then, she supposed, that was the point.

His moments of tenderness were never what they seemed. Invariably, just when she feared she might be warming to him, he would undercut his apparent humanity. He would leave her wanting when he had promised delights; he would reveal onlookers when she'd thought they'd been alone; he would be understanding, caring, and then he'd laugh at her for taking his words at face value.

Clarissa preferred it when he was unremittingly, openly cruel. It made him easier to hate.

But, even though she hated him, she loved being his. One time, with Jake watching, he had coupled with her in the stables, the straw prickling her arse. Clarissa had gloried in it. She'd flaunted her lust and her soft open thighs, because the stablemaster could not touch her.

She wished Alec would come to her now. She pined for him, pined for his dangerous attentions, and her body ached constantly with desire. Yet in this room she feared tending to her needs. Many times she'd covered the spy-hole; many times it had been uncovered. And she knew not how many more there were. Only in the dead of night dared she pleasure herself, and it was always quietly, stealthily, her hand nudging beneath the bedclothes. The satisfaction she gained from it was weak and impoverished.

The bolt grated at the door. She turned, trying to urge herself to pessimism, and started as her former lady's maid bustled into the room.

'Pascale!' she exclaimed. 'What are you doing here?'

The Frenchwoman appeared ready for work, an apron over her gown, her dark hair drawn back into a bun, emphasising that large, strange nose of hers.

Pascale arched her brows. 'You need someone to help with your toilette, do you not?' she replied imperiously.

'His lordship says the other woman cannot dress hair. Tish! I see it is very true.' She squeamishly lifted a long black tress from where it trailed over Clarissa's shoulder.

Clarissa gave a vexed flick of her head and slapped away the maid's hand. 'My hair will fall out before I accept your help,' she hissed. 'You're a nasty, deceitful little piece of work, Miss Rieux. Get out of my sight.'

'I take my orders from Lord Marldon,' replied Pascale grandly, tossing some silks on to the bed. 'Not from you. You are to wear that.'

'When my stepmother hears of this –' began Clarissa, colouring with anger.

'*Je m'en fiche*,' said the maid, shrugging. 'My loyalties are with the earl. His pay is so much better. Alicia, oh she also paid well, but that is because my job was to be difficult. She wanted me to seduce you. Faugh! I prefer to work for his lordship. He does not ask such things of me.'

She smiled triumphantly at Clarissa's shocked, bewildered expression.

'To seduce me?' echoed Clarissa. 'Alicia asked that? You are being ridiculous, Pascale. Utterly ridiculous.'

'*C'est vrai, mademoiselle*,' she replied calmly. 'Mrs Longleigh, she wanted you to be a more suitable bride, not so closed, not so *naïf*. Tish! I believe it was for your sake, but Lord Marldon, he liked the idea also. *Et moi?* I found it very fatiguing.'

With a rustle of silk, Pascale swished away to the dressing table. Clarissa stared after her, turning over in her mind incidents from the past. There was the time the woman had touched her in the bath, times when she'd been suggestive, others when she'd been lewd. And oh, how encouraging she'd been when Clarissa had spoken of Gabriel, promising to conceal her whereabouts should she wish to spend the night with him. Could it really be that it had all been at Alicia's request?

Clarissa suddenly questioned the sincerity of everyone she knew, and she looked back on her stay in London with fresh eyes. Lucy had been so eager for her to find a beau. Had she been part of her stepmother's plan? And Gabriel? Had he simply been trying to make her ready for Lord Marldon? She felt foolish and used. With a heavy heart she realised other people wanted to control her life. She was surrounded by puppeteers who made her dance to their string-pulling. And she'd thought them friends.

But no. It was inconceivable that Gabriel could be anything but true; he had not been working to mould her into something Marldon would approve of. His love was real, perhaps the only real thing she had. But that was surely over now. Some day he would learn how she'd betrayed him, and never again would he look at her with those soft, yearning eyes. She put the thought from her mind. It was better not to think of him; it could only bring her sorrow.

Pascale turned to her. 'Will you please put on the gown,' she said, gesturing to the silks.

It was hardly a gown, thought Clarissa, lifting it from the bed. It was little more than two wisps of fabric, stitched at the side.

'What for?' she asked sulkily.

'His lordship requests your presence,' said the maid. 'Do you wish me to help you dress?'

'No, I do not,' replied Clarissa firmly.

The prospect of seeing Alec again made her stomach churn excitedly. She walked over to the chest of drawers and pulled out a chemise.

'*Non*,' said Pascale. 'This gown, it does not require underclothes.'

'But it's far too thin,' protested Clarissa. 'It will show everything.'

Yet, even as she spoke, she knew that was the intention. The idea of greeting Marldon in such flimsy drapes covertly thrilled her. She slipped off her wrapper, baring her naked body, and dropped the gown over her head.

The shot silk rippled down, shimmering purple and deep blue.

She stood before the mirror. The garment was cut low at the neck, with no sleeves to speak of, just thin straps over the shoulders. It was not waisted or gored. Yet it was cut in such a way that it clung to every curve and dip. Her dusky nipples were clear beneath the delicate fabric and her pubic hair pushed a crinkled patch in the smooth fall of the garment.

'Ah, it is quite beautiful,' purred Pascale. 'Now we must do something with your hair. His lordship is expecting a guest, so it will be something elegant and grand.'

'I cannot wear this in company,' exclaimed Clarissa. 'It's indecent. And it's the middle of the afternoon.'

'Tish! Of course you can,' replied the maid. 'And, if it is of help, you will not be received until later in the evening.'

'Then why are you attending me now?' demanded Clarissa. 'So that I can wait and wonder? So I can agonise about what lies in store for me?'

The Frenchwoman smiled and shepherded her to the dressing table. '*Bien entendu, mademoiselle,*' she murmured, taking a brush to Clarissa's hair. 'No other reason.'

Clarissa gave a low, weary breath, all thoughts of defying Pascale now gone. She hoped the maid would curl and dress her hair as she used to. Clarissa wanted to look her finest for Lord Marldon, though she wished more than anything that the two of them could be alone.

'And our guest?' she asked forlornly. 'Am I to know about that?'

Pascale leant low over her shoulder and met her eyes in the glass. 'It is a foreign doctor,' she said. 'With strange mysterious powers. He is going to read into the hearts of both yourself and his lordship.'

'Well, at least one of us should prove a challenge to him,' muttered Clarissa.

In the soft glow of evening sunlight, Gabriel's carriage rolled along Knightsbridge, past the trees of Hyde Park. His heartbeat quickened as they neared Piccadilly. He thought little of what might befall him should he be discovered; his drumming pulse was for Clarissa.

It seemed an eternity had passed since he had last set eyes on her, but in truth it was no more than thirteen days. And, for most of those days, Gabriel had been perfecting his disguise, allowing his reputation to swell on the tide of London gossip. An audience with Lord Marldon had not been difficult to secure. Dr Irfan was greatly in demand, and Gabriel half-fancied that as a fraudulent soothsayer he could earn a pretty decent living. Superstitious nonsense was much in vogue.

But he knew Marldon did not subscribe to the current fashion. His invitation, he suspected, had come about because the earl wanted to outwit him. He wanted an opinion on the latest society tittle-tattle; then he could show those who'd fallen for the ruse what deluded fools they were.

But Gabriel did not care. As long as he had the chance to be near Clarissa, nothing else mattered. How he yearned to look into those deep-blue eyes, eyes that were sometimes slumberous, sometimes brilliant. He was desperate to know if she was well, to ascertain how Marldon was treating her.

Lucy's suggestion that Clarissa might be residing there of her own free will was ludicrous. The letter she'd written him, although it was in her hand, had not been composed by her. Those words in which she'd retracted her feelings for him had been lies, as patently obvious as the lie that she was ailing in Chelsea. Marldon had forced her to pen such things, just as he was forcing her to stay at Asham. And the vicious old libertine was no doubt forcing her into deeds as black as his heart.

Gabriel looked out of the window as the carriage passed Hyde Park Corner. The sun's last rays gilded the bronze statue atop Wellington Arch, and then they were rattling past the grand mansions of Piccadilly. Asham was unique among them. High, bleak walls surrounded it, and only a glimpse of the house could be seen through its vast iron gates.

He checked the garnet clasps of his brocaded robe, pulled the hood over his head, and patted his beard. The disguise was good. Thanks to Octavia's skilful application of stage paint, even those he knew well had failed to recognise him. It was perfect, right down to his hands, which were aged with lumps and lines. He hoped Clarissa would see through it, that his presence would reassure her that help was close by.

Gabriel had been advised not to attempt anything foolhardy. Or he could, said Octavia, end up badly wounded, in a prison cell, or quite simply dead. Stick to the plan, she'd said. Find an opportunity to slip away; take a look about Asham; discover how guarded it is, where the doors are, which windows might be forced; then bloody well get out. The rest would come later, when Kitty had found a place at the brothel and wormed her way into Marldon's favour. There was a busy trading of places between the man's whores and his servants, and with someone on the inside they were more likely to secure an easy release for Clarissa. Don't put him on the alert, Gabriel.

But Gabriel was impatient. He fancied that somehow, tonight, he might manage to leave with Clarissa.

The wrought-iron gates of Asham House opened. Gabriel hunched his shoulders as the horse clopped slowly across the forecourt to the wide red-brick building. The row of mullioned windows on the ground floor looked in upon rooms of glittering splendour. The carriage came to a halt and Gabriel's heart grew nervous as his coachman opened the door and folded down the steps.

173

'I'll get a hansom back,' he whispered, not wanting to have his servant mingling with members of Marldon's staff. He was a trustworthy fellow but slips of the tongue happened and Gabriel did not want to take the risk.

At the head of the stone steps, the oak door swung back. Gabriel made heavy labour of being handed down from his carriage, leaning on his coachman as he shuffled up to Asham's imposing entrance with its great portico and glittering white hall.

He handed his card to Marldon's butler and he was no longer Gabriel. He was Dr Irfan Paya of Constantinople, Soothsayer to the Sultan. And he was inside Asham House.

The blue drawing room was in near-darkness.

'My dear,' said Marldon, rising to greet Clarissa as she entered. 'How ravishing you look tonight.'

He lifted her hand and pressed a kiss to it. After so long an absence, merely seeing him was enough to stir her desire. The touch of his lips was a taper to her hunger. Lustful anticipation flared within her and she resented him for showing no inclination to pursue it.

'The gloom is for Dr Paya,' he hissed. 'Apparently it helps his concentration.'

Taking Clarissa's arm, he led her to a small table and offered her a seat opposite the cloaked, huddled figure. Lord Marldon stood behind her and rested his hands on her bare shoulders.

'Doctor,' he said, massaging her neck lightly. 'Permit me to introduce Miss Longleigh. What, pray, can you tell us of our future? Can you say if we are well matched, for we are quite set upon marriage?'

The man muttered from within his voluminous hood and stretched out his hand, gesturing for Clarissa's.

She repressed a sigh of impatience and did as requested. She could not understand this game; she did not know where it was leading. What did Alec care whether they were matched or not? And, more to the point, why bother with this mumbo-jumbo? Alec was surely too cold and rational to believe in it.

Dr Paya lightly took her fingers in his, uncurling them to display her palm. His ageing hands were fine and elegant. His touch was gentle, familiar. Clarissa's heart lurched. It could not be. No, it could not.

The man spoke, something about loss, but she did not hear his words. She listened only to his voice. He held it croakily in his throat and faintly accented it, but beneath there was that soft resonance she knew. The doctor kept his head low, allowing the hood to conceal his face. Flee, she wanted to say, flee at once. And her hand shook.

He raised his head for a moment. She recognised nothing but the eyes, eyes the colour of brandy in firelight, eyes which flashed a warning intensity. Gabriel clasped her hand a little more firmly, stilling her tremors. She felt a surge of tender passion, so painfully recalled, so mockingly strong, that her limbs grew weak. She fought for control, praying no one would ask her to speak.

She stared at her hand, her quivering fingertips held by his. The pretence of strangeness, of a touch which was nothing compared to what they'd once had, was desperately poignant to her. This was the man she had first given her body to; this was the man she had loved – did love.

Gabriel rambled on, weaving nonsense with seeming perception. There were many truths he could have spoken of, both profound and light, but to her relief he said few of them. He did not take the risk of appearing too clever. He was no better or worse than any other man touting himself as a seer.

Guilt overwhelmed her. She did not deserve that he should put himself at risk. She could have fought harder against Marldon; she could have clung to her love for Gabriel, and thought of him endlessly. But she had not. It was easier to yield, and more bearable when emotions were blocked out.

'And I see . . . ah, a need for ease,' Gabriel was saying in slow, throaty tones. 'A body hungering for something, for simple pleasures.'

'Balderdash,' said Marldon sedately. 'My betrothed cares little for such vapid pursuits. She has an appetite only for bitter and sour. Sweetness, alas, she cannot taste.' He slid his hands from her shoulders, down into her iridescent gown. His fingers squeezed her soft, naked breasts.

He knew. Of course he did. Why else was she dressed like this? Why else was he standing there, touching her so possessively? It was to torment Gabriel. She tried to catch her lover's eye, to caution him of the danger, but he would not look at her. She could not begin to think what his plan was, and she feared for him. Surely he realised this place was like a fortress.

'You see how she allows me to touch her, Doctor?' continued Marldon. 'Even before one as eminent as yourself? She does not flinch from it because it arouses her greatly. She thinks of your lust, Doctor. She knows you want her, as any man would, and she is proud. She is proud of her power, and proud to have given herself to me. Because only I can truly satisfy her. Isn't that so Clarissa?'

He teased her nipples and they sprang erect. She swallowed hard, wishing she could deny him and shake off his hands. But she did not for, while Marldon was flaunting his dominance, Gabriel was surely safe. But it crushed her heart to think he must be suffering so.

'My lord,' she said, affecting calm, 'I fail to understand why you have invited this gentleman here when you yourself read me with such confidence.'

'A mere diversion,' he answered pleasantly. 'I thought perhaps you would appreciate some entertainment other than my body. After all, you've had it so often, Clarissa. Aren't you tiring of it yet?' He palmed her breasts and kissed her neck, his teeth scraping, his sideburns scouring.

'No, I am not,' she said, offering a truth she hoped would tempt him. 'However, I tire of this gentleman. My lord, I have not seen you for almost two days.'

Marldon gave a harsh laugh. 'I wonder if it is within the doctor's powers to divine how often you masturbated during that interval.'

Clarissa felt the heat rise in her face. 'My lord, send him away, I beg of you.'

'How I enjoy it when you beg,' he replied, releasing her breasts. 'It's rare that I show mercy, but for once I think I shall oblige you.'

He crossed to tug on the velvet-tasselled bell-pull. Clarissa kicked Gabriel lightly under the table. He raised his head and looked at her with eyes full of pain and anger. 'Go!' she mouthed urgently and he gave a sharp nod, acknowledging the danger. When the butler entered, Gabriel left the room, stooped and shuffling like an old man.

Clarissa watched Marldon anxiously, wondering if he knew she had seen through the disguise. It would be better, she thought, to feign innocence. There was a remote possibility that Marldon did not know the doctor's true identity, and she did not want to enlighten him.

'How touching that you missed me,' he said, bidding her rise from the chair. 'Thank God I'm not a fool or I might take that for a sign of fondness. Lift your dress, Clarissa. Show me exactly where you missed me.'

Obediently, she rucked up the purple-blue fabric and held it bunched about her waist. Her mind raced, wondering if Gabriel had made a safe exit. Perhaps there were others within the walls of Asham ready to help him overpower the servants. They might return within moments and rescue her.

She widened her legs for the hand Alec slipped between her thighs. His skilled fingers wandered, tantalising her sex and sensitising her clitoris. She groaned faintly, feeling her wetness gather. She hated him for tormenting Gabriel, yet she could not stem her desire for him. She tried telling herself she was sparing the man she loved by offering herself so wantonly, and so soon after his departure. It was a way to deflect Marldon's attention.

But her conscience did not ease. She knew that, even when Gabriel had been sitting there, Marldon's touch had aroused her.

'Take it off,' said Marldon, and Clarissa swept the loose silks over her head. 'I shall have more such gowns made up for you. Perhaps one slashed at front and back, then I can reach for you at any time. Would that please you, Clarissa?'

Not caring, she murmured that it would. Her sex ached to feel him and she rolled her hips desirously. Lord Marldon unbuttoned himself.

'Forgive me if I sit for this one,' he said, drawing the chair. 'I've expended more energy than you the last couple of days.'

The remark stung, reminding her that she was not as much of his life as he was of hers. She did not wish to know where he had been, or muse on what depravities he might have indulged in. She hoped he would not insist on telling her.

Alec pulled her to stand astride his lap. His stiff prick stood from his open trousers, ruddy at its head. Clarissa lowered herself on to it, moaning soft bliss as her vagina slid wetly down. She sank herself to his root. Her pliant flesh enveloped his thickness and his glans pushed high. She breathed quickly and stayed there, immobile, relishing how his solid virility filled her so entirely.

'Ah, how greedy you are,' Marldon whispered.

He closed his mouth over a hard nipple, sucking and nibbling. Clarissa arched her spine, rocking on his penis. With every roll forward, her inflamed pleasure bud pressed through his crisp curls to rub against his body. She raised herself high, sucking with her sex muscles, then dropped back on to his cock. Her urgency swelled and she grasped the chair and bucked with a driving hunger.

Her breasts bobbed from Marldon's mouth. His strong hands spanned her waist, encouraging her movements, and he watched the eager bounce of her bosom with delight. Clarissa gave a shrill cry as she reached her crisis.

'Don't stop,' he said. 'Prove how you've missed me, Clarissa. Work to make me come. Sweat for it.'

Clarissa lifted herself, her thighs trembling with the effort. Her vagina glowed with the dying pulse of her pleasure, and she felt his cock-tip butting at the core of her. Again and again, she sank deep, impaling herself on the hard, hot pole of his prick. Marldon's lust was hard to release. He held himself back until she thought her legs would fail her. She panted and pleaded, feeling the sweet, rising tide of her second peak.

'Yes,' urged Marldon. 'Ride me hard, Clarissa.'

He thrust urgently beneath her, clutching her waist, controlling her balance. With increasing speed he plunged upward, slamming her body down to meet his furious, jolting strokes. His lips stretched, baring his white teeth, then with a long throaty growl he spent his fulfilment. The searing heat of his orgasm pushed Clarissa to her limit. Wrenching ecstasy burst open and her climax shuddered around the last squeezes of his cock. Then she sagged against his chest as the throbbing force drained away, her breath coming in quick gasps.

'It seems our soothsayer was correct,' said Marldon. 'Your body *has* been yearning for simple pleasures. How insightful of him. Perhaps I shall invite him back sometime.'

Gabriel moved down the marble stairway with slow, faltering steps. The need to maintain the charade was frustrating beyond measure. All he wanted to do was get out of Asham House as quickly as possible before anyone questioned him.

Clarissa's warning had proved timely, confirming what he feared: the earl was suspicious of him. And that little show, with Clarissa barely dressed and Marldon handling her so intimately, had most likely been for his benefit. Gabriel's blood seethed at the memory of it. The man was a cruel tyrant, a Caligula who deserved a lingering death. It had taken Gabriel every ounce of control he had not to throttle the despicable fiend there and then.

But that would have meant certain exposure. At least he had made a start. He now knew that a tighter plan was required, one which took into account Asham's lurking employees, its maze of corridors and securely locked doors. If Lucy and Julian could not come up with anything decent then to hell with them. He would summon the police to Asham and he'd damn well accompany them to make sure there was no foul play. Marldon would get his comeuppance somehow, and it had to be sooner rather than later. Every minute Clarissa was under his roof was a minute too long.

At the foot of the steps stood the waiting butler, staring into nothing. Gabriel eyed him with concealed suspicion, knowing he was not safe until he was on the pavements of Piccadilly, perhaps further. He shuffled over the final marble slab and stepped delicately on to the tiled hall floor. The butler strode stiffly towards the door and rested a hand on one of the bolts.

When Gabriel reached the centre of the hall, the man drew back the shaft with unnecessary sharpness. The bolt rasped loudly. Quick footsteps followed. Gabriel twisted his head round, catching a glimpse of a rushing figure before an arm was hooked violently about his neck. He uttered a strangled cry and jabbed his elbow fiercely into his assailant's stomach. The grip on his neck slackened. Gabriel swung free of it, sweeping back his hood.

The thin fellow was bent double, then he raised his head, green eyes flaring, and made ready to lunge again.

Gabriel landed a tightly balled fist into his face. Blood trickled from the creature's nose and he staggered back, groaning.

His cloak whirling, Gabriel spun around to see two more men fast approaching.

'You cheating blackguards,' he snarled, and cracked a solid upward punch beneath the jaw of one. He turned to thump the other but a clenched hand, broad and strong, struck him on the temple. Dizziness rocked him for a second. Then he hit the brawny fellow square in his brick-hard stomach. The man grunted, barely affected, then addressed Gabriel with a tobacco-stained grin.

From behind, something thudded against Gabriel's skull. The room twisted, the colours blurred, then everything went black.

Chapter Ten

*L*ord Marldon had barely left Clarissa's side all day. She did not trust him. He watched her with a furtive smile and there was a gleefulness in his manner which made her taut with apprehension. And now they were eating in the state dining room instead of the usual, smaller one. They sat either end of the long table, a line of candelabras and fruit pyramids stretching between them. Silver dishes, decanters and flagons gleamed strangely against the dark wainscoting.

'Are we expecting company?' she had asked on seeing the display. And Marldon had replied with an enigmatic 'maybe'. But only two places were set.

Clarissa feared his behaviour had some connection with Gabriel. Seeing him yesterday had raised her hopes: her friends knew of her whereabouts and were attempting to help her. Yet, at the same time, despondency weighed on her heart. In the face of Marldon's cunning, they could surely accomplish little. She toyed with the food before her, too anxious to swallow a morsel.

'Perhaps dessert will tempt your appetite,' said Marldon, signalling for the footmen to clear away the main course. 'You are preoccupied, Clarissa. Are you wondering whether finally to accept my offer of marriage?

Perhaps I should ask for your hand once more, just to test the air.'

Clarissa said nothing as the liveried servants, Beckett and Simms, removed plates and cutlery. 'The question is beginning to bore me,' she replied eventually.

'Now there is something I have not tried,' said Alec with a contemplative gaze. 'Boring a woman into submission. Still, I don't suppose I would be successful at it. That's the trouble with charisma: it narrows a man's options.'

Simms, oval-faced and balding, brought a decanter of wine to the table and made to pour it into Clarissa's glass. She put out her hand to stop him.

'Have some,' insisted Marldon firmly. 'It's a Muscadet. Its sweetness will be a perfect complement to the next dish.'

Clarissa shot him a worried glance. There was an edge to his voice; his words sounded ominous. Marldon smiled as his glass was filled, then raised a toast. Clarissa did not join him.

'To sweetness,' he said, and drank.

Clarissa watched him, her body tense with grim expectation. What pestilent thoughts were going on in that mind? What was he anticipating?

A movement at the far end of the room caught her attention. She looked beyond Alec to see the double doors open wide. Brinley and Jake entered and between them, hands behind his back, arms locked in theirs, was Gabriel.

'No,' gasped Clarissa, leaping to her feet.

She rushed to him, emotion robbing her of breath. A purple-black bruise, shiny at its centre, marked one of his cheeks and, though he did not struggle, his strong, beautiful face was shadowed with fury. She drew up short when she saw the blade glinting at his throat. 'No,' she whispered.

She threw a fearful, pleading glance at the knife-wielding valet. Brinley's left eye was blackened and he grinned, vengeful and smug. She turned to Gabriel. Her heart flared with pity and love, and culpability pulled a sombre knot in her stomach. She had brought him to this.

Her hand trembling, she reached out to his wound. Her fingertips hovered above it before she brushed a touch over his lips.

'They hurt you,' she said quietly. She gazed at him for a long time, seeing tenderness beyond the anger in his rich-brown eyes. Hot tears smarted in her own and she turned to Marldon slowly but feverish with rage.

He had positioned his chair so as to observe her better. He rolled the stem of his glass between thumb and fingers, and his lips were curved in a triumphant smile.

'Release him,' she said, her voice low and quivering. 'Release him, or I swear I will not be responsible for my actions.'

'Ah, the passion of young love,' said Marldon lightly.

Clarissa screamed, incensed, and ran to hurl herself at him. The impact of her body almost unbalanced him and his glass crashed to the wooden floor. She slapped and battered at his chest, tugged at his clothes, clawed wildly at his face. She shrieked curses at him. She clutched great fistfuls of his hair, pulled him low and shook his head savagely, wanting to tear it from his neck.

Then harsh fingers gripped her arms and the footmen wrestled her away. She kicked and squirmed in their grasp, still screeching abuse at Marldon.

The earl crossed to her, his eyes barbarous, his hair dishevelled. With swift force, he cracked a hard stinging slap across one cheek.

Clarissa choked a heaving cry, then fell silent, stunned.

'You bastard,' spat Gabriel.

'She was hysterical,' barked Marldon. 'And she's my business.'

There were threads on his frock coat where a button should have been, and part of his high starched collar was undone. It poked above his skewed tie at a gawky angle. With the calm of one attempting to regain his dignity, Marldon swept his thick sable hair into place and adjusted his clothing.

'Release her,' he snapped, and the two footmen at once stepped back.

Marldon walked to the sideboard and poured himself a glass of claret. His face was flushed and scored with red lines, and his mouth was pinched and wrathful.

'You spilt my drink,' he said to Clarissa. 'Mop it up.'

She stared at him, too shocked and breathless to respond. Her mind seemed to float in a tranquil space, vaguely aware of some far-off violence. She felt serene, dazed, and she could not recall what Alec had just said. Then a suppressed groan of agony penetrated her trance. She twisted around to see Gabriel half-bent and writhing, his face contorted in pain. His wrists, she saw now, were manacled, and his captors were forcing his arms high behind his back.

'I'll do it,' she whispered to Marldon. 'What is it? I'll do it.'

Alec signed for Brinley and Jake to cease their cruelty then repeated his command: 'Mop it up.'

Clarissa turned to address Simms. 'Could I please have a cloth?' she asked meekly.

'No, you cannot,' said Marldon sternly. 'Soak it up with your drawers.'

A tiny whimper escaped her lips and she closed her eyes in wretched despair.

'Do not,' shouted Gabriel. 'Clarissa, do not allow him to abuse you so. I will bear anything for you, any amount of pain.'

'That's as may be,' said Lord Marldon. 'Although you will not be as quick to say it when your throat is slit. And, if I am merciful and merely slash your face until the skin hangs from it in ribbons, then I perceive great disappointment. Clarissa is not, I can assure you, averse to a scar or two. But a patchwork of them would be unlikely to appeal.'

'It's nothing, Gabriel,' she said imploringly. 'Please, don't make it worse for me.'

Alec's threats of murder were hollow, she was sure of it. Oh, he was doubtless capable of it, but he was far too wise to do it. Yet she feared he would have no compunction about inflicting pain. While Gabriel might be able to bear the suffering, she could not.

She reached beneath her petticoats, bending double in a bid to conceal herself. With useless, shaking fingers, she worried at her strings. It seemed an age before the knots came undone, then her drawers rippled down and crumpled about each ankle like white silken shackles.

'Must the servants watch?' she asked timorously.

Marldon teased her with a frowning, meditative expression. 'Let me think,' he began. 'I don't suppose we require the footmen. No, I'm not quite ready for port to be served. However, I'm afraid Brinley and Grimshaw must stay. Your lover needs their support.'

When Beckett and Simms had left, Clarissa reluctantly stepped free of her undergarment. She knelt like a drudge before the splashes of wine, folding her skirts to make a pad for her knees. Bunching the drawers in her hand, she pushed at the spillage, nudging back splinters of glass. Emotion scorched her eyes, and her face was hot with shame. This indeed was a new form of humiliation.

'And here,' said Marldon, tapping his foot.

She placed her hand carefully on the floor, wary of the broken glass, and stretched to reach. She was powerless to defy him. Gabriel's presence was a weapon in his hands, and only Alec's imagination limited her abasement. Such a limit did not cheer her. She rubbed feebly at the wine, demoralised into true servitude.

Marldon moved behind her and she felt, to her horror, his hand on her skirts. In a sharp movement, he flung back every layer, exposing the pale ovals of her buttocks. Jake grunted in the background.

Clarissa gritted her teeth, fighting back the tears. She must not show her distress, for Gabriel would be certain to try defending her. And Marldon's brutish servants would not hesitate to punish him for it.

'Oh dear, how clumsy of me,' said Alec, tilting his glass and pouring a stream of red wine to the floor.

Droplets splashed on to her face and she dashed a forearm across her cheek, catching back a sob of desolation. On hands and knees, she shuffled to wipe up the liquid. Marldon deliberately spilt some more wine. Clarissa crawled after it. Her movements, she knew, were designed to make her bared mounds more visible to Gabriel. The presence of Brinley and Jake hardly concerned her: they had seen her degraded before. But for Gabriel to see her like this was mortifying.

'A tempting sight, is it not, Mr Ardenzi?' said Marldon, moving behind her. 'Although, of course, not one entirely new to you.'

He stooped beside her and moulded a cool hand to the curve of her buttocks. Gently, he stroked its rounded flesh. Then he brushed his fingers over the dusky folds of her vulva, up and down, light and teasing. Her treacherous sex-lips tingled in response. She screwed her eyes tight, trying to will away the sensation, and swept her sodden drawers in blind arcs over the parquetry.

'I've finished,' she said in a quiet shaken voice.

'No you haven't,' countered Alec, withdrawing his caress.

She heard liquid splash. Forcing open her eyes, she mopped up the dark wine. Then another little splash landed, and another. She could not outdo him; it was futile to try. She made a charade of lingering over the spillage and Marldon returned his hand to the lush, swelling pouch of her loins.

He tantalised her there, drawing out her wetness with an experienced, knowing touch. She rubbed mechanically at the floor, repressing every groan that fought for release.

'You're a devil, Marldon,' came Gabriel's low, angry voice.

'So I'm told,' he replied impassively. 'In fact, I believe Clarissa is of the same opinion. However, it does not appear to concern her overmuch. Truth to tell, I believe it rather excites her. Watch. Listen.'

In the silence, Marldon pushed two hard fingers deep into her moist, warm canal. He probed thoroughly, stirring her juices to faint wet sounds. Clarissa uttered inarticulate noises, half-protest, half-pleasure. It was unbearable that he should make a performance of her arousal, yet she could not quell her body's lust; and she dared not resist, for Gabriel's sake. She heard Grimshaw's gurgling, lecherous breath and felt nauseous with revulsion and self-loathing.

'Jake, you're a pig,' said Marldon. 'Shut up or you'll feel my hand again.'

The stablemaster uttered a final throaty grunt and fell quiet.

Marldon slicked Clarissa's milky warmth down to her clitoris and rubbed, angling his touch this way and that, varying his pressures, until she moaned wildly, pleading for more. He knew exactly how and where to caress her. It was a knowledge he had gained from her, from her abject failure to resist him. He massaged and stimulated every hot tender part, taking her close to her peak but never granting it. Her sex wept tears of fire.

'Mr Ardenzi, I must thank you for leaving me both virginities,' said Marldon. 'I'm so grateful.'

His finger drifted back and drew her secretions up to the dark, wrinkled mouth of her anus. He rubbed hard little circles there, pushing against the tightly closed orifice. Clarissa groaned uncontrollably, delirious with vulgar, forbidden wanting.

'Shall I take the second, Clarissa?' he asked. 'You can,

of course, say no. Gabriel will not be harmed and I shall abide by your request.'

Clarissa did not reply. For a long time she had ached to feel him there, and now her need for him was like a fever in her veins.

'You see,' continued Marldon, 'I do not wish your lover to think I do everything by force. He would gain quite a false impression of our relationship.'

His teasing finger persisted, nudging repeatedly at her anus, tempting her with a foretaste of penetration. She whimpered, needful and breathless, and pressed back against his touch, seeking his intrusion. She uttered no words of refusal.

Marldon helped her to her feet and, smiling, guided her to the table. He leant the upper half of her trembling body across it and raised her skirts. The linen cloth was cool against her cheek and she gazed down its white expanse to the foot of the table. She edged her feet apart, brazenly offering herself to Alec.

A groan from Jake, rumbling like thunder, broke the quiet. She could sense them all watching her: the servants eager, and between them Gabriel, revolted and dismayed. But at that moment she was awash with reckless excitement. Her demands were so strong that his disapproval and her shame could not temper them. All she cared for was the depraved violation Marldon offered. Modesty no longer had a part to play.

She felt him behind her, close. Her heart pounded and her body waited. She saw him reach across to lift the lid from the butter dish and scoop up fingerfuls of it. Then he slipped his hand into the cleft of her buttocks and smeared the grease there. Its initial coldness disappeared as he rubbed it in, concentrating on her resistant hole. She felt her pinched entrance yielding, loosening to his steady, slippery massage. He drove a finger inside her, then another, lubricating her richly within. She moaned wantonly. She felt wide open for him, so relaxed, so ready.

'Methinks the lady doth not protest enough,' taunted Marldon.

He parted her cheeks and the air briefly chilled her buttery crevice. She felt his bared prick, heavy and threateningly erect, rest deep in the split. It slid down and the domed head of his phallus butted at the tender rose. He pushed and his cock, with steady force, breached the oiled ring of muscles. Searing pain burnt there for an instant and she cried out. Then with exquisite ease the massive whole of his shaft was sliding greasily into her, plundering her dark, velvet depths. He drove gently until her narrow virginity was utterly, unspeakably packed full of flesh.

Marldon lodged himself there, pausing as he released a long, contented sigh. The warmth of his tightened balls rested against her soft vulva, and his strong, solid bulk, stretching her apart, was crammed into her most intimate passage. The pleasure was fierce, black and sordid. He drew back, as languorously as he'd entered her, and began slowly to thrust. Ah, how he filled her. Knives of heat sliced into the immensity of his assault, and each stroke he took was harder, faster than the last.

Clarissa groaned, her elation mounting, intensifying wildly. She clutched the table edge, her buttocks surging back, greedy for every lunge of his brutal prick.

'You should have asked for this sooner,' breathed Marldon. 'I failed to see how impatient you were.'

He slammed to a quickening rhythm, kneading and pummelling her satin-smooth haunches. The heavy, hanging purse of his balls knocked against her labia, sending tremors through her swollen lips, making her clitoris thrill hotly. Alec grunted, short, urgent grunts.

'Touch yourself,' he rasped.

Clarissa flinched at the request. To be seen receiving pleasure was one thing; to be seen wanting it, chasing it, was far worse. 'You do it,' she pleaded.

'No,' he replied huskily.

His refusal was absolute, and her sex, teased then

forsaken, craved a touch. She dipped her fingers in the wetness of her creases, plunging and agitating. She tantalised herself, delaying a climax she could take if she wished to. But she wanted to prolong the pleasure, to stay on the maddeningly sweet plane of nearness.

Marldon growled, ramming himself into her again and again. She reached her hand back and his taut, pulsing balls brushed over it as he plunged mercilessly on. He snarled and gasped, pounding so eagerly she thought her body would split. Her ravaged virginity blazed like a furnace, and she wailed in agonised bliss. His furiously swollen cock, thundering into her tightness, seemed almost to reach her spine. Her whole body was suffused with hot, throbbing ecstasy. The tension was at its height. She could take no more.

Three rubs on her pleasure bud were enough to release her. She came, abandoned and sobbing. Paroxysms of delight clutched fiercely at her centre and sensation soared, lifting her to rapture. Marldon had been waiting. He gave several violent thrusts and, on a raucous cry, buried himself deep in her slick, stretched tunnel. His cock shuddered wildly, emptying its burning liquor into the trembling crash of her orgasm.

When his spurts ebbed away, he released a low, heavy groan of satisfaction. His hands ran idle strokes over her fleshy rear. The sudden silence was immense.

Clarissa drew shallow breaths, feeling his size diminishing in her sore, tainted passage. Her consciousness, no longer marred by lustful fumes, grew sharp. Her surroundings, her audience, returned to her perception. Remorse filtered into her mind and she felt sickened to the core of her being, hating herself for sharing Marldon's depravity so willingly.

He slipped out of her. 'Delightful, isn't she?' he said.

Clarissa ruffled back her skirts with flicking, apologetic hands, and sluggishly raised her exhausted body. Alec brought her a chair and she sat, her head bowed, unable to look at Gabriel.

She wished he would speak. She wanted to hear his words of contempt and disgust. She wanted him to castigate her, to ease her conscience by punishing her with the abuse she deserved. But he said nothing, and her shame intensified.

Marldon strode over to the three men and Clarissa looked up, anxious, curious. Jake's mouth sagged open, lewd and wet, and Brinley gave her a salacious grin. Their hunger was evident in their bulging crotches. So was Gabriel's. She noted it with both relief and guilt. She wanted to catch his eye, to exchange a glance of understanding, but he kept his gaze resolutely fixed on the ground.

Only when Alec stood before him did Gabriel raise his head. The two men were virtually the same height, Marldon a little broader. They looked each other full in the face, Marldon gloating, Gabriel glaring defiantly.

'As you can see,' began Marldon, 'your knight-in-shining-armour attempt is wasted on Clarissa. She takes to captivity with relish. It gives her the freedom to indulge her baser appetites, and to Clarissa that is paramount. However, your visit has not been entirely without its reward. The entertainment, I discern, you found quite enjoyable.'

He cupped a hand to Gabriel's swollen groin. 'Very enjoyable,' he said, rubbing.

Gabriel glowered at him, his shoulders lifted, and his chin tilted up. Then he spat directly into Marldon's face. For a moment, Marldon was perfectly still. Then he took a backward step, pulled a silk handkerchief from his trouser pocket and calmly wiped away the sliding foam. His features were clouded with rage.

'You will pay for that,' he said, slow and controlled. 'You will truly pay for that.'

Octavia, in a wrapper of apricot chiffon, lay across Lucy's bed, propped on one elbow. Her vivid auburn locks were half-pinned and a few loose waves streamed over one shoulder.

'So when do we start worrying?' she asked, reaching for a grape.

Lucy, seated at the dressing table, cast her a shy glance in the mirror. 'I'm worrying now,' she said with a nervous smile.

'Darling,' said Octavia, her voice rich and chocolaty. 'You know perfectly well that I was referring to Gabriel.'

Lucy shrugged and made a fuss of powdering her nose. 'Tomorrow, I suppose,' she replied. 'He did promise to call today. But you know Gabriel: he gets distracted by something or changes his mind. I'm sure it all went quite, quite smoothly.'

'I do hope so,' said Octavia, rising from the bed. 'And I do hope you're right about that little housemaid too. I have deep reservations about securing her a position with Jane. It's not any old bloody knocking shop, you know. The girls there have a certain refinement.'

She stood behind Lucy and scrunched handfuls of blonde ringlets, fingertips rubbing lightly at her scalp. Lucy shivered nervously.

'Julian's teaching her to waltz,' she said. 'Kitty's been slipping out at night and they've been practising. And she doesn't curse quite as much. Not when she's concentrating anyway.'

'Well, it's a start,' replied Octavia absently. 'Are you sure you want to wait for him, Lucy?'

She ran her fingers beneath the frilled edge of Lucy's chemise, moving from one shoulder to the other. Lucy's heart fluttered. She felt terribly ashamed to be exploiting her friend's desire in this way, even though Octavia professed not to care. Lucy's tastes were for men and men alone, and this was engineered solely to snap Julian out of his complacency. Her affairs and flirtations so far had affected him not in the slightest, and Lucy was tired of his confidence in her hunger for him, tired of being taken for granted. And she hated the fact of his marriage. Yet she could not let him go.

His wit delighted her and her appetite for the games he played was insatiable. He could be both wicked master and tender lover. But what she loved most was that his taste for subjugating her was not borne out of a corroded soul as it was with Lord Marldon. Julian knew how to play. The earl, as she'd discovered, did not.

She met Octavia's gaze in the mirror. The older woman had promised to pleasure her in such a way that Sir Julian would soon stop believing he was indispensable. Lucy was less convinced, and now the moment had arrived she was starting to regret having been persuaded into it.

Ready words of doubt formed on her lips, but Octavia was looking at her with such yearning that she was crushed to silence. A sudden thrill coursed through her body and she shuddered, excited and fearful.

'No,' she said quietly. 'Let's not wait for him.' It was less insulting to Octavia this way, she thought, and she did not want to appear hesitant when Julian finally arrived.

'You'll love it,' whispered Octavia. 'You'll love it.'

She slid her hands either side of Lucy's back, smoothing down the thin ivory fabric, dipping into her waist and swooping over the flare of her hips. Leaning forward, she ran her hands along Lucy's thighs and nuzzled beyond her rich fall of curls to kiss her neck. Her breath was soft and warm, her touch slow and lingering. Her hands moved back, wrinkling up the chemise on Lucy's legs, then skimmed over the slight rise of her belly to press beneath her breasts. She ran a finger below each underswell, gently pushing silk into the creases where her rounded flesh hung.

Lucy drew a tremulous breath. Her body tingled to Octavia's easy, soothing caress. She closed her eyes, feeling hands cup the weight of her bosom, thumbs scuff across her nipples. A whimper caught in her throat and her full orbs took all the sparkling sensation to their tips. Beneath the silk her crests hardened, erect and lustful. The pleasure was unexpected, but it was sweet and strong.

She looked at Octavia in the glass. 'Have you always preferred women?' she asked coyly.

Octavia gave a kind smile. 'No,' she said. 'I've always liked both. I've never understood desiring just muscles or just curves. I'm attracted to people first, bodies second.' She kissed Lucy behind her ear. 'It just happens that of late the nicer, more interesting people in my life have been women.'

Lucy unfastened the top two buttons of her chemise, a tentative offering of her eagerness. Octavia encouraged her with eyes that were needy yet understanding. Lucy continued to open her shift, still a little timid.

'Why do you keep so quiet about it?' Lucy asked.

Octavia eased the silk from Lucy's shoulders, exposing her white, coral-peaked mounds.

'Because it's better that way,' she replied, brushing back Lucy's hair. 'Considering the line of business I'm in. Some men are funny about it: they feel threatened or revolted. And there are others completely enchanted by the idea. Both are bloody tiresome.'

She nibbled Lucy's earlobe and massaged her bared flesh. Arousal trickled through Lucy, and she moaned faintly.

'You have beautiful breasts,' murmured Octavia. 'Come, stand up.'

Slowly, Lucy stood. She faced her friend, looking steadily into her hazel eyes, aware of each breath she took. With deft, soft fingers, Octavia slipped the half-open chemise down Lucy's body. The silk whispered to the ground.

'Ah, how luscious and white,' purred Octavia.

Her gaze roved over Lucy's nakedness as she unfastened the gold ribbons of her own wrapper and let the chiffon fall from her shoulders. Octavia's pale skin was smooth and lustrous, her body superbly firm and buxom. The peaks of her ample bosom were tight points, surrounded by great rosy circles. She stepped to Lucy, and drew her close. Their breasts squashed together, soft and yielding, and their nipples chafed.

Octavia touched her lips to Lucy's, and fluttered a brief kiss. Drops of lust spilt into Lucy's groin and stayed there, quivering. She had thought about their bodies together, but for some reason she had not thought about kisses. Its intimacy roused her and she answered with a hungering mouth and caressing hands. She swept over the woman's back, palmed her fleshy buttocks, and stroked the scoop of her waist. The feel of silky, supple flesh delighted her and she swayed her hips languorously, pressing her pubis to Octavia's. A warmth drummed in her sex, heavy and rich.

The door creaked and Lucy jumped. Sir Julian entered, stopping abruptly as he saw them.

'What the devil –' he exclaimed, staring hard, his mouth agape.

Lucy looked at him. She had expected, hoped for such a reaction when she'd arranged this. But now it seemed misplaced and foolish.

'Go away, Julian,' she murmured, and she meant it.

'Let him stay if he desires to,' countered Octavia, giving her a gentle, unseen pinch. 'We can be alone at other times if you wish. Three is often interesting.'

Lucy was disappointed. She did not want to compete or be competed for. She did not want to prove anything. All she wanted was to explore these new sensations and other ways of pleasuring. But she relented, knowing the opportunity would be wasted if she let it pass.

'Would you like to stay?' she asked, her voice betraying her lack of enthusiasm.

'I seem to recall you invited me,' said Julian flatly. 'Did you change your plans or is this part of them?'

Lucy shrugged and received another nip from Octavia. Putting on a brilliant smile, she sauntered over to him, and laid her hand to his crotch. His prick was swelling and the pulsing maleness of it charged her with a fierce need.

'We got a little distracted,' Lucy said, gazing seductively into his steely blue eyes. 'Why, what else is a girl to do when her lover is over half an hour late?'

She rubbed at his burgeoning erection and kissed him deeply, relishing the scouring bristles of his moustache against her upper lip. Octavia came to join her, helping Julian off with his frock coat.

'Indeed,' he said, whipping undone his tie. 'I must remember to be late more often.'

He undressed quickly, and his cock jutted from his light-brown curls, deliciously stiff. Lucy fell to her knees and took his tumid length in one lavish mouthful. Octavia sank behind her and slipped a hand into the parting of her legs. Her busy fingers quested in the hot, juicy folds, dipping into Lucy's rich well and nudging at the bead of her clitoris. Her touch was glorious.

Lucy moaned her delight around Julian's rigid shaft, drawing back and forth with keen strength and an agile tongue. He gasped at her zeal, and pulled away from her.

'You'll make me spend, my sweet,' he cautioned.

He knelt before her, his mouth seeking her breasts. He suckled on a tight, crinkled cone, and his hands roved over her flesh. Lucy exhaled deeply, wallowing in the luxury of two skilled eager lovers. It was sheer heaven to have them tending to her most sensitive parts. Her sex burned to Octavia's expert caress, her moisture running quickly, and her nipples throbbed as Sir Julian moved from breast to breast, bestowing his wet attentions upon her.

Octavia bore her gently back to the floor, and Lucy lay supine, moaning softly. She parted her legs, her hips tipping for someone's, anyone's, ministrations. Julian's fingers slipped briefly within the soaked petals of her vulva, finding her readiness. But Octavia urged him out of the way. She knelt over Lucy and lowered her head to the juncture of her thighs. Her mouth was wide open, hot and wet, as she engulfed Lucy's folds in a voracious sucking kiss. Her tongue slipped through Lucy's plump lips, its tip gliding along her deep juicy valley. Then she lashed and nibbled at the knot of her pleasure bud, teasing back its hood to seek the hard pearl within.

Lucy whimpered and writhed. Octavia's sumptuously heavy bosom rested on her belly and her legs were astride her face. Russet hair cloaked her mons, and her sex, split before Lucy's gaze, was pouting ripely, shimmering with dew. She found the sight deliciously indecent and fiercely exciting. With a rush of appetite she clutched Octavia's hips, urging her open thighs down to her mouth. She sipped at the other woman's rich, briny nectar. She explored the succulent pleats of her flesh, exquisitely tender and moist, and revelled in the intoxicating scent of her musk.

Octavia mumbled throatily and Julian released a quick groan of disbelief and wanting. Lucy, aware that for the moment he was excluded, was thrilled. She knew how erect he was, how impatient he must be to take her. Let him wait, she thought, reaching to fondle Octavia's generous breasts and toy with their great puckered tips. This was bliss beyond compare, made all the sweeter by Sir Julian's thwarted desire.

The two women squirmed and moaned with rising pleasure. Softness pressed on softness, and Octavia guided them, rolling over, shifting positions. They lavished kisses on mouths and nipples; they rubbed their mounds together, meshing golden hair with amber; they delayed their orgasms and luxuriated in the newness of each other's body. Julian stole an occasional caress, or snatched a fleeting kiss. But Octavia was possessive and alert, at once claiming any flesh he covered.

Eventually he huffed in frustration. 'Are you going to let me in?' he asked sharply. 'Or would you prefer it if I took my leave now?'

Octavia looked at Lucy with questioningly raised brows. Lucy smiled at Julian and ran a slow gaze down his broad torso to his towering prick, deliberately critical and ponderous. He was rearing potently, his glans empurpled and glistening in the half-light. Her vagina ached to be filled by the driving strength of him, but she was guarded enough not to reveal it.

'Don't be churlish,' she said, gentle and placating. 'Stay. I'm sure you can play a part. Just try a little harder.'

With that she edged back to the bed and levered herself on to it, spreading her bent legs wide. Julian scrambled to be with her, and caught her upper body to his. His demanding mouth met hers, fiercely taking all the kisses he'd been denied. His fingers sought her wetness and he plunged three of them, over and over, into her hot swollen opening. Lucy gasped frantically. She drove herself into his hard thrusts, grinding her pubis to the heel of his hand.

'Ah, that's what you like, isn't it?' he snarled, ramming his crushed fingers deep. 'A foretaste of fucking. You cannot fool me, Luce. A woman could never satisfy such a greedy orifice.'

'But there are other pleasures,' insisted Octavia, squirming into their embrace. 'Pleasures the three of us can find.'

Her lips closed over one of Lucy's nipples and her hand reached to clasp Julian's cock. She pumped his rigid shaft while sucking and tonguing Lucy's crests.

Lucy thrashed beneath them, rubbing against a hard body, a soft one. Her caresses moved everywhere, finding muscles and fleshy contours, stiffness and moisture. In the tangle of limbs she did not know whose mouth touched this place, whose fingers touched that, nor did she care. It was sublime to have such an abundance of skin and heat, to receive so much attention.

Julian knelt between her splayed thighs, cradling her buttocks, and heaved her loins towards his. The stout knob of his phallus brushed and teased her inflamed labia. He delayed entering her, making her beg and cry for him. Her hips arched, searching for him, shaking in anticipation. But still he lingered.

Octavia straddled her belly, blocking her view of Sir Julian. She edged up, smearing her wetness over Lucy's undulating body until her pulpy, scarlet sex was pressed to Lucy mouth. Lucy lashed and probed with her tongue, burrowing into the heat of the pliable folds, tasting the woman's juices.

She felt the head of Julian's cock poised at her hot openness, and she gasped urgently, her sounds muffled by Octavia's smothering flesh. Her need for him was torment, pushing her to the very edge of endurance. Then with a brisk force, he penetrated her, shoving his gorgeous thick shaft to its limit. Her slick orifice cleaved to his warm sturdy rod, and she whined her joy, drawing Octavia closer in the fever of her excitement.

Julian slammed and jabbed with furious lust. His fingertips dug into her buttocks and he jerked her body to meet each powerful lunge. Octavia's breath came short and fast, as Lucy nibbled eagerly on her clitoris. Then the woman climaxed with a series of husky moans, and her mouth and hands were suddenly everywhere, kissing and kneading Lucy's creamy white curves.

'God, you're divine,' mumbled Octavia, her warm lips fluttering over Lucy's lifting bosom.

Lucy panted, her near-orgasm starting to clutch at her groin. Her clitoris seethed; her vagina throbbed, slipping and gripping around Julian's cock. She pounded to match him, stroke for stroke, until extremity claimed her. She wailed as an eddy of pulses exploded and gushed, but Julian allowed her no respite. He snorted and gasped, driving himself on to his ultimate fulfilment.

With a hoarse shout, he tore himself free of her. His release jetted in pearly arcs, splashing hotly on to Lucy's belly and breasts. Octavia gave a long, sonorous breath and lovingly massaged the silky fluid into Lucy's skin. Lucy murmured contentedly, her body sinking into the relaxation of her calmed orgasm.

Octavia smiled at Julian's softening penis. 'Well, that's you finished,' she said, without malice. She nuzzled up to Lucy and rubbed the swell of her pubis against Lucy's plump thigh.

'If you insist,' replied Julian, easing himself back on to the pillows.

Lucy turned away from him, twining her legs about Octavia's. They exchanged warm, languid kisses and gentle, snaking caresses. They tantalised each other, teasing and sucking, stirring up arousal where it tingled still.

'Perhaps I should put up at my club tonight,' said Julian, a note of irritation in his voice. 'I doubt this bed will afford me much sleep.'

He did not move, and Lucy did not answer, too involved in Octavia's flesh even to enjoy his vexation.

'Or perhaps I should ring for some refreshments,' he continued, pettishly seeking to be noticed. 'A cognac would be much appreciated.'

'Then get dressed and ring from the drawing room,' mumbled Lucy, worrying he might call up a servant just for spite.

Julian grumbled to himself and moved from the bed to retrieve his clothes. From the corner of her eye, Lucy watched him. His face was devoid of its collected ease, and instead his brows were pinched in a frown, his lips compressed in a tight line. She felt a moment's pleasure, recognising that she had managed to ruffle him, but the satisfaction was not as brilliant as she'd anticipated.

'How the mighty are fallen,' said Octavia as he left the room. 'You'll soon have him eating out of your palm, darling. Or your lap.'

'Mmm,' replied Lucy, taking a rigid nipple between her teeth. She grated lightly on its hard, roughened texture, then drew away, tense.

An urgent hammering of the door knocker resounded through the house.

'Bit late, isn't it?' said Octavia, a quiver of concern passing over her face. 'You don't suppose –'

'Gabriel,' said Lucy. 'Oh, fudge, it must be Gabriel. And, at this hour, his news can only be dreadful.'

In a panic, she set about covering herself, pulling on a petticoat and hunting for her shift. Low voices reached her from the hall and she grasped Octavia's wrapper, hurrying into it as she stole out on to the landing to listen. She heard the front door close, then footsteps – more than one pair – on the first flight of stairs. She fumbled with the ribbons, struggling to make the wispy garment a little less indecent.

'Kitty!' she exclaimed, seeing the flaxen-haired girl rounding the foot of the steps with Julian. 'What in heaven's name are you doing here?'

'It seems Gabriel hasn't returned home,' answered Julian. 'Which means the situation is worse than we thought. Or better, but I doubt that.'

'You can't bring her up here,' hissed Lucy, crossing her hands to conceal her bosom, visible beneath the sheer fabric. 'You can't bring her into the bedroom.'

'Of course I can,' he returned. 'We have things to discuss. I think Kitty will need to gain a place at Madame Jane's with some urgency. So she's going to have to accustom herself to sights far more depraved than our half-clothed aftermath.'

Lucy swung round as the bedroom door creaked open behind her.

'Bloody right she is,' declared Octavia. She stood there, magnificently calm, utterly naked.

'Lord ha' mercy,' said Kitty in a low breath, gawping at Octavia's large breasts.

'Do come in, Miss Preedy,' said Octavia. 'I feel you have an awful lot to learn.'

202

Chapter Eleven

Marldon's servants were not as other servants. They took their orders but they also took their pleasures, as blatantly and crudely as their master.

Throughout the night, their laughter and groans of lust had echoed around the basement's sleeping quarters. The sounds had drifted into Gabriel's ugly dreams, dreams in which the valet, the steward, footmen and grooms had queued up to couple with a willing Clarissa; dreams in which she had jeered when it was his turn to take her; dreams in which Marldon lay dying, a dagger sticking from the place where his heart should be.

Gabriel paced restlessly. The room seemed to grow smaller with each passing moment, but at least it was quiet now. Escape seemed nigh on impossible. The window was a mere slot of glass, high on one of the walls. The door was securely locked from the outside and whenever a servant entered, to bring food or issue an order, they were always backed up by the gruff stable-master. Gabriel's prospects seemed bleak.

He stepped up on to a chair beneath the window and peered out of the oblong pane, as he had done a thousand times since being cooped up in the spartan little room. Level with his eyes, the stableyard stretched out to the cheerless red-brick wall engirdling Asham House. A youth jogged alongside a horse, trotting it about in wide circles. Sunlight glinted on the animal's hooves and, though Gabriel could not see the sky, he knew it was of the fiercest, cruellest blue.

The brightness of the afternoon mocked him: his hurt did not darken the world, nor did his agony shape brooding clouds. It was all crammed into his heart and mind, and no one but he suffered for it. Clarissa did not love him. Any fool could see that. He did not need the servants to tell him that last night, when she'd submitted so utterly to Marldon, was not a rare occasion. She had not done it to save Gabriel from harm; she had not done it under duress. She had done it willingly, hungrily, without a thought for his pain. Marldon was the man she wanted, not he.

The key turned in the lock and Gabriel stepped wearily down. A woman entered the room and, as ever, Grimshaw stood in the doorway, his thuggish bulk blocking the potential exit. It was Charlotte, the curly-haired maid who had brought him shirts and trousers yesterday, garments which Lord Marldon apparently no longer required.

'Perhaps,' she'd said, 'he'll give you Clarissa too, once he's cast her off.'

Gabriel had balked at wearing the earl's clothes but thought it marginally preferable to wearing the robes he'd arrived in. He hardly cared that the costume was now ridiculous. He simply did not want to be dressed in a reminder of his deceived heart and hopes.

'Feeling creative?' asked Charlotte, fixing him with her mocking jade-grey eyes.

Gabriel sat on the narrow bed and leant against the wall. 'Not particularly,' he replied.

The woman tossed an assortment of equipment on to the mattress: pencils, pens, inks, charcoal sticks and pastels.

'Well, you'd better try getting in the mood,' she said. 'His lordship wants some sketches doing.'

Gabriel rummaged idly through the materials. 'Landscapes?' he enquired sardonically.

Charlotte smiled. 'Of Clarissa.'

'Ah, nudes,' said Gabriel, nodding with mock sagacity. 'My favourite art form. How perceptive of Lord Alexander.'

Despite himself, the thought of seeing Clarissa made him ache with wanting. It could only be a bitter pleasure, one designed to torment him, but logic could not quell his yearning to be near her. And there was, he told himself, a chance that she might give him a word or a look to show her feelings for him were still as strong. He knew it was a false hope, but nevertheless he clung to it, allowing deception to overrule his judgement. He would not refuse Marldon's request.

'Paper would be helpful,' he said.

'Upstairs,' said Charlotte. 'Select what you need and we'll go. Handcuffs, Jake.'

'They're not necessary,' sighed Gabriel, rising from the bed.

But they paid him no heed and he was taken, hands bound, up to the first floor.

There, without knocking, Charlotte quietly opened the door to a drawing room of blue and silver. Clarissa, playing Chopin at the pianoforte, did not see them. Her body swayed gently and her elegant fingers rippled over the keys, filling the room with a melancholy sound. Lord Marldon was seated in a fireside armchair, his legs crossed, one foot bobbing gently in the air. He smiled serenely, raised his hand for their silence, then resumed his meditative demeanour.

It was, thought Gabriel, a parody of domestic contentment. For a few moments Clarissa played on until something made her aware of the intrusion. She turned slightly; the notes faltered, then she hastened to her feet.

'Gabriel,' she said, in a whisper so full of longing that it tore through his heart.

He had been mistaken. She truly did care for him.

'Clarissa,' he responded softly. Could he convey how he loved and needed her with a single word?

She ran a few eager steps towards the small group. Then she checked herself, snapping her head round to Marldon. Her face darkened and her eyes grew narrow, darting suspicious, uncertain glances from one man to the other.

'What is it?' she demanded of Lord Marldon. 'What do you mean by this? What is it you hoped I would do?'

Lord Marldon rose from his chair and strolled over to her, smiling coldly. The scar on his strong, cruel jawbone shimmered like the silver track of a slug, and everything about him spoke of cruelty and cynicism. He looked like a man who, having tried and tired of every known perversion, was now intent on devising his own.

'Ah, how guarded you've become,' he said. 'Whatever happened to those simple, open passions, Clarissa? Once you would have thrown yourself at his feet, begged for his forgiveness just as you have begged for my mercy.'

Clarissa was motionless, her expression stony as Marldon pinched the end of a curl hanging by her ear. He pulled it down, stretching it to tight straightness. Her head tilted a little and the merest grimace of discomfort twitched on her face. Then he released his grip and the hair sprang up to a shining ebony tendril.

'Your self-control spoils my fun,' said Alec mildly. 'Alas, alack, such a pity. Won't you at least humour me by pleading for your lover's forgiveness?'

Gabriel drew quivering breaths, his anger rising hotly. 'There's nothing to forgive, damn you,' he said fiercely.

'No?' returned Marldon with inflated surprise. 'Most men would be a little put out at the sight of their sweetheart being buggered, and loving every minute of it. But not you? Ah yes, I recall it well now. You found the sight quite pleasing, didn't you, Mr Ardenzi?'

Gabriel wriggled in frustration, his handcuffs clanking. 'You bastard,' he snarled.

It shamed and enraged him that he had no defence.

When he'd witnessed Clarissa being taken so intimately, his lust had proved stronger than his censure. He had tried closing his eyes to the scene, but the sounds of her pleasure had still inflamed him, and the compulsion to watch had been overwhelming. His arousal, however, had not detracted from his hatred of Marldon. Nothing could do that.

'Leave him,' implored Clarissa as the earl stalked over to Gabriel. 'If you must torment someone, my lord, then torment me.'

She followed him like a whipped dog, tugging on the sleeve of his frock coat. Jake sniggered.

'But you enjoy it too much,' retorted Marldon, pulling his arm from her clutches. 'Besides, I'd rather torment you both.'

Gabriel breathed deeply, attempting to calm himself. He recalled Octavia's advice: a cat would not toy with a mouse if it lay still; seeming indifference was the best defence against Lord Marldon. He forced his lips into an agreeable smile.

'Then, please, try your damnedest,' he said with a charm he did not feel.

Marldon returned the smile and looked at him keenly, his eyes black as pitch.

'Perhaps later,' he said eventually. 'But for now, Mr Ardenzi, will you cooperate with my request for some sketches of Clarissa? I can, of course, force you to draw, although I doubt I could force you to produce your best. However, I would so appreciate it if you tried. I'd like a record of Clarissa before it's too late, before she turns into an irredeemable slut.'

Clarissa cursed him.

'My pleasure,' replied Gabriel with assumed urbanity. 'How else am I to earn my keep? I fear the handcuffs might present a problem, though. And I do not work with an audience.' With a nod he indicated the servants flanking him.

'Ah, the sensibilities of an artist,' said Marldon. 'I find Clarissa thrives in company. However, as you wish.'

He bid Charlotte release the manacles then dismissed her, and ordered Grimshaw to remain outside the door. Gabriel rubbed at his wrists and flexed his fingers.

'Hardly the best preparation,' he said affably, settling into his role as the earl's match. 'Would you mind if I took a look around the room, my lord? I need to judge the lighting.'

'Be my guest,' said Marldon, following him with watchful eyes.

Gabriel took his time, relishing his slight increase in power. He wondered if the man genuinely did want some sketches or if this was solely to induce heartache. But either way it mattered little. He could spend time with Clarissa, and that counted more than anything.

He strolled past the tall mullioned windows which looked down on Piccadilly. A few carriages rumbled along the wide, cobbled road, gleaming in the brilliant afternoon, and beyond were the verdant treetops of Green Park. The sky was of the deepest azure, and the sun was a blaze of gold, high and blinding. Gabriel eased a shutter to, lessening some of the glare, and gazed contemplatively about the room. Clarissa regarded him with a confused, cautious expression. He smiled openly at her.

'When you're ready,' urged Marldon tetchily. 'Mr Ardenzi, will you help your model undress? I don't wish to interfere overmuch.'

'No,' murmured Clarissa. 'No, I won't have it.'

Marldon sighed. 'What? Do you want me to threaten his life again, Clarissa? Or is it that you would rather I helped you?'

Clarissa pressed her lips together, and threw Gabriel a troubled glance. He was on the point of reassuring her that it did not matter, that it was a trifling thing, when she spoke.

'Yes,' she whispered, guiltily lowering her eyelashes. 'I would rather it were you, my lord.'

The request pierced Gabriel to the quick. Was she ignoring his feelings or trying to spare them? He felt a surge of hostility towards her: she could have at least granted him those few moments of closeness. The pleasure of touching her skin would have far outweighed the anguish it was meant to provoke. Perhaps, he thought, she could not bear the pain of him being near. Either that, or Marldon had the preference.

Gabriel pulled out the pencils from his pocket and took up the paper and board set out for him on a small table. If she wanted Marldon to help her disrobe, then so be it. He was certainly not going to watch them. He sat on a brocaded couch, an ankle resting on the opposite knee, and laid the board on his lap. With a casual air he began sketching various pieces of furniture: a rococo console table, a jardinière holding a great potted palm, a chair with ball-and-claw feet.

He hummed as he worked, only once stealing a glimpse of Clarissa and Marldon. And, when he did, he regretted it deeply. He saw the earl slipping her chemise from her shoulders, his hands sliding down her bare arms, his lips pressing kisses to the nape of her neck. And, in the same moment, he saw Clarissa close her eyes luxuriously.

Jealousy, sour and vicious, twisted his guts, mocking his nonchalant façade. Oh, how quickly she surrendered to the man; how she cherished his dominance and his polluted sensuality. This was not the woman Gabriel had fallen in love with.

'Where in the room would you have her positioned?' asked Marldon.

Gabriel raised his head from his determined sketching. Clarissa was naked, her hair unpinned. A thick black lock streamed over one shoulder and hung in a soft curl, half-concealing the breast below. A shell-pink nipple poked shyly through the lush curtain, and she appealed to him with eyes that were imploring, apologetic. Her expression sent tender emotions flaring high, and his phallus pulsed at the sight of her pale, beautiful nudity. But he girded his heart with stoicism and coolly surveyed her up and down.

'Very nice,' he said in a neutral tone. 'Anywhere over there, please. Away from the windows.'

Gabriel saw a disconcerted shadow cross Marldon's face. It was the briefest loss of poise, but it rallied his spirits. Octavia had been right: the man disliked the taste of his own medicine.

Lord Marldon arranged Clarissa on a blue damask chaise. She was a rag doll in his hands, her compliant limbs flopping this way, spreading that. When he had finished she was lying full length, her head on the armrest, one foot on the floor, one on the upholstery.

'What I would like, Gabriel,' began Marldon, 'is for you to capture the expression on her face when she's in ecstasy.'

The earl drove his fingers into the crimson-throated entrance between her thighs. Clarissa gasped quietly. She squirmed on the couch, uttering small objections, but her legs widened and she tilted her hips, pursuing his invasion.

'Ecstasy is a fleeting thing,' asserted Gabriel. 'And it seldom stays still. The task will be somewhat difficult.'

Lord Marldon pushed in and out of her pouting orifice, slow and teasing, his thumb rolling on her clitoris. Clarissa's eyelids dropped shut and she gave in to his caress. Her breath grew short and she moaned shamelessly.

'Then you'll have to watch her come, again and again,' said Marldon softly. 'Commit it to memory, Gabriel, then set it down on paper.'

Gabriel felt his face flush with a surge of loathing, but he was resolute, convinced he could better Marldon – as long as he could control his emotions. He inhaled deeply and quietly.

'Very well,' he replied. 'I think the times I've spent with Clarissa will give me a head start.'

Lord Marldon slid him an uncertain glance then smiled benignly, returning his eyes to Clarissa. He probed rhythmically in her open, dewy sex, answering her groans with murmured words of approval. As his glazed fingers worked he studied her face, his own rapt and adoring. But it was delight, not in her enjoyment, but in her subjection which gave him such a look.

Gabriel's resentment swelled apace with his arousal. Clarissa's abandonment, her writhing body and her sounds of bliss stirred his prick to hardness. And it was at her that he began to direct his anger. This was the Clarissa he had seen yesterday, the one with the restraint of a whore and the constancy of a weathervane. Those victimised looks she'd cast him had meant nothing: they were as hollow as her declarations of love.

And while he detested Marldon with a violent passion, Gabriel decided that he was not the one to denounce. Clarissa was the one who had claimed devotion and spoken of forever, not Lord Alexander. She was the one who now betrayed him. She was the faithless slut.

He watched, inflamed with fury and lust, as Marldon thrust into her greedy wet flesh. She ground herself against his hand, gasping frantically, body shivering, eyes closed, lips parted. Gabriel had seen such an expression before, but then it had been at the touch of his fingers. Now she was blind to his presence. The girl did not care who gave her pleasure, or who observed it. As long as she got her fill, she was happy. Any man would do, any cock.

Marldon brought her, panting and thrashing, to the edge of her crisis. Then he stepped away from the couch and turned to Gabriel, holding his gaze.

'She's all yours,' he said disdainfully. 'Do what you will with her. I recommend her arse, but it's entirely your choice.'

Clarissa gave a cry of alarm and pushed herself on to one elbow. She looked beseechingly at Marldon, her face a confusion of disbelief and desperate, lascivious need. Then she turned to Gabriel, and her countenance did not change.

Gabriel had been right: she could transfer the object of her desires within the blink of an eyelid. And now she'd been denied, she wanted *his* prick inside her – his prick because it was the only one on offer. Well, he would give her what she wanted. He was rock hard and more than ready for it.

He shoved aside his drawing board and got to his feet, tearing off his shirt. He strode over to her, unbuttoning as he approached.

'No, Gabriel,' she gasped, cowering in the corner of the chaise, her hands raised as if to ward him off. 'Don't be like this. Don't give him the satisfaction.'

Gabriel scoffed, stripping till he was naked. 'I think it's you who wants satisfaction,' he rasped.

He scooped her upper body to his, and kissed her harshly, his tongue thrashing hot and quick. She whimpered in his arms and when he urged her off the couch she sank with him to the floor. Her hands swept eager caresses over his back and her mouth searched for his. But Gabriel did not care for such pretences of fondness. The brazen doxy was only trying to appease her guilt.

He pressed his hands to her inner thighs, forcing her wide. Her sex, red and slick, gaped for penetration. He lay over her and, on a violently swift lunge, slammed his cock deep into her. He began driving furiously, thumping his prick high, venting his anger in an onslaught of thrusting madness. Her slippery wet heat hugged his shaft. She moaned deliriously, protesting one moment, begging the next. He brooked her no mercy. She liked cruelty; she liked to be mastered.

Her body shunted back along the carpet, jolting with the force of his stiff, plunging phallus. Gabriel clutched her firm breasts and kneaded urgently, his fingers

212

tweaking and twisting her tightly pinched nipples. Clarissa wailed and wrapped her legs about his waist, encircling him, her vagina thirsty for every thick swollen inch. She ground herself against him, her loins pumping upward, her actions belying her gasps of complaint.

'Shut up,' barked Gabriel. 'Stop pretending you don't want it. Bitch. You grasping, greedy slut.'

She looked up at him, her half-closed eyes full of pleading and hurt. Amid moans of hunger, she uttered words intended to soothe and calm. She tangled her fingers in his hair, pulling his mouth to hers. Gabriel snatched his head away. He felt her lips brush against his neck, soft, gentle, moist. He did not want those touches from her; he did not want her deception.

He fucked her hard, driven more by rage than desire. He rammed his prick to its root, and clawed at her tits, abused and cursed her. He blocked out every care he'd ever had.

She loved it. The hot little bitch loved it. A ruthless fuck was all she wanted, and that's all she would get from him. No more love, no more tenderness.

As he powered into her, she gasped frantically, her fingernails raking his back. She peaked, her head tossing, her humid sex trembling around his solid pounding length. Gabriel gritted his teeth, driving wildly. His climax would not build and he begrudged Clarissa bitterly for taking hers.

'Lift her on to your prick,' came Lord Marldon's voice.

Gabriel glanced up and saw the earl striding over to them. He was naked, his phallus hugely erect and forbidding.

'I want to share her with you,' he continued. 'I want to take her arse while you're taking her more romantic orifice.'

Gabriel's blood ran cold. The idea of having another man so intimately near filled him with horror and revulsion.

'Damn you, no,' he growled, feeling suddenly possessive.

Marldon was at his side in an instant. He grabbed Gabriel's curling locks and twisted them, forcing back his head. Gabriel, his spine arched, held still, his penis pressing deep inside Clarissa.

'My faithful stablemaster is just outside the door,' sneered Marldon, bringing his face close to Gabriel's. 'Jake Grimshaw – not a pretty fellow, I'll grant – is desperate to get his hands on Clarissa. Would you enjoy watching him fuck her? Seeing his great oafish arse pumping between her spread thighs? Seeing him slaver and grunt over her soft white body?'

Clarissa screamed. Lord Marldon clamped his free hand to her mouth, stifling her cries.

'Well, Gabriel?' he enquired smoothly. 'What's it to be?'

Gabriel gave a jerk of his head, wrenching his hair from Marldon's fist. Clarissa looked up at him, mumbling urgently behind Marldon's fingers, her blue eyes wide with terror. Gabriel glared at her, making her wait for his answer, wanting her to suffer. She deserved Grimshaw, he thought spitefully. But he could not do it to her; he could not do it to himself.

He acceded to Marldon's request with a curse and a quick movement, holding Clarissa tight and rolling over so she was sitting astride his cock. Clarissa protested, whining thinly, but she did not struggle.

'Ah yes,' breathed Marldon. 'It's what she's wanted for a long time: the two of us inside her.'

He spat on his fingers and moved to kneel in the gap of Gabriel's bent, open legs. Clarissa whimpered her excitement as Marldon worked his spittle into the crack of her buttocks. His touch brushed once or twice against Gabriel's balls. Gabriel tensed, fighting to quell his abhorrence: he did not want to appear cowed by the earl's perversions. But Clarissa, oblivious to his ordeal, moaned gently and began rocking back and forth.

Gabriel's resentment flared and he gave a snort of derisive laughter.

'Isn't one enough for you?' he jeered.

Clarissa dipped her head, holding herself immobile. Her hair hung in black waves over her bosom. Gabriel jerked his pelvis upwards, bouncing her passive body with each thrust. She looked down at him, her wet lips parted salaciously, her indigo eyes, full of amethyst shards, searching for his sympathy. Gabriel had none to offer.

'Yes,' urged Gabriel. 'She's a sordid little whore. Give it to her hard.'

Lord Marldon laughed with unrestrained delight, and Gabriel felt a moment's acute embarrassment.

'So you think you can give the commands, do you?' teased the earl. 'How charming.'

He tipped Clarissa's upper body until she was leaning over Gabriel, her weight supported on her arms. His thighs pressed against Gabriel's as he edged forward, then with a blissful sigh Lord Marldon entered her. Gabriel felt it. He felt Marldon's thick, turgid shaft rising in her greedy little arse. It pushed against the silky flesh separating them, moving against his own organ, rubbing upward as it forayed into Clarissa's darkest depths. The pressure of the internal caress was unexpectedly gratifying.

Marldon held himself deep and shifted position, moving back until his arse was flat against Gabriel's, his legs either side of his torso. Clarissa groaned, sitting upright, impaled on two swollen hungry cocks.

'Work for us, Clarissa,' ordered Marldon. 'Show us how much you care.'

Clarissa released a tortured cry and tilted her racked gaze to the ceiling. Her sex muscles rippled around Gabriel's erection and he grunted sour enjoyment. Tentatively, she rose from the dual penetration then sank down, groaning as their hard, rigid columns bored into each orifice.

Increasingly passionate, she rode their engorged pricks, her pert breasts jiggling with her body's lift and fall. She gasped and sobbed, wanton lust contorting her face.

'Faster,' urged Marldon. 'Squeeze us hard.'

And she obeyed. Gabriel felt the tight clench of her inner muscles as she moved on their solid, fleshy staffs, rising and sinking with frenzied need. The two men set up a conspiratorial rhythm, both of them thrusting up to meet Clarissa's hot, swallowing holes. Marldon's balls, warm and tense, crushed against Gabriel's. Gabriel did not care. He cared only that Clarissa would look back on this with overwhelming shame.

With a surging anger, he rammed himself high into her, driving faster and faster, setting the pace for Marldon. His loins throbbed, his prick ached, and yet still his climax eluded him. Clarissa's tear-stained face, though it rewarded his vengeful fury, was doing little for his lust.

The earl cursed, growled, then matched a fierce lunge to a snarl of fulfilment. His phallus pulsed against Gabriel's, then moments later he slipped out of Clarissa's rear. She was all Gabriel's again.

Gabriel clutched her buttocks to his thighs and, with a twist of his body, jerked her on to her back. She gasped beneath him, and he clamped his eyes shut, plunging into her with animal passion.

'Watch her,' commanded Marldon. 'Watch her as she comes. Commit that expression to mind then you can set it down on paper.'

Gabriel paid him no heed. He knew well enough what she looked like. He slammed relentlessly, and the pressure in his cock burnt as it strained and quivered. Then at last he claimed his satisfaction, groaning as the hot release tore through his groin and into Clarissa. She cried out, joining him in dissolution, before he collapsed on top of her, exhausted and emotionally numbed.

Clarissa sniffled against his shoulder. Her body trembled and she coiled a strand of his hair about her finger. Her lips moved on his neck, kissing and sobbing. She whispered in his ear, Gabriel, oh Gabriel. Misery and loss echoed in her soft tremulous voice. She was vanquished, devoid of hope, but Gabriel felt none of the victor's triumph he'd anticipated. Her gentle intimacy kindled a flame in his heart, and he felt a sudden upsurge of compassionate, debilitating love, so raw that his eyes prickled with emotion.

He pulled away from her and snatched up his crumpled shirt. He dressed in haste, his gaze steadfastly averted. He knew Clarissa was still lying there, naked, tearful, threateningly pathetic, but not once did he look at her. When she called his name on a plaintive, breathless howl, he did not turn, because he did not hear it. He heard only a whore's solicitation.

He would not let his feelings hold sway; they would destroy him. And she was not worth it.

Marldon stood between two windows, leaning against the blue wall, his arms folded across his body. He smiled vaguely, watching the boy tug on his clothes.

Clarissa might be fooled by that stern exterior, those attempts at nonchalance and cruelty, but Marldon was not. Oh, Gabriel had been good at first, unsettling even, but the poor sop couldn't sustain it. He loved the girl too much. Marldon was grateful. The artist, in his futile bid to gain the upper hand, had deprived his lover of all hope.

After this, Clarissa – and her dowry – would truly be his. Alec's only regret was that Gabriel hadn't suffered more overtly. It would have been most entertaining to see the young pair tormented by each other's shame. Still, there was time.

Marldon crossed to Clarissa, who was curled on the floor, snivelling. 'Are you ready to pose?' he enquired, offering her his hand.

For a while she did not move, then sullenly she accepted his help and rose to her feet.

'Let him go,' she murmured, cupping her hands behind her neck to shield her breasts with her arms.

'But I want some pictures,' replied Alec. And he did. He wanted the lovers to sit in concentrated silence, to drink in each other's beauty knowing it was not theirs – only yards away but far out of reach. He wanted thoughts of broken love and lost futures to eat away at their innocent young hearts. And most of all he wanted Gabriel to continue spurning Clarissa with his indifferent façade. The sooner she realised she had lost the boy's passion, the sooner she would accept the alternative: life as Marldon's countess and plaything.

'Mr Ardenzi,' said Marldon. 'I trust you are also ready. Because, if you aren't, then I shall not hesitate to force you. Rape is the threat that appeals to me the most, and I see you as a man who treasures his anal virginity. Am I correct?'

Clarissa made a choked noise of shock and fear.

Gabriel shrugged, attempting aloofness. 'Exactly how many drawings of the girl do you require?' he asked indifferently.

Marldon smiled. Ah, yes, Clarissa was definitely his.

Kitty had been working at Madame Jane's for over a week. It was a dandy place, full of sparkling lights and deep-red silk, and a stone's throw either way to the Haymarket or Leicester Square. The customers were well-to-do fellows: lords and society types. Most of them were all right and easily pleased, although there were one or two Kitty didn't much care for. But she'd scrubbed enough floors in her time to know that you didn't have to concentrate on a job to do it.

She sat now in a wooded alcove of The Royal, one of the Haymarket's better cafés. Decent girls didn't go into Barron's or The Blue Post, and Kitty, for all her sins, was still a decent girl. As was Laura, her companion. They didn't spend their afternoons prowling the streets and arcades in search of lusty gallants. They worked late into the night, and that was plenty. The days were for sleeping, eating and shopping in Regent Street.

'Let us have a wee peek, then,' said Laura, nudging at the large brown parcel on the table between them.

Kitty smiled and, moving aside their glasses of negus, untied the string and folded back a little of the wrapping.

'There,' she said proudly, ripping at tissue paper to display a triangle of her new gown.

The sunlight, softened by the frosted windows of the bar, gleamed on the watered silk. It was gin-bottle green, and quite the loveliest thing Kitty had ever owned. Lucy and Octavia had started her up with a fine enough wardrobe, but this she'd bought with her own money and it was all the more special for that.

'Ah, that's a lovely cloth,' cooed Laura in her lilting Irish voice. 'Will you be wearing it tonight?'

Kitty said she would, if the creases fell out, and if Laura wore scarlet. Laura had thick sandy curls and a sprinkling of freckles, almost the same colour as her hair, and a tiny upturned nose. She was one of the prettiest girls at the nighthouse, and together they made a dazzling pair. Parading about the dance hall in green and red, they'd be sure to catch many a gentleman's eye.

'Very well then, scarlet it is,' said Laura. She took a few healthy sips of her negus then set down an empty glass. 'We ought to be getting back soon. Drink up.'

It was their turn to go out that evening, which meant lots of preening and an early start. Sometimes they just stayed at Jane's, entertaining whoever came in; other nights they wandered around the West End, visiting casinos and dancing saloons, luring back those who had money to burn and lust to spend.

Kitty drained her glass and tidied up the wrapping of her new gown. Outside, the low sun was bright after The Royal's wooded darkness. The two women sauntered along the busy Haymarket, Kitty holding her cumbersome parcel in a tight embrace. A gang of grimy-faced street urchins danced around them, offering to help the lady with her parcel. Laura shooed them away, scattering a few farthings on the ground when they persisted.

'I shouldn't be much surprised if Lord Marldon pays us a wee visit soon,' said Laura. 'Let us hope it is tonight or another when we're about on the town.'

'Oh?' replied Kitty. 'Why's that then?' She trusted Laura but was under strict instructions not to tell a soul her reason for working at Madame Jane's. She did her best to appear conversational and casual.

'Because I can't be doing with the man,' declared Laura, raising her voice above a swell in the clatter of cabs and shouts of costermongers. 'Ah, a nasty piece of work, that he is. He swans in, checking this, changing that, and he looks at a girl so hard it sometimes makes your blood curdle. And he surely puts Jane's back up. I tell you, the last time he came, he –'

'No,' interrupted Kitty. 'I mean, why do you think he'll be visiting us?'

They reached the corner where, as usual, a crowd of men gathered around the local trickster, jostling to get a view of whatever was set out on his box. Kitty and Laura skirted past them, ignoring one or two jeers, and turned into Panton Street.

'The season's coming to an end,' answered Laura as the noise faded behind them. 'He always pays us a visit before disappearing to the country. Business isn't nearly so good in the autumn, you know. For the moneyed ones, they all go off hunting. But at least his lordship doesn't pester us, and you have to be thankful for small mercies.'

Kitty felt a pang of alarm. She hadn't banked on Marldon going away. Was he planning to take Clarissa with him?

'They reckon he's to be wed,' continued Laura.

'Though, myself, I cannot see it. One look's enough for anyone to see the fellow's a wicked old pervert. Who'd say "I do" to that? Not me, that's for sure.'

'The bride might not have a choice,' suggested Kitty, trying to tease out more information. 'He might have some sort of power over her.'

Laura gave a little laugh. 'God love you. You mean he might have got her in the family way? Well, even so, if it were me, I'd sooner suckle a bastard then marry one. Wouldn't you now?'

'That's not what I meant,' mumbled Kitty, unsure of what she did mean.

Clarissa's friends had never agreed on whether she was a willing guest at Asham House or a prisoner. Octavia had said it was easy to rescue someone if their body had been captured but, if their mind had been captured, then it was much more difficult. It was all rather odd to Kitty. But, now that Mr Ardenzi had gone missing, she was sure something was badly wrong.

She was growing impatient with this half-baked plan, and the others didn't seem to be doing much in the way of finding out more information. She wished Charles and Alicia Longleigh would return, but that wouldn't be for another month or so. They'd know how to sort it all out.

She hoped they wouldn't mind that she'd left her old job.

The two women reached the small sidedoor of Madame Jane's. Downstairs, on the large glass windows, green and gold lettering spelt out, so Laura had said, 'Wines, Beers and Spirits'. Officially it was The Balmoral and it looked, for all the world, like any other café. You could just drink and sup there if you wished. But if you had the right face and enough money, then you could go on up to the real Madame Jane's with its glittering dance hall, its bawdy shows, private gallery and booths.

Laura unlocked the door and led the way along the dim corridor. As they climbed the flights of stairs, Kitty wondered whether she ought to confide in her new friend. Laura knew the clients and the other girls better. Perhaps she could find something out.

'So,' she began tentatively, 'is it true that this Marldon . . . Well, it's just I heard he sometimes took girls from here to be his servants. Is it true?'

'Ay,' replied Laura. 'But you needn't worry yourself. It's only the truly bad ones, and only if they want to. There was a wee lass by the name of Charlotte and she went away with him, oh about a year ago now. And before that there was – Eleanor, I think her name was, Eleanor Gracely. Now she was a scandal, I tell you. In love with her brother, so they said. Or was that Charlotte? Jesus, I can never remember.'

Laura gabbled on. Kitty scarcely heard a thing. She felt relieved that she wasn't likely to be whisked away and made to be a servant once more. But she felt dreadfully worried too. Poor Miss Clarissa. How were they meant to get help to her now?

Kitty and Laura entered the lodging part of the building on the upper floor. In the low-ceilinged drawing room, a few of the girls sat around, reading, mending clothes, chatting idly. Madame Jane, seated in her great leather armchair, looked up from her book as the two of them strolled in. She raised her pince-nez to her eyes, and gazed intently at Kitty.

'Come here, would you?' she said, her voice kind rather than commanding.

Kitty set down her bulky parcel and crossed to stand before her.

'You've been in service, haven't you, Katherine?' said Jane.

Kitty nodded. Jane insisted, for the sake of dignity and distance, that everyone in the brothel used their full name. It still sounded strange to Kitty's ears.

'Housemaid,' she replied. Then she added, 'Upper,' although it wasn't true.

'Then you won't have any trouble carrying trays of

222

drinks and responding when someone clicks their fingers?' said Jane.

Kitty eyed her a little warily, half-fearing she was about to be fired. Or, worse still, that Lord Marldon was after employing her. Had he heard she was truly bad? She shook her head, frowning.

'Good,' declared Jane. 'Marldon's been here today. He wanted to check you over but I said you'd be fine. He trusts me.'

A couple of the girls sniggered. It was an open secret that Madame Jane cooked the books and creamed off some of the earl's profits. They were all grateful, for they benefited as much as she.

'He wants a few girls to go to Asham,' continued Jane. 'He's having a bit of a party. You too, Laura.'

Laura threw herself on to a couch and groaned. 'I'm not dancing,' she said firmly. 'I'm absolutely not dancing, no matter what he's paying.'

'No need,' said Jane with a sympathetic smile. 'The dancers are organised. You'll just have to wait on and entertain his guests.'

Kitty gnawed at her lip. This was more than she'd ever hoped for: just a party; no clearing grates and beating dust from carpets. But the prospect frightened her. The responsibility was immense. She'd have to send word to Lucy. And she would definitely have to confide in Laura.

'When is it?' enquired Kitty, her voice coming as a nervous squeak.

'The night after next,' stated Jane. 'And I recommend you don't wear such a scared rabbit expression when you're up there. His lordship might take a fancy to you.'

There was more knowing laughter.

'Well, Jane,' said Laura with a resigned sigh. 'What's the devil celebrating this time?'

'His betrothal,' replied the madam, returning her attention to the book on her lap. 'Apparently some woman by the name of Longleigh has agreed to marry him. Damn fool whoever she is.'

Chapter Twelve

Clarissa had moved bedrooms. This one, with its silk hangings, gilt flourishes and painted ceiling, was, according to Lord Marldon, more befitting to a countess. And it led directly on to his room.

At least, thought Clarissa wryly, she would not have as far to walk when he cast her from his side in the dark hours.

'*Voilà*,' declared Pascale. She tossed the shaving blade into the bowl of soapy water and sat back on her heels. '*Regardez*, mademoiselle.'

Lord Alec sat, elbows on the chair-arms, fingertips pressed together, watching Clarissa with a remote smile. He looked, not at her nudity and her newly bared mons, but at her face.

Even now, she could scarce believe he was to be her husband. But she could see no other choice. The loss of her virginity was enough to ensure no decent man would ever touch her; and she had lost far more than that. She had lost Gabriel. She had seen it in his eyes, so hard and contemptuous; felt it in every deep, bitter thrust he had taken inside her. She had lost him, and because of that she had lost what little will she had left to fight.

'Take a look,' said Marldon, nodding to the mirror.

Obediently, Clarissa padded over to the cheval glass and hesitantly eyed her reflection. Gone were the dark curls cloaking her sex, and instead was a moon-pale mound, split by a high line. Her torso seemed strangely elongated, its unbroken whiteness drawing attention to the lascivious lips of her vulva.

'C'est magnifique,' sang Pascale proudly.

'It's obscene,' countered Clarissa, her mouth turning in a sullen pout.

And it was. Yet the image, so wickedly unabashed, caught at those black delights within her.

'Then it suits you,' said Alec, standing.

He walked to her and touched a finger either side of her sex. His face impassive, he stroked along the smooth pouch of her labia, stirring an eager pulse in her heart and her loins. She wished her body did not thrill so to his detached mastery, yet it did. She craved his cruelty, courted his humiliations, and for that she hated herself almost as much as she hated him.

She moaned faintly as his slender fingers played within her folds, teasing and questing, rocking her clitoris. He did it because Pascale watched, to stimulate that excitement which flourished from her shame.

There could be no other man but he who would understand her base desires. He cherished and nourished them; he satisfied them. Gabriel could never do that. When he had shared in her abasement, he had seen the pleasure she'd struggled to quell, and he had loathed her for it. She was lucky to have Marldon.

He caressed the shaven swell of her pubis, his fingertips tracing gentle scrolls over the satin-soft skin.

'Very nice,' he whispered, his lips moving to her neck.

Clarissa stretched away from him. Marldon laughed and drew back.

'How pleasing,' he murmured. 'You can still manage those moments of reluctance. I'd thought you beyond such charming affectations.'

225

He raised her hand and printed a soft kiss there.

'Until later,' he said, and with that he left the room.

She watched him depart, hoping for a parting glance. But he gave none, and the door clicked shut.

A slut and a whore Gabriel had said, and he was right.

If further proof were needed, it was there in the sketches he'd made of her. In every line of those drawings, she saw herself as Marldon must see her, as Gabriel must see her: shameless, abandoned, prisoner to an appetite that was corrupt and voracious.

She reached for her chiffon peignoir.

'*Mais non*,' said Pascale, wafting away the flimsy gown. 'We have not finished with your body, mademoiselle. It is in need of some colour, *n'est-ce pas*?'

Clarissa made no demur. She would appear before Alec's guests as he wanted her to appear. There was no longer any point in resisting. She just hoped that in the crowd tonight there would be no faces from the life which had once been hers. She could cope, just, with the avaricious stares of Marldon's servants; but attention from those she'd met on the London circuit she did not think she could bear.

At least Gabriel would not be there to watch. He had been released; he was no longer useful to her betrothed.

Pascale, blue silks swishing, brought a pot of rouge from the dressing table and scooped a small amount on to one finger. She hummed gently as she smeared the waxy cream into Clarissa's nipples.

'Do you remember that little housemaid of yours?' asked Pascale with a conversational air. 'The troublesome one – Kitty Preedy?'

'Of course I do,' replied Clarissa, a note of resentment in her voice. Did the Frenchwoman really think she would forget her friends so easily?

'*Bon*. She has left her position in your household,' stated Pascale, kneeling and taking more of the red stuff on to her finger.

Delicately she began to rub it over Clarissa's labia. Clarissa flinched slightly, hating the efficient intimacy of the maid's touch.

'I don't blame her,' said Clarissa. 'It seems Ellis is master of the house, and you, when you are there, mistress.'

'Tish, it is so,' replied Pascale with feigned regret. 'We have offended also the housekeeper, the butler, the laundrymaid, the ... ah, I forget them all. But Aunt Hester, it is us she likes and so the others, they go. We stay.'

'Kitty must have been difficult to get rid of,' said Clarissa sardonically. 'I fancy she does not shock or scare easily.'

'We had good fortune,' answered Pascale, dabbling her fingertips in the water and wiping them on the skirt of her apron. 'She had to return to care for her family. Her mother is dead.'

She looked up at Clarissa, smiling, her dark eyes sparkling with gleeful expectation. She wanted to hurt her, to see her saddened by Kitty's loss, appalled by the callous delight she took in it.

Clarissa turned away from the woman's scrutiny. She could not satisfy Pascale's malice: Kitty's mother was already dead. The young maid had lied, for whatever reason. Clarissa shrugged it off, silently wished Kitty luck for the future, and said nothing to Pascale.

The Frenchwoman rose to her feet and lifted Clarissa's chin.

'Mademoiselle, do not look so melancholy,' she whined, reading Clarissa's aloof gaze as gravity. Her mouth curved in a mocking smile. 'You have much to be happy about: a party in your honour, a wedding in the autumn, a husband who –'

'Oh, shut up,' snapped Clarissa, with a little flare of temper. 'Leave me alone.'

She had barely thought about the wedding ceremony and the reminder was unwelcome. How proud her father would be as he escorted her down the aisle, and how sickened he would be if he knew of the sordid pleasures she and Marldon shared.

'Leave me alone,' she repeated fiercely, seeing Pascale had made no move to obey.

'I must dress you and arrange your hair,' replied the maid, defiant and smug.

'Do it later,' ordered Clarissa, snatching up her peignoir. 'We have ample time before the guests arrive.'

'Later, I will be gone,' smiled Pascale. 'I do not wish to remain here to be used by his lordship's friends. I am above that. Tonight, I have leave to visit Sebastian. Ah, *mon amour.*' She coaxed the thin dressing gown from Clarissa's hand. 'I shall give Aunt Hester your very good wishes, *non*?'

'How kind,' replied Clarissa tartly. 'And while you're there, perhaps you could travel a few doors down and give my very good wishes to Mr Ardenzi.'

'Ah, the artist,' said Pascale airily, bundling up the chiffon. 'Such a pity his lordship permitted him to go. Charlotte, she was so, so disappointed. She said to me he was very good, a very good fuck. So hard and rough, she said. And always he was so angry and passionate. Myself, I did not try him. *Quel dommage!* Perhaps, as you say, I must call on him when I go to Chelsea.'

Sudden tears scorched Clarissa's eyes. Had Gabriel really been with that brassy little whore? With that incestuous piece who would not know a hairpin if she saw one? She thought of them coupling, of him tangling his fingers in the girl's abundant curls, kissing her, thrusting.

'How dare you speak of him in such a way,' she fumed.

Pascale gave her a steady, challenging smirk. Without thought, Clarissa landed the flat of her hand across the impudent maid's cheek. Pascale, recovering quickly from the slap, fixed Clarissa with the same infuriating gaze.

228

'*Bon*,' she said. 'It is what his lordship requested: a little fire in you. He grows bored of your compliance. You have become too easy, mademoiselle. It is not to his taste. *Alors*, shall we dress?'

Carriages had been arriving all afternoon. Gabriel had listened to them clattering across the forecourt, most of them passing by his high, narrow window then on, he assumed, to the stables or the kitchens.

So it was true: she had accepted his hand in marriage. And tonight was to be their betrothal party – the one the servants had teased him about, the one where Clarissa would submit to every degradation. Well, long may she suffer for it. She deserved to be Marldon's wife.

Gabriel stalked over to the door, fists balled, and battered furiously on the wood.

'Let me out,' he raged. 'You bastards. Let me out.'

Sometimes, his anger, his hurt, his frustrations reached such a pitch he thought his body would explode, or the room blast apart. The more his emotion swelled, the more the walls seemed to close in on him, until he felt he would choke from want of air.

His hammering on the door was rewarded. Footsteps clicked and tramped down the corridor.

'What is it?' came a voice. 'What's the fuss this time?'

It was the randy little bitch, Charlotte. Apart from pacing this room and an occasional handcuffed walk outside, fucking her was the only exercise he got.

'My prick's hard,' he lied, pressing his ear to the wood. He heard only mutterings. 'Jake with you?' he enquired.

'Of course,' said Charlotte, and there was a grunt of affirmation.

Gabriel huffed impatiently. He wished he were a boxer instead of an artist. He would fight his way out, flooring all those who stood in his path. But Jake was a gorilla and there could be few men capable of over-powering him.

The key turned, the bolt grated, and the door opened, just enough for Charlotte to sidle in before it was banged shut and locked again. The woman, brunette hair tumbling wantonly about her shoulders, put a hand to his crotch.

'It's not hard,' she said, smiling.

'Then make it,' returned Gabriel. 'I'm bored. Why don't you give me some books to read or something?'

'Haven't been told to,' she shrugged, efficiently flicking open the buttons at his groin. Her thin fingers reached in to weigh his phallus. She teased and rolled, capping and uncapping him until he was pulsingly erect. 'Anyway, you're leaving tomorrow. This could be our last encounter.'

'How tragic,' replied Gabriel, propelling her backward to the wall and leaning against her body. His stiffened cock jerked against her skirt, pushing between her spread thighs. 'Then let us make it memorable.'

He tucked his fingers into the neckline of her bodice and, with a backward step, tore open the muslin. Charlotte gave a shocked, delighted laugh and he scooped her breasts free of her corset. He squeezed the taut half-globes, bending to bite and suck on the firm pale flesh.

'Yes,' she gasped. 'Yes. Harder.'

'You want it harder?' spat Gabriel. He grasped a fistful of her lush brown curls and tugged her head to one side. The girl liked it to hurt, and he was just in the mood for obliging her.

'Yes,' she said challengingly. 'Be rough.'

Gabriel clawed at her skirts, hitching up her petticoats until they were bunched about her waist. His rigid cock nudged beyond the slit of her drawers to find the deeper slit of her sex, then he drove himself into her hungry, easy passage. He slid himself up and down, his strong legs powering his fast, high thrusts.

Charlotte wailed and groaned. Her vagina rippled about his shaft. She was just like Clarissa, always wanting it, always ready. He hammered into her, jerking her up against the wall, making her insolent little tits bounce and shudder. He crushed her nipples and pounded her breasts, leaving red marks and promises of bruises. He bit her neck, gnawed her lips. He pulled her hair and dug fingers into her sinewy upper arms.

Without waiting for her, Gabriel climaxed. It was honest; it was satisfying. There was no emotion wasted between them, and if she wanted to come then she could do it herself. Neither of them engaged in this to please the other. It was utterly selfish and blissfully simple.

He quickly withdrew and, moving away, covered himself. Charlotte swore and her hand delved beneath her skirts to quest within the crotch of her drawers. With a frantic action, she rubbed and plunged, panting and moaning.

Gabriel turned from her and stepped up on to the chair beneath the window. He peered through the oblong of glass, scanning the meagre view. Nothing but evening sunlight on the stretch of gravel.

He sighed restlessly. So tomorrow, at last, he would be out of here. He would put it all behind him, forget Marldon, forget Clarissa. They were not even worth his vengeance. He listened to Charlotte's wail of fulfilment then stepped down from the chair.

'Why can't I leave now?' he demanded. 'Am I expected to attend tonight's celebrations? Did my invitation get lost?'

Charlotte shrugged. 'Don't ask me,' she said, disconsolately arranging her torn bodice. 'As far as I know, Clarissa thinks you're gone. I don't see the point of you staying.'

'Let me go then,' he ventured, knowing it was a futile proposition.

Charlotte laughed. 'More than my life's worth,' she said. 'Anyway, perhaps his lordship wants you as security, to threaten you if Clarissa refuses him something.'

She rapped on the door for Jake to release her.

'I can't imagine that,' replied Gabriel.

'No,' murmured Charlotte as a gap widened for her. 'Neither can I.'

The leather-padded doors swung open at the footman's knock. Clarissa, her heart pounding, gazed down the length of the shadowy room.

It was heavy and churchly, panelled in dark wood with richly carved archways and niches. Hazy spots of light seemed to come from a hundred different points: there were octagonal lanterns, flaming torchères, candles everywhere, and from the ceiling hung a gloomy, medieval-style gasolier. On couches of silk and faded damask, on vast cushions of embroidery and tapestry, lounged people in twos and threes.

All eyes were on Clarissa as she took a few hesitant steps forward. The violins melted away. Whispers rushed. Then a fascinated calm stilled the chamber.

At the far end, raised on a dais, was Lord Marldon. He was sprawled indolently across a couch – a great couch draped in tiger skins – and he looked like an Eastern prince. His chest was bare beneath a jewelled waistcoat; his legs were swathed in dark silk pantaloons, and he wore no shoes.

A pair of twisted iron cressets, full of dancing fire, lit the small stage, dappling him in coppery light. He smiled and motioned for Clarissa to enter.

She could not move. She was to be honoured as the future Countess of Marldon, yet she looked like a whore from some exotic, bygone age. Her black hair was heaped in an elaborate mass of curls, of red scarves and golden ribbons. Her lips and cheeks were rouged; and in her ears she wore great gold loops, almost as large as the bangles at her wrists.

A vermilion corselet, laced tightly at the back, was cut low to display the whole of her bosom. Her nipples, artificially reddened, were brazen and lewd. Her long, flowing skirt was gossamer fine: ivory and gold threads interwoven with nothing. Through it, her shaved, rouged sex could clearly be seen. She had no secrets from this crowd.

Lord Marldon rose sinuously from his couch. Silently, he sauntered towards her, smiling. His glinting waistcoat showed a broad, pale stripe of his torso, and his pantaloons, slung low on his hips, exposed almost the whole of his muscled stomach. He lifted her fingertips to his lips. Her bangles clanked down her forearm.

'My betrothed,' announced Marldon, holding Clarissa's hand aloft and stepping aside.

There was a whistle, followed by an outbreak of cheering, laughter and riotous applause. People stood to welcome her.

Clarissa flushed, wanting to throw herself into Alec's embrace, to beg for his protection, but she did not. She had resolved to be compliant throughout, knowing how he wanted fire. It was a small gesture of defiance, but one she thought would serve her well tonight. She would not give Marldon the chance to flaunt how he could defeat her, not before these ogling guests.

Clarissa held her head high as Lord Alec escorted her across the room. The musicians began to play again, a low swooping tune. Censers burnt, puffing up cloudlets, and the air was languid with scents of jasmine and musk. As they meandered through the crowds, Marldon paused occasionally to introduce various people: the Marquis de Chouard, Viscount Quigley, a Prussian count with eyes so lecherous that his name did not register. Clarissa nodded graciously to them all.

Most were men. The two or three female guests were noticeable for their velvet half-masks, and the other women were servants, both familiar and unknown. They circulated with trays of drinks, dressed as fashionable ladies save for their too-low necklines and too-painted faces.

Three shallow steps led up to the dais.

'How envied I am,' said Alec, reclining on the couch.

'In you I have a wife, a whore and a lifetime's prosperity.'

Marldon stretched out his arm and Clarissa placed her hand in his.

'And I?' she enquired, joining him on the fur coverings. 'What do I gain?'

'Satisfaction of your lust,' he answered, drawing her to lie alongside him. 'What more do you require? I cannot guarantee how long you will have that, Clarissa, although for the moment you delight me. You've sustained my interest remarkably well.' He stroked the nape of her neck, a feather-soft touch, then teased down a tendril from her ornate coiffure. 'I never knew courtship could be so enjoyable.'

Clarissa nuzzled closer, trying to conceal herself, and also wanting him. The guests paid them scant attention, more involved now in other things. On a heap of cushions a serving girl in canary yellow, spread-legged and smiling, was inching back her skirts, tantalising the men around her with more and more blue stocking. Her onlookers urged her on with quickening handclaps, their shouts and ribald laughter soaring above the music. Yet still Clarissa felt vulnerable.

'Seeking to hide your charms?' taunted Marldon. He reached between their bodies to handle her naked breasts. 'A fit of modesty. How endearing.'

Clarissa rubbed against him and toyed with his hair. The jewels of his waistcoat pressed against her skin, cold and hard. 'My lord, please tell me what will happen tonight,' she said. 'What is it you expect of me?'

'Patience, child,' he said. 'Of all the things I've taught you there have been few virtues. But patience is one I thought you might have acquired.'

He sat, urging Clarissa to do the same, and signalled to a serving maid who stood waiting by the dais. She ascended the steps bearing a salver holding two golden goblets. Marldon passed one to Clarissa, took the second for himself and clinked the rims together.

'To us,' he said, taking a large draught.

Clarissa sipped delicately at the red wine. It was spicy, with a bitter undertone, and a little thicker than wine. She grimaced slightly.

'What are you waiting for?' said Marldon to the maid, who had not moved. 'Serve this to my guests.'

The sandy-haired girl bobbed a curtsey and made to leave. As she did so, she stumbled heavily and fell sprawling on to the couch, her body slamming against Clarissa's. Clarissa squealed as the goblet flew from her hand and the viscous red liquid spilt over her skirt and on to the tigerskin.

'I'm so sorry, ma'am. I'm so sorry. Forgive me, I beg you,' appealed the maid vociferously. She pushed herself up, flapping uselessly at the upset wine.

Lord Marldon shoved away the girl's hand.

'What's your name?' he demanded crisply.

'Laura, milord,' announced the maid, quickly recovering her aplomb.

'Ah, yes,' he said, nodding with vague recognition. 'Well, Laura, I imagine Lady Marldon needs another drink. Make sure it isn't you who brings it. In fact, make sure I don't set eyes on you again tonight, you clumsy halfwit. Begone.'

The maid curtsied and scurried away.

'I'm wet,' said Clarissa, plucking at her sodden skirt. 'I want to get out of these clothes.'

Marldon laughed. 'You'll get out of them when I say so, Lady Marldon, and not before.'

'I am not yet Lady Marldon,' she said stiffly.

Marldon shrugged indifferently. 'It doesn't hurt to practise.'

He drained his wine just as another serving girl, carrying a single goblet, stepped up to the dais. Clarissa's heart missed a beat.

It was Kitty. It was Kitty with fashionably styled hair, a gown of green silk, and peridots dangling from her ears. But, for all the finery, Clarissa recognised her at once. That pretty little face was unmistakable.

Kitty shot her a cautionary glance. Clarissa accepted the goblet Alec handed her, betraying no hint of consternation. She hardly dared hope that Kitty might be able to help her, but hope she did. Merely seeing the young maid was enough to make her feel less isolated, less doomed.

'Try to drink it this time,' said Alec.

Clarissa, resisting the urge to follow Kitty's movements, sipped. It was not the same concoction. There was no spiciness, no bitterness, and it flowed as easily as wine. It was wine. Clarissa's hopes surged higher still. The difference could not be accidental; Kitty was up to something. Unable to think what that might be, Clarissa drank quickly to hide the evidence, commenting on the liquor's strange taste. Marldon smiled his satisfaction.

'You'll find its aftertaste even stranger,' he said. 'Now, shall we relax a while?'

He raised his arm and clicked his fingers, two loud snaps. The music ceased. People muttered eagerly and shifted positions, turning their gazes to a stage set against one wall, curtained with deep-red velvet.

'A little entertainment,' he said quietly, pulling Clarissa near.

Her stained skirt, clammy and cold, slithered against one thigh.

The music began, a mournful tune, and the red drapes parted. On stage a woman wrapped in sheer lengths of blue and green stood within a great half-shell. Crouched at her feet was a ring of slender chiffon-clad girls, immobile. One by one they began to move, earthy-coloured wisps fluttering about them, hinting at graceful nudity.

'Ah, God, Botticelli,' muttered Lord Alec. 'I've seen this one, the fools. And I doubt it's improved. Suck me, Clarissa.'

He placed her hand on his groin. He was fiercely erect, and the sudden, unexpected hardness of him sent a thrill through her body. She slipped a hand into the vent of his baggy silk trousers, releasing him, and clasped her fingers about his stiff, veined shaft. Its vitality throbbed quick and warm within her fist. Marldon sighed and wriggled into a position of luxurious ease, his head lolling back on to the plump cushions.

Clarissa looked warily about the room, grateful to see that all attention was fixed on the titillating show. The dancers were stripping diaphanous scarves from the woman in the shell, and piece by piece her pale contours were emerging. Clarissa watched, intrigued, as a bearded spectator stepped up on to the stage. To whoops and cheers, he clasped a slinky, olive-skinned girl about the waist and wrestled her away from the performance.

'A delay of pleasure can be very tantalising,' said Marldon above the noisy applause. 'But at the moment it is most irksome. Suck me.'

He put a hand to the back of Clarissa's neck and pulled her down to his rearing phallus. She trailed the tip of her tongue over his plum-hued glans, following the ridge of retracted skin and lapping wetly at his smooth, shining knob.

'I want sucking, not a light dusting,' he said urgently. 'Make me come, and make it fast.'

Clarissa complied, closing her mouth over his great, pulsing length. With her lips circled tightly, she drew along his swollen cock, taking him in generous, far-reaching gulps.

'Ah yes,' breathed Marldon. 'You'll refuse me nothing tonight.'

He pumped his hips, driving himself deep into her wet caress. Groans rumbled in his throat, then, with a rasp of pleasure, he peaked. He clutched her head to his loins, and she drank his hot pungency, licking away every last trace of flavour.

Marldon murmured contentedly, stroking Clarissa's half-bared, silky back.

'One of your many wifely duties,' he said in a gentle tone. 'And how well you perform it.'

His prick was still erect in Clarissa's mouth. She withdrew, eyeing his powerful, upstanding organ. It showed no signs of slackening. She looked at him suspiciously and he caught the glance.

'The drink,' he said by way of an explanation. 'My lust will not be assuaged tonight, Clarissa. And nor will yours.'

The drink. The spiciness. Clarissa's mind whirled. He was still erect because of the drink. An aphrodisiac then. But she had not drunk it.

'Don't you feel your appetite swelling?' he asked. 'Don't you feel yourself on the verge of a hunger that knows no bounds?'

Clarissa hugged up close to his body, squashing her bosom into his warm, hard chest. She kissed his neck, his face, the satin streak of his scar. She nibbled his earlobe.

'Yes,' she murmured over and over. 'Yes.' And she laid his hand to her breast, moaning breathy pleasure when he palmed her yielding flesh.

Her heart thundered with hope, a hope dulled by unease. Alec was shrewd. Was he luring Kitty into a trap just as he had lured Gabriel?

'Soon,' continued Marldon, 'you will be so desperate and needful that, when I lead you on to that stage, you will writhe and plead for a man's cock. My guests will queue up to satisfy you, Clarissa. One by one, they will give you what you beg for, and still you won't be sated, still you will be crying for more.'

He caressed her white mounds, pinching her rouged nipples, and Clarissa turned a whimper of alarm into an inflated groan of arousal.

'Kiss my breasts,' she whispered. 'Put your hands

between my thighs, my lord. Make me come. I want you so much.'

'All alone, Brinley?' said Kitty in her best suggestive voice.

She sashayed into the kitchen and set down a tray of dirty glasses. The curly-headed valet, sitting there slouched over the enormous oak table, raised a listless glance.

'It hardly seems fair,' she persisted. 'Not when everyone else is having so much fun.' She moved round to him, placed a daintily shod foot on to the bench and stepped up to perch herself on the table. She took his hand and rested it in her lap. 'Why you?' she murmured sympathetically.

Brinley eased himself to sit upright and stroked along her thigh with a firm caress. He regarded her attentively, his mouth twisting in a wily smirk.

'Because he trusts me,' he said. 'You're from Jane's, aren't you? Haven't seen you before.' His smudgy green eyes twinkled.

Brinley, she had discerned, was there to keep watch over the basement because Gabriel was somewhere nearby. Most of the other men had gone into town, drinking and whoring, and the few that remained were there to usher in guests, or guard the doors. Escape was not going to be easy, and it would be quite a task to find a way in for Lucy and Sir Julian. She'd managed the side gate for them, but so far that was it. Kitty was determined though, and Brinley at any rate would be a piece of cake.

'New girl,' she breathed, lying sideways along the table. 'Still full of enthusiasm.' She drew one leg into her body, and pulled back her skirts a touch, offering him a tempting glimpse of black embroidered stockings.

The valet grinned and his hand strayed to a slender ankle, sliding slowly upward.

'Then why aren't you with the party, servicing Marldon's guests?' he enquired.

Kitty gave a weary sigh. 'Oh, his lordship has chosen me to serve him his drinks. It's very frustrating, very dull. Especially since we were all asked not to wear drawers. I had hopes of doing something more exciting than waiting on.'

Brinley's hand travelled quickly along her leg to find the warm, pouting flesh between her thighs.

'You're a little floozy, aren't you?' he said, smiling broadly.

Without preamble he pushed two fingers into her vagina, quickening moisture that already flowed. Kitty's lust had been bubbling under for some time, sparked by the debauchery she'd witnessed upstairs. She'd seen her friends writhing on cushions, being tended to by competitive men; muscled arses, bared and pumping; bawdy stage shows and hungry, leering eyes.

It was shockingly bad, worse than she'd expected, but it was all very thrilling. She was quite glad that seducing Brinley was necessary to her plan.

She moaned an enthusiastic response to the valet's probing fingers. He stood hurriedly, the bench scraping on the tiled floor, and slipped his other hand into her low décolletage. He caressed her small pert breasts, tweaking her puckered nipples.

Kitty trailed her fingers over his crotch, feeling the small bulge of keys nestling below the larger bulge of his prick. Perfect.

'Hurry,' she urged, swivelling round so her legs were either side of his body. 'Someone might come down.'

She ruffled up her skirts, baring her glossy pink sex, and Brinley hastened to unbutton himself.

'On the table,' implored Kitty, edging back across the dull, knife-marked wood. 'I've never done it on a table.'

Brinley scrambled to join her, his cock poking through his open flies. Kitty lay on the great oak surface, frogging her legs wide, and with a big, hungry lunge Brinley penetrated her. Grunting away, he drove himself into her soft and juicy channel. Arousal swarmed deliciously in Kitty's groin. She circled her legs about his hips, rising to meet him, frantic to yield to the pleasure. But she could not allow herself that luxury. At any rate, not just yet.

Her hands flailed beneath her buttocks, searching for the valet's trouser pocket. Her fingertips skimmed over the bump where the keys lay, but she could not reach inside. Brinley thrust on, oblivious to her intentions. His pounding length drove deep and fast, urging her to a distracted passion. Kitty moaned eagerly, her orgasm gathering force, her rational senses drifting away.

But no, she had to do this for Clarissa, for Gabriel. She held on to that thought and managed, bit by bit, first to unhook the valet's braces, next to loosen his trousers so they sagged about his knees. Finally, in a moment of great heroism, Kitty feigned her crisis. She wailed, long and loud, dropping her legs from him in an assumed excess of passion. His penis slipped from her, and she continued to howl, the sound covering the clink of metal when her fingers closed around the keys.

'I'm ever so sorry,' she pleaded. 'I lost control.'

But Brinley's prick was already nudging at her entrance, ready to take her once more.

'I thought you were a professional,' he muttered, slamming his cock deep.

'Oh, but you're so good,' cooed Kitty. 'I could probably spend again. Soon.'

Brinley powered into her, taking quick, hectic strokes. Kitty clenched her sex muscles to his strong solid shaft, indulging in the heavenly feel of him with an uncluttered mind. Her near-orgasm pulsed and swelled, lifting her desire to its dizzy peak. She cried out as the force of it seized her.

'Greedy little devil,' gasped Brinley, unable to suppress a boastful grin.

His breath came fast; his thrusts were hot and hard.

Then a grunt turned into a growl and he snatched his cock free. Kitty felt his warm liquid splash on to her thighs and while he knelt over her, panting satisfaction, she secreted his keys into the beaded reticule fastened at her waist.

'Thirsty work,' she said, smiling up at him. 'I reckon you and I deserve a drop of something.'

She tensed as the valet yanked up his trousers, fearing he might notice the missing bunch of keys.

'I hardly ever come twice,' she went on, eager to keep his attention. 'You've got a good thrust on you. I like that in a man.'

Brinley visibly swelled with pride, his chest puffing out like a wood pigeon's in mating season. Oh, men could be so disappointingly easy, thought Kitty.

'You sly little wench,' said Brinley, eyeing her fixedly. 'I've spotted your game.'

Kitty's knees went soft. 'Oh?' she replied in a tiny squeak. This was it; she was done for. She was going to be slapped in a cell, tortured and raped.

'You're just after a drink, aren't you?' he said. 'You're only saying I was good. You don't mean it.'

'Oh, but I do, I do,' protested Kitty, her relief giving her words great enthusiasm. She trailed a finger down his torso. 'I just thought it'd be nice for us to have a bit of wine or something. Then I'll have to go upstairs for a while, but I could come back later if you like.' She gave him a coquettish look.

Brinley beamed. 'Go on then,' he said, nodding to the dresser. 'Pour us some Burgundy.'

'Hark at the gentleman,' chided Kitty, wiping his seed from her thighs with her petticoat.

She sauntered across the room, hips swaying, looking back at him with alluring smiles. He was riveted. At the dresser, she gently placed her reticule on the pine surface. While her right hand moved glasses and bottles, her left opened the beaded pouch and withdrew one of the four phials. She glugged wine into two goblets, chattering gaily, then eased the tiny cork stopper from the small glass tube. Into Brinley's drink, she tipped a generous measure of chloral. She hummed, swirling the liquid, waiting for the crystals to dissolve.

Within minutes, he would be sleeping like a baby.

She returned to him, goblet in either hand.

'I propose a toast,' she said. 'To us, and to a night of endless passion.'

In the silvery, moonlit darkness, Lucy and Sir Julian crept around the rear of Asham House. It was eerily calm, the only sound that of their footsteps crunching lightly on gravel, and the muted rattle of carriages from Piccadilly.

'This is utterly impossible,' complained Lucy under her breath.

Julian, several yards ahead, beckoned her over to him.

'Look,' he whispered, pointing down to a small window. 'I'll bet we can get in there.' Then, with a stoop and a swinging leap, he jumped softly down into the alleyway which ran alongside the basement.

'I can't get down there,' hissed Lucy. 'I'll go and find some steps.'

'No, you won't,' replied Julian, quiet but insistent.

He reached up his hands to her. With a huff of irritation, Lucy sat on the cold ground, legs dangling over the wall, and levered herself into Julian's awaiting arms. He staggered a little as he caught her, then when her feet touched the floor he clasped her tightly, reassuring and strong.

'Perfect,' he said, pressing a congratulatory kiss to her lips.

'It would have been perfect if Kitty had opened a door for us,' she retorted, her voice low.

'Indeed,' he replied, stroking back a blonde curl that had escaped its pin. 'But that hasn't happened. Lucy, my sweet, you are quite delicious tonight.'

They were both dressed in their evening finery: Lucy

in taffeta of aqua blue, sapphires and diamonds at her neck. They had hoped to sneak into Asham, then merge inconspicuously with the guests. So much for that. If things continued in this vein, by the time they reached the party – if they ever did – they would be battered, bruised and outstandingly dishevelled.

'I should have worn a sack,' answered Lucy, her skirt hissing softly as she swiped at the creases.

'And still you would be beautiful,' murmured Julian, gazing at her with intense blue eyes.

Lucy regarded him steadily, curious and more than a little suspicious. He had changed. Ever since the episode with Octavia, he'd been far more earnest and attentive, less urbane and flippant.

'Hmm,' she said cagily. 'Shall we attempt to find Clarissa, or stay here exchanging flatteries?'

Sir Julian smiled. The sash window was open a few inches at the bottom, and he hooked his fingers under the wood, heaving it up. It scraped loudly in the silence, and they both held their breath, waiting. But there were no answering sounds.

'You first,' whispered Julian. 'I'll keep watch.'

Lucy clambered over the ledge, pulling her trailing skirts around her, and jumped neatly into the room. Its corners were shadowy, the only light coming from the moon. Its opaline tints fell upon washtubs, mangles and presses. Lucy scowled and wove through the clutter to try the door. Julian landed quietly from the windowsill.

'We appear to be locked in a laundry room,' she said in a sharp whisper.

'Lucy,' he said softly. 'Will you marry me?'

She swung around, glaring. He was on bended knee.

'We are locked in a godforsaken laundry room,' she snapped. 'This is no time for japes.'

'I'm serious,' he persisted. 'Marry me, Luce. I adore you.'

Lucy, prickling with exasperation, could barely speak.

'I seem to recall you have other commitments,' she said eventually. 'Like a wife in Oxfordshire.'

'Forgive me,' replied Sir Julian. He dropped his other knee and clasped his hands together as if praying. 'It was a lie. I invented her.'

Lucy stared at him, dumbstruck.

'It started some years ago,' he continued apologetically. 'There were so many husband-hunting females around and I ... Damn it, I just wanted protection. Forgive me, Luce. Please.'

'Ha,' she said, incredulous and piqued. 'You mean you wanted to play the philanderer without offering a thing in return?'

'Something like that,' mumbled Sir Julian.

'And now what?' she demanded, struggling to keep her voice low. 'Time's moving on? Tired of being a bachelor? Worried you might be out of the market in a few years?'

'No,' he answered firmly. 'I've found the woman I want to spend the rest of my life with. Say yes.'

Lucy's heart leapt. It was everything she wanted: Julian's love, his undivided attention, his ceaseless ability to pleasure her and, to top it all, he was offering her respectability.

'Well,' said Julian, raising one knee again. 'Will you do me the honour?'

Lucy looked at him, her face showing no sign of her joy, only lingering disbelief.

'I'll think about it,' she said sniffily. 'Now, how do we get out of here?'

Clarissa writhed on the couch, murmuring eager delight.

Between her thighs Lord Marldon's expert fingers moved, slow and arousing. His caresses and whispered words cocooned her. She felt alone with him, oblivious to the crowd. She had drunk none of the spiked wine, but her natural lusts transported her. For the moment, with Alec once again taking her close to a peak, Clarissa's hunger blocked out everything.

'Aren't you ready yet?' he asked softly, his breath tickling her neck.

Clarissa made a beseeching moan. 'No,' she replied in a weak voice. 'Don't make me do it. Take me here if you must, my lord, but nothing else, please.'

'But I do not want to take you here,' he countered. 'I want to observe you on stage, legs spread, offering yourself to my guests. Offering, that is, Clarissa. I'm not of a mind to force you. Not yet anyway. Far more satisfying to see you debased of your own volition. Well?'

He pressed his thumb against her clitoris, a sweetly fierce pressure, and chafed harder. His fingers played within her wet opening, stroking the fleshy sensitivity of her inner walls. Clarissa's orgasm beckoned, and she cried aloud, teetering on the brink. Then Marldon's fingers stopped.

'Well?' he asked. 'Are you any nearer to agreeing?'

Clarissa was, desperately so, but she shook her head. If she had not seen Kitty earlier, she might have submitted to him. She might have gone on to the stage and pursued her satisfaction, no matter how shaming it was. But the housemaid was here for a reason, and Clarissa, for once, clung to thoughts of the future, not the present.

'This stubbornness is most surprising,' said Alec, eyeing her sharply. 'I fear you have not drunk enough, Clarissa. And I thought you would require but a sip.'

He gestured to Kitty, who stood a few feet from their dais, awaiting orders. People in various states of undress were scattered about the sombre room. They sprawled, squirmed and jerked, limbs entangled, inhibitions gone.

'Bring the wine,' ordered Marldon.

Kitty approached with her salver, appearing tense and nervous.

'Didn't anyone ever tell you,' said Alec to the maid, 'that two drinks should be presented side by side, not one in front of the other? Still, if you're one of Jane's girls I suppose your expertise lies elsewhere.'

He took the nearest goblet and handed it to Clarissa. Kitty's shoulders sagged with a released breath, and she smiled slightly. Clarissa assumed the maid was still controlling the drinks. She half-wished it were not so. She did not know how much longer she could refuse Marldon without arousing his suspicion. If only she knew what Kitty's intentions were. Perhaps she was keeping back the aphrodisiacs to protect Clarissa's modesty. Poor innocent.

Lord Marldon took the second goblet. 'Follow my lead, Clarissa.' He drained the goblet, flicked out the dregs, then set it back on Kitty's tray. 'Not very becoming to a lady, I grant you –' he smiled '– but that's of little concern to you. Now drink.'

Kitty gave Clarissa a covert, reassuring nod. She sipped once, twice.

'Drink,' repeated Marldon. 'Then I'll escort you on to the stage. And I vow, after every man has had you, you'll still be . . . be begging for mmm . . . begging . . .' His voice faded away, and he looked at Clarissa strangely, his eyes narrowing, squinting, his head swaying back and forth. 'Begging for me,' he resumed, his voice thick and slurred.

His lips parted, as slow as a tortoise, and he uttered something incomprehensible. Then his eyelids drooped, lifted heavily again, and shut as his head lolled sideways. He slumped on to the couch, mouth ajar, motionless.

'Come on,' urged Kitty, tugging Clarissa to her feet.

A figure hurried on to the dais. It was the clumsy maid, Laura. She hastily draped herself over Marldon and fluffed her skirts high.

Clarissa and Kitty moved calmly down the steps, attracting no one's attention. Clarissa stole a backward glance to see Laura squirming against Marldon's inert body, her fingers twisting in his hair.

'I haven't killed him,' whispered Kitty, guiding her to the nearest door. 'I couldn't get enough chloral. Sorry.'

Chapter Thirteen

Kitty, her hand fastened about Clarissa's wrist, led the way along dimly lit corridors.

'Please, tell me where we're going,' implored Clarissa, struggling to keep pace with the young maid. 'Why can't I simply leave?'

'Because the doors are guarded and you look a mess,' replied Kitty sternly. 'And because we're going to see Gabriel.'

'But he's gone,' wailed Clarissa, frustrated and close to tears.

'No, he hasn't,' snapped Kitty. 'Now come on, before someone spots us.'

Clarissa pulled up short, refusing to budge. She struggled to wrench her arm from the maid's fierce grip, but Kitty's hold on her was implacable.

'I cannot,' said Clarissa. 'He hates me.'

'Of course he doesn't,' retorted the maid. She looked hard at Clarissa, her young elfin face alarmingly severe. 'I've done a lot to get you this far, miss. So stop acting like a spoilt child and do as I say.'

Clarissa gave a whimper of defeat and hurried after Kitty, scurrying past door upon door. Occasional gaslights broke into the gloom with halos of feeble yellow lambency. Finally Kitty stopped and tapped on a bolted door.

'Gabriel?' she hissed. 'It's Kitty.'

'Kitty!' came the soft response, a voice full of hope and relief, so familiar, and yet hauntingly strange.

Clarissa's blood pounded as Kitty slammed back the bolt and jangled keys. Six did not fit the lock – six agonising attempts in which Clarissa both willed the door to open and willed it to remain shut. Her mind spun with a confusion of memories, of distant tender pleasures eclipsed by vivid depravities. And she did not know which she preferred. She crossed her arms over her bared, rouged breasts, wishing she were not dressed so lewdly, wishing her skirt was not wine-stained like a slattern's.

The seventh key slid into the lock and turned. The door swung back and Gabriel, his eyes bright as topaz, stepped forward. He looked wild and unkempt, his jaw darkened with stubble, his chestnut hair curling in an unruly tangle. And still he was heart-stoppingly beautiful. The eagerness faded from his face the moment he recognised Clarissa, and he froze.

Despair plummeted into her stomach and she bowed her head, bitterly ashamed.

'What's she doing here?' he demanded. 'She's supposed to be celebrating. Betrothal party, isn't it?'

Kitty exhaled a sharp, angry breath. 'You two need to sort things out,' she said impatiently. 'And you're not leaving Asham until you do. Get along that corridor. If you make one whisper of protest, I shall scream the place down and then you'll both be back where you started. Go on. Move.'

Clarissa and Gabriel exchanged glances of assent. Heeding Kitty's orders, they walked down the corridor, sullen and shy. They did not speak, and they touched only once, an accidental brush of arms as they turned a corner. Both of them pretended not to have noticed.

Kitty marched behind them, snapping out directions,

guiding them through passageways. At length they came to a corridor with walls tiled in majolica, a large oak door at its far end.

'Where are you taking us, Kitty?' enquired Clarissa in a small timid voice.

'Somewhere you'll be safe for a bit,' she replied. 'Somewhere you can wash that muck off your body and talk.'

At the door she fiddled with keys while Clarissa and Gabriel stood by, impassive and accepting.

'Marldon was hoping to bring his guests down here,' said the maid, inserting the correct key. 'But I don't think he'll be in a fit state to suggest it.'

She opened the door, and a great waft of steam billowed into the passageway. She nudged them both forward.

'You might get a bit warm with your togs on,' said Kitty, giving a parting grin.

The door closed on them; the lock clicked and Kitty's footsteps clattered down the corridor, fading to silence.

They were in an antechamber, surrounded by marble, enveloped in mist. It was hot. Clarissa felt her face dampening and a droplet of moisture trickled a cool path down her back. She opened her mouth to speak, but Gabriel turned abruptly and stalked towards an archway hung with green silken drapes. His movements were quick and angry.

Clarissa rushed forward, catching him around the waist, and uttered his name in a cracked, pleading cry. He stood rigid and she pressed her cheek to his warm, solid chest, whispering apologies. Then, suddenly shocked, she stepped back and glared at him.

'You smell of another woman,' she said accusingly.

'I?' exclaimed Gabriel, his eyes wide with astonishment. 'You dare to reproach me?'

Clarissa shook her head vehemently, at once realising the folly of her words. She began to protest but Gabriel ignored her and, with a vicious swipe, drew back the

251

green curtains. He stood gazing, gave a short, bitter laugh, then jogged down a small flight of steps. Clarissa, motionless in the archway, stared after him.

Few things surprised her about Asham now, but she had known nothing of this extravagance. A large room of pale marble walls and columns stretched below her. Candle flames, diffused in the mist, glowed high and low like blurred amber stars. Along the sides ran ledges of marble, carved at intervals into deep basins. At the centre was a pool, a rectangle of pale-green stillness, watched over by Grecian statues.

Gabriel jerked his shirt over his head, casting it to the ground as he strode swiftly into the room. He paused to tug off his remaining clothes then ran gently towards the pool, diving with tense, elegant strength. His lithe sinewy body seemed to hang in the air, quivering, before he arrowed into the clean, calm surface. He moved in the water's depths, his outline fractured and shimmering beneath spreading ripples.

Clarissa gnawed at her bottom lip, not knowing how to placate him or make amends. Perhaps it was futile even to try. She could not explain why she lusted after a man she loathed; she could not explain the pleasures and agonies she'd found in her shame.

Kitty had been wrong to bring them here. She should have secured Gabriel's release and left Clarissa where she belonged, with Marldon.

She watched Gabriel emerge from underwater. He shook his head vigorously, sprinkling a shower of diamonds, then pushed his shiny, wet hair from his face. Without acknowledging her, he began to swim, his arms flicking in a powerful crawl, a white froth splashing in his wake.

Clarissa slipped off her shoes and padded down into the room. The marble was cool and a little slippery underfoot. Small pewter bowls lay here and there, and deep single shelves, containing bottles and towels, were cut high in the walls. Clarissa crossed to one of the broad ledges and sat there beside a sturdy marble basin, hands folded over her lap, prim and tense.

Still Gabriel swam.

She sighed and turned on the basin tap, dabbling her fingers in the warm running water. She set the plug in its hole and cupped her hands beneath the flow. She splashed her face and rubbed at her rouged lips and cheeks. She filled a pewter bowl and tipped it at her neck, the water streaming down her body like a liquid silk caress. She squeezed and pulled at her nipples, trying to rid them of their stubborn red pigment, and still Gabriel swam.

Clarissa blinked hard, fighting back tears. She had lost him, and now she had to endure the torment of waiting until Kitty freed them. Doubtless the maid expected them to mend their differences with a few kisses and a simple act of sex. But Clarissa knew their differences were too great. Her body found its heights in her depths, and Gabriel could not give her that.

She clawed at her hair, tugging out combs and snatching at ribbons. If nothing else, she could cleanse herself of this whorish garb. Her ebony locks came out of the coiffure in untidy, pin-tangled clumps. The bangles clanked at her wrists and she twisted them off and pulled at her earrings. Golden loops scattered at her feet, glinting in the wetness which glossed the marble floor. Then the splashing stopped.

She looked up to see Gabriel, his hands on the edge of the pool, the anger gone from his face. He heaved himself from the water, his bronzed arms flexing, and walked towards her. The thin mist made him nebulous; he moved as in a slow dream. Droplets fell from his long, dark hair and trickled down his graceful body, sliding over his abdomen like beads of quicksilver. They glinted in the curls at his groin where his penis nestled quietly.

'Ah, God,' he said as he reached her.

Then, without another word, he began gently to

253

remove pins from her disordered, straggling tresses. Clarissa trembled, and her heart swelled with guilt. How could he be like this when she had betrayed him so completely?

She did not know what to do. Would sorry be enough? Would an embrace be misconstrued, taken as lust instead of feeling? She sat, meek and still.

When her hair was freed, Gabriel dipped the pewter dish into the overflowing basin and scooped up water. He poured it over her jet-black waves, scooping and pouring until her locks were saturated, and her diaphanous skirt was sticking wetly to her thighs.

'I need to wash before we leave,' she mumbled, her hand wafting awkwardly at her breasts. 'This rouge. I need to wash.'

Gabriel reached for soap and began rolling it to a lather. Clarissa flinched back. She could not let him touch her, not there. It was an invitation to more, and she feared his tenderness.

'I don't want sex with you,' she said flatly. 'It wouldn't work.'

Gabriel was still for a long moment, the only sound that of water trickling into the basin and spilling over its brim. Then, softly: 'What do you want from me, Clarissa? I'll do anything to please you, to have you back. Just tell me.'

She stifled a sob. His forgiveness and humility were devastatingly painful to her.

'Why?' she pleaded. 'I do not deserve this.'

Gabriel gave a half-smile, attempting playfulness. 'I know,' he replied.

Then he knelt at her feet and reached up to wind a spiral in her soaked, squeaky hair. He traced a finger over her brow, as if to smooth away the frown, and gazed at her. In the deep-orange half-light his honeyed skin glowed. Shadows played over the angelic perfection of his features and darkened the sweet hollow of his throat. His eyes were sleepy velvet, full of brooding sadness and desire.

'But I've tried to hate you and I can't,' he said quietly. 'I can only love.'

Clarissa stared into her lap. 'Even after all you've seen me do?' she said, her voice breathy with disbelief. 'Even when you know of the ... the deplorable things which give me pleasure?'

'It's only your body,' he whispered. 'And your body isn't you. I'd love you if you were a disembodied soul, Clarissa.' He pushed her hair back over her shoulders and lightly stroked along her jaw. 'But I am quite fond of the packaging,' he smiled, tilting her chin then skimming a touch over her lips.

She returned the smile, just, and took his fingertip in a tiny, nibbling kiss.

'Let me wash you,' he breathed.

Clarissa stiffened. She wanted his intimacy yet the prospect of being unfulfilled terrified her. It would be confirmation of her unassailable taste for debauchery, for Marldon, and she did not think she could bear such a truth.

'Take the risk,' he said, reading her reluctance. 'Or you'll never know.'

With tensed shoulders Clarissa swivelled to one side, allowing him to unlace her corselet. He eased it from her then unfastened the cord of her skirt. But she did not stand and he did not ask her to. She was not ready for him to see her shaved mons and her rouged sex.

Gabriel was lingering and cautious, soaping her fingers, her arms, her neck. His slippery, massaging touch lulled her into near-relaxation and her skin glowed with a languid sensitivity.

He washed her feet, rubbing suds between her toes and over the arches of her insteps. He trickled water over her, rinsing away the lather. Foam swilled on to the floor and swirled rainbow bubbles about her discarded pins and bangles. For a long time he avoided her breasts, until it began to feel unnatural.

But then he touched her there, and she murmured encouragement. He kneaded her full yielding mounds, his soapiness gliding fluidly over lily-white skin. Firm yet gentle, he stroked his thumbs over her soft nipples, pressing lather into the rouged peaks. They tingled lightly in answer and, when he streamed crystal water over the contours of her bosom, her tips were crinkled cones, as naturally pink as rosebuds.

'Sacrilege to hide such a perfect colour,' he said, sweeping his fingertips over her flesh and scuffing her tightened crests.

Clarissa made small noises of enjoyment. Her body thrilled to the forgotten pleasure of delay, of delay that was designed not to torment but to indulge her in blissful luxury and heartfelt attention. She felt heat gathering in her sex, and a precious humidity bedewed her cleft. It was so very different, and for once her insides did not have that knot of tension. She knew that, unlike Marldon, he would not depart on a whim and leave her wanting.

She cupped her hand to his neck and, a little shy, drew him to her breasts. He kissed her taut, pale globes, his mouth warm against the wetness of her skin, his stubble rasping lightly. He lapped at her erect nipples, the tip of his tongue circling moistly over the dusky tips. He plucked at them with grazing teeth and Clarissa gave a gasp of intense delight. He nibbled and bit, his hands suddenly urgent, roaming over her thighs, her waist, her bosom, squeezing hard.

The flare of roughness excited her. She knew he could be as forceful as he was tender, but she had only ever seen that force when he'd ravished her with Marldon. Then, anger had fuelled his passion, but the thought that love could be a spur quickened her blood. A flutter of lust stirred in her groin and her pleasure bud began to beat like a tiny warm heart.

She slid her hands over the smooth wet slab of his back, dropping down to kneel with him on the soapy floor. His phallus was hard and upright, standing proudly from its cluster of dark, crisp curls. Shivering inwardly, Clarissa trailed a finger along his inner thigh and hammocked the plush pouch of his balls. She rolled the tautness within, and a soft sound of hunger caught in Gabriel's throat. Gently, she stroked the underside of his swollen prick. Beneath stretched silken skin his shaft pulsed, so solid and potent. Clarissa began to ache.

She gazed at him, offering her willingness with a steady look. A candle flame shone in the black depths of his pupils, a tiny diamond in each limpid brown eye. Then he clutched her to him, his mouth and fingers moving in her wet hair. She pressed her cheek to his strong, sleek chest, listening to the thud of his eagerness within. For a time they were as the statues around them, just holding, until Clarissa looked up, wanting him now, offering him her parted lips.

And they shared a hungering kiss, a kiss that erased cruel memories and revived a past of love and gleefully secret pleasures taken in Gabriel's brass bed. They embraced, damp skin slipping and sticking, and Gabriel peeled down Clarissa's flimsy, sodden skirt. She wriggled uncomfortably as he removed it. Quickly she knelt again, pushing her fists between her legs to conceal her shorn mound of Venus.

'It'll grow,' she said, her cheeks colouring slightly.

He eased away her arms and gently widened her thighs, gazing down.

'It's beautiful,' he murmured, his voice snagging with desire. 'It shows your sex.'

His words sparked a sudden surge of arousal in her loins. A flickering warmth swirled low in her body and hung there as a fierce, rhythmic throb. It was not obscene; it was beautiful, beautiful. The word echoed in her mind and relief overwhelmed her.

She passed Gabriel the soap. 'The rouge might not

taste very nice,' she said with a coy smile. How heavenly it was to ask for something and know her needs would not be mocked.

Gabriel lathered his hands and cupped her blushing vulva. He rubbed the slipperiness into her crimson petals, his fingers gliding within her crevices and pulling gently on her labia, teasing out the redness. He stroked her hairless mons, his soapy caress sliding back and forth, from her pliant folds to the satin swell of her pubis. It was more intimate than any intended pleasuring, and somehow all the more rousing. Perhaps she did not need restraints and degradations to satisfy her. Perhaps love and purity could be enough.

She moaned blissfully at his sweet, slithering attentions, wanting more of him with every beat of her heart. He rimmed the entrance to her vagina, a fingertip circling round and round, tarrying on the mouth of her openness. He slicked soap over her clitoris, loading the smouldering pearl with creaminess, and he teased her there. The little bead moved beneath his touch, light, fluid, deliciously easy, driving her to a needful agony.

She lowered herself to the floor and lay supine on the wet marble, her legs stretched wide for him. Her hips heaved and she groaned, yearning to feel him within her. His fingers sunk into her aching emptiness, pushing forward and stroking back, slow, strong and exquisitely indolent. His thumb nudged at her flaring pleasure point and his other hand reached to fill the pewter bowl with water. Slowly he trickled the clear, warm liquid over her folds, fingers and wetness mingling, bathing the whole of her sex in rapturous sensation.

Clarissa uttered soft repeated cries. The onset of her crisis, sumptuously thick, swam deep in her loins, rolling to an ever tighter coil. His head dipped between her thighs and he possessed her with his mouth, nibbling and sucking. He plunged his tongue into her ready opening, trailed it over her lips and burrowed into every crease. He sought her clitoris, nudged back its hood, and lapped at the inflamed, peeping bud.

It was enough, too much. Clarissa's orgasm soared, an intensity shivering open, consuming her utterly. She cried hoarsely, hanging on a euphoric peak, before tumbling into the fall of shattering ecstasy, of a thousand melting pulsations.

Gabriel kissed her inner thighs then edged up to lie beside her. He trembled almost as much as she, and he studied her face, his brown eyes searching and intense. Clarissa lay silent, the spreading afterglow of her peak soothing away the shudders from her limbs.

'Say you won't ever leave me,' he whispered. 'Even if you don't mean it, just say it. Make this moment perfect.'

'I won't leave you,' she replied quietly, holding his gaze. 'I promise that with all my heart.'

He kissed her, his lips rich and sweet with the taste of her sex. His jutting phallus pressed insistently against one thigh, and she let her hand drift over his body, teasing him with soft sinuous strokes.

She drew back a little to admire his strong, spare physique. His chest was a wedge of muscularity, smooth and firm, with nipples like bronze halfpennies. She traced curves there, sliding down to his ridged abdomen and sweeping over his hard, slender hips. His cock reared from his thatch of dark hair, throbbing with virility, straining for her touch.

But she lingered as he had done, moving around his body, massaging his tight, lean buttocks and swooping her hands over the polished, beautiful plane of his back. Her wet hair trailed on his skin as she kissed his shoulder blades, the nape of his neck, the insides of his elbows, his wrists. She blew gentle breath over his prick.

A droplet of fluid formed there, as clear and smooth as a cabochon moonstone. She licked it away and Gabriel groaned, tormented and needy. He rubbed his fingers into her scalp and his pelvis lifted in a tiny, questing jerk. She moulded her lips to the flushed crown of his knob and suckled there, her tongue teasing around the collaring foreskin. Slowly she moved down his warm shaft, taking him deeper into her mouth with open, pulsing kisses.

Gabriel gave a guttural cry, and he pressed at her shoulders, urging her away.

'I cannot bear it,' he rasped. 'Stop.' His breath was shallow and he gazed up at her, his eyes burning beneath lust-heavy lids. 'I remember when you would suck me to my crisis because your maidenhead was sacred. Please, do not continue for I fear you might do the same. And I want you.'

He brought her down into his arms, and rolled her on to her back. She spread her thighs, her sex gaping in moist invitation.

'I'm yours,' she whispered. 'Take me.'

As she spoke she felt him penetrating her. The domed head of his cock was easing past her entrance, pushing into her yielding depths with a slow, steady force. He stifled his urgency, and when he had buried himself to the hilt he was motionless, the thick flesh of his prick lodged solidly within her.

Clarissa released a low feverish groan. Her groin tingled and she squeezed her vagina around his hard girth, clutching at his embedded stiffness with rippling inner muscles. She looked up at him and saw his mouth open in a silent inhalation of pleasure. His eyes fixed on hers, Gabriel began to move, driving gentle bumps against the neck of her womb, his pelvis lunging tensely, rocking into hers.

She moaned and gasped, and gradually his withdrawals became longer, his glans teasing at the warm rim of her sex before gliding once more into her sheathing heat. Each stroke was exquisitely controlled, powerfully stern. She lifted her loins, her wetness slipping up to meet his slow-shunting cock. It was as if they were caught in quicksands of bliss, their shared, heavy movements drawing them deeper into a realm of delight, prolonged and unbearably sweet.

In a surge of mutual lust, they ground against each other, their rhythm accelerating with their eagerness. Gabriel slammed himself harder and harder, his chestnut curls flicking about his face. The hair at his groin scoured her naked mons, and his pubis nudged at her clitoris, quickening it to a wild, demanding beat. His passion thrilled her.

Hot sensation lapped at her core, taking her to a second climax. She peaked, and Gabriel dropped his mouth to hers. He drank in her cries of joy with fierce liquid kisses. His muscled chest, humid with sweat, rubbed against her softness, and his swollen phallus thrust on, pounding into her quivering sex.

She felt the pulsations of his cock, his kisses groaning against her neck, kisses with teeth. And as he climaxed he called her name, his voice a splintered, dry sob.

'God, I love you so much,' he whispered.

He gathered her to him and they rolled to lie chest to chest, Clarissa's thigh over his. The strength of his penis slowly ebbed away. Their breathing grew steadier and their lips moved constantly, kissing, murmuring endearments, and sometimes just touching.

'I want to leave now,' said Clarissa. 'I want us to be far away from here.'

'So do I,' replied Gabriel. 'But we seem to be in Kitty's hands, my angel. And until she opens that door I want to fill every moment with pleasure.'

He stroked her throat, trailed his fingers down her breastbone then swooped a caress below the underswell of her bosom.

'Tonight's your betrothal party after all,' he said, printing kisses to her shoulders. 'We should honour that commitment, celebrate it anew.'

Clarissa looked at him, frowning, then buried her face in his mane of dark hair.

'Oh, Gabriel,' she said. 'My father –'

'Hush, hush,' he whispered, holding her tightly. 'We'll run away, live elsewhere. I can support you with my painting.'

'Yes,' she breathed, looking at him steadily. 'Anything.'

'Then, for now, this is our night,' he said, stroking damply curling tresses from her face. 'I hope you don't mind the paucity of guests.'

It was dark. The gas lanterns of Chelsea Embankment cast split reflections of light on to the Thames' inky surface. A carriage, its side-lamps burning, rumbled along Cheyne Walk and drew up outside the quiet Longleigh household.

Without waiting to be handed down, Alicia Longleigh gathered in her skirts and stepped out on to the pavement. She breathed deeply, the chill night air refreshing her senses. It was an appalling time to arrive, and the unlit windows proved their passage had been quicker than their letter's. She'd predicted as much and, if Charles' bed was not made, his room unaired, then he could blame no one but himself.

She tiptoed up the stone steps and fitted the key into the lock. Charles, escorted by the coachman, limped after her. In the gloomy hallway, Alicia fumbled for a tinder-box and lit the oil lamp, turning the wick high. Its white luminosity glowed on dusty wood. She wiped a finger on the oak table, frowning at the gleaming stripe she left.

Lantern in hand, Alicia bustled from room to room, her anger rising at the sight of evident neglect. The carpets had not been shaken, burnt coal was scattered in the hearths, and nothing shone. In the dining room there were unwashed plates stacked on the sideboard and the table had not been cleared of an unfinished meal.

Had everybody died? Their return was not expected but that was no excuse for such filth. She stormed up the stairs. This could not wait until the morning. What the devil was Hester Carr thinking of to allow this disgrace? If the old maid could not manage affairs then why hadn't Clarissa taken charge? At the spinster's door, she quietly turned the handle, and glided into the room.

Alicia gasped as the pearly haze of the oil lantern fell upon the bed. There were three people there: Hester Carr, the footman and Clarissa's lady's maid, limbs tangled, all breathing the rhythm of deep, contented sleep.

No sound came when Alicia first tried to speak, then she cried out in a high-pitched rage: 'What the hell is going on here? Wake up! Wake up at once!'

The figures stirred and groaned. She set down her lamp and impatiently shook Miss Carr. The woman's eyes slowly opened and she frowned in confusion. Then she smiled, her thin, pendulous cheeks lifting.

'Oh, you're home,' she murmured, patting her long greying hair and looking at Alicia with a beatific vagueness.

'Gracious heavens,' snapped Alicia. 'You've taken to laudanum again. Pascale! Ellis! Explain yourselves.'

The Frenchwoman came to her senses with a start and struggled to pull a twisted bedsheet over her nudity. Ellis cursed.

'I asked you to keep her occupied,' hissed Alicia, close to his face. 'I did not ask that you allow the house to fall down while you were doing so.'

From the hallway downstairs Charles called out self-pityingly.

'Get dressed,' ordered Alicia. 'Then make our room decent while I divert his attention.'

The two servants sullenly pulled on their clothes and Alicia shouted down to Charles, reassuring him she would be there in a flea's breath.

'Where is Clarissa?' she demanded of the threesome. 'I cannot believe she would live in such a pigsty.'

Pascale smiled, infuriatingly triumphant. 'I did my job

so well that she could not wait for her wedding night. She has gone to live with Lord Marldon.'

Alicia looked at her doubtfully. She could not quite believe it, but then the Longleighs seemed to have a taste for strangeness. And Clarissa's absence would go some way to explaining the chaos.

'Hmm,' she said. 'Well at least some good seems to have come from this shambles. Now start acting like servants.'

And after that I shall fire you, she thought, swishing out of the room.

Dawn was just breaking, and Green Park was an expanse of spectral violet light. Hand in hand, Clarissa and Gabriel ran across the dewy grey lawns.

No one had seen them go, no one but Kitty. She had found clothes for Clarissa, guided them through scenes of calcified dissipation and past slumped, drunken servants. Lord Marldon, she'd said, was still out cold, and Lucy and Julian were slumbering happily in a laundry room. It seemed Clarissa's friends had not turned traitor as she'd once thought. They had tried; they were true to her.

As the two lovers neared Constitution Hill, they slowed, breathless. Clarissa glanced back across the soft, shadowed landscape. In the phosphorescent gloom everything was still and sombre, and Clarissa felt as if they were the first people to walk the earth. She looked at Asham: just a bit of brick peeping above the trees.

'Don't,' said Gabriel, touching her cheek and turning her gaze to his.

The half-tones of daybreak gave him an unreal air, making his face paler, his hair and eyes darker. He seemed an essence rather than a physical thing, a beautiful essence.

Clarissa shook her head. 'I just wanted to see how small it was.'

Gabriel held her close and printed a kiss on her forehead.

'The things you did there . . .' he began. 'The things you said were deplorable –'

'Please,' she interrupted. 'I want to forget everything.'

'No,' said Gabriel firmly. 'It's wrong to deny what you enjoy. I want you complete, Clarissa. I don't want you to hide your desires from me, however terrible you think they are. Because love can make all things beautiful, even obscenities. And, when trust is involved, they can only be better.'

He swiftly grasped one wrist and twisted her around, bending her arm behind her back. 'Do you trust me, Clarissa? Do you?'

Clarissa squealed in pain and surprise. 'Yes,' she laughed. 'Yes.'

Gabriel sank his teeth into her neck and urged her forward, shoving. She stumbled and protested, unnerved yet excited by his sudden brutality. He pushed her up against a vast elm, pressing heavily behind her so her breasts were crushed against the trunk. The rough bark grated against her cheek, and scraped at her arms.

'I want you now,' he hissed, ruffling up her skirts in a flurry of white lace.

He held her layers high with his body, the bulge of his cock digging into her buttocks. She wriggled and cried, begging him to stop. Someone might walk by; they could be seen; they ought to go home. But Gabriel paid her no heed.

He snatched at her drawers, tugging until they dropped to her ankles. Cool air wafted against her bared cheeks and breathed into the folds of her naked sex. It was thrilling to be so exposed, and the risk of being discovered aroused her greatly. She struggled, for decency's sake, and for the added pleasure of having him conquer her.

He pinned her to the trunk with his slender strength, his hands swooping down to clutch her inner thighs.

His fingers dug into her flesh and, with remorseless insistence, he spread her legs wide. She felt the head of his prick nudge at her swelling lips, and then he drove himself savagely into her tingling passage.

Clarissa groaned. His thick rigidity, so quick and fierce, filled her completely. Her body lifted with the surge of his penetration, and her breasts slammed into the tree bark. Again and again he thrust, plunging furiously. His pounding hips made her soft buttocks bounce, and then she felt a wet fingertip, very wet, sliding down the cleft of her cheeks.

Clarissa wailed, knowing what he was about to do, relishing it. He sought the rosy pit of her anus then drove his moistened digit deep into her narrow tunnel. As his engorged cock thundered into her, he worked his finger in her darker hole, pumping eagerly.

'You like that, don't you?' he hissed. 'Don't you?'

'God, yes,' she breathed.

She felt a rush of pride, of delight in her wantonness. The tide of her orgasm billowed and she moaned frantically, crying aloud when ecstasy possessed her. Gabriel chased her crisis, driving fast, and caught it with a deep shuddering thrust. He gave a roar of exhilaration then fell panting against her body.

His ragged breath puffed against her neck and he covered her skin in tiny, exhausted kisses.

Above them, the canopy of leaves rustled in a soft breeze, and birdsong, shrill and urgent, shivered across the park's tranquillity.

'Was I right?' murmured Gabriel. 'Are trust and dominance better bedfellows than cruelty and dominance?'

'Yes,' whispered Clarissa. 'Yes, they are.'

And she was truly overjoyed to trust and be trusted, and more than anything to love and be loved. She had almost forgotten the power of such things.

As the sun rose, they walked through London, touching all the time, pausing to kiss, to look, to whisper feelings and desires.

They skirted Belgravia and dawdled towards Chelsea. They would call at Clarissa's first, collect clothes, boast silently to Pascale, then spend time at Gabriel's, making plans.

Bit by bit, the pale morning light shrank the long, soft shadows, and the streets came alive. Carts laden with market produce, and omnibuses without passengers clattered over the cobbles; curtains opened at small, top-floor windows; one or two people passed by.

They reached Chelsea Embankment, and the sun was a ball of hazy gold, low in the sky. Barges and wherries moved sluggishly on the water, and the wharves were clanging into being.

'I think something's wrong,' said Gabriel as they neared Clarissa's house.

At the foot of the steps was a heap of trunks, band-boxes, portmanteaux, and travelling bags. A rugged fellow was loading them on top of an awaiting carriage. Pascale, glowering, descended the steps, slapped a hat-box on the pile, then stomped back up to the house.

Cautiously, the young couple advanced. When Alicia appeared in the doorway, red hair aflame, Clarissa flew to her, forgiving her everything in an instant.

She clasped her stepmother in an urgent embrace: What was happening? Was Father all right? Why had they returned early? Something was terribly wrong, wasn't it?

'Gout,' said Alicia, giving Clarissa's hands a reassuring squeeze. 'Charles merely has gout. He eats too much. Hardly enough to warrant shortening our holiday, but I could not bear his endless complaints. And may I ask what you're doing at this hour?'

Before Clarissa could reply, Pascale edged past with another box, followed by a scowling Ellis. The two servants glared at Clarissa but said nothing.

'You need a new lady's maid,' said Alicia, pitching a scornful look as Pascale made her way back into the house. 'Well, Clarissa? Why, pray, are you wandering the streets at dawn?'

Clarissa cast a glance down to the street, smiling shyly. Gabriel was hovering there, half-hiding behind the pillar of the gate. She beckoned him discreetly and he approached, squeezing past the luggage. Alicia regarded him intently.

'Are you in love, Clarissa?' she asked in a conspiratorial hiss.

Clarissa nodded earnestly, trying to stress with her eyes that it was a secret. She took Gabriel's warm hand as he reached them. Alicia shook her head, perched herself on the wall, then stared out at the river.

The silence was long. The sun was rising. Shadows might have moved.

At length, Alicia turned. 'I didn't think it could be true,' she said softly. 'About Marldon. I'm afraid Pascale's been talking rather loudly. Your father's slept through it all, thank God.' She indicated Gabriel and smiled. 'Well?'

Clarissa mumbled over introductions, then the two lovers, at times awkward and halting, at others clamouring to share sentences, gave a confused, half-truthful tale of Marldon, Asham House, cruelties and dowry contracts.

'Please,' said Alicia, raising her hands. 'Spare me further details.'

'Oh, Alicia,' breathed Clarissa. 'We were going to hide from you, run away. We want to marry but Father . . . He'll never ever agree to it.'

Alicia stood. 'Don't worry about him,' she replied confidently. 'I shall have a word in his ear.'

She brushed a strand of hair from Clarissa's furrowed brow, gazing kindly at them both.

'Charles Longleigh,' she continued, 'despite his stubbornness, has a very obedient streak. He'll yield.'

Gabriel laughed quietly, drew Clarissa close and nuzzled into her neck.

'Much like his daughter,' he whispered, and she shivered with desire.